WHITE
LINES

WHITE LINES

TRACY BROWN

ST. MARTIN'S GRIFFIN
NEW YORK

WHITE LINES. Copyright © 2007 by Tracy Brown. All rights reserved. Printed in the United States of America. For information, address St. Martin's Press, 175 Fifth Avenue, New York, N.Y. 10010.

www.stmartins.com

Library of Congress Cataloging-in-Publication Data

Brown, Tracy, 1974–
    White lines / Tracy Brown.
        p. cm.
    ISBN-13: 978-0-312-33648-6
    ISBN-10: 0-312-33648-9
    1. Cocaine abuse—Fiction. 2. African American women—Fiction. 3. Inner cities—Fiction. I. Title.

PS3602.R723W47 2007
813'.6—dc22

2006052210

A WORD FROM THE AUTHOR ABOUT WHITE LINES

I grew up in the eighties and nineties, decades when the crack epidemic destroyed families and communities. I witnessed the epidemic up close and personally, and I watched people fall prey to drug addiction. I've grieved with friends who lost loved ones to AIDS and other drug-related illnesses. At seventeen, I went to the first of several funerals for my peers, all gunned down in drug wars being waged in the streets where we lived. I watched helplessly as even more of my peers were hauled off to prison for crimes related to the game. The drug trade touched each of us in my generation profoundly. It affected our lives, our politics, the movies that we watched and the music that we listened to. And it destroyed our community piece by piece.

In telling the story in *White Lines,* I want to shed light on every aspect of the drug game to show that no one *ever* wins in this game. There are only losers. The hustlers, the drug addicts, the family members, the friends. Everybody loses in the game. We lose loved ones to addiction, young men and women to tragic early deaths, and we lose years of our lives to incarceration. We lose. In every possible way. Many times the game is glamourized in the entertainment industry. Movies glorify the game, as do music, magazines, and even books. In *White Lines,* my objective is not to glamourize the lifestyle, but instead to call your attention to the pain that the game inevitably causes those who are bold enough to play it.

This story is dedicated to the children of the drug game. To the lost little boys and little girls dealing with the pain of watching a loved one slip away a day at a time. To the husbands and wives forced to pick up the pieces for a spouse who can't kick their habit. To the dealers, the pushers, the hustlers who supply the needs of these victims without realizing the destruction of families and communities taking place at their very own hands.

This story is dedicated to love, which conquers all and costs nothing. May it help heal all our wounds, past and present.

ACKNOWLEDGMENTS

Thank you, God, for both the sun and the rain. Without the rain, the sunny days would be taken for granted. So thank you for the lessons and the joy in all things good and bad.

My children, you make every sleepless night, every stressful deadline, and every early morning flight worthwhile. I love you. You are my inspiration.

And, to the love of my life, you inspire me every single day. Thank you for all the ways you contributed to this story and for all the ways you've opened yourself up to me without fear. Your insight helped me to breathe life into these characters, and your honesty made me fall deeper in love with you than I ever imagined possible. Even though I have a way with words, your love leaves me speechless. It feels like my life was lived in black and white until you came and filled it with color. Each day together we write a new chapter of our love story—each one more beautiful than the last. I pray that our story never ends.

WHITE
LINES

Prologue
A BLAST FROM THE PAST

January 9, 2007

Born placed the card inside the envelope and handed it to the clerk behind the counter. He walked toward the door of the flower shop, thinking about what he'd written. He hoped Jada would know who the flowers were from, since he hadn't bothered to sign his name. But more important, he hoped she would be happy to hear from him. After all, so much time had passed, and yet sometimes the pain of their split still felt like a fresh cut. He walked out of the store and toward his Denali parked at the curb. Now all he could do was wait and see if time really did heal all wounds.

Born thought about something his mother had often told him over the years. She said that whatever you claimed to be in life, you'd be tested at. He had always thought that he knew what she meant. God knows he'd been put to the test in his life. Most times, Born had passed those tests. But when the time came for him to be tested at love, it was a different story. That was one test that Born wasn't so sure he'd passed.

Jada opened the door and saw a deliveryman standing there, smiling. In his hands he held a huge flower arrangement. "Jada Ford?" he asked. Jada did not return his smile but nodded, confirming her identity, and signed for the arrangement.

"Thank you," she said, in a soft voice. The deliveryman headed back toward the van parked at the curb.

Jada had been accepting flowers for the past two days, all condolences for her mother's death. Most of the flowers had been sent over by members of her mother's small Baptist church congregation, who had become the dead woman's extended family for the past several years. For years Jada's relationship with her mother had been nonexistent. And then when one did exist, it had been complex. For years Jada had never seen her mother in charge or in control of her own life, or theirs, when Jada and her sister, Ava, had been kids. It had always seemed like they had been responsible for finding their own way in life, responsible for learning all their lessons on their own. The hard way.

But then Edna had finally come out of the shadows, and had claimed her place at the head of her family. She had fought the toughest battles and found solace in the only comforter she ever needed. Then cancer claimed Edna Ford's life. It was a sad time for Jada, compounded by the fact that she'd spent so much time consumed with the fruitless pursuit of happiness in the gutter of drug addiction. Prior to her death Edna had begun to pick up the pieces of her shattered relationship with Jada. She had watched Jada come back from the dark side, and seen that she had gotten her life together, that she'd regained custody of her son. But there had been some unfinished business between the two of them. Things they still had yet to conquer together. And now it was too late.

Edna's passing made Jada think about so many things that she had not allowed herself to remember for so long. She could still hear her mother's terrified voice, still feel the fear that surged through her body every time she watched her mother beaten by J.D. Jada remembered the terror etched on her mother's face as she curled in on herself to block her husband's drunken blows. Jada remembered how she used to try and cover her little sister's eyes and ears, to block out the horror they were forced to witness. Jada had resented her mother for not being stronger. She had wanted Edna to fight back. It was no wonder that a woman who had never been able to fight back in her own defense had been unable to fight for her children's survival.

Realizing that she was still standing in the open doorway of her home, Jada shut the door and placed the new flowers on the only available space on the table in the foyer. She removed the card that accompanied the latest delivery, and walked into her cozy living room. She sat down on the sofa and tucked her feet snugly underneath her. Opening the card, she read its message:

> I'm sure that losing your moms has you feeling real emotional right now. I know what it feels like to lose a parent. I just want you to know that even though we haven't spoken in a while, I'm here for you, if you need me. Believe it or not, I still think about you all the time. And I'm sorry for your loss. Call me if you wanna talk. (347) 555-1992.

Jada tucked the card back into its envelope. It bore no signature. None was necessary. She recognized the handwriting, and the familiarity caused a shiver to travel down her spine. Jada laid her head back against the sofa, her back flush against the mountain of pillows. Her eyes were fixed on the smooth surface of the ceiling, and on the prisms of light reflecting through the partially open Venetian blinds, her thoughts far away. Some place so long ago and so bittersweet.

JADA

1

A HOUSE OF CARDS

Brooklyn, 1990

"You don't fuckin' listen! I told you to come out of that room, Ava. I was knocking on the door, and all I heard was your nasty ass moaning."

"Whatever, Jada!" Ava smoothed her hair out of her face, and popped her gum.

Jada and Ava knew they were in trouble. They were supposed to be home by the time the streetlights came on. But it had been dark for a while now, and they knew they were in for it. At sixteen and fourteen years old, respectively, boys were their favorite pastime, and they had snuck off to meet a couple of them.

"Whatever my ass. I told you to stop letting these li'l niggas touch on you and hump you and shit." Jada looked at her sister with disapproval all over her face.

"Jada, stop fuckin' preaching all the time. I only let Derek do all that. And you ain't no saint. Don't sit there and act like you wasn't in the living room with Marlon being just as nasty. So—"

"So, nothing! I knew when it was time to go home, though. We should have been home a long time ago, but your nasty ass didn't want to leave. And you never listen to me when I tell you that we gotta go. Whenever we go somewhere together, and you don't want to leave, I can't leave you behind. You're my sister. Anything can happen out here.

And now 'cause of you, we're late. You know this muthafucka J.D.'s gonna be beefing all night now."

They walked through the streets of Brooklyn, silenced by worry. Neither of them wanted to face the fury that awaited them at home. They were pretty little ghetto superstars, mulatto girls with glowing complexions and encompassing eyes. Their mother was a blend of French and black, and their father was of Jamaican descent. They had a look that made them stand out from the rest, yet they still had a grit about them that was undeniably hood. The sisters were quite different in personality. Jada was bold, almost wild and adventurous. Everybody in the neighborhood—even the grown folks—knew Jada by name. She was always on the scene. Always with the latest slang and the loudest mouth. Jada's soft brown complexion, shoulder-length dark hair, and striking bone structure made her quite stunning.

Ava, on the other hand, was beautiful, but she was timid and delicate and tended to blend into a crowd. Not that she was innocent. Ava was quieter than Jada, but she was just as much a Brooklyn girl as her sister. Ava was boy crazy, and would often intrigue Jada with her stories of passionate make-out sessions with guys. Ava hid this side of her well. So while Jada was usually in the center of the crowd, with everyone hanging on her every word, Ava would be sitting on the sidelines—with some boy usually whispering in her pretty brown ears. Ava was a little shorter than her sister, but had a lighter skin tone, longer hair, and the prettiest pink lips anyone had ever seen. She was lovely, and her body was shapelier than average at her age.

Realizing that her sister was right, Ava cleared her throat. "I'm sorry," she said, avoiding her sister's gaze. "I should have listened to you, Jada. But Derek is so cute."

Jada grinned at Ava and shook her head. "He *is* cute. But, not as cute as Marlon."

"Whatever!" Ava laughed, and shoved her sister playfully. They walked the rest of the way home giggling about how they'd spent their afternoon. Derek and Marlon were the cutest boys in school, and they just happened to be cousins. Both of them hustled, despite their young ages, and they were well-known around the way. Jada and Ava had spent many a giggle-filled night talking about how two boys that fine *had* to fall from the same family tree. All the girls in school wanted Derek and Marlon. They were always fly, always had dough. But despite all the girls who wanted them, they wanted Jada and Ava. So when the opportunity arose for the four of them to be alone, the girls had jumped at the chance. They'd met at Marlon's house and proceeded to spend several unsupervised hours with the boys of their dreams. For the next few hours, both girls were on cloud nine, as they French-kissed and were caressed by the two cutest boys in school. Now it was almost 8:30, and they had a lot of explaining to do. Their time with Derek and Marlon had been a welcome distraction from the ugliness they experienced both at home and in their neighborhood.

The crack epidemic had taken over ghettos across the country, and Brooklyn was the worst. Bodies showed up every night up and down Flatbush Avenue, and throughout the borough of Brooklyn. Gunshots rang out, and everybody knew the drill. They'd hit the deck and wait till it ceased, wondering if this time the victim was someone they knew. Crack vials littered the sidewalks, the stairwells, and even the school-yards. Drug dealers fought over corners, and over customers. Car radios blared rap music at all hours of the day and night. This became the canvas of the girls' young lives as they journeyed toward adulthood.

They arrived at their building, and entered the littered lobby. They rode up on the urine-scented elevator, the walls lined with tracks from spit. Garbage littered the elevator floor, and for the millionth time both girls wished they lived anywhere except the projects. As soon as Jada turned the key in their apartment door, she could hear the yelling coming from the kitchen. It was going to be a long night. J.D. was in the middle of one of his tirades. Both sisters knew that the night would end in the usual manner—with their mother balled up on the floor, crying as she tried to block her man's kicks and punches.

Life hadn't always been so hopeless for the girls. Edna Ford had gotten married and given birth to Jada and Ava when she was fresh out of high school. Their father, Sheldon Ford, a man five years older than

Edna, married her when she was very young and easily manipulated. Sheldon had been the hardworking, financially stable father and husband that every woman dreams of. Edna had stayed home and cooked and cleaned, while Sheldon went out every day and worked as a truck driver, in and out of state. Jada grew up adoring her father. It was easy to do, since Sheldon had been such a handsome, strong, and charismatic man. Whenever Sheldon was away—often for days at a time driving his truck—Edna seemed eager, almost anxious for his return. She had a hard time making decisions on her own, or thinking for herself. And Jada sensed this early on. She could tell that her mother was not comfortable in a position of authority, that Edna needed Sheldon's input and his direction. This was evident in everything, from selecting new furniture for the house to which dress she should wear when they went out. Edna always sought Sheldon's approval. So whenever he returned it was a relief for both Edna and her daughters, all of them thirsting for the comfort they found in Daddy's presence. Edna loved and doted on her husband. She knew that she was lucky to have a man like Sheldon. Someone who wasn't in and out of jail, a man who worked hard and looked good doing it. What Edna didn't know was that Sheldon was living a double life, and was secretly seeing other women.

He left exactly four years after Ava was born. It was her birthday, and they were having guests to celebrate their baby girl's special day. Jada and Ava had been decked out in their best dresses, and all the mothers from the neighborhood had brought their children to the party. Edna had been so busy flaunting her well-furnished home and her beautiful daughters in front of the jealous women from the block that she never realized so many of them had already slept with her husband.

Ava was sitting shyly in the corner at her own birthday party while Jada was center stage, dancing her heart out with all the other kids. Edna was so distracted, as she soothingly encouraged Ava to join in the fun, that she only half acknowledged Sheldon when he told her that he was going to the store to get some more soda. Edna had waved him off and mumbled something about them needing napkins too. But Sheldon never returned. And Jada had watched her mother make feeble ex-

cuses for the rest of the night about where her man was. She entertained their guests while discreetly wringing her hands, eager for his return. But Sheldon never came back. Long after the guests were gone
and the house was clean, he was nowhere to be found. When he finally
had the decency to call his wife, he told her that he'd found somebody
else with whom the grass seemed greener. And he never looked back.
Edna had been heartbroken. She had stayed in her room and lain in her
bed, crying for days at a time. Jada had been the one to put on a brave
face and shield her younger sister from her mother's sobs, by keeping
Edna's bedroom door closed and turning on the living room stereo in
order to drown out their mother's crying. While Ava asked where their
daddy had gone, and why Mommy wouldn't come out of her room,
Jada changed the subject and made sandwiches for her sister. Despite
being a mere six years old, Jada knew in her heart that their daddy
wasn't coming back. She knew that Sheldon had walked away, never to
return. And she thought she must have been the most heartbroken of
all. Yet she kept her game face on and played the role of the rock for
both her sister and her own mother. Jada did a lot of growing up, and
would later wonder who had been the parent and who had been the
child.

Sheldon had met lots of women in the course of driving in and out of
state. But he fell in love with a woman who didn't want or have the patience for kids. Despite the voice in his head telling him that he was
wrong, he abandoned his own daughters and began a life with the
woman he couldn't live without. But it turned out that the woman
wasn't quite divorced, and in an unexpected altercation, he was killed by
her jealous husband with a gunshot to the heart. After being contacted as
next of kin, Edna and the girls had buried Sheldon in what was the saddest of funerals. As his wife, she had inherited all of his benefits. But
Edna was overcome with grief and disappointment. She felt that she had
failed as a wife. She wondered what she had done wrong to cause him to
love someone else. Was she not pretty enough? Was her cooking not up
to par? Had she asked for too many frivolous things? Was she too talkative? Too conservative? She was full of questions and no answers were

forthcoming from the dead man she had loved so much, who was stretched out in a casket at Roosevelt Funeral Home.

Edna seemed not to notice her daughters' pain. But Jada and Ava both felt a huge void. After Sheldon died, Edna had sold and given away most of his belongings in order to rid herself of all the pain she seemed to grow more consumed by day after day. All the girls had to remember their father by was a five-by-seven-inch picture that he had taken before he had broken out. Jada would always remember staring at that picture night after night, wishing he would come back. Ava mourned her father's loss in silence, internalizing her pain. And Edna seemed to miss him, too. She was visibly sad and seemed lonely without him. She no longer entertained company, because now that Sheldon was gone she began hearing all the stories about what a ladies' man he had been. Edna was embarrassed, and felt like a fool. She imagined that everyone was laughing at her behind her back. She hung her head in shame, and withdrew from almost everybody. Her daughters were the only ones with whom she shared an occasional smile.

Those were the times in her childhood Jada would always reflect happily on. Edna spent time teaching them to play cards. They played Bingo for loose change and baked cakes together. The girls would help her cook, and Edna would let them brush her long hair. It was a time of contentment for the girls. And yet for Edna, those years were so lonely. She felt incomplete without a man to share her life. This wasn't how she'd pictured life as a mother. Where was the man in her life? What had happened to happily ever after? Edna longed for the comfort of a man—the comfort of not having to work and make decisions. She longed to relinquish her control. Somehow her daughters sensed their mother's loneliness. So when she met J.D., the girls thought she had found happiness at last. They thought she would have somebody to help her smile more, and they were excited for her.

Soon Edna seemed like a whole different woman. She started going to get her hair pressed, and started dressing better and putting on makeup and perfume. Every Saturday she played Betty Wright records. Candy Statton and Evelyn Champagne King. She was happier then. She smiled more, and the house was filled with music instead of so much silence and structure.

Edna and J.D. had met at her job. She had been working several odd jobs to make ends meet, but she met him when she was working as a waitress at a diner in downtown Brooklyn. He flirted with her until he broke down her wall, and then he wined and dined her. She was so shy and so quiet. But he made her smile. He made her laugh.

J.D. made Edna feel good. And he was good to her daughters, bringing them candy, and talking with them about whatever was on TV. Everything was fine and dandy, until he moved in. Edna let J.D. move into her two-bedroom apartment on Parkside after they had been together for about eight or nine months. And that's when the truth came out. He started hitting her about a month or two after he got there.

The first time J.D. put his hands on Edna, the girls heard their mother fighting with him and they ran in to help her. J.D. was instantly remorseful, and he started apologizing to all of them. He was so sorry, so very sorry. But after that time, he was never sorry. He would get drunk, beat her ass, and then if they were lucky, he would go out for a few hours.

The girls were little then. Jada was ten, and Ava was eight when he moved in. Edna did what she could to explain what he was doing. She always had an excuse, some lame explanation for his unprovoked rage. When he was in bed sobering up the next day, dead asleep and snoring like a fucking madman, she would attempt to explain his behavior. She told them that he was an alcoholic, that he had a sickness, and you don't leave people just because they're sick. She said that he had had a hard life, and he was frustrated sometimes. She would tell them that she provoked him. It was her fault that he hit her. She found some way to justify it, found a way to make it her fault. Either it was because she had decided to get her hair done that day, when the money she spent on her hair could have been J.D.'s carfare to go and look for a job, or it was the pressure of being a black man in America, and never being good enough. Or it was his frustration over never having children of his own. Or maybe it was because he didn't know how to express his anger any other way.

Edna had a million excuses for J.D.'s behavior. But excuses are never good reasons, and being a very mature ten-year-old, Jada could tell that her mother was feeding them bullshit. As they grew older, J.D. turned his fury on them. This was the environment in which the girls became young ladies, trying to sidestep a madman living under their own roof.

Jada proceeded inside the apartment with Ava right behind her. But when they shut the door and locked it, J.D., visibly drunk, and their mother were standing with their arms folded, looking at the two of them.

"Where the hell were you two?" J.D. demanded. Jada looked at her mother, hoping she would intervene. But Edna stood there humbly, behind her man as he took charge of the situation.

Jada spoke up. "We were at the park."

"What time did your mother tell you to be in this house?" J.D.'s voice was loud, and Ava moved closer to her older sister.

Jada fought the urge to tell him that it was none of his muthafuckin' business where they'd been, and that he wasn't their father and he had no right to question them. Looking at her mother cowering behind J.D., Jada knew that she wouldn't be able to hold her tongue much longer. She was tired of living in fear of this son of a bitch. She spoke calmly once more. "We always come home when the streetlights come on. But today—"

"But shit! You two think your little asses is grown. That's the fuckin' problem!" J.D. got in Jada's face, scowling. "Your mother told you to be in this house before it got dark. And here it is damn near nine o'clock, and you two *hos* come strolling up in here—"

"I ain't no ho!" Jada yelled defiantly, in his face, and not backing down.

J.D. slapped Jada hard in her face. Edna recoiled, as if she herself had been hit, but said nothing in her daughter's defense.

"Don't hit my sister!" Ava yelled, and stepped between her sister and J.D. J.D. felt that Ava was challenging his authority by stepping in front of him like that, and he whaled on Ava.

"Oh, you wanna challenge me? Bitch!" J.D. shouted, and he slapped Ava so hard that she staggered back.

Ava looked stunned at first. Then her expression went feral, and she launched herself at J.D., arms swinging and legs kicking.

"*Stop!*" Edna and Jada yelled and screamed, as J.D. and Ava fought. Jada pulled at J.D. But rather than let up, J.D. fought both girls full on, while Edna stood cowering on the sidelines, continuing to beg and plead for them to stop.

J.D. was bigger, but he was also drunk. And it didn't take long before Jada and Ava had him on the floor, scratching, biting, and punching him. Ava grabbed the broom leaning against the wall and proceeded to knock J.D. all upside his head with it. Finally, Edna rushed forward and pulled the girls off of him.

"Stop it!" she screamed. "Stop it right now!"

Jada backed away and stared at her mother in outrage, while Ava continued to whale on J.D. J.D. could beat their asses from one end of the apartment to the other. But the minute they started to stomp J.D. into the ground their mother came leaping to the rescue.

Jada reached down and grabbed Ava, who was practically snarling like a demon. J.D. lay across the living room floor, almost passed out from the booze and the beating. With Edna crouched over him, Jada had to hold Ava back to keep her from pouncing on him again. Ava turned her fury on her mother.

"He gotta go, Ma!" Ava yelled. "Put his punk ass out!"

Jada looked at her sister in disbelief. Ava never cursed in front of their mother.

Edna shook her head. "Ava! Stop it. Just calm down for a second—"

"Calm down for what, Ma?" Jada asked, still panting. "You saw him hit us. So what are you gonna do about it? Every time he hits us, you sit there and act like you can't do nothing."

Ava glared at her mother. "I'm not staying in this house if he's living here! I can't live like this, Ma!" Ava started to cry. "*He's gotta go.* I'm tired of coming home to fights every day. I'm sick of this nigga putting his hands on us, and there's nothing we can do about it. He has to get outta here tonight."

Edna looked into her daughters' eyes, and they stood there, staring at her angrily. Edna wondered why they were putting her back against the wall. She felt that they were forcing her to decide between them and the man who took care of her. Edna was truly torn.

J.D. had gotten off the floor by now, and he stood against the wall getting his bearings. Then, turning to glare at Ava, he said, "You can go. Go 'head. 'Cuz I ain't going nowhere."

Edna had never felt so torn. She knew she had an obligation to her daughters. But she was so tired of being lonely, so scared of being single. And while J.D. was far from perfect, in her eyes he was better than nothing. So many nights she had longed for the company of a man. She had needed to be held, needed someone's touch. J.D. had provided these things in the beginning. And even now, when they had good times, they were really good times. The downside was that the bad times were horrible. And this was one of those times.

"Girls, go to your room until I tell you to come out," Edna stood up and said, calmly. Jada began to protest, but Edna raised her hand in warning, and yelled, "*Now,* Jada!"

Both girls stormed off to the sanctuary of their bedroom. When they got there, Jada plopped down on her bed and began cracking her knuckles, while Ava walked to the bedroom window and stared outside. Jada finally broke the silence.

"I hate him," she said. "I don't know why she don't throw his ass out! Just get rid of him. He's a fuckin' bully. All he does is fight women. But you never see him out in the street fighting no men. He's a punk. What the hell does she see in him?" It wasn't long before Jada realized that she was talking to herself. Ava's mind was somewhere else as she stared out their bedroom window. Jada knew how it felt to be mad to the point of speechlessness, so she allowed her sister several minutes to herself. But finally the silence became too much to bear.

"What's the matter, Ava?" Jada sat on the overturned milk crate that doubled as their chair.

Ava was still crying, but softly now. She turned to her sister. "I can't take it anymore, Jada. Every fucking day he starts a fight." Ava spoke each word slowly, deliberately pronouncing each syllable. "Either he's beating her ass or he's beating ours. And she won't make him leave." Ava looked completely fed up, and Jada wondered if this evening's battle had finally pushed her sister over the edge. Jada felt that Ava had never been as strong as she, that Ava couldn't take as much stress and drama as Jada could. True, Jada was also fed up with the bullshit, but not as fed up as Ava appeared to be now.

"What are you gonna do? Run away again, Ava? What's that gonna prove? You already tried that, and Mommy let him stay right here. It won't fix nothing." Ava was a professional runaway. She took flight whenever the going got too tough, and her disappearances had always ended when she came home to Edna's empty promises that J.D. would change, and that things would be different. But they never were.

Ava stared blankly out the window. "Well, I can't live like this no more. It's one thing for him to beat on *her*. If she's dumb enough to let him hit her, what the hell! But me and you haven't done shit to deserve what he does to us." Ava closed her eyes and shook her head. "And lately he keeps making comments about my body, talking about how big my ass is, and telling me that Mommy don't have to know if I let him fuck me." Ava's voice was almost a whisper, yet the force of her words was like thunder in Jada's ears. "He waits until I'm by myself, and he corners me. And I want to tell her. But I know she's gonna take his side, Jada."

Jada's blood was boiling. "How long he been doin' that to you? Why didn't you tell me?"

Ava shook her head. "He's crazy, that's why. That nigga will kill you if you confront him. And Mommy would probably even forgive him for doing that!"

"Fuck him, Ava! He ain't nobody. You can't be scared of him. You want me to say something to him?"

Ava shook her head, looking downcast. "I gotta tell Mommy. I gotta tell her so she can kick him out."

Jada walked over and hugged her little sister. She shook her head in dismay. Ava was only fourteen years old. It didn't matter how well developed she was. She was still only fourteen years old, and that sick son of a bitch was violating her. It was only verbal right now, but Jada knew it was only a matter of time before J.D. touched Ava. And Jada knew that if he ever did that to her sister, she would not hesitate to kill him. Jada consoled Ava, and they talked about what had been taking place. How J.D. had made her too scared to say anything, telling Ava that her mother would never believe her over him. Jada and Ava cried together, frustrated by what was being done to Ava by a man more than three times her age. They talked until J.D.'s snoring could be heard coming from their mother's bedroom across the hall. By then it was 11:30 P.M., and Ava—still teary and upset—decided it was time to go and try to talk to their mother. Jada wanted to come, too. Wanted to provide some support for her little sister, but Ava insisted on going alone. She insisted on talking to their mother one-on-one. So Jada watched her sister leave the room, and listened as Ava summoned their mother and the two of them walked down the hall toward the living room.

Jada sat alone in her room, furious about what her sister had told her. She was disgusted, and so confused. She could hear her mother's and sister's voices as they rose and fell when their conversation got heated. Jada couldn't make out exactly what was being said, but she could tell things had gotten out of hand. J.D. was still snoring loudly, passed out from all the liquor, as Jada climbed out of bed and walked toward the sound of her sister's anguished voice.

"Why can't you believe me? I'm telling you, he does it all the time. Why do you think he always insists that I stay home when you go places—when you go to the supermarket and stuff?"

"J.D. ain't like that, Ava. You can't tell me that he would say those things to you. No way. I know you want me to put him out—"

"Why can't you believe your own damn daughter?"

"Watch your mouth!"

"He told me you wouldn't believe me. I kept my mouth shut for so long because I didn't want to hurt you. But you don't even care that he's hurting your kids!"

"No." Edna shook her head. "You're wrong. You misunderstood."

"No, I didn't! He told me he thinks about me when he's having sex with you and—"

"Ava, go to bed. I can't do this right now!"

"He told me that he wants to feel my pretty lips on his dick." Ava was in tears. "He's always talking about my body, and telling me that you never have to know." Suddenly, Ava's tears of anguish turned to tears of rage, and she began to breathe heavily. "How come you don't believe me? I'm telling you the truth!"

"He couldn't be thinking of you that way, Ava! You're only fourteen."

"He is! And he's making me nervous around him."

"Ava, you would have said something then, if he was doing that to you. Why didn't you tell me when he said it? Why wait till now? J.D. is not that kind of man. No way. Maybe you *want* him to look at you like that. You just want him for yourself."

Ava stood up and walked closer to her mother, towering over her. "What the fuck would I want with a nigga that beats my ass every day?"

Edna hauled off and slapped Ava so hard that she saw stars, momentarily. "You watch your mouth in this house, you hear me?" Suddenly, Edna was the angry one.

Ava couldn't believe that her mother had slapped her. She stood holding her face, the pain throbbing in her cheek. But that pain was nothing compared to the pain of knowing that her mother wasn't on her side. She never fought J.D. Not even when he was beating Jada's ass, or when Ava was being emotionally and verbally molested. But here Edna was slapping her so hard that her face stung something terrible. How could she fight her and never fight the monster sleeping in the bedroom? Ava felt so close to the edge. One last time, she told her mother the truth. "I swear to God, Ma." Ava was crying no more tears. Now she was firm, her eyes locked on her mother's. "I swear. I'm not lying." Ava shook her head. "And he said you wouldn't believe me. He said you would take his side."

Edna stood in silence, staring blankly at her baby daughter.

"Ma!" Jada made her presence known as she entered the kitchen. "What is wrong with you? Why can't you listen to her?"

"Go back to your room, Jada. This is none of your business." Now Edna was crying, her ears ringing with the allegations against the man she loved, the man she had invited into her home, and into her heart. Her tears turned into gut-wrenching sobs, and Edna cried her eyes out. For a few minutes both girls thought their mother might hyperventilate. They watched Edna's breath come in audible gasps as she clung to the wall for support. She was coming undone.

Ava glared at her mother, her anger increasing with each second that passed. Jada stood motionless as Ava suddenly lunged toward her mother, grabbed her by the throat, and made every attempt to squeeze the life out of her. Jada rushed over and tried desperately to loosen her sister's grip on their mother's neck. "Let her go, Ava. Let her go!" Jada spoke through clenched teeth.

"I'm telling you the truth!" Ava yelled so loudly that Jada expected J.D. to wake up. "I'm telling you!"

Edna's fingers clawed at Ava's as she tried to pry them free from her neck. She gasped for air.

"Let her go, Ava! Let her go! Come on!"

Finally Ava came to her senses and released her mother. Edna sat holding her neck and breathing heavily. Jada walked over to her sister, put her arms around her, and tried to calm her down. But Ava shrugged Jada off her. She didn't want to be touched. She turned and stormed toward the kitchen. Jada followed her, but Ava ran into the bathroom and slammed the door behind her. Stomping back into the living room, Jada pounced on her mother. Edna was sitting in the corner, holding her neck and crying.

"How could you do that to her?"

"Jada, enough!" Edna was crying so hard, and still trying to catch her breath. "You and your sister made this shit up. You know J.D. wouldn't do nothing like that to her. Has he ever said anything like that to you?" Edna was standing now.

"No," Jada admitted. "That's 'cause he knows I would kill him if he tried that with me."

"Jada, I'm going to bed. And your sister is gonna go and get some help! You both need help!" Edna stood, trembling, almost eye-to-eye with her young daughter as she prepared to leave. Jada's gaze was penetrating. She shook her head, amazed.

"You know she's telling the truth. You just don't want to admit it to yourself."

"Jada, shut your mouth!"

"She's never gonna forgive you." Jada said it bitterly.

Edna walked down the hall, still teary, and into her bedroom, closing the door behind her. Jada stood dumbfounded in the kitchen by herself for several minutes. She couldn't believe what had just happened. Soon she walked down the short hallway and knocked on the bathroom door. She could hear Ava's muffled sobs through the door, but Ava refused to unlock it.

"I love you, Ava. I believe you. We're gonna take care of it, okay?"

No answer.

"Ava, come to bed." Jada could still hear her sister's soft sobs. "Stop playing, and come out."

"I'm not coming out, Jada. Go to bed." Ava's voice was faint.

Jada sat there for another fifteen minutes, trying to persuade her sister to come out, but to no avail. Ava wouldn't budge. Eventually, Jada made her way back to bed, where she sat waiting for her sister. J.D.'s snoring was still audible across the hall as Jada's eyes closed involuntarily, and she drifted off to sleep.

Early the next morning—so early the hood was quiet—Jada woke to the bloodcurdling scream of a distraught mother. Jada realized that her sister was nowhere in sight as she sat up in bed and looked around her room for Ava. Rushing from the room, she ran past J.D., who stood in the hallway with his head in his hands. She ran toward her mother's anguished cries and found Edna in the bathroom on the floor, cradling Ava's limp body. Both her wrists were slit, and a steak knife lay nearby. Ava was bleeding to death at the age of fourteen. And Jada slipped further down the slippery slope of her sanity.

2

THE GREAT ESCAPE

Amazingly, Ava survived her suicide attempt. But she wouldn't talk to the social workers. She wouldn't cooperate with the psychologists. They talked about putting her in a mental hospital for a while because she wouldn't talk about what had happened. But one social worker, Mrs. Lopez, took an interest in Ava's case. And once Ava was released from the hospital, Mrs. Lopez managed to convince Edna that her daughter could benefit from a good program outside of the home. Edna was reluctant at first and uncomfortable with the idea of placing her child in the state of New York's care. But she gave in after Ava showed no signs of improvement. Eventually, they placed Ava in a girls' home in Staten Island, on Maple Parkway.

To Jada it sounded like some June Cleaver shit. And compared to where they were living in Brooklyn, it was. Edna and Jada went out to Staten Island to visit Ava once in a blue moon, because for Edna it was still all about J.D. Jada hated him. And it became harder and harder for her to hide it.

Jada began to spend more and more time away from home. She learned how to get to Staten Island on public transportation, and would slip away and go visit her sister. Jada wasn't used to riding in boats, so the Staten Island Ferry was an uncomfortable experience for her. She hated it. But she visited Ava whenever she got enough time, money, and courage to do so. Jada was always out in the street, trying to escape the loneliness she felt after her sister's departure. Looking for the peace she never found at home.

But as fate would have it, close to a year after Ava went into the group home, J.D. crashed his car into a utility pole and killed himself while driving drunk. Edna was a wreck. She cried all the time. The dishes went unwashed; the house became a mess. Jada found herself mothering her own mother, and she hated it. This was the second time she'd had to pick up the pieces of Edna's broken heart. Edna was lost without J.D., both emotionally and financially. She couldn't handle the bills. She had a little money that he had left behind, but soon that was gone. With no place else to turn, Edna went to Mrs. Lopez and explained that she had few options left. She had no money, and was in need of assistance. So Mrs. Lopez pulled some strings and helped Edna get an apartment in Staten Island, so that she and Jada could be near Ava. When they found an apartment that was affordable and wasn't too far from where Ava was staying, they packed up and headed for Staten Island. Edna and Jada moved into an apartment on Wayne Court in West Brighton.

3

MOTHERLESS CHILD

They moved to Staten Island. And every day after that, Edna was home alone while Jada was always out with newfound friends, missing curfew and smoking weed. Ava introduced her sister to all the local bustas. The two of them would drink with all the niggas from around the way, hang out, and mess with older cats. They were growing up way too fast. But they felt like they had no one. It was them, and the streets.

One night, as they hung out smoking with some guys Ava knew, they discussed their mother. They were in a subleased apartment in the Mariner's Harbor projects, getting high while baby hustlers bagged up their product in the kitchen. Jason, Harvey, and Dean were high school dropouts getting their feet wet in the drug game. Since Jason had a crush on Ava, whenever he was around she and Jada could get high free of charge. That was just what the doctor had ordered on this particular evening.

"Pass that blunt, nigga!" Ava said, reaching toward her sister anxiously.

"Ill, you're fiending." Jada was smiling as she passed the weed to Ava.

Ava took a couple of tokes and exhaled. "So, what time you gotta go home?" she asked facetiously. "Won't the warden be worried that you ain't home before dark?" Ava didn't miss Edna's rules one bit.

Jada shrugged her shoulders. "I don't give a fuck what Mommy says.

She knows what she can do with her curfews. I don't have to listen to shit she says."

Ava grinned. "I know you get sick of hearing her mouth, though. She gotta be lecturing you, telling you that you'll turn out like me if you keep it up."

Jada nodded. "Yeah. She complains all the time that I'm always in the street. She threatens to put me in a home like she did to you. Either that, or she'll change the locks, and I'll have to make it on my own. She would never do that. She ain't strong enough to stand up to nobody. I don't pay her no mind. She's all talk."

Ava shook her head. "I hate the way she is, Jada. She cries and whines about everything. She's so weak. I hate how pitiful she is." Ava looked at Jada, her eyes low as the weed mellowed her senses. Still, her sincerity was obvious. "I don't ever wanna be like her. I don't ever wanna be that help-less and that scared." She took the blunt her sister passed to her. "I was acting like her when I tried to kill myself. But I'll never let myself be that weak again."

Jada nodded. "I'm glad to hear that. 'Cuz if you ever tried some shit like that again I'd kill you myself."

Ava laughed, and passed the weed to Jada. Jason called out from the kitchen, "Ava, wassup with me and you, ma? You come up here every day and smoke my weed, and you ain't trying to give a nigga no play?"

Jada frowned and looked at her sister. "No, this muthafucka is not calling you out in front of his boys."

Ava turned in Jason's direction and said, "Okay, so we'll leave then. I'll go smoke my own weed." She reached for her jacket and pretended to be leaving. Jada also gathered her things.

Jason took the bait. "I ain't saying it like that. Y'all ain't gotta leave."

"So, why you complaining that we're smoking your weed and you ain't getting no play? It takes more than some weed to get all that from us. We ain't those kinda bitches." Ava popped her gum when she was fin-ished speaking. Jada tried to suppress a smirk.

Dean stood behind Jason, both of them staring at the girls. "So, what it take?" Dean asked. Harvey and Jason burst out laughing, and Jada did, too.

Ava shook her head, smiling. "More than a fuckin' blunt, nigga."

"Be easy, ma. I was just playing. Sit down and smoke." Jason tossed her a small Ziploc bag filled with the good shit. The ladies quickly made themselves at home, and kept talking.

"What's up with you and Jason?" Jada asked. "I thought you was feeling him." Ava had always talked about how fine Jason was, and how nicely he dressed. But judging from the lack of chemistry between them tonight, Jada had surmised that something must have changed her sister's mind.

Ava looked around to make sure the coast was clear, and lowered her voice. "That nigga is a backward ass hustler. He always got weed, stay getting high, and never got money to do nothing else. I don't understand how he always broke, and he hustles all day, every day. That's not the kind of guy for me."

Jada slapped her sister high five. "No romance without finance, you know what I'm saying?"

Ava concurred and crossed her legs. They thought they had it all figured out. The sisters smoked and talked for another hour or so. When Jason, Harvey, and Dean ran out of weed, Ava and Jada decided that it was time to go. They said good-bye to the guys and walked off to catch the bus. Ava promised to call Jason the next day, and the evening ended with everyone happy and high. Ava returned to her group home, and Jada went home, knowing that Edna would greet her at the door with complaints about her lateness. It was well after midnight, and she had school in the morning. Just as she suspected, her mother greeted her at the door.

"Where the hell have you been?" Edna demanded as soon as Jada walked in the door. She stood with her hands on her hips, glaring at her daughter.

"Out," Jada answered, as she breezed past her mother and walked into the kitchen.

"I know you were out, Jada. Out where?" Edna asked, following Jada closely.

"Ma, I went out. What's the problem?" Jada asked, nonchalantly. She poured herself some juice and stood there in the kitchen and drank it. When she'd drained the glass, she looked at her mother and grinned. Then she turned to wash out her glass.

"The problem is, I told you to be home by ten o'clock. It's almost one o'clock in the morning, Jada. You've got school tomorrow."

Jada frowned, seeming confused by her mother's concern. "Oh, so now you care about my education? Since when? *Oh, that's right.* I almost forgot, J.D. is dead. So *now* you have time to worry about me. I'm having a hard time getting used to that. *Now* you wanna be a parent?"

Edna stood silently and soaked up her daughter's cold words. Jada knew that whenever she brought up J.D. and Edna's failure to protect her daughters, Edna was defenseless. There was nothing she could say to that. Edna's voice was low as she spoke. "Jada, I need you to be in this house at a decent time every night. I'm not gonna keep putting up with you coming in here this late."

Jada smirked. "What you gonna do?" Her tone was defiant. She was challenging her mother. "What are you gonna do if I don't listen to you, Ma?"

Edna picked up on the mockery in Jada's tone. "I can put you out of here. You can make it on your own, just like your sister."

Jada laughed. "You can do that. That's what you want, anyway. To get rid of both of us, so you don't have to worry about us no more. Go ahead and put me out. Ava already hates you. Go 'head and make me hate you, too."

Edna stood, silently fighting back tears. Disgusted, Jada rolled her eyes and walked off to her bedroom and shut the door, knowing that Edna's threats were empty ones. Jada knew how to manipulate Edna's emotions and break the woman down. She thrived on her ability to reduce her mother to tears.

What Jada had said to Edna was true. Ava did hate her. But Jada didn't. What she hated was the weakness in her. She hated that about her. But other than that, Jada felt sorry for her mother. Edna was a pitiful excuse for a woman, in Jada's opinion. She was powerless and too fragile. She was too strict, and she had waited too long to try to play the role of a parent. For too many years the girls had witnessed one emotional meltdown after another from their mother. So to have her suddenly attempt to enforce rules was something neither of them welcomed. Jada wanted freedom.

But what she needed was a firm hand. She needed her mother's strength and control. But Edna had neither and she couldn't even hide it. She felt useless and unloved by all the men in her life. And now her own daughters were against her. Edna felt as guilty as Jada and Ava wanted her to. And she was too timid and guilt-ridden to do anything other than sit by and let her daughter get away with murder. Part of her was frustrated by Jada's strong will and rebelliousness. And another part of her was just unwilling to *try* to control her child. Edna had spent her whole life handing over control to someone else. So she allowed Jada to have control over her own destiny. In essence, Edna gave up.

Ava was out of her jurisdiction. Edna didn't even really try to control what Ava did or how she behaved. She knew that she had done Ava wrong, so she never gave her much grief or really tried to parent Ava. She left that up to the people running the home. Her life had turned out in a way that she had never imagined it would. So Edna began to seek solace in the arms of Jesus Christ. Him, and Mr. Charlie.

"I told you, ain't nobody gettin' high!" Jada yelled.

"Come on, now!" Edna's attempt at yelling fell sadly short. "Your eyes are bloodshot half the time. I found them cigars in your room. I know what that's about, Jada. Don't take me for a fool!"

Jada laughed, wondering why she should think of her mother as anything but that. In Jada's mind, her mother was just that—a fool.

Edna continued her rant. "Your teacher called and said that you ain't been to school in days. Now, you leave this house every day. So since you're not going to school, I wanna know where you've been?"

"I go to school." Jada kept eating her cereal, hoping to provoke her mother into having a backbone. She almost wanted Edna to throw a fit, and to take charge for once. But she had no such luck.

"Jada, you're *not* going to school. That teacher has no reason to lie on you."

"Well, I don't know why she's lying, then. But I've been in school. Maybe she made a mistake." Jada shrugged.

"She didn't make a mistake, and you know that. She told me that you're failing her class—"

"So what?" Jada bellowed, drowning out her mother's voice. Edna fell silent, and was tempted to hit Jada. But she knew that if she did, Jada might just hit her back. She didn't want to go toe-to-toe with her daughter.

The doorbell interrupted them, and Edna stormed off to answer it.

"Hi, Charlie," she gushed, when she opened the door. "Come in. Excuse the mess. I was just about to straighten up." Edna smoothed her shirt, making sure her outfit was perfect.

Mr. Charlie was their neighbor. He was dapper at forty-nine years old, and had an old-school, buttery smooth demeanor. His style was reminiscent of Richard Roundtree's Shaft, or a modern-day Samuel Jackson. He had a woman in his life, who no one saw very often. She didn't live with him, but she did come around every now and then. Spent a couple of days at most with him, and then she'd leave. She never socialized with any of the neighbors, but Mr. Charlie sure did. He was like everybody's super. All of them lived in Section 8 houses and rent-controlled apartments. Edna's was a town house in the Markham homes on Wayne Court. It was humble, but it was home. Charlie's apartment was across the street, in the projects. He lived at 240 Broadway, but he made himself known to all the people in the hood. He was the guy who fixed your toilet, helped you get a part for your car, and got you an air conditioner for cheaper than normal. He was the go-to guy. And everybody liked Charlie.

Edna ushered him in, gushing all the while. Charlie smiled at Jada, and she barely returned the gesture. "I came to put in that air conditioner you wanted," he explained.

"Thank you," Edna said, smiling. She seemed to almost forget that Jada was in the room. She seemed mesmerized by Charlie.

Jada took her cue. She stood to leave, and carried her bowl to the sink. Edna turned toward her. She didn't want her daughter to think she'd forgotten about her behavior. Edna turned back to Charlie. "Excuse me for a minute. I was just talking to Jada. You know how hardheaded these young girls are." Edna's voice took on the sweetest lilt whenever he was near. "Where are you going?" she asked Jada, sweetly.

"Outside," Jada answered flatly. She didn't even glance at her mother. But she noticed Mr. Charlie looking at her from across the room.

"Well, you better not come in here as late as you did last night." Edna's attempt at sounding authoritative was unconvincing to Jada. "I don't want you over that boy Sean's house, neither. His mother ain't even home half the time. I ain't stupid, Jada." Edna shook her head. "That's where you were last night, ain't it?"

Jada shook her head, preparing to lie and say that she hadn't been. But to her surprise, Charlie did it for her. "Nah, Edna. I saw Jada last night in my building with her friend Shante. Shante lives in my building. I know her family. Her mother works every day. They good people. Her and Shante are good girls. They don't be getting in trouble like these other girls around here. I look out for her, you know." He smiled at Edna, and she seemed to relax.

Both Edna and Charlie looked at Jada. Jada's brow furrowed slightly, wondering what was going on. She *had* seen Mr. Charlie the night before. But she hadn't been with Shante at all. She had been in the corner store with Sean. While she had gone to get a soda from the back, Sean had been at the counter asking for condoms. When Jada had joined him at the register, Charlie had walked in. She had cringed while Charlie ordered a pack of cigarettes and watched her walk out of the store with Sean's hand on her ass. And here he was lying for her. As her mother searched her face for confirmation, Jada nodded. Charlie winked at her.

She suppressed a smile as she left. Charlie followed her out, as he went to retrieve the air conditioner from his car. When they were out of Edna's earshot, Charlie said, "You know I saw you last night, right? Now, what would your mother think about what you were doing with that boy?"

Jada looked at him. "I know you came to give my mother more than an air conditioner. And what would your wifey think about that?"

Charlie smirked. "I'll keep your secrets if you keep mine," he said.

Jada smiled back. "Deal." She strutted off toward Broadway, and Charlie couldn't help watching.

From then on, Jada felt that Mr. Charlie was her ally. He saw her from time to time, being fast and acting grown. And she turned a blind eye and a deaf ear to the loud fucking he did with her mother twice a week. Charlie treated Edna as his chick on the side. Whatever she needed, Mr. Charlie could provide. Charlie always brought them something. He gave Edna money, groceries—whatever. He'd give her money to take Jada shopping, and he drove them to the mall. But what Jada liked about him was that he seemed to understand *her*. He seemed to remember what it was like to be young and to want to have freedom—to have fun. Whenever Jada told her mother that she had been at the after-school center, while she and Ava had really been riding around with niggas smoking weed, Charlie knew the truth. And he never told their mother. He would even cover for Jada if Edna caught her in a lie. He became her coconspirator.

One night Charlie bumped into Jada as she stood in the stairwell of his building smoking weed with Shante. He stopped and warned her that she would get in trouble if the cops caught her smoking there. "You should be careful where you do your dirt," he said. He could tell that she was moving in the wrong direction, because she was hanging out with Shante more and more. Shante was bad news, and everybody knew it. Her mother seemed blind to it, and she was grown long before the law said so. She was a booster. She smoked weed all day, boosted her shit, and got her money. Shante hardly ever went to school, and she seemed to be able to come and go as she pleased. Her mother worked all the time, and was obsessed with her younger boyfriend. Shante's mom had time for little else than young Raymond, so her apartment was the hangout spot. Shante was fast, and she didn't give a fuck. Jada would get high with her just about every day after school. Some days they would invite guys over and get busy with them, but usually they would just chill, drinking and smoking, talking and acting grown.

Jada nodded. "I'll be careful. Thank you, Mr. Charlie."

He walked up the stairs, and she kept right on smoking. She took his advice, though. And after that they started smoking at Shante's house. They opened all the windows and sprayed air freshener to keep the scent out. By the time her mother got home, the place was always back in shape. This became their routine. It was on one such occasion that smoking with Shante changed Jada's life forever.

They were smoking at Shante's place with her friend, Lucas. Lucas was a guy everybody knew yet no one was really close to. He was ugly, loud, rude, and often dirty-looking. The only reason anyone even bothered to socialize with Lucas at all was because he always had weed, always had money. Hanging with Lucas always meant a good time. Jada was beginning to suspect that Shante and Lucas had something going on. It seemed that every time Jada visited Shante these days, Lucas was there already. She couldn't understand what Shante saw in him, but figured it was none of her business, as long as he kept the weed coming. On this day, everybody was smoking Lucas's blunt. It wasn't unlike them to experiment with different types of weed: hydro, blueberry, chocolate, purple haze. They mixed it with hash, and smoked with bongs, different cigars, and rolling papers. Almost every time they got together, they tried something new. So when Lucas rolled up a blunt and passed it to Shante, Jada thought nothing of it.

Jada watched Shante puff eagerly on the blunt, and how that look of complete peace washed over her friend. The expression on Shante's face was similar to how someone would look after taking a long drink of water after being thirsty for days. She seemed relieved. *That must be the good shit!* Jada thought. When Shante passed the blunt to her, Jada took a long, hard toke, and exhaled. Then she took another one. Immediately, a fog swept over her. She could feel her heart galloping in her chest, and yet she felt better than she could ever remember feeling. Jada took another toke and felt all the nerves in her body tingle. She felt higher than she ever had in her life. Jada had never felt more alive than she did at that moment. She felt like she was floating, and all her senses were heightened. She took another toke. *Damn!* she thought. *This is the best shit I ever had.* Reluctantly, she passed the blunt to Lucas, who sat grinning at her in the most sinister way. But Jada was oblivious to Lucas's grin. She was off in space, her mind taking her on a trip unlike any she'd ever experienced before. By the time the blunt made its way back to her, Jada took it anxiously. She relished the feeling it gave her, and took long puffs as she enjoyed it.

When it was finished, the three of them were extremely high, Jada most of all. Shante and Lucas held an animated conversation about something that Jada paid no attention to. She sat in silence, enjoying her high. The music seemed louder, the colors in the room somehow brighter. She started laughing to herself at jokes no one but her could hear. She felt completely carefree. As it wore off, and she began coming out of the fog she had been in, Jada looked over at Shante and cleared her throat.

"What was that shit we just smoked, Shante?"

Shante smiled at her friend. "Girl, that was a woolah."

Not wanting to sound like a lame in front of streetwise Lucas by asking specifically what kind of weed it was, Jada simply nodded her head. "Damn. Woolahs is the bomb!"

After the first time they smoked a woolah together, Jada loved it. The high was unlike anything she had ever experienced before. And for the rest of the night, Jada thought about that feeling. It wasn't until the next day, when Lucas wasn't around, that she finally asked Shante why the previous night's high had been so much better than normal.

That's when Shante explained to her friend that they had been smoking weed with crack mixed into it.

Jada was stunned. "We're smoking crack?"

But Shante acted like it was no big deal. "Nah. It's not like we're smoking straight-up crack. That's the shit that gets you addicted—when you smoke it straight, no chaser. We mix it with weed, and it takes some of the potency out of it, so you won't get addicted. Stop worrying," Shante said, nonchalantly. "I'm surprised you ain't never heard of it, with you being from *Brooklyn* and all!"

Jada frowned, and Shante knew she'd touched a nerve. Jada often liked to behave as if she was so far ahead of the girls her age in Staten Island. She entertained them often with stories about her Brooklyn days, and about the things she'd seen and lessons she'd learned there. So when Shante mentioned Brooklyn, Jada felt like she was questioning her gangsta.

"I have heard of it. I just never knew anybody that smoked it before," she explained.

Shante shrugged her shoulders. "Well, it ain't no big deal. Everybody smokes these. There's so much weed and so little crack that it don't get you hooked." Shante smiled at Jada. "But that high was the bomb, wasn't it?"

Jada smiled back and gave Shante five. "Hell, yeah!"

After that, Jada and Shante smoked woolahs all the time. They naïvely assumed that Shante's theory was correct, and that they couldn't get hooked as long as they mixed it. But it wasn't long before Jada was strung the fuck out. The first time Jada had experienced a high that was so wonderful that soon she was chasing it all the time. The feeling was so intense. But it seemed as if the highest high was always just out of her reach, and she just had to have it. It was like trying to grasp an elusive dream. And then she would come down, and find herself craving it all over again. Now she had a problem.

4

KILLING ME SOFTLY

Jada and Ava spent less time together as Jada's addiction blossomed. She had a boyfriend she had met around her old neighborhood in Brooklyn. He was rugged and ruthless, and he turned her on. While Jada was only seventeen, her man, Rico, was twenty-three. She convinced herself that she'd found love. He flaunted her around his boys, and she loved every minute of it.

"Come here, *mami*. Suck my dick." Rico sat sprawled across his water bed, watching Jada masturbate in front of him. Rico was selling crack and was no stranger to recreational drug use. So when Jada told him that she liked smoking woolahs, he didn't mind. He gave her a vial or two of crack to mix in with her weed whenever he reupped. He liked the sex she gave him when she was high on that shit. Today was one of those days, and she eagerly obliged him. She placed him in her mouth and sucked him like a Popsicle. "That's it, *mami*." Rico enjoyed the ride as Jada took him to paradise. He watched her and voiced his approval.

Jada stopped abruptly, straddled him, and plunged him deep inside her. She rode him, and their lips locked together before she pulled back a little and bit his lip until she drew blood. Rico pried her off of him, and turned her over on her stomach. She writhed as if she was going to resist him, and he slapped her ass hard. Sucking the blood off his lip, he stroked her from behind. Rico wrapped her long hair around his hand and pulled it roughly.

"Fuck me!" Jada yelled, defiantly. "Fuck me, Rico!"

He pounded her furiously, turned on by her yelling. "Yeah? Like that?" He fucked her, and pulled out right before he came. He splashed off on her ass, and turned her over roughly. "You a fuckin' freak!" Jada smiled at him in a way that he thought was sexier than anything he'd ever seen before.

Rico's mother had been a heroin addict. He had a father who snorted cocaine. He, himself, snorted a little from time to time. But he managed to keep it together enough to be a contender in a hood full of hustlers. Drug use, drug sales, drug trafficking, it was all familiar territory to Rico. So while he didn't exactly discourage Jada's habit, he did warn her that it could get out of hand if she let it.

After taking a shower Jada sat at the foot of his bed and took another hit.

Rico shook his head. "It's too much now, Jada. Your shit is out of hand. Every time I turn around you're doing that shit again."

Jada sighed and rolled her eyes. "Come on, Rico. Not now with that shit!"

"What you mean, not now? If I didn't care about you, I'd let you go 'head. But I'm telling you, you got a problem now, baby girl. You should trust me on this one. You need some help."

Jada stood up and angrily threw her clothes back on. She was sick of Rico's cryptic warnings that she was headed for trouble. She ran a quick comb through her hair, grabbed her bag, and turned to Rico. "Fuck you, Rico. I don't need nobody's fuckin' help!" She bounced and headed back to Staten Island. She went straight to Shante's house—a place where she could get high in peace.

Jada told Shante about her fight with Rico. Shante listened, and then said, "You know what it is? He feels like he can say that shit to you because he thinks you need him. Right now, he's your main source for getting high, but you don't need him for that shit. I ain't met a bitch yet who had a hard time staying high. As long as you use what God gave you, you should never go without." Jada grimaced, and Shante laughed. She figured it was time to explain the power of the pussy to Jada.

"Whenever you give it up to any man, you should be compensated for it. Pussy has its price, you know what I'm saying?"

"I'm not a prostitute, Shante. I ain't putting no price tag on my pussy."

"It ain't prostitution," Shante reasoned. "That shit is fair exchange. The nigga wants some ass, and you want some cash. One hand washes the other, right?" Jada's expression was unsure, so Shante clarified her position. "I'm not saying you walk around with a dollar sign on your shit. But no man touches me without giving me something. Ain't shit for free over here."

They got high together, and Jada contemplated Shante's advice. She knew that she didn't want to have to ask Rico for shit anymore. She hated hearing the condescension in his voice when he told her that she needed help. She didn't want to give him the satisfaction of being her sole provider.

Soon Jada adopted Shante's philosophy, and the guys she dealt with knew that they had to pay to play. She was a high-maintenance fly girl with a habit that was growing out of her control. She was in Mr. Charlie's building pretty often, copping weed and crack from Lucas on the third floor and going up to Shante's place to smoke her woolahs.

The nineties in New York City were plagued by an out-of-control drug epidemic, and with police eager to stop the young hustlers from making a killing. But plenty of them were still getting dough. Shante and Jada tried to rub elbows with all of those types. They used their looks and flair for fashion, as well as Shante's talent for stealing, and they gained access to all the biggest parties. It wasn't hard for two young ladies in an error of excess to gain entry into the drug-induced fog of addiction.

But the drug use started to become evident in Jada's appearance. She was strung out, and she looked it. Her face was sunken, her hair often uncombed. She rarely bothered to iron her clothes, or even to change them from day to day. Still she was in denial. She reasoned that she just had a little habit. Eventually, Charlie warned her that her mother had begun to notice the change in her appearance. He told her to clean up her act, and Jada worried for a moment that he knew her secret. "Your mother thinks you're losing too much weight. I told her you was probably on a diet, and that I think she should get off your case. But you need to stop upsetting your mother. You know what I'm saying?"

Jada nodded, and made an effort to keep her appearance intact. Shante was boosting. Jada told her that she wanted to learn how to do that, too. So one day Shante took Jada with her. She taught Jada how to take off an alarm, and that was it. Jada was stealing whatever she could steal. She did it all the time. She was enrolled in high school at the time, but hardly ever went. The only time she would go was when she had a new outfit that she knew would make the other bitches sick. Jada looked fierce every day, always one of the best dressed around the way. Her clothes were fabulous. She was making money to do what she wanted by stealing and running niggas' pockets. She was still in school, coming into her mother's house all hours of the day and night, dressed to kill and hiding a drug problem.

Edna noticed the change. Jada was thinner than she'd ever been, and wearing clothes that Edna hadn't bought her. Her motherly instincts told her that something was amiss. She could feel it in her gut. But never one to really rock the boat, Edna questioned Jada about her weight loss only offhandedly. She didn't want to spur Jada's wrath. So in soft tones she would question, "Jada, those jeans used to be tight on you, right?" Jada would always react defensively, and Edna would always retreat. When Ava finally saw her sister she told Jada that she was concerned about her rapid weight loss, but Jada didn't think it was a big deal. She had only been smoking crack for about a year. It wasn't that bad. That's what she told herself. She knew other people who were using, and she saw them maintaining. Jada figured she could do that, too.

When too many people raised their eyebrows at her weight loss, Jada made even more of an effort to stay presentable. She was a lovely young lady. Her long hair was natural. Her pretty face was chiseled, showing off a flawless bone structure that was enviable. To top it all off, she had the gift of gab. Jada had the ability to look a person in the eyes and make them feel as if all she was concerned with was them. She had a smile that people yearned to be on the receiving end of. Jada was likable. And that made it all the easier for her to find new "friends." It also made it easy for her to smile at and distract store security guards when she went to work.

"Work" is what Jada called the boosting she did to get the clothes and funds she needed to get high the way she wanted to. She got up every day with stealing on her mind. She soon became a compulsive thief. It got to the point where she would steal even when she didn't need anything. It was an obsession. She enjoyed the rush of getting something nice for free and of using it to get money. She liked the high she was always rewarded with afterward, and the whole thing became a routine for her. And one that she rather enjoyed. Jada was giving her sister a lot of things, too. Ava was the recipient of bags of designer clothes, courtesy of her sister. Jada wondered if her sister knew what she was doing. And, indeed, Ava suspected that her sister was doing something shady to get all those things. But Ava loved the way nice clothes made her feel. So she didn't rock the boat. They were in high school in a new borough, each with a gorgeous face, a nice figure, and the best outfits. Needless to say, she and her sister stood out.

On an afternoon in mid-August, Jada scoured the shelves in Victoria's Secret and grabbed as many B and C cups as she could. She'd already gotten all the girls' sizes around the way, and figured she could get rid of all of them for twenty dollars a pop at least. She was busily stuffing her bags. Yet she was so on point that she noticed the security guard watching her discreetly. She knew it was useless to put everything back. By the time she noticed the guard casually glancing at her, she realized that he had probably seen her stash half the store in her bag. She had a bag full of merchandise she'd stolen from other stores, but she wasn't going to jail. In a flash, Jada ran like Flo-Jo, without a warning. By the time they realized that she had suddenly taken flight, they couldn't catch up to her. She ran faster than she ever had in her life. Her heart raced as she ran down the escalator, bumping other shoppers and shoving people out of her way. She ran straight through the doors and through the parking lot. Mall security canvassed the area and radioed Jada's description across the airwaves. But Jada took off like a runaway slave. And a slave she was, indeed. To the very drug she thought she had control of.

After that she was scared to steal. Jada didn't do it for a long time after that day. But she still had a jones for the crack, so she needed money. One afternoon, she went to Mr. Charlie and asked him for a favor.

"Can I borrow twenty dollars?" she asked, shifting her weight from one leg to the other. She was thirsting to get high, and it was obvious.

Charlie gave it to her, no questions asked. "You don't have to pay me back, either." He put the money in her palm and held it for a couple extra moments. "You're like a daughter to me."

"Thanks, Mr. Charlie," Jada said, smiling innocently. She went right away and copped upstairs. After she got her drugs she scurried out into the hallway; her next stop would be Shante's apartment. But as she was coming out of Lucas's apartment, she ran smack into Mr. Charlie.

"Oh. Hi," Jada stammered. She didn't know what he was doing on that floor, since he lived two floors down. But she was stunned and embarrassed that he had seen her coming out of there. Everybody in the hood knew that that was the drug spot. So Jada knew she was busted.

But to her surprise, he said, "I figured you'd be up here. Don't be out here like one of these fiends, Jada. Don't be smoking in the staircase and shit. Come downstairs and smoke at my place, where it's safe."

To say that Jada was shocked was an understatement. Her heart beat rapidly, and she was momentarily at a loss for words. So she silently followed him back to his apartment, and stood awkwardly in the living room once inside. Charlie shut the door and locked it, and he gestured toward his sofa. Jada sat down, and cleared her throat.

"I'm not about to smoke weed," she began.

Charlie nodded. "I know what you're smoking. Go 'head. I won't judge you." Charlie went into the kitchen, leaving Jada alone. She sat there on his sofa, and smoked her woolah. Charlie let her have her space, and she sat and got high. When she was done, she felt slightly awkward.

"Umm," Jada played with her hair, and barely met Charlie's gaze. "I don't do this all the time, so I don't have a problem. Thank you for not saying nothing to my mother. If it gets out of hand, I'll stop—"

"Listen," Charlie interrupted. "Everybody has their vices. Who am I to judge you for yours? But since I don't wanna see your mother hurt, I'm trying to keep you from getting in trouble. You can't be out there getting high off that shit in the stairways. Shante's house is hot. Lucas's dumb ass is up there every day, and the cops been looking at him for a while now. All your mother needs is to hear that you got arrested in a drug spot. If you wanna get high, you come here. I'd rather you do it where you're safe."

Jada nodded, grateful for his understanding. After that it was her routine. Jada was there every day, and Charlie let her handle her business. She would go home after school, and do what she had to do around the house in order to keep Edna quiet. Then she would go outside and cop, then head to Mr. Charlie's apartment and smoke her woolahs. Soon the woolahs turned into straight crack pipes.

He never smoked with her, just watched her get high and go through her changes. Jada would bug out, talk to herself, sing, whatever the crack told her to do. Then she would come down and compose herself enough to go home.

Charlie was still seeing Jada's mother throughout this period of time. He would come by every now and then, like usual. But he never let on that he knew her daughter was developing a very powerful addiction. And Edna never knew the secret between Charlie and Jada. And, as twisted as it was, Jada was grateful to Mr. Charlie for that. He kept her secrets.

5

SUGAR DADDY

1992

Charlie Harmon sat in his armchair, Al Green smoothly crooning "Let's Stay Together" in the background, and he stared at seventeen-year-old Jada hungrily. He'd watched her get high for the thousandth time, and he knew she was twisted. He could tell by her restlessness, her silly face, her drowsy half smiles. He watched her tripping, waiting for the right time. All of a sudden she started rubbing her arms rapidly, as if she was trying to warm herself.

"What's the matter, Jada? You cold?" he asked. "Let me help you out, sweetheart."

She was twitching and laughing to herself. Then she started looking to either side of herself, picking at her shirt unnecessarily. But she was calm enough, in Charlie's opinion. He inched closer to her, and sat beside her on the couch. "Let me warm you up." Jada didn't protest when he touched her.

She rocked back and forth, twisting a long strand of hair and staring blankly at Charlie. She wasn't seeing him, though. Jada was some place far off in her mind. She looked around, trying to see the cloud on which the room appeared to be floating. She felt herself drifting, felt the whole world spinning, and she smiled. Her eyelids squinted, Jada hazily watched his hands come closer.

Charlie pulled her sweater up so slowly that Jada almost didn't notice. She felt it all in slow motion and felt the air on her body as he sat back and looked at her black lace bra. Charlie unleashed her breasts and he stroked them. He seemed to know just how to make a woman melt, because Jada had never been caressed like that before. She smiled wider at the sensation, at the man stroking her perfectly. By her smile, he was encouraged. It seemed like every nerve in her body felt every sensation in the atmosphere at the same time. She felt a breeze across her skin, and her hairs stood on end. She felt his hands on her body, and was convinced that nothing felt better than what Charlie was doing to her at that moment.

"Ain't this alright, Jada?" His breath felt warm against her face, and sent a tingle up her spine. She nodded, as he watched her facial expressions change. "Yeah," he said. "It's alright."

Jada nodded, foggily. Then she was laughing, and moving around to a rhythm only she could feel. She nodded so slowly, her head rolling to the rhythm of Charlie's fingertips. He licked and sucked her breasts, with his hands up her tiny skirt. Jada exhaled loudly.

Jada was dancing in her head, still twitchy and jumpy. But what his fingers were doing to her pussy was spellbinding. "Yeah." He said it again. "It's alright." As crazy as it was, Jada fantasized that she was in control. She still would not admit that crack had her by the throat. Instead she watched him, smiling and thinking, *Look at this old muthafucka licking me. He knows he wants me and not my mother.* Charlie worked magic with his tongue. He toyed with her young pearl and didn't stop until she bubbled over with pleasure. Jada was spent, having just loudly achieved the first orgasm of her life at the age of seventeen.

Charlie sat back and calmly stared at Jada's young body. She sat in the same position he had left her, her leg propped up on the arm of the couch to reveal all of her goodies. Her bra was pulled up over her breasts; her sweater was bunched up as well. She sat there, high as ever, naked before Mr. Charlie.

He stood up and pulled down his pants. He looked at her, half naked and high, and smiled as he put himself inside the tightness of her young walls.

"Yeah," he moaned in her ear, over and over.

Jada pulled back from him, as if uncomfortable. The thought of resisting him registered somewhere in the corner of her mind. But Charlie held her gently, and said, "It's alright." He held her thighs open, and she was still jumpy, but moaning. He stroked her slowly, enjoying each and every thrust. Jada didn't protest, and she smiled, enjoying her high and the ride Mr. Charlie was taking her on. He knew he had her now. He stroked her until his old penis couldn't hold out any longer. Charlie had sense enough to pull himself out and spill his seed on her stomach. Afterward, he sat beside her and caught his breath, his dick lying limp across his thigh.

Jada sat zoned out for a while, somewhere far away in her mind again. He watched her come down slowly, unaware, it seemed, of how perfect her body was. He gave her space until she was composed enough to go home. She never mentioned what had occurred. She simply washed herself off and fixed her clothes, and Charlie sent her on her way, knowing that she had what it took. She was young, and pretty, and had some tight pussy and a crack habit. He knew it wouldn't be long before he turned her out.

6

STORMY WEATHER

Jada finally knew she was a crackhead, even though she hated the thought of it. She had always been the street-smart one—the tougher one of Edna's daughters. Now she was someone weak enough to submit to an addiction. She was disappointed in herself and felt guilty for all that she had done. But that guilt didn't outweigh the hunger she had to get high. Charlie was having sex with her on a regular basis, giving her drugs each time she came to see him. He dominated her, and seemed to enjoy making her feel good. She no longer had to go upstairs to cop. She got all that she needed right from Mr. Charlie's wrinkled hands. She was his sex toy, doing whatever he wanted. Part of her felt comforted by her relationship with him. He was a father figure, and she was even turned on by the thought of calling him Mr. Charlie while she fucked him.

In between her highs, Charlie taught her things. Mostly about sex. He made her feel beautiful—too beautiful for the young gangsta wannabes she hung around. She began to recognize game, because Charlie taught her what he knew. Those conversations felt privileged to Jada. Like Charlie was letting her in on the ground floor of Hustlers, Inc. She learned how to get what she wanted from men of any age. Mr. Charlie taught her what to say, how to dress. He was schooling her, telling her how to hold her liquor when she drank, how to roll a dutch properly. He told her that he was going to make her the baddest bitch ever. He would show her how to be every man's fantasy. Soon nothing a nigga said sounded as good as it used to. Jada recognized their game, and she shot them down left and right. Only Charlie was getting it at that point. He seemed genuinely interested in her. She thought he was the only one who understood her.

Charlie introduced her to the art of oral sex, to all kinds of different positions. He showed her how to work her hips when she rode him. Jada felt like he was teaching her how to be his woman, grooming her to keep him happy. She would have done just about anything to keep old Charlie happy, because old Charlie was keeping her high. And she liked it like that.

He was also showing Jada how to survive in the mean streets. He taught her how to navigate all kinds of situations, and how to protect herself. He gave her a knife and showed her how to stash a razor without being detected. He taught her how to get what she wanted out of the men she came in contact with. Jada felt like a grown-up in his presence, and Mr. Charlie fed into that. When he spoke, she listened, and he knew she was like putty in his hands.

With her eighteenth birthday drawing near, Mr. Charlie was carrying on a physical relationship with both Jada and her mother. In her mind, usually in the midst of her drug-induced fog, Jada felt that she was getting back at her mother somehow. She convinced herself that what she was doing with Mr. Charlie was payback for her mother letting her and Ava down. It was revenge for the fact that Edna had failed her daughters when they needed her most. It was her way of rationalizing what she knew was wrong, so that she could continue to be selfish.

He continued to visit her mother periodically, bringing her money, giving her attention. But Edna was blind to the winks Charlie would toss Jada's way, to the way he would touch Jada's ass when her mother's back was turned. Their secret was theirs alone. Until the day it came crashing down.

It was a Sunday afternoon, and Edna hadn't returned from Sunday church service yet. After two nights of smoking crack, Jada had just woken up, at four o'clock in the afternoon. She stumbled out of bed, and almost immediately felt the urge to get high. She started scratching at her skin, itchy after two days in the same clothes. She needed a shower, and had hardly eaten a thing. But all she could think about was how soon she could get high again.

The doorbell rang, and Jada stumbled to answer it. When she opened the door and found Charlie standing there, she gladly ushered him inside. She had planned to take a shower, get dressed, and go looking for him. But now she wouldn't have to go looking after all.

"Hey," she said, smiling. Her mouth felt cottony and dry, but she licked her lips, happily. "Mommy ain't back from church yet."

Charlie gave Jada a once-over and shook his head. "You look a mess," he said. "Go clean yourself up before your mother sees you like this." Charlie knew that Edna was beginning to grow suspicious of Jada's behavior and her appearance lately. He'd done his best to reassure her that Jada was too smart to do anything as stupid as use drugs. But with Jada walking around looking like the neighborhood crackhead, he was having a harder time convincing Edna that her daughter wasn't slipping.

"I will," Jada said. "But let me get you off real fast before I go wash up. Then you can give me a couple of dollars—"

"I'm not gonna fuck you in your mama's house, Jada. You must be crazy," Charlie protested, before sitting down on the sofa. He shook his head at her.

"I didn't say you had to fuck me, Mr. Charlie." Jada smiled at him again, and without further discussion, she dropped to her knees and frantically unzipped his pants.

"Stop playing, Jada," Charlie protested, halfheartedly. "Wait till later on."

But Jada ignored him. She knew that her head game was the best, and estimated that within five minutes tops she could make him bust a nut. Then she could go and get high while he hung around and waited for Edna to come back. Deaf to his protests, she engulfed him with her mouth, earning what she needed. His penis was limp, and she sucked all of it, until it began to grow inch by inch in her mouth. Still offering a weak protest, Charlie reminded Jada that her mother would be on her way home. But Jada was persistent, and she tightened the suction in her cheeks, sucking all of him into her mouth and establishing an intoxicating rhythm. His head fell back against the sofa, as he enjoyed the sensation of Jada's warm mouth on his old penis. He closed his eyes, and held on to her head, pushing Jada down on his dick as far as she would let him. He felt the cum throbbing within his dick as it made its way to the head. Jada felt it too, and sucked harder as she felt Charlie about to cum. But Edna's scream brought him out of his trance.

Jada pulled herself to her feet and faced her mother, wiping the spit from her chin, as Charlie came involuntarily. Edna stood crying in shock only feet from where Jada stood. The apartment door was still open behind her, and both Jada and Mr. Charlie wondered how they hadn't heard her come in. Charlie sat with cum all over him, dumbfounded. He grabbed a nearby pillow and wiped himself off, quickly. Then he adjusted his pants and stood between the two women, wondering what the hell would happen now.

Edna charged at Jada, tearing, scratching, clawing, and ripping at her daughter's face. "You dirty bitch!"

Jada was screaming, trying to block her mother's wild blows. Jada had never seen her mother act so aggressively, and she had never expected her mother to hit her. Gone was the woman who always let the men in her life batter her both physically and emotionally.

"Edna, come on, now. Get off the girl, you're hurting her." Charlie tried to coax Edna to stop, but even he was hesitant to step into her pathway for fear of being hurt. He cautiously pulled Edna off of her daughter.

Jada tucked herself into a ball, weeping and trying to shield her face from further damage. *"You and your sister!"* Edna was yelling. "You and your fucking sister!" Finally, Charlie pulled Edna off of Jada with enough force to send her tumbling backward.

Edna sat panting, with her back against the wall. "You get the hell out of my house!" She looked at Charlie, and was tempted to kill him. How could he mess with her daughter? She was sobbing, seeming as if she was on the verge of a nervous breakdown.

Mr. Charlie tried to intervene. "Edna, hold on a minute—"

"Get out, Charlie. You're dead wrong! Oh, my God! Both of you get out! *Get out!*"

Jada felt shame and regret, but couldn't bring herself to offer a pitiful apology. There was no apology that could excuse what her mother had just witnessed. Without protesting, she went to her room and gathered some of her belongings. Her face felt hot from all the scratches and slaps. When she finally looked at herself in her bedroom mirror, she saw the crisscross scratches and bruises from her mother's attack. She was bleeding in some places, and her own tears stung, as she gathered her things. She could hear Mr. Charlie trying, unsuccessfully, to calm Edna down. By the time Jada emerged from her room, Mr. Charlie was standing by the door looking defeated. Edna looked at her daughter and then at Charlie—another man who had made her feel like she was special, and then broken her heart—as tears fell from her eyes. She walked quickly into the bathroom, slammed the door, and slid to the floor, her sobs echoing off the walls. Jada left with Mr. Charlie that day and moved into his apartment; it was the beginning of a whole new life for her.

7

ROCK OF AGES

By now Jada and Shante were straight-up fiends. Whenever her mother was home and she couldn't do her drugs in her apartment, Shante would come to Mr. Charlie's apartment and smoke with Jada. He would let them do their thing, and he would go on about his business. Jada started smoking more than ever. She stopped going to school, and dropped out in her senior year.

After Jada moved in with him, Mr. Charlie kept her as high as she wanted. He made sure she had three square meals a day, a roof over her head, and anything else she asked him for. He used her physically, and she let him. Their arrangement was mutually beneficial. Jada wasn't disillusioned enough to believe that she was Charlie's one and only. His "wife"—Kelly—still came by every now and then. Charlie explained to Jada that Kelly was really no more than a lady who'd been down for him over the years, and she still made money for him. Whenever she was there, Jada would go and stay at Shante's house until the woman had left, and Mr. Charlie was alone again.

Shante was amazed by this. "You're telling me that you fuck him, you live there, he gives you dough. But when his wifey comes over, you just leave, and she don't say nothing to you? Y'all don't fight? What kinda shit is that? You're both sharing the same man."

Jada shrugged. "I'm not in love with Mr. Charlie. I don't need to have a confrontation with his wife. We never had any drama." Jada didn't know how Mr. Charlie explained their relationship or the fact that she was living with him to his wifey, and she really didn't care. Shante shook her head in disbelief. Jada tried to explain once again. "For me . . . I'm grateful to Charlie for what he's done to help me. But he's only a means to an end. He looks out for me. I may care about him. But I know he's not my man."

Charlie was getting serviced sexually, and Jada was having her habit sustained. Jada had all of Mr. Charlie's money at her disposal and no mother to hide from anymore. She was high all the time. Within three months, Mr. Charlie had her selling her body.

There was a side to Charlie that Jada had not yet seen. He began to show his true colors in September of 1993. Slowly Charlie began to stop giving Jada money. It started with an occasional no, when all Jada had been accustomed to hearing from Charlie was yes. This caught her by surprise, but Charlie still gave her *some* money, so she didn't complain. He was still giving her crack, although he wasn't giving it to her as freely. Charlie started demanding more from Jada in order for her to get high.

She woke up one afternoon from an eleven-hour "nap" and took a long shower. She got out, dried off, and threw on some shorts and a T-shirt. She was hungry, so she headed for the kitchen to fix a sandwich. As she passed the living room, she saw that Charlie's friend Gordon had stopped by. She greeted him and proceeded toward the kitchen. She listened to the men laughing and talking in the next room while she fixed her sandwich. She sat down and ate it, and drank close to the whole half gallon of juice in the refrigerator. She was wondering how to get Charlie's attention, so that she could get high without being rude and interrupting his conversation. But as if he'd read her mind, Charlie joined her in the kitchen and greeted her smiling.

"Hey, sleeping beauty. Good to see you up and at 'em."

Jada smiled. "Can I get something to smoke while you talk to your friend?" she asked.

Charlie tilted his head to the side. "Well, I was hoping you would come and talk to my friend, too," he said. He smiled again, though this time it seemed a little wicked. "I told Gordon about that thing I taught you last night, and he wants to see it."

Jada stood, dumbfounded. Surely he wasn't asking her to give him head in front of his friend. "I can't do that in front of him. I don't feel comfortable—"

"I thought you wanted to get high." Charlie lit a cigarette and blew the smoke in her direction. The cloud loomed in front of her, and she trembled nervously. She did want to get high. She looked at Charlie, hoping he would tell her that he was only kidding. But instead he walked back into the living room, leaving her with the option of following him and getting high, or sitting in the kitchen and fiending. She stood there and debated within herself for several minutes, before reluctantly following him into the living room.

She looked at Gordon. He was a nice-looking older man—older than Mr. Charlie. He lived in the neighborhood with his churchgoing wife. He smiled at her, and she looked away. She looked again at Charlie, hoping he would spare her this indignity. But he unzipped his pants, unbuckled his belt, and spread his legs, allowing her easy access.

Jada slowly walked toward him and kneeled before him. She took his dick in her hands, blocking out the third person in the room and pretending she was alone with Mr. Charlie, like usual. She wrapped her hand tightly around the base of his dick and sucked the head. Her hand matched the rhythm of her mouth, and Charlie was in ecstasy. He moaned and fondled her; Gordon watched closely. Finally, he came, and Jada waited anxiously for her reward.

Charlie sat collecting his breath, and Jada stood to her feet and waited. Gordon sat back with an aroused expression on his face. To Jada's surprise, he unzipped his pants and stroked his dick as he stared at her. Jada looked at Charlie confused, and he nodded in his friend's direction. "Now, be nice, baby girl. Show Gordon some love, too."

Jada stood frozen in disbelief. "Charlie, please," she protested, her eyes pleading with Charlie not to make her suck his friend's dick. That was too much for her, and she didn't want to do it. "I don't wanna do that."

Charlie looked at her silently for several moments. "I'm asking you to do something for a friend, and you tell me no? I don't think you like it when I tell *you* no."

Jada fought back tears, and looked at Charlie with new eyes. She wanted to be high badly, so she did it. She got on her knees in front of Gordon and tried not to notice his unfamiliar scent. She wanted to cry the entire time, and she felt sick. But she held it together, knowing that Charlie didn't like tears. If she cried, she ran the risk of not getting what she wanted. No matter how hard he fucked her or how nasty he treated her, she wasn't allowed to cry. So as she sucked Gordon's dick she was determined not to cry. Jada stepped outside of herself and separated her mind from what she was doing. She imagined herself someplace far away, and only her body was involved in the act she was engaged in. She wandered off in her mind until Gordon burst on her favorite shirt. When she was done, she desperately grabbed the crack from Charlie's hands and ran to the bedroom to get high. She felt dirty all over again, until the crack took her to a place where nothing even mattered.

Another time, Charlie demanded that she have anal sex with him in exchange for some crack. That time she did cry, the entire time. And Charlie didn't even seem to care. He kept pounding away at her, ramming her with no mercy. "You like that?" he panted as she bit the sheets, her body tense. "You know you like it."

It seemed to take him forever to cum that night. When he finally did, he passed out, and Jada spent the rest of the night getting high. She was beginning to see that living with Mr. Charlie came with a bigger price than she could afford.

One day Jada was jonesing and she knew Charlie had money. But for some reason, he wasn't so willing to part with it anymore. She had her period, and therefore had little to offer Mr. Charlie. She didn't feel like being passed around like a toy among Charlie and his friends this time. She had five dollars she found in the pocket of one of Charlie's jackets. All she needed was four or five more dollars to get high at least one good time.

Jada was in the corner store, and she was itching for a scratch. "Come on, *papi*. I just bought this shit from you yesterday. I don't need it, so just let me get my money back." Jada pushed the container toward the man behind the register. She was trying to return some laundry detergent she had bought the day before.

"I don't even know that you bought that here," the Hispanic store clerk argued. "You could have bought that anywhere. Now you want me to give you money back for it. Where's your receipt?"

"I don't have the fuckin' receipt. But I'm in here every day, and you know I bought this here. It's four fuckin' dollars. Just let me get it so I can get out of your store." Jada was desperate. She stood there and argued with the clerk, until he finally gave her the money back. She could tell as the man muttered in Spanish while he reached in the register that he was giving her the money just to get her out of the store. She almost snatched the four one-dollar bills out of his hand, she was so anxious to get them. Then, as she turned to leave, Jada saw her mother standing near the front of the store, as if she had just walked in.

Jada stopped dead in her tracks, and wondered how much Edna had seen and heard. Edna looked in Jada's eyes. And for a moment, Jada swore that her mother knew everything. The look on her mother's face made Jada feel like a child caught with her hand in the cookie jar. It was almost like Edna could see right through her, and could tell that her daughter was jonesing. She could see that Jada was out there. Edna looked at her daughter's disheveled clothing, her sloppy ponytail, and her thin frame. She wanted to cry. But despite the obvious angst written all over her face, all Edna did was move aside and walk toward the back of the store. As she walked past her, Jada thought for a moment that her mother was going to stop and say something. But she didn't say a word. Edna simply walked past her, and Jada walked slowly out of the store. After Jada left the store, she cried all the way back to Charlie's building. She was so hurt that her mother hadn't said anything to her. Not a word. In a way, Jada had wanted her mother to reach out to her somehow. To hug her and say that she would help her get clean. But as usual, Edna was unwilling to help her daughter. And now Jada really felt alone in the world.

Two days later, Jada was pacing in the apartment, wondering how long it would be before Charlie came back. He hadn't come home the night before, and Jada hadn't been high in far too long. Shante had gotten arrested for stealing, which left Jada with no partner in crime. Her friend's arrest made Jada hesitant to do it herself. More than anything, Jada feared going to jail. And that fear was only bolstered by Shante's predicament. To make matters worse, Lucas was nowhere to be found. She searched frantically through the pockets of Charlie's clothes and in the cushions of the sofa, to no avail. When he was leaving the previous day, Charlie had told Jada that he couldn't give her any money. He said that he had bills to pay, that his wife needed money for his kids. Jada had never even known he *had* kids, but all of a sudden his kids needed money. She wasn't concerned about all that, though. All she wanted was to get high. She was alone in the house with no means of getting her fix.

Charlie finally came home at nearly two o'clock that afternoon. Jada was thirsting for a hit.

"Damn!" she said, beads of sweat forming on her forehead. "I was dying for you to get back, Charlie. Can I get something? I need it."

That's when Charlie saw his opportunity.

"I think I might be able to help you," he said. He stroked her ass as he said it. He looked at her, still pretty, even after all the abuse she'd put her body through. He sighed. "I like having you to myself, Jada. You're my favorite girl. But you got a habit I can't afford to keep supporting."

Jada looked like she was surprised by his words, but she knew in her heart that he was right. Her habit had ballooned out of proportion. "So how can you help me?" she asked. She prayed that he wouldn't suggest rehab, like Rico had. That's not the kind of help she wanted. All she wanted was some help to stay high.

"Kelly, my wife, she can set you up on 'dates' with men. They can help you make money to feed your habit."

Jada let his words sink in. She thought about being a call girl or some kind of prostitute. She thought about Shante's advice about the "power of the pussy." She wondered how much she could make. "I don't know. I don't know if I can do that every night. I don't want to be fuckin' with dirty men—with strangers. They could be psychos."

Charlie nodded. "I understand that, and I'll keep it real with you. You're a star, baby girl. Even though right now you got a real jones for that crack, you're still pretty. You look good naturally. You're a freak in bed. You're a high-class bitch. Don't ever let a nigga tell you that you ain't worth nothing. I almost wanna keep you for myself and let you shine. But you're worth more than what I can give you. I can't afford you. You need to work what you got, and Kelly can help you do that." Charlie was being truthful. It pained him to turn the sexy young lady out. Jada had given him some of the best sex he'd ever had. But it was time for him to make back the money he'd invested in her.

Jada thought about it. Charlie could see the look of anguish on her face as she considered his words.

"Let me call Kelly over to talk to you. I'll let her tell you like it is. And then you can see what you wanna do."

Jada nodded, and off he went to retrieve the phone. She sat, and took another hit, while Charlie arranged for his lady to come and add another worker to their stable. Kelly was there within the hour.

"This is Jada." Charlie finally introduced the two women. Kelly looked Jada up and down, thinking that Charlie sure had chosen a pretty one this time. Jada seemed nervous in the presence of Charlie's main chick. Kelly was taller than Jada, and her face seemed unaccustomed to smiling. She was dark skinned and heavyset, and she didn't waste a lot of time before she cut to the chase.

"I hear you need to make some money," she said.

Jada nodded, and shifted nervously. "I do need to make money. But I'm not sure about doing what Charlie suggested. I don't know if I can sell my body to strange men."

Kelly nodded. In her mind she was relieved that Charlie was finally willing to set Jada out on the track. He always broke the young ones in before he cut them loose. Usually Kelly managed to keep her jealousy under wraps. But with Jada, for the first time she felt threatened. Jada was prettier than most of the girls Charlie normally attracted. And Charlie had kept her around as his own companion for far longer than he usually kept the girls. Kelly had begun to wonder if he was feeling for Jada, and she was relieved when he called and told her that he was ready to put her to work. Kelly tried to keep her voice sincere as she began. "I met Charlie when I was nineteen and broke. My stepfather was fucking me and my sister, and I wasn't going back to that. When Charlie found me I was homeless, sleeping in the project stairwells, because I had no place else to go. I was out running them streets, and I was living dangerously. Charlie helped me out, and I'll never forget that."

Jada nodded, feeling that she had her own reasons to be grateful to Mr. Charlie. Kelly continued.

"I remember what it was like for me starting out on my own and not having nobody to lean on. Nobody cared if I ate, or where I slept, or how I survived. All I had was me, and I was scared to death. Thank God I found somebody to help me." Kelly paused and looked at Jada. "You have somebody who's willing to help you, too. Charlie has a big heart. He doesn't judge people. And he sees something special in you. We wanna try to help set you up on dates with good men. Men with cash and class and none of that other bullshit. You're gonna be safe, and you'll make a lot of money. And it'll be your money. You won't have to ask no-body else for shit. You'll have your own." Kelly promised Jada that she wouldn't send her any dirty, disgusting men. "You have a very pretty face, and your body is close to perfect. I'll have no problems getting the good dates for you."

Jada relaxed and felt better about the prospect of working for Kelly. Kelly seemed so nice. Almost like a mother figure. Jada liked her, because she was being so comforting, and she seemed as if she genuinely wanted to help her. But mostly Jada liked her because Kelly had devised a plan to keep her high. And her plan was beginning to sound like it wasn't such a bad one after all.

8

ROCK BOTTOM

It wasn't long before Kelly got Jada started. She took her first "date" in the fall of 1993, when she was only nineteen years old. Kelly brought Jada to a spot out in Harlem. It was something like a boardinghouse, with three separate rooms and one common bathroom. Jada was understandably nervous, and even had second thoughts about the whole thing. What if the men smelled bad or looked disgusting? What if they wanted her to do something that she didn't want to do? Kelly calmed her fears, telling Jada that she would only send her the cleanest and most decent-looking men. Jada was still not fully persuaded, until Kelly held out her hand, and in it sat two crack vials. Jada reached for them eagerly, but Kelly closed her hand in time to stop Jada from taking them.

"You get *one* now, and one after the night is over. The first one will relax you enough for you to do what you need to do. The second one I'll hold for you until it's all over. That way you can get high after you're finished, and you won't have to think about it when all is said and done." Kelly gave her a half smile.

Jada nodded, thinking that this was a perfect plan. She took the one vial that Kelly extended to her. She made Jada go down to the basement to smoke it. The stairs that led to the basement were covered in cobwebs. She could smell the scent of cheap perfume mixed with cigarette smoke. It was obvious that downstairs was the part of the house where the women went to unwind. Jada noticed a black girl nodding in the corner.

She wondered if it was fatigue or heroin that made her nod like that. She descended the last step and looked around. The furniture was old and worn, the windows dingy, but to Jada, none of that mattered. She was here to get high, get paid, and go home.

Once she was down there, Jada saw another young lady. Judging from the pipe the white girl puffed on eagerly, she was a young lady with a crack habit to support. Just like Jada. Between hits, the white chick introduced herself. "My name is Cara." She had shoulder-length red hair and pretty green eyes. Her clothes looked cheap and raggedy, but her beauty couldn't be denied. What cracked Jada up was that when she opened her mouth she sounded like a black girl from around the way.

"This is your first time?" Cara asked.

Jada nodded, feeling a little like a fish out of water.

Cara smiled. She had a smile that would light up a room. "You'll get used to it real quick." Cara was very animated and energetic. She didn't mince words, and she told Jada point-blank that she loved to suck dick, and she was good at it. "That's my claim to fame. I can even teach you how to do it."

Cara proceeded to do just that. Using an empty bottle of Poland Spring water, she demonstrated her techniques. While Jada sat in the basement getting high, Cara launched into step-by-step instructions on how to make any man holla. She made no apologies for her addiction, nor for her means of supplying herself with cocaine. Cara had no shame.

When Jada was sufficiently high, she went back upstairs to find Kelly. She found her standing with a man who looked like he was about fifty years old. He wasn't very handsome, but he wasn't exactly ugly, either. He had a medium build and graying hair. But he seemed nice enough, and he didn't smell bad. But he did smell old. Like Old Spice. Kelly showed Jada and the man into one of the empty rooms and closed the door behind her as she left. Jada was all alone with the stranger who would usher her into the world of prostitution.

He sat down on the edge of the bed, and smiled at her. "You're really pretty," he said.

"Thanks." Jada was high, and fidgeting. She plucked at imaginary lint on her shirt, and her eyes darted back and forth between her clothes and the man sitting on the bed.

"Can I see you?" he asked.

Jada didn't know what he meant, and the confusion was evident on her face.

"Take off your clothes," he clarified.

Jada began to oblige him, unbuttoning her shirt swiftly.

"Slowly," the man said. "Do it slowly."

Jada looked at him. She was disappointed that he wasn't going to be quick about it. He wanted to see her—all of her. She undressed awkwardly, knowing that this was a moment she would never forget. Somehow this was different from Mr. Charlie and his friend. Charlie was familiar. He was always the common denominator. This time, with this man, she was all on her own. Selling herself. This whole situation was blowing her high. Slowly she undid the buttons on her blouse. She took it off, and laid it on the chair next to the bed. Then she slowly peeled off her jeans and stood before the man with only her bra and panties on. As she reached to remove her underwear, he stopped her.

"Come here," he said.

Jada obliged, and walked over to him. He sat before her and began to rub his hands across her body. Jada felt awkward with such an older man touching her this way. But she didn't stop him. She was high, and she retreated into that safe place in her head. The place where she didn't have to be Jada and face all the consequences of her actions. She didn't have to dwell on the guilt she felt without the drugs. Jada drifted into a zone, somewhere her body never mattered. The man exploring her body didn't bother her anymore. He rubbed her breasts and fingered her pussy for a few long moments. Then he finally got undressed himself and asked her very politely to suck his dick. Jada was dreading that request, but she did as she was asked. The whole time she did it, he rubbed her breasts and called her "Sugar." She had never felt so dirty in her life. She felt like she was sucking her grandfather's dick. Jada's high was being challenged by her pride, and she realized then that she would need to be someone else in her head. She pretended she was a porn star. She had the cameras set up around her and everything, all inside her head. She gave that man the best head he had ever experienced in his life. When his dick was rock hard in her mouth, he laid her down and climbed on top of her. He entered her slowly and proceeded to hump and sweat all over her, moaning in her ear. She thought about getting high again and how good it would feel. She thought about having money of her own and not having to ask Mr. Charlie for it. These were the things that motivated her to keep quiet while the old man pounded away at her young pussy. When he was close to cumming, Jada could tell by the increase in his pace and in the volume of his moaning. Before she knew what had happened, his old ass had pulled out of her, and he spilled his seed all over her face. Jada was mortified. With cum dripping from her lips and nose, she stumbled out of the room naked and ran to the bathroom to clean herself off. She shut the door behind her, slid to the floor, and cried. She felt so unclean, and so worthless. She stayed in there for several minutes, trying to pull herself together. Her high was officially over, and reality had hit her like a brick. She had nothing left. Not even her pride. Jada wept quietly until the tears dried up. When she emerged and went back into the room, the man was gone. Instead, Kelly sat on the edge of the bed, looking at her coldly.

"The next time you run out on a client like that, I'm not paying you," she said. "Do you understand?"

Jada nodded, amazed by Kelly's lack of compassion. Then Kelly stood up and walked out of the room without another word. Jada sat alone, and thought about leaving. She could leave and get clean, and never have to worry about having strangers inside of her, raw, for no more than a couple of rocks and a warm room. It didn't have to be like this, she reasoned. But if she left, Jada wondered where she could go. She couldn't go back to her mother. Edna would turn her away, and the pain of that would be too much to bear. Ava was doing better for herself and didn't need Jada's troubles weighing her down. There was no one else. No one who could help her find the strength to leave the drugs alone.

Ten minutes later Jada got another client. This time she did what was required of her without reacting to the discomfort she felt. She simply found a way to step outside of her body until the client was through with it. At the end of the night she got her fix from Kelly, along with her money, and she went downstairs with Cara. The two of them got high and exchanged stories. It was a relief to meet someone who understood her pain and her struggles. Jada laughed with Cara, and they talked until they were both exhausted. And for a little while, Jada was free of the guilt and the shame.

9
CHANGING FACES

Jada went to Kelly's brothel every night for two hours. She would see as many men as Kelly sent to her room. Some nights it was one or two. Other nights it was as many as five. Jada learned to put on a make-believe identity. She wasn't Jada while she was with these men. She was "Melissa." And when Melissa was working, Jada was nowhere around. Melissa was fearless, and there was nothing she wouldn't do for a fast buck. Melissa was all about the Benjamins.

On one occasion Kelly sent a couple to Jada's room. A black man and a white woman. They looked normal, but what they wanted to do was something outside of Jada's comfort zone. She almost said no, but she needed the money in order to feed her habit. So she called on her alter ego, and handled her business. The guy sat and watched while Jada gave the woman oral sex. When the woman spread her legs and put her pink pussy in Jada's face, Jada thought she might throw up. She held her breath and licked it gingerly at first. While she did it, the man rubbed all over Jada and caressed her body. She felt disgusting with the woman's pussy in her face, as she moaned and pulled Jada's hair softly. Jada felt like it went on forever, but she didn't dare stop out of fear that if she didn't get the woman to climax she wouldn't get paid. It was all a means to an end for Jada.

Once the woman had a very loud orgasm, they informed her that it wasn't over yet. The woman joined Jada on her knees, and the two of them sucked him off. The man was in ecstasy, as Jada and the woman's tongues mingled in a serenade to his big dick. When they were done, the man left to go and get their car, while the woman fixed her clothes and put on her shoes.

"You can call me if you ever need to make some extra cash," the lady said to Jada. She handed her two crumpled ten-dollar bills and a piece of paper with her phone number on it. "Next time, we don't have to invite him." The woman winked, and Jada felt nauseous.

Jada thanked her, and told her that she would call. But she knew in her heart that no matter how low she sank, she would not resort to giving another woman head ever again.

There was another guy who Kelly sent to Jada, and it wasn't long before he became a regular. He told Jada that he was a movie producer, although she wasn't sure that she believed him. He did wear some expensive watches, and his shoes looked like they cost a fortune. He told her that he lived in a pricey condominium overlooking the water. Jada wondered why a successful man with so much money would want to fuck a crackhead for a couple of dollars. But it wasn't just the sex. He liked Jada to do really kinky shit to him, and he just loved to be dominated. Jada spanked him, peed on him, spit on his face while she rode him, and all sorts of twisted activities.

Surprisingly, she actually enjoyed herself with him from time to time, because he made her feel powerful. She spent most of her time feeling weak and powerless against her addiction. So being with the skinny, kinky white man was a nice change of pace. He always gave her money, even though the procedure was that he paid Kelly before he even got to Jada's room. But no matter what, when they were finished with one of their erotic episodes, the man always pressed a twenty-dollar bill into Jada's palm.

Jada didn't question the money Kelly gave her at the end of the night. She would get fifty dollars, sixty dollars, sometimes more. As long as she made enough to stay high and buy something to eat, Jada didn't complain. But after a month or so, that began to diminish, becoming twenty dollars, thirty dollars. Then, the before and after crack vials that Kelly once supplied Jada with each night became a thing of the past. Jada was starting to notice that she was being played.

There were a few other girls who worked for Kelly. Cara was one of them, but there were a number of others who seemed to work in shifts. All of them were battling addictions in various stages. One was a black girl who didn't talk to anyone without a scowl or a sneer. Jada didn't like her, didn't trust her, and made a point of not interacting with her if she could help it. Another was a Hispanic girl with terrible acne and a thick accent. She was nasty, and Jada could often hear her moaning and cursing through the walls that separated their rooms.

But Cara was someone who Jada grew to like a lot. She talked to Jada whenever the two of them were waiting for dates. And to Jada's astonishment, Cara's interaction with Mr. Charlie had been eerily similar to Jada's own.

The two of them discussed it one night after they'd both finished their work for the night. Jada was telling Cara how much Charlie had helped her out, and she was surprised that Cara didn't feel the same way.

"Charlie and Kelly are full of shit," she said. "I didn't realize it until I got in too deep with them to get out. But all they care about is themselves."

Jada frowned, wondering what she meant by that. "What makes you feel like that?"

Cara shook her head and exhaled the smoke from her Newport. "My mother was a dope fiend, and Charlie used to supply her habit. I was little then. Nine or ten years old. My moms was strung out, but she wanted more than that for me. She tried to make me do good in school, and she always wanted me to stay out of trouble. But I was hardheaded and rebellious. All the kids at school made fun of my cheap clothes and my mother with the toothless grin. By the time I was thirteen, I had a habit of my own. Charlie knew about it, but he kept my secret. He didn't tell my mother about it, and I was grateful. Then my moms OD'd, and I was left behind. After her overdose, Charlie let me stay with him. He didn't force me to go to school, and he supplied my habit. It wasn't long before our relationship turned physical. And then came Kelly, with her plan for me to make money. I've seen so many other girls come through here with the same story that I finally realized that this shit is Charlie and Kelly's hustle. They don't care about us girls. They use us to get what they want. Them crooks haven't paid me right in years. But they know my time has passed. I don't look like I used to, and I only have an eighth-grade education. So now I'm stuck. And they know it. So it is what it is."

As Cara told Jada all about Kelly and Mr. Charlie, it all began to make sense to her. She had been manipulated into a life that Cara said was a dead-end street. Jada thought about her mother and about how Charlie had helped her hide her addiction. She had been grateful to him for not telling her mother. She wondered now if he had been helping her after all.

"I've been working for Kelly for four years," Cara said. "Still I have no money saved, no place to go, and the little family that I have left disowned me because of the drugs." Cara paused, and seemed pained by the truth in her statement. "I would stop fuckin' for Kelly and Charlie if I could, Jada," Cara said, sadly. "But I don't want to go back out there on my own. I got no family, no friends. I'm not kicking this habit. And I know I'm not. But you could do it if you wanted to." She smiled at Jada. "You're too young and too pretty to keep selling your pussy for crack."

Jada began to realize that as long as she kept dealing with Mr. Charlie and Kelly she would be in an endless cycle of tricking to feed her habit. Cara was proof of that.

Still Jada kept getting high. Charlie was still fucking her and giving her money, though not as much as before. But after listening to how Charlie and Kelly had manipulated her into this lifestyle, Jada made up her mind that one day she would leave. She had no place to go, no plan, and very little money. But she knew she didn't want to fuck Mr. Charlie anymore. And if she wasn't fucking him, she knew he wouldn't let her stay in his house. So Jada started sleeping at the boardinghouse where she met her tricks. But that wasn't safe, and she hated sleeping in the same room where she had fucked all those men. She started going back to

Brooklyn to stay with the friends she still had out there, sleeping on her friends' couches when she could. Shante got probation for her shoplifting charge, and since she was back in the hood, Jada crashed at her house a lot. Shante's mother didn't like Jada, though. So Shante had to sneak her into her room when her mother was asleep. Whenever she wasn't high, Jada fell further and further into depression and self-loathing.

One night Jada lay in her room at Kelly's brothel, crying herself to sleep. She had just spent a night of humiliating sex with three undesirable men—the kind of men Kelly had promised Jada she would never send to her room. One smelled like a distillery. Another looked like King Kong. Then, finally, Kelly had sent a middle-aged man to Jada's room who called her every degrading name imaginable while he ravaged her. His words had cut Jada like a million knives and made her feel like the lowest scum on the face of the earth. As she lay in the cum-stained bed, Jada made up her mind to quit. No amount of money was worth feeling as low-down and disgusting as she felt at that moment. Jada got up and went to get her last little bit of money. She walked downstairs and found Kelly in the foyer, counting money.

"Kelly," she called to her.

Kelly turned around, stuffing the fistful of cash into her pocket. "What's the matter Jada?" she asked.

Jada shrugged, avoiding Kelly's gaze. "I think this is gonna be my last night. I can't come back here anymore to sell my ass. Each time I leave here, I feel lower and lower. And pretty soon no amount of getting high is going to be able to cover up how bad I feel about myself. I think this is it for me."

Kelly calmly looked at Jada and nodded, understanding. Then Kelly reached into her pocket and handed Jada a ten-dollar bill. Jada stood with her hand outstretched, waiting for more. She had just seen Kelly shove a knot of bills into her pocket. When Jada saw that Kelly wasn't about to give up any more dough, she thought about the three men who had just humped and sweated all over her, smelling musty and disgusting, and she flipped out.

"What the fuck is this?" Jada demanded. "I know you're not giving me no muthafuckin' ten dollars after I just laid upstairs and fucked three men—"

Kelly didn't bat an eyelash. "You're free to go now, Jada. You don't bring in the kind of money that you used to bring in anyway. That ten dollars is the last money you'll be getting from me."

"Kelly, I know you must be joking. You can't be serious." Jada stood open-mouthed, shocked that Kelly would treat her this way after all the work Jada had put in for her.

Kelly just looked at Jada blankly and shrugged her shoulders.

"You fuckin' bitch! You old, washed-up, beat-up bitch!" Jada was infuriated. Kelly smirked at her. Cara and the scowling black girl emerged from their rooms to see what all the commotion was about. From where they stood it looked as if Jada was losing control while Kelly was cool as a cucumber.

Jada took a deep breath, made her voice calm and soft, and said, "You seem like a smart woman, Kelly. Charlie calls you his wife, but why do you think he fucks all of us? Because your pussy is dry and your sex is whack, that's why. Has he ever told you that my pussy is better than yours? 'Cause that's what he told me. He told Cara that, too." Jada paused, smirking. "You can have your fuckin' ten dollars. You know why? 'Cuz all I gotta do is go back to Charlie and let him hit this pussy one more time. I'll be running his old ass pockets again in no time!"

Kelly felt anger building inside her. She knew that Charlie had a weakness for young pussy. Charlie liked to pretend that he was just trying the young girls out to set them out on the track. But she knew that was bullshit, and that he really loved sexing young girls. Charlie would hit it again if he could, and this enraged Kelly. So she did the only thing that came to mind. She hauled off and punched Jada dead in her face. Jada stumbled back, but quickly recovered and came at the older woman like a cat. To Jada's surprise, Kelly was strong. She tore Jada's shirt off, and Jada fought the old bitch bare-chested. Then Kelly whipped out a razor and began to cut Jada's torso all up. She left one big gash right down the center of Jada's chest and a couple of other cuts and scrapes across her upper body. Jada just kept on coming. But before Cara and the

scowling girl could pull Kelly and Jada apart, Jada came away with half
of the knot of cash that Kelly had in her pocket. Cara peeped this, and
quickly pulled Jada outside and covered her with her jacket.

Jada was enraged that Kelly had resorted to scarring her body with a
blade. She refused to go for stitches, although it was clear that she
should. Cara tried to reason with her.

"Jada, that shit is wide open. You need to go to the hospital and let
them—"

"I'm not going to the fuckin' hospital!" Jada bellowed. Her blood soaked
Cara's jacket, and Jada seemed not to care. She was only thinking about
the fact that Kelly had violated her. All she felt was outrage that Kelly
had resorted to disfiguring her.

Realizing that Jada wasn't going to listen to reason, Cara shook her
head. "Well, you have to get that closed up," she said. "Come with me."

Cara took Jada to a nearby crack house. She brought Jada to one of
the rooms in the back and gestured for her to lie down on a tattered old
bed. "Here. Drink this." Cara handed Jada a bottle of gin and told her to
drink it straight down. "Don't sip that shit. Guzzle it. You're going to
need the buzz. Trust me." Cara left the room, and returned moments
later with a needle she had sterilized over the kitchen stove and some
thread.

Once Jada had gulped most of the liquor, Cara straddled her and
sewed up the wound in Jada's chest. With nothing to numb the pain but
the gin oozing down her throat, Jada cried out in pure agony.

"Come on, ya tough bitch. You didn't want to go to the hospital, remember? If you don't lay still and let me do this, you're gonna get an in-
fection. And if that happens, you're gonna be in even worse shape."
Ignoring Jada's cries, Cara continued to sew her up.

Jada was in excruciating pain. But she bit her lip, drawing blood to
keep from crying out too often. Whenever Cara paused, Jada drank the
gin as if it were an anesthetic. When Cara was done, she sat beside her
now drunk friend, and held her as she cried on her shoulder.

Jada knew that there was no going back now. She couldn't work for
Kelly anymore, and she wouldn't go back to Mr. Charlie. She wanted the

pain to go away. She wanted the nightmare to end. She gave Cara a couple of dollars for helping her out. Then she and Cara sat in the crack house and got high together, both of them seeking refuge from a reality too harsh for them to endure.

10

A BLESSING IN DISGUISE

Without Charlie and Kelly to set her up on dates, Jada began to free-lance. She got money or crack from the local hustlers by sucking their dicks on the roofs of the project buildings for four or five dollars. She was still an attractive girl, despite the toll the drug abuse had taken on her body. And she accentuated it as much as possible. It was her business to stay pretty, to look sexy. Jada had always been petite, so she could wear cute little outfits from the cheapest stores. But when a woman has a nice body and a pretty face, it don't matter what you have on. It's the ass that gets men's attention. True, Jada had lost weight. She was skinnier than she once was. But she still looked good. Jada was often seen walking around in tight pants, miniskirts, or painted-on jeans. She went braless most days, wanting the attention.

Jada and Shante had resorted to robbing bitches. Shante got hold of a .38 Special from Lucas, and they set out sticking up white women heading home from work, or at ATMs. She and Shante had gone back to boosting as well. The fear of getting caught was secondary to their need for the narcotic. Then finally they discovered the most convenient hustle of all: They started selling crack for Lucas and his crew. He would pay them in crack, rather than in cash, which worked perfectly for all involved. So everything had a purpose. The boosting was to keep them looking good, and to keep them with money in their pockets from all the stuff they were able to sell. The robberies gave them jewelry to pawn (although they did keep some things for themselves), and working for Lucas fed their habits. Once they got rid of the package Lucas had given them, they would scurry to find him to collect their take for the work they'd put in. At the end of the night, they could count on that high. It made them work harder.

As she prepared to go outside to work on this day, Jada felt a sense of uneasiness. She had a strange feeling that something was going to happen that day. Still, she was determined to go out and get her high. Jada waited until Shante's mother had left the house to go food shopping. She dragged herself out of bed, still teary and sad. She took a hot shower and got dressed, putting on her tightest jeans and a little tank top, and no bra. She did her makeup, and she brushed her hair.

They went to work that day for Lucas, selling in the lobby of 240 Broadway. They had been down there slinging their package for quite a while, and they were almost finished with their pack. Jada was anxious to finish selling what was left. She peered out of the lobby windows looking for another customer. Finally, one arrived. The Hispanic guy who came in asking for Lucas wasn't familiar to either of them. Still, Jada went into the stairwell to sell to him, while Shante stood in the lobby standing watch. Jada and the man made the exchange, and he walked out of the stairwell. Jada stood there counting the money, making sure everything added up. The last thing she wanted was for any of Lucas's money to be missing, which would give him an excuse not to pay them. She took her time, recounting the money, confident that Shante had her back. Then she checked her pack to see how much was left before she could go and get high herself. Only five left. Jada wondered how long it would take her to sell these few remaining cracks, as she headed back to the lobby. But to her surprise, when she walked out of the stairwell and stepped into the lobby, handcuffs were slapped on her wrists.

"You have the right to remain silent." A plainclothes officer began reading Jada her rights.

"What the fuck is this?" Jada demanded.

"The guy you just sold to was an undercover," the cop explained. "Anything you say can and will be used against you."

Jada stopped listening, and looked around desperately. She saw four plainclothes cops. Shante was standing there in cuffs as well. Jada glared at her in contempt. "Why the fuck didn't you say something, Shante?"

"They told me to be quiet, Jada!"

"*So what?* What part of the fuckin' game is that, Shante? You were supposed to have my back." Jada scowled at her friend, pissed. They got arrested for the sale and for possession, and Jada was going to jail.

Jada was put in jail for ninety days, and then was sent to a mandatory drug program in a prison hospital for ninety days as well. Being in rehab at the prison hospital was no better than being in the prison itself. She was not free to come and go as she pleased, and any vistors needed to be searched thoroughly in order to gain access to the facility. Being in prison was torture for her, mainly because she was unable to get high. She thought about it every day, and she longed for that feeling more than ever. Once she was in the program, Jada couldn't wait to get out. She wanted to get high so badly that it was all that she could think about. Rehab was not what Jada wanted at all. She didn't want to hear that she had a problem or that she needed help. What she wanted was to get out, get high, and get back to where she had left off. She was resistant at first, unwilling to allow the counselors to convince her that she had a serious problem. She was irritable and nasty toward them because she wanted a fix. That was all she was able to focus on. Without that, life felt unbearable to Jada. But after a few weeks, she began to see the truth in what they spoke about.

The counselors at the rehab clinic were helpful. They told her about the pitfalls of addiction; about how, going back out into the world, she could be exposed to all the same shit again. They told her about how certain situations, certain people, even certain *smells* could trigger memories and make her want to use again. Jada was proud of the fact that she hadn't used drugs in weeks. But she began to wonder if she'd be able to keep it that way. Now that she wasn't high anymore, all she could think about was what she'd done. She thought about all the men she'd sold herself to. She looked at her body, at all the scars that Kelly had left her with. The large scar that was left when Cara had stitched her up so poorly particularly bothered her. It all reminded her of how she'd de-graded herself. She couldn't stand the scent of musky men. The smell brought to mind all the nasty strangers who had humped, sweated, and come all over her precious body. And more than ever she wanted to es-cape. Sensing that she may not be strong enough to stay clean on her own, Jada decided to try to reconnect with her family. She sat down one Sunday afternoon while she was in rehab and wrote a letter to Ava.

Dear Ava,

By now, I'm sure you heard that I got busted for drugs. The cops contacted Mommy once they arrested me, but she didn't post my bail. I'm not sure if she didn't have the money or if she just didn't want to come and help me out. But, anyway, the judge gave me six months. I have to do ninety days here in rehab, and I had to do ninety days on Rikers. Rikers is no joke, and since I survived that, I believe I can sur-vive anything. In here, they teach you that you have to accept respon-sibility for your actions. I can accept mine now. I was using drugs and the shit got out of control. I never thought that would happen to me. I thought I was too strong to ever get addicted. Remember when I used to tell you that only weaklings become drug addicts? I was wrong about that. Because, I did get addicted. But, I'm strong enough to beat this shit, and that's what I'm gonna do. I just wanted to write to you and tell you that I love you. I miss you a lot and I need you to be there for me. You may be all the family I have left. Mommy is disappointed in me, and I can understand that. I'm disappointed in myself, and I'm sure you feel the same way. I'm sorry.

I hope you write me back soon. I need to hear from you.

Your sister,
Jada

Ava received her sister's letter, and she was heartbroken. She wanted so badly to help Jada find her way. She wrote back to her sister, and after doing so she cried her eyes out. Their lives had taken such tragic turns. Ava looked at her sister's plight and knew that she had to turn her life around before she wound up just as lost as Jada was. Ava was getting high every day. She told herself that it was only weed, but she saw how quickly smoking weed had escalated for her sister. She didn't want to go the same route. So Ava slowed down. She started smoking less, and eventually she quit altogether. She focused on graduating, and began to take her counselor, Mrs. Lopez's, advice. For once, she began to see life through different eyes. Her dreams took on richer colors.

Jada received her sister's letter, and she was so excited that she practically tore it in her eagerness to read it.

Jada,

I love you. You are my sister for life. Nothing can change that, and nothing can change the fact that I have your back all the time. No matter what happens I'm here for you. I mean that. We're in this shit together.

I'm glad you got caught. I'm so happy that you're finally going to get some help. For a long time I suspected that you were using drugs. But, I didn't want to question you and offend you. I didn't want to accuse you of something like that without knowing for sure. But, you had lost so much weight, you were stealing all kinds of expensive clothes and giving me all sorts of shit. I noticed you would disappear for days and weeks at a time. Then you got arrested and there was no more doubt about it. And I was upset when I heard about it. I still wonder how the hell you got caught up in smoking crack. Crack, Jada. We have a lot to talk about. But, I still love you. I will be here for you from the moment you get out of that program. I'll walk with you through this every step of the way. I promise you that. You're not alone. Remember that.

I love you always.

Ava

Jada smiled. She understood where Ava was coming from. She knew that Ava was disappointed. But she still loved her. And it made Jada feel good to know that her sister was still on her side. She felt so good about

Ava's letter that she decided to write to her mother. Maybe this whole thing would be what brought her family back together again. Maybe her addiction would be what reunited them after all of the pain. She tried her luck.

Ma,

I'm not really sure where to start with this letter. But, I guess I should start by saying that I'm sorry. I really am sorry. I was probably the worst daughter any mother could get stuck with. I betrayed you, and I disrespected you. But, I never meant to hurt you. Not when I was with Charlie, and not when I started using drugs. Causing you pain wasn't what I wanted. I only wanted my own pain to go away. You might not have ever known that I was in pain. But, I was. I was hurt because you never fought for anything as hard as you fought for the men in your life. It felt like you cared about them more than us. I know there's no excuse for some of the things I've done. And I'm sure you probably don't really want to forgive me. But, I am asking you to forgive me. And, I forgive you, too. I hope you still love me. Because I still love you. I want to put our family back together again. I hope you want the same thing.

Please write me back.

Your daughter,

Jada

Jada's mother never wrote her back. She told herself that it was no big deal. But the child inside of her cried a little for the love her mother had never given her. Getting through rehab without her mother's support and forgiveness was hard for Jada. She didn't admit that, not even to herself. But the fact that she never got a response from Edna cut her deeply. She felt as if she'd been kicked while she was down. Soon the counselors and their speeches and rhetoric became noisy belligerence to her. Jada heard them. She listened to what they said. And she knew she had a problem. But she wouldn't allow herself to really believe that she couldn't handle her problem on her own. She got tired of going to group. "Group" was what they called the group therapy sessions. She was tired of it. She didn't want to hear about other people's struggles, and she was sick of thinking about her own. She felt that since she couldn't change her past, she would much rather try to forget it. All she wanted now was to try to stay clean, and to pick up the pieces from where they'd fallen. Jada was ready to get out of there and get back on track. She felt like she had the power to control her need for cocaine. She thought she was strong enough, mentally, to never use crack again. And she left rehab in early 1995, feeling in her heart that she wasn't going to smoke crack anymore. They wanted her to stay for another thirty days. The counselors felt that she could benefit from more time in the structured environment. But since they could only force her to stay for ninety days, Jada didn't stay a day longer than she had to.

She was determined to make a clean start. So she steered clear of West Brighton, where she'd been lured into a life of drugs and crazy living in the first place. She hooked back up with Shante, after running into her at a party, when Shante told her that she'd been off the crack for four months and was determined to stay that way. Shante had moved out of her mother's place and gotten her own apartment on Steuben Street. Shante let Jada stay with her from time to time. She had a man, though, and he was there quite often. Shante had a studio apartment, so there was no way Jada could stay there and go unnoticed. So she was homeless again, living hand to mouth and staying with Shante when she could. Jada was sleeping on a different person's couch every other night. She got sick of that and didn't want to go into a homeless shelter. She didn't want to admit that she was that alone in the world. Months passed. Then Jada went back to West Brighton one day. She decided to go and see her mother.

It was about four o'clock on a Saturday afternoon, and Jada figured Edna would be home. Her schedule had always been predictable. On the weekends Edna normally woke up early and went out to pay her bills, and then to the supermarket. Jada knew that Edna would be home by this time in the afternoon. As she approached her mother's home, Jada was nervous. She had no idea what she would say when Edna came to the door. She tried to come up with an opening line, and she couldn't think of one. So she decided to wait and see what her mother's reaction would be to seeing Jada after so long. She figured the words would come to her once she saw Edna's face again. Jada went to her mother's door, and listened. She could hear the TV in the background, and she wondered what her mother was watching. She wondered if she still watched the same shows at the same time every day. Nervously, Jada stepped back from the door and knocked on it. She thought she saw her mother's eye appear at the peephole, yet there was no answer. Jada stood there and knocked for the longest time, unwilling to accept the fact that Edna wasn't answering. Jada knew that her mother was in there. She had heard the TV on when she got there; and then, when she started knocking on the door, the TV volume was suddenly muted. Jada could hear her mother's footsteps, even though Edna thought she was tiptoeing. Jada knew she was home. But Edna wouldn't let her daughter in. Finally Jada resigned herself to the fact that Edna wasn't going to open the door. Crushed, Jada decided that that would be the last time she ever went back to her mother's house.

Feeling rejected, and tempted to go back to the numbness of getting high, Jada decided to go to the group home to see her sister. She got on the bus and headed for Mariner's Harbor. The bus ride seemed to take forever. All she could think about was the fact that her mother wouldn't let her in. Her own mother didn't want to see her or talk to her. Edna hadn't answered her letters when Jada had written to her from rehab. Sitting in a seat near the window, Jada gazed out of it with tears cascading down her face.

When she finally arrived at the group home, Jada was disappointed to find that Ava wasn't there. She fought off the feeling that she was alone in the world again. She told herself that Ava would probably be back pretty soon. So since she had no place else to go, and she didn't know where any of her friends were after all the time she'd spent away from Staten Island, Jada sat outside the home and waited for Ava to come back. She was feeling sorry for herself and wondered if she should give up on trying to stay clean and just go back to what had made her feel good—crack. But still she waited for her sister, trying to block out the urge to backslide.

While she was sitting out in front of the group home, waiting for Ava, a black Benz drove by three different times. The windows were tinted, and Jada couldn't see who was driving. But she knew it was the same car, and she wondered why the driver seemed to be circling the block. About an hour passed, as she sat there in the front of the building. The next time the car passed her by, she was walking to the store on the next corner. The car pulled up beside her, and the driver slowed down. He lowered the power windows, and he called out to her.

"Excuse me, do you mind if I talk to you for a minute?"

"Yes. I mind." Jada didn't break stride. She kept walking at the same swift pace, switching her ass in her Lee jeans. Jada had gained back some of the weight she'd lost. She looked thick and sexy in all the right places as she strolled along.

"Well, I'm gonna follow you, anyway." He smiled at her, still driving slowly alongside her.

Jada kept on walking, only glancing once at the cutie behind the wheel of the black luxury car. His smile was disarming, but she knew it was the jiggle in her jeans that had him driving at twenty miles below the speed limit. She had sold herself for drugs enough times for her to resent any man who pulled up in a car next to a lady walking alone. She felt that she knew his intentions right away. He was adorable, but Jada wasn't in the mood for some local wannabe trying to get some play. She was still upset about what had happened at her mother's house, and was upset that Ava was nowhere to be found. She kept right on walking, her focus on the store up ahead.

"What's your name?" the guy in the car asked.

No response.

"Wow. You really don't wanna talk to me, huh?"

"Nah." Jada reached the store and walked inside, hoping the stranger would take the hint and keep on moving. She had no such luck. The unfamiliar young man parked his car and followed the unidentified beauty into the store. Once inside, he scanned the tiny aisles until he found his mark. Jada stood by the freezers, scanning the sodas, looking for a Cherry Coke.

He walked up behind Jada, smiling at the apple bottom she possessed. He loved a nice ass, and Jada's was certainly a work of art. Her waist was small, and her bad-girl stance was intriguing him. "I can't believe you ain't gonna give me a chance to talk to you."

Jada rolled her eyes dramatically, turned around, and faced him. "I can't believe that you really can't take no for an answer."

"I don't like hearing no. Especially when I have my heart set on something." He sized her up tastefully, wondering why he was so mesmerized by her eyes. It wasn't every day that he noticed something like a woman's eyes. That wasn't really his style. He usually noticed the obvious, the most prominent bodily features: tits and asses. But this girl's eyes were so delicate, almost innocent. And so very sexy. He was captivated.

"Okay. You're in my way," Jada said. "Excuse me."

"Let me get your number." He stated it, rather than asked it. He made his intentions very clear. "I'll leave you alone after that, I promise." Jada laughed at his aggressiveness but was secretly intrigued by his confidence. He had an arrogance about him, which strangely turned her on. He was about six feet tall, well-built, and very handsome. He had a honey-colored complexion, a fresh haircut, and a very costly gold chain on his neck. He wasn't gorgeous, but was a nice-looking guy, with a smile that was absolutely disarming. Jada liked what she saw, but kept her game face on. When he asked for her number, he crossed his arms on his chest, and Jada took note of the watch, but didn't recognize the maker; something called "TAG Heuer" that she'd never heard of. But it sure looked expensive. His smile was amazingly contagious, and he had a pair of lips that just begged to be kissed.

"I don't know who you are." Jada's voice was silky as she spoke.

"They call me Born. What's your name?"

"Nice to meet you, Born. I'm not really looking for a man right now—"

"I didn't say I want to be your man." He looked directly in her eyes, and noticed that she was scanning the room, looking for a way out. "I just want to talk to you. That's all." Born really wasn't looking for love, or for commitment. He was looking for a good time with a pretty young woman. And Jada fit the bill perfectly.

Jada finally looked directly at him. "I don't have a phone." She put her hands on her hips, certain that now he would leave her alone. Jada wished that her statement was false, but it was pure truth. She had no phone, no place to really call home, no plan. She felt so lost. She didn't want to go back to the drugs, to the sex and the misery. But at the moment, she had no idea where else to go. All she really wanted was her sister, and she had no idea where Ava was.

Born entertained the idea of giving her his pager number. But she might not use it, and he didn't want to take the chance. Thinking on his feet, he said, "So, then let me take you to eat, somethin' real quick. If I bore you to death, you can walk out and leave me."

Jada looked at him, visibly unmoved. She didn't know this guy, and she wasn't about to go off somewhere with this stranger. Sensing her hesitation, Born spoke up.

"I ain't the boogeyman, ma. You ain't gotta be nervous around me." He smiled. "Plus, you look like you could probably beat my ass, anyway."

Jada chuckled, and still wavered. She wasn't sure it was a good idea to go off with some dude she had just met. But she was broke, her sister was missing in action, her mother was shutting her out, and she was hungry. The man standing before her was a welcome distraction, and she hesitantly accepted. She followed Born to his car, which was parked unlocked, with the key still hanging in the ignition. For Jada it was easy to surmise that this young man in the Benz, with the gold chain, fancy watch, and movie-star smile, was a hustler. Born knew that no one would dare touch his car, even with the key in the ignition in the middle of the day. Jada had been around all kinds of players in the game during the days she spent living in Brooklyn, as well as in the streets of Staten Island. She knew the signs of a baller, and she could tell that Born was a man to contend with. She could sense his abundance of confidence by the way he had approached her. Jada suspected that he was used to having his way, and that he was cocky. But she also noticed his charm and his wit. She figured that at least for that afternoon, Born could be someone who she might not mind spending time with. She sat back against the leather passenger seat and gazed out the window as he looked over at her, nestled comfortably in his car.

"So, what you feel like eating?" Born asked, stealing glances at the beauty on his right.

Jada shrugged her shoulders. "It don't matter. Whatever you want is fine."

Born raised an eyebrow, slyly. "Don't tell me that. Because I think I see what I want already."

Jada looked at him snottily, and then rolled her eyes. Looking out the window once again, she said, "Well, for now, just stick to food. That's all."

Born smiled and nodded, directing his attention to the road ahead of them. He wondered what he should make of this girl with a lovely face and a nasty attitude. He wasn't sure if she would turn out to be a headache or had some potential. But there was something about her that made him want to dig deeper. He felt that under all that toughness was a sensuality that hadn't been tapped into yet. He figured he might as well find out if it was worth the trouble. He pulled into the parking lot of the diner on Forest Avenue and parked his Benz. He couldn't wait to see if this first date would prove to be their last.

Turns out, it was the start of something big.

BORN

11

A HUSTLER IS BORN

1980

Marquis Graham stood proudly, watching his father work the crowd. They were in a shopping plaza on Targee Street, standing outside of the Zebra Lounge, and Leo was chatting animatedly with a group of his cronies. They laughed and talked about the Knicks game that had been on TV the night before. Marquis watched his dad, soaking up his aura and marveling at how easily he stole the spotlight whenever he stepped onto the scene. At eight years old, Marquis was like a sponge. He soaked up everything around him, particularly the words and actions of his father and his friends.

The thing that made Marquis the proudest was the fact that he had the coolest father in the world. Leo Graham was a living legend in the hood. Everywhere he went people respected him, some almost bowed to him. Whenever he walked into a room, it was all eyes on him. Leo's role in the life of his son had not been a traditional one. Leo had been arrested for manslaughter when Marquis was two years old, and had served five years for that crime. He got to know his youngest son through occasional visitation up north, and through the updates his wife, Ingrid Graham, gave him. He was released when Marquis was seven years old. Leo was in and out. He was here and there. But when he finally came home, everything was alright. For Marquis, every day was sunshine now that Daddy was home.

Marquis saw a familiar man walking swiftly in their direction. He recognized the man's face but didn't know his name. He was walking very fast, and his face was set in a frown. His eyes were focused on Leo. "Dad." Marquis tugged at Leo's shirt. "Here comes your friend."

Leo looked in the direction his son was pointing at, and he shook his head. "This muthafucka ain't nobody," he said. He looked at the man as he approached, and greeted him halfheartedly. "What's up, Nick?"

"Don't give me that 'what's up?' shit, nigga! Where the fuck is my money at?" The man was fuming. He was taller than Leo, and heavier. But Leo didn't seem at all intimidated.

Leo smiled at the menacing man. "Fuck you," Leo said, puffing on his cigarette. "I brought that money by your house last night. You wasn't home, so I was gonna give the dough to your wife. But after I got finished fucking her, she said it was so good that *she* shoulda been paying *me*. So I don't owe you shit."

Leo's audience laughed at angry Nick, and Marquis watched to see what would happen next. To his amazement, his father went right back to talking to his boys, as if Nick wasn't even there. Furious, Nick pulled out a gun, and everybody scattered. He started firing at Leo, aiming for his face. Using his arms to block his face, Leo ducked and tried to ward off the gunshots. The first bullet hit him in the forearm as he fell to the ground. Marquis stood frozen in fear, crying loudly. Leo tried desperately to wriggle out of harm's way. But the shooter continued to fire, hitting Leo several times.

Mayhem erupted as the shopping plaza exploded in screams and chaos. Leo tried to go for his gun, which was on his ankle. But the shooter was still firing, and Leo was badly injured. Marquis watched his father and was disturbed by the obvious pain that he was in. Leo was like a giant to his son, and so seeing him sprawled on the ground, with his face twisted in agony, was difficult for Marquis to witness. Marquis stood crying as he watched his father cringe in pain. Finally out of bullets, Nick ran off in the opposite direction from which he'd come, and Marquis ran to his father's side.

"Dad," he cried. "Dad, are you okay?" Marquis's tear-streaked face was all that Leo could focus on as he drifted in and out of consciousness.

The madness that followed seemed to swallow Marquis right up. All of Leo's boys came out of their hiding places, and began to talk to him, trying to keep him lucid and alert. Someone called 911 from a nearby pay phone. All the while Marquis clung to his father and prayed that he wouldn't die. After close to twenty minutes, an ambulance finally came, followed by several police cars. Cops swarmed the plaza as the paramedics tended to Leo down on the pavement. Marquis stood off in the corner, scared to death that his father would die. Leo struggled to remain conscious as they loaded him into the ambulance. He was rushed to the hospital while Ingrid hurried to the scene in order to get to Marquis. She arrived to find the police questioning her son about the shooting.

"Son, you have to try to remember more details. Do you remember the man's name? Was he a friend of your father's?" One officer grilled Marquis.

"Excuse me, he ain't answering no more of your questions," Ingrid interrupted, taking her son by the hand and hugging him close to her body. "He don't remember, and that's just that."

"Ma'am, we're trying to find the guy who shot your husband—"

"Good luck. Now I'd appreciate it if you leave us alone, so that I can get to the hospital." Ingrid stood calmly, and patted Marquis on his back reassuringly. But inwardly she was agonizing, wondering if this time Leo really might not make it. All the accounts she'd gotten from his boys had sounded grim. She knew that her husband had been shot at close range and that Marquis had witnessed it all. She knew that Nick was responsible. But she also knew that, if Leo survived, he wouldn't want the cops to do his dirty work. Leo would want to handle Nick all by himself.

The officer reluctantly allowed Ingrid to leave, handing her his card and instructing her to call him if her son remembered something. She lied and told him that she would, and then she took her baby and headed toward her car. Once inside she hugged and kissed her traumatized child, who was still crying from the trauma of what he'd witnessed. Ingrid tried her best to assure him that his father was tough and that he would survive. As they headed to the hospital, she assured Marquis that Leo would pull through.

When they arrived at the hospital, Ingrid left Marquis in the company of Aunt Betty while she stood vigil outside of Leo's operating room. Even with five bullets in him, he was talking shit and giving the doctors a hard time.

"Don't . . . put me to sleep! I don't . . . wanna go under. Don't put me . . . to sleep. I'm serious. I'm . . . serious." Leo was yelling at the doctors, nervous that if he was sedated he might not wake up.

The doctors argued with him, but to no avail. Finally a doctor came out to speak to Ingrid to explain the situation. "Your husband is refusing to allow us to sedate him. He wants to remain awake during the surgery. He's got several bullet wounds—one each in his forearm, his hand, his shoulder, and his stomach. He also has a graze wound on his neck. That's a lot to stay awake for. Maybe you can talk some sense into him."

Ingrid shook her head, knowing that it would be pointless to try to talk to Leo when his mind was made up. Leo always followed his instincts. He was superstitious at times—he was the kind of man who would never lay his hat on a bed or walk under a ladder. If his gut instincts told him not to go somewhere, Leo didn't go. And if he was apprehensive about being put to sleep, nothing she said to him would change his mind.

"Can't you give him something to numb the area where he was shot and still allow him to stay awake?" she asked. "He doesn't want to be put to sleep, and if he's strong enough to handle it, I think you should let him have his way."

The doctor was surprised by her response. He stood speechless for a long while. Then he nodded and returned to the operating room. He explained to the anesthesiologist that only a local anesthetic would be used. Leo lay there with his teeth clenched, sweat streaming down his face and his fists tightly balled, while the doctors removed the bullets and closed up his wounds. They saved the abdominal wound until last, hoping he would succumb to the pain and beg for anesthesia. Leo was stubborn. But he eventually passed out from a mixture of exhaustion and pain. The doctors tended to his abdominal wound then.

The next several hours were tense for Ingrid and Marquis. They waited anxiously for Leo to wake up. When he finally did, Ingrid cried for the first time all day. Leo looked at his wife and his son and was so happy to see them. As long as he could see them, that meant he wasn't dead. Leo's dry mouth made it difficult for him to talk. So he simply squeezed his wife's hand and winked at her. Ingrid smiled, feeling that her husband would be strong enough to survive. Marquis thanked God for bringing his father through the whole ordeal alive.

When Leo was finally released from the hospital, Ingrid waited on him hand and foot. His recovery was slow and deliberate. And she was with her husband every step of the way. While Leo had always been a far from perfect husband, he was a good man, and a good provider. Ingrid loved him intensely.

Ingrid had grown up in Marietta, Georgia. Her sister, Betty, had been bold and adventurous, and had ventured out of the small town they'd grown up in, opting for life in a big city. Soon Betty was living in New York City. She was three years older than Ingrid, and she'd gotten a sleep-in job in Manhattan, cleaning house and working as a nanny for some wealthy white people. Eventually Betty got her own place in Harlem and worked odd jobs to get by. Her sister, Ingrid, came to New York in the fall of 1970. Ingrid was seventeen. She left her mother, her father, and her four brothers, and came to stay with her sister in New York, looking for something better.

Ingrid had been living with her sister for about ten months. She loved New York, just *loved* the city. And it was nice for her to be back in the company of her sister. They had always been close, since the two of them were the only girls in a family of so many boys. But Betty had a man. His name was Calvin. Calvin would get high, and he'd get a wandering eye. It wasn't long before he started making comments and staring at Ingrid, leering at her. Betty seemed not to notice, and Ingrid didn't want to upset her sister. Instead, she made up her mind that as soon as possible, she would find a place of her own and vacate the uncomfortable surroundings in which she was now living. She and Betty spent a lot of time at supper clubs on Friday and Saturday nights. They would hang out there whenever Calvin was tripping. On one such night at a supper club, Ingrid met the man who would sweep her off her feet and change her life forever.

There was a card game in the basement at Jack's after-hours spot. Only the "in" crowd was allowed downstairs, and Betty qualified as part of that crowd. With her sister in tow, she gained access to the exclusive club, and the two of them watched the card game in progress. A baller by the name of Leo was there. He was with his crew of fellow ballers, and Betty was familiar with one of them. His name was Wes. He was from Bed-Stuy, and he ran numbers for Simon. Ingrid felt grown, living in a big city, coming from a small town, and she wanted to see everything. She stayed in the middle of things, and got to know all the characters in the neighborhood. She watched Leo doing his thing. And she also saw him checking her out. But Leo was there that night with some high-yellow broad from Harlem. She was shining, too, with some diamonds in her ears and a mink wrap on her shoulders. She was stuck-up, though, and she sat all night long in the corner, away from the party. Ingrid was with Betty, and Betty had an ass as big as Rhode Island. With all that junk in the trunk, it was no wonder Betty commanded the attention of half the men in the room.

Betty started dancing when her song came on. She was out there in the middle of the floor, grinding and twisting. Soon all eyes were on their little corner of the basement. And when the song went off, and the cards were dealt, Leo won the card game.

It all got rowdy, with the losers grumbling and Leo and his boys gloating. He sent over a bottle of champagne for Ingrid and Betty, and the high-yellow ho he had come with jumped up and got in his face. She yelled, "Leonard! You got me sittin' over here all night, and when you win, the first thing you do is send them bitches a bottle?" Betty jumped up, about to mop the floor with that bitch. She was really going to hurt the girl. But Leo's boys held her back, and Leo just laughed. He looked at the chick, and said, "You better sit down somewhere before you get embarrassed." But the redbone didn't sit down. She hauled off and slapped Leo dead in his face. The whole room stood still. And then Leo hit her right back! Slapped her so hard, Ingrid just knew the woman must have seen stars. The redbone soon recovered, and when she did, she started *swinging*. The two of them fought each other so bad in that basement that Leo's boys pulled her out of there and put her in a cab. Leo sat right there at the bar and bought drinks for everybody. It was the funniest thing Ingrid had ever witnessed.

Leo's friend Wes was sweet on Betty. He was over there all night, whispering in her ear and all that. And with the rowdy redbone long gone, Leo would not leave Ingrid's side. He was glued to her, but he wasn't too aggressive. He was as smooth as butter. Ingrid fell in love on the spot.

Ingrid and Betty decided to leave at around one o'clock in the morning. They had come alone, so they were prepared to leave alone. But Leo insisted on driving them the seven blocks to Betty's place. They piled into his Cadillac, and Ingrid was thoroughly impressed. By the time they pulled up in front of Betty's house, Ingrid had her mind made up that she was gonna see that man again. He asked for her number, and she gave it to him with no problem. He kissed her hand before she got out of the car, and said, "I'm gonna marry you someday, Miss Ingrid Bourne. You can take that to the bank." Leo said all the right things. He was so confident, so charismatic. Within months Ingrid had married him, and was expecting their first child. Their son, Marquis Lamont Graham, was born on a rainy night in 1972.

After Leo recovered from the shooting his youngest son had witnessed, he went right back to the streets he loved so much. Nick was killed in a "botched robbery" soon after, and Leo even went to his funeral. Everybody knew that Leo had killed Nick, but no one went to the police. Everybody knew that the penalty for fucking with Leo was death. Nick had only gotten what his hand had called for.

As he grew up, Marquis watched his father with much awe and re-spect. Leo had had six kids with three other women. But Marquis was his youngest and his favorite, whether he ever said it or not. Wherever he went, Leo had his baby boy by his side. Marquis saw a few of his siblings often. His half-brother Michael and his half-sister Bridgett were the closest ones to him. And they were only closest to him because they lived in close proximity to his mother. Marquis had always felt like an only child, even though he had so many brothers and sisters. In his house, it was only him, his mother, and his father. It was easy for him to forget, at times, that he was the youngest of seven of his father's children. And be-ing his father's child definitely had its perks.

Once Marquis had gone with his father to an arcade in Staten Island. When they got there, a couple of kids were playing the video games. Marquis couldn't wait to get in there and play, too. But judging by the looks of it, every game in the arcade was already being played. Leo saw the look of disappointment on his son's face and told him not to worry. Marquis watched his pops walk over and say something to the guy who ran the place. The owner walked over and spoke in a low voice to the kids who were playing, and suddenly every video game became available. The kids gathered up their stuff and left. No one was allowed access to the games except Marquis, and he got to play all the games by himself. It was then that he knew that Leo Graham was a powerful man. Without being told, Marquis knew his father was into something serious.

But as much as Marquis admired his father, he longed for a more con-sistent relationship with Leo. When they spent time together, Leo taught his son all that there was to know about being a hustler. He constantly pointed things out to Marquis, and explained the intricacies of the game to him. But soon Leo's absences from home became more frequent and prolonged. Ingrid was working harder than ever. And with Leo pulling more disappearing acts, Ingrid was forced to look for a babysitter. Mar-quis was only ten years old, and Ingrid didn't feel comfortable leaving him home alone. Especially in their home, which was filled with guns, drugs, and cash hidden in the most unexpected places. Sometimes her sister Betty would watch Marquis. But he was bored at her house, and would protest whenever he was forced to go there. Betty didn't tolerate noise and childish nonsense, so the hours spent at Aunt Betty's were almost unbearable for him. Marquis would cry and throw a fit whenever his mother suggested sending him there. Ingrid would often give in, and bring Marquis to work with her. Ingrid worked the overnight shift at a home for the mentally retarded. She was well liked and well respected by both the staff and the residents. When Marquis came to work with her on the overnight shift, Ingrid would let him play records or watch TV in the lounge. They also spent hours playing cards, talking, and laughing, until Marquis fell asleep in one of the vacant beds. Once her shift ended in the morning, she would bring her son to school and go home to get some rest. Marquis's bond with his mother was solidified during his father's unexplained absences. Those evenings spent at work with his mom would form memories that he would forever carry with him. They became closer than ever. Marquis loved and idolized his father, but his mother was the one he depended on and counted on to be there for him day after day. She was the one consistent factor in his life, and he loved her for it.

Leo's absences only made Marquis more excited whenever he did come home. He would see his dad and light up like a Christmas tree. To Marquis, Leo was the ultimate gangster. He adored his dad. Every moment with him was packed with excitement.

One day, Leo had Marquis riding in a car with him and two of Leo's boys. Their destination that day was a mystery to Marquis. But wherever they were going, everyone seemed to be in a big hurry to get there. Leo was speeding along the expressway, when all of a sudden sirens sounded behind them. The cops pulled the Cadillac over, with their weapons drawn and everything. They patted everybody down, including young Marquis. They searched every inch of the car as well. But after a while they had to let them go, since everybody was clean. The cops gave Leo a ticket for speeding, and let him leave. It seemed like the police wanted to find something on Leo badly—anything! But they found nothing. Marquis had had no idea that his father and his cronies had just been involved in a major bank heist. All Marquis knew was that his father had stopped off at the bank and gone inside, leaving him in the car. Leo's two friends had gone inside with him, as had another carload of Leo's associates, who had been riding behind them. When he came out, Leo had strode confidently over to his Cadillac, followed by his two friends, and they'd peeled the fuck up out of there.

Marquis never noticed where the other carload of Leo's cronies had gone, but would find out much later that their car had been the one with the money in it. Marquis was clueless as to what types of day-to-day activities Leo was involved in. But to him, at such a young age, getting pulled over and patted down by the cops was just another exciting story for him to entertain his friends with. He loved telling them about the things he saw while with his father, the places he went, the excitement he experienced. He grew up feeling like his dad was the man, and he was proud to be his son. Leo taught his son the streets as if it were a science. And Marquis studied those streets, studied that man. Leo did what he could to capitalize off of anyone else's success, and that included a lot of different activities. Be it extortion, loan sharking, illegal numbers, prostitution, or gunrunning, he was a man who got all his gains by questionable means.

As he got older, people would ask Marquis what he wanted to be when he grew up. He didn't know how to explain what it was that Leo did. So he would tell them that he wanted to be just like his dad. Once he asked Leo what his job title was: "What do you do for a living, Pop?"

Leo had smiled, and shrugged his shoulders. "I do what I can. That's all there is to it."

Marquis accepted that answer, and from that day on whenever he was out with his dad, watching him handle his business, Leo would remind him of his motto. "Do what you can, young man." Marquis would always remember that phrase.

But Marquis began to have mixed emotions about some aspects of his father's life. Leo thought nothing of bringing Marquis with him whenever he went to visit one of his many girlfriends. Marquis didn't understand the relationship his father had with these women at first. It didn't dawn on him that there was anything out of the ordinary when Leo first began bringing him to the homes of various women. Marquis had assumed they were friends of Leo's, just like the men he hung around with, until Leo began to bring him to the home of one woman in particular, who really seemed special to him. The woman, whose name was Audra, lived in Park Hill. She went out of her way to make Marquis smile whenever Leo brought him by, cooking for him and being very nice to him. The pretty young woman always offered him something to drink, made sure he was comfortable, and asked him all kinds of questions about himself. Marquis was polite to Miss Audra, and he enjoyed her cooking. And his father seemed to really like her. Marquis could tell by how Leo smiled around her, how he acted, that he had feelings for this woman, more than for the rest of his mistresses. This began to tug at Marquis's conscience, because as much as he loved his father, he loved his mother as well. And the last thing he wanted was to see his mother hurt.

Feeling, even at that young age, that what his father was doing was wrong, Marquis told his mother about the incident. He knew that it wasn't right for Leo to cheat on Ingrid. But his mother's reaction had been completely unexpected. She did absolutely nothing. There was no argument, no fight, no hostility between his parents. Ingrid had simply thanked Marquis for telling her the truth, and assured him that everything would be alright. He never pressed the issue out of the sheer respect and admiration he had for his dad. But over time Marquis came to realize that his mother knew about the other women. She knew about *all* of them, and there were several. Ingrid didn't make a big issue out of it. She never tripped about Leo's cheating ways, because she felt that those women were only getting whatever they were getting. She was the *wife*, she had the name, his youngest son, his home. Ingrid didn't trip about the other women. Because as far as she was concerned, all they provided for Leo was an assortment of pussy. Ingrid was Leo's number one, and no one was going to take her spot.

But for Marquis, it was intriguing how his dad juggled so many chicks. It was almost admirable that he could manage to have a wife with a few mistresses on the side. Marquis was impressed. In fact, he later came to realize that women were a part of Leo's big business. This fact came to light during an episode that happened when he turned thirteen.

"Marquis, get your shoes on. I'm taking you out with me today."

Leo didn't need to say another word. Marquis sprang to his feet and ran to his room to look for his sneakers. He felt like a man whenever he went out with his dad. Puberty was having an obvious effect on him. His voice had deepened, there was more muscle definition in his arms and torso, and he had even begun to have wet dreams. Ingrid had embarrassed him upon discovering her son's sticky sheets and pajamas balled up at the bottom of the hamper. *What's all this shit on your sheets, Marquis?* Ingrid had demanded. He felt mortified, and was grateful when his dad had intervened, telling Ingrid to "stay out of the young man's business." A young man. That's what he was. And Marquis felt like that whenever Leo was around. He adored Leo. Being in his father's presence made him feel invincible.

They got into Leo's car, and Marquis rolled the passenger-side window down all the way. He wanted all his boys to see him. He wanted them to see how lucky he was to have a father as gangsta as Leo. They drove down the block with Marquis calling out to his friends, and Leo singing along to a Marvin Gaye hit that was playing on the car stereo. A Newport dangled from Leo's lips as he maneuvered the car through the streets of Staten Island. Finally they got to a house on a dead-end street that Marquis didn't recognize. He often accompanied his father to collect money that was owed him or to deliver mysterious packages to his henchmen. So he assumed that this was one of those occasions.

A man answered the door. Marquis didn't recognize the dapper older man, but Leo greeted him warmly. They walked inside, and Leo introduced his son. "James, this is Marquis," he said, smiling proudly. "My boy turned thirteen, and it's time for him to get his feet wet. You know what I'm saying?"

Leo's friend laughed. "I don't think it's his feet that he needs to get wet."

Both men laughed while Marquis stood there wondering what was so funny. Without any further discussion, James ushered Leo and Marquis down to the basement. Once they got there, Marquis couldn't believe his eyes. Four young women—all of them appeared to be in their early twenties—sat in various stages of undress. One girl, a petite, light-skinned sister with long brown hair, wore only a bra and panties. She sat with her legs spread open like a man, and she smiled at Marquis. Another lady was a thick, dark-skinned chick with a flimsy bathrobe pulled tightly around her full frame. She sat with her legs crossed as she smoked a cigarette. Two sexy Spanish girls flanked her. One wore her long hair in a tight ponytail, and she stared at Marquis as she chewed her gum. The other was short and wore her hair in cornrows. Both of them were topless. Marquis couldn't take his eyes off of them.

Leo smiled approvingly at his son. Marquis stared hungrily at the four women before him, and Leo urged him to take advantage of the opportunity before him. "Happy birthday, son. This is my present to you. You pick any of these fine young ladies you want, and your wish is their command."

Marquis looked at his father in astonishment. He couldn't believe this was happening. He was speechless as it dawned on him that Leo had brought him to a whorehouse. Marquis didn't know it at the time, but this was an establishment that Leo had a financial stake in. Leo had personally sampled every one of them, and he knew that his son was in for a good time. All Marquis knew was that there were four women in front of him. And he could have whichever one he wanted. He smiled.

James and Leo smiled as well. "I like this kid," James said to Leo. He looked at Marquis standing there with a Kool-Aid smile on his face. "Since me and your father go back like bread and butter, I'm gonna make your birthday even more special," James said. "You can have all four of them."

Marquis's mouth fell open in surprise, and Leo patted him on his shoulder encouragingly. "Do what you can, young man," Leo said. "I'll be upstairs when you're finished." Leo and James headed back upstairs, leaving Marquis alone with the four hos.

His heart was beating so fast he could almost hear it. Marquis stood awkwardly on the far end of the room, staring shyly at the women before him.

The Spanish girl with the long ponytail smacked her gum, sassily. "You can come over here," she said. "We won't bite. Unless you want us to." She smiled at Marquis, and he felt himself blushing.

He walked over to where the women sat, and stood with his hands in his pockets. The light-skinned girl motioned him closer and opened her legs wider. She motioned toward her protruding pussy, signaling that she wanted him to come close. Marquis did as he was instructed and nearly fainted as she unbuckled his jeans and unzipped them. Sliding his pants down around his knees, she smiled at the woody in his boxer shorts.

"Looks like you're happy to see me," she said. The other women chuckled and began to surround Marquis.

He stood there nervously as the girl in front of him took his dick out of his pants. She kissed it, and Marquis thought his knees would buckle. She took the head in her mouth and sucked it softly. He couldn't help but moan. The two topless girls each took one of his hands and placed it on their breasts. Marquis stroked them and marveled at the way their nipples stood at attention. By now, the light-skinned girl had all of him in her mouth, and she was sucking him like a Popsicle. He felt light-headed, and euphoric.

"Sit down, baby," the short, thick, brown-skinned girl said. "You look like you need a seat."

The one sucking him off paused while he sat beside her. Once he was seated, she leaned over and continued her professional blow job. While she took him to paradise, the chocolate shorty knelt before him and began licking and lightly sucking on his balls, stroking them and making him want to scream in ecstasy. One of the topless girls put her titty in Marquis's mouth, and he sucked on it like a newborn child. The other one took his hand and placed it in her pussy, and he finger-fucked her as she moaned, enjoying it.

Marquis knew he was about to cum. It seemed that the shorty giving him head sensed that as well. She abruptly stopped what she was doing as Marquis came in spurts. He became light-headed, and his heart galloped in his chest. The light-skinned girl stood up. Marquis's dick lay limp across his stomach.

He was somewhat embarrassed, because he had cum so fast. He didn't know what to say, so an awkward silence filled the room. Finally, chocolate said, "You want to lose your virginity?"

Marquis looked at her and nodded. But he felt so drained that he wasn't sure he could go another round. His mind was willing, but his flesh might not cooperate.

She nodded. "Which one you want?" she asked.

He looked at all the girls, and all of them were sexy. But she was his favorite. "I want you," he said. "But I might need a few more minutes."

She smiled. He thought she was so pretty. The other girls began to touch each other. They rubbed one another and kissed each other in places that stunned Marquis. Before long, his dick was once again at attention. Chocolate stood before him. She took off her robe and peeled off her panties. Discarding her bra to reveal her DDs, she let him touch her body. He liked the way she felt. Soft, like Charmin. She was so soft. He touched her, and she moaned for him. He really liked that. It made him feel so good. She didn't rush him, and she stood confidently as he explored her body.

Straddling him, she said, "Put it in."

Marquis's hands trembled as he grabbed his dick and rubbed it against her pussy. He didn't know what to do, and was nervous and slightly uncomfortable. Seeing his inexperience, she took his dick and slowly inserted it inside of her warmth. Marquis had never felt anything so wonderful in his life. He couldn't believe that he was losing his virginity to a grown-ass woman, and having an orgy to boot. She rubbed herself as she rode him. She seemed to be really getting off on what he was doing, and this boosted his confidence.

After several minutes, Marquis couldn't hold back anymore. He began to moan loudly.

"That's it, baby. I feel you cummin," she said breathlessly. She stood up in the nick of time and Marquis burst all over the place.

"Aaaaagh!"

Chocolate girl kissed Marquis, her tongue mingling with his. Then she pecked him softly on the lips, and smiled. "Happy birthday," she said.

Marquis was drained. He was also slightly uncomfortable. He wasn't sure why, but he was. He adjusted his clothes, and stood up. He wasn't sure what he should say, and the women went right back to talking among themselves, as if nothing had ever happened. He cleared his throat and fidgeted nervously, with his hands in his pockets. "Thank you," he said, not knowing what else to say.

They smiled at him, and told him he was welcome, and that he could come back any time. He turned and walked upstairs and found his father and his friend James sitting at the kitchen table sharing a bottle of Jack Daniel's.

Leo smiled at his son. "How'd it go?" he asked.

Marquis smiled, shyly. "I did what I could," he said.

The men laughed, and shook hands with him in a congratulatory way. Leo poured his son a drink, and Marquis took it eagerly. The hot liquor burned his chest, and more than ever before Marquis felt like a man.

When they went home, neither of them mentioned the incident to Ingrid. Marquis lay in his bed all night replaying the scene in his head. He would tell all his boys what had happened. And once again, he'd be the envy of all his friends.

The year that he turned thirteen was a year of a lot of change for Marquis. He was no longer a virgin, and he began to feel and act like a grown man. He felt more privileged than ever to be the son of a man with so much power, so much control. He was the heir to the throne, and he was being groomed to take over when the time came. But suddenly, his father began to be absent for more prolonged periods of time. Suddenly Leo wasn't coming home every night, and days would pass before he saw his father again. Then, when Leo did come home, he would sleep for hours and hours, and it seemed that not even an atomic bomb could rouse him from his sleep. Being the perceptive young man that he was, Marquis began to notice that his mother was putting in far more hours at work than she had before. She was always tired, falling asleep almost as soon as she got home from work. Ingrid was exhausted, trying to keep things from falling apart in her husband's absence. And Leo was becoming more unpredictable—and unreliable—than ever.

Marquis was thirteen years old, and already his relationship with his father was fractured. The man Marquis had once idolized and adored was now absent from his life more often than not. It seemed that the facade he'd been shown of a father who could conquer the world had suddenly crumbled, to reveal a man as tainted and as human as any other.

Marquis was friends with a couple of young men from around the way. Sammy and Martin were brothers, and then there was Chauncey. These were his boys. All of them grew up in the same building, and soon they became known collectively as the 55 Holland niggas. They got into all kinds of mischief together, all of them enduring differing levels of poverty in the era of President Ronald Reagan. Not many male role models existed in most of their families. All of their mothers were struggling to make ends meet. So the hood, and the camaraderie they found within it, became their family. And together, they grew up.

One afternoon in 1985, Marquis sat on the edge of his bed, fully engrossed in his Atari game system. Pac-Man was chomping up points, as Sammy and Chauncey looked on. It was always fun to hang out at Marquis's house. His mother wasn't fussy, and she didn't mind the noise. Plus, he was the only one in their building with an Atari. Marquis was defeated by the game, and he relinquished the joystick to Sammy. As they continued watching the game, Chauncey started a conversation that would change Marquis forever.

"Yo, I forgot to tell you I saw your pops yesterday."

Marquis looked at his friend, wondering about the specifics. He hadn't seen his dad in three days. Whenever he heard his father was in the hood, Marquis would get excited at the thought of seeing him. Someone would tell him that his father was on South Avenue at the store, and Marquis would head there immediately, in anticipation of seeing his dad. He thought back to the last time he'd seen his father. Marquis had been walking down the block, feeling good and thinking he was looking that way, too. Out of nowhere, it seemed, his father came calling his name. He stopped and greeted Leo Graham, the always well-dressed gentleman of his time.

Leo had stepped back dramatically, and looked at his son's sweat suit. "Where you going looking like that?" he had asked.

Marquis smiled and held his hands up, defensively. "What's wrong with how I look?" Leo shook his head. "As long as you look like that, you won't never get money. Not looking like that! You got it all wrong."

Marquis frowned, and laughed his father's comments off.

"Let me tell you something," Leo said animatedly, leaning close to his son. "Even if you ain't *got* no money, you gotta always *look* like you got money. That way you can always *get* some money."

Marquis had to sift that through his mind for a couple of moments. But when he figured out what his father was telling him, it had made perfect sense. He meant that a man who has nothing can always get something, if he looks like he already has it all. These were the types of jewels Leo often gave his son. Little tidbits of wisdom that Marquis could tuck into his mental Rolodex.

Marquis remembered that encounter now, as Chauncey mentioned seeing his father. He was wondering what Leo was up to, and how he was getting money. Like any young man coming of age, he wanted to understand his father—his first male role model—fully, and Leo's life was anything but an open book. "Where'd you see him at?"

Chauncey laughed in reaction to Sammy's demise in the video game, as his man was gobbled up. Then he turned his attention back to Marquis. "In front of 55 Holland. He was out there copping from A.J. and them. I think he saw me, but he just kept it movin' and shit."

Marquis sat silently, mulling over what he'd just heard. Sammy and Chauncey were focused on the game, not noticing the troubled expression on Marquis's face. Everybody knew A.J. sold crack on the block. That was common knowledge in the hood. So naturally, Marquis probed further. "Copping from A.J.?" he asked with a frown. "Copping what?"

Both Sammy and Chauncey looked directly at Marquis, appearing confused. Chauncey said, "Crack, nigga. You knew your pops was smokin', right?"

Marquis laughed, uneasily. "Get the fuck outta here," he said. "My pops ain't smokin' crack. You must be crazy." Sammy and Chauncey exchanged glances, knowingly. Marquis watched the exchange, and felt his insides bubbling with anxiety. He'd come to some conclusions about his pops. He wasn't *that* naïve. He knew about Leo's drug use. As a young child he had witnessed his father snorting cocaine with his friends on numerous occasions. Marquis had been too young to understand that it was illegal, but he had seen some odd behavior. Eventually, Marquis had asked his mother about what he had witnessed. He had surprised her one day when he was nine years old by asking, "Why's daddy always sniffing soap powder?" That question had sparked a big fight between Ingrid and his father, whose drug use had been beginning to spin out of control. That argument was still etched in Marquis's brain. So he knew that his dad had his struggles. He knew that his father was using *some* drugs. But to think of him smoking *crack*—being a fiend—was more than he could imagine. His father was no crackhead. He was supposed to be the king of the world.

Sammy spoke up. "Nah, Marquis. The nigga's smoking. Trust me." He set the joystick down, and gave his friend a look of sincerity. "A.J. and them niggas been serving him. I thought you knew." The boys grew silent as Sammy continued to play the game, and Marquis's world came crashing down. They became engrossed in the game once more, Chauncey and Sammy teasing each other about their lack of skills. But Marquis's mind was reeling. His father was a crackhead, and it seemed that everyone was aware of it except for him.

They heard a knock at the front door and listened as Mrs. Graham answered it. After a few moments, Martin entered the room, greeting all his boys and plopping down on the beanbag chair in the corner.

"Where the fuck you been, nigga?" Sammy chided his brother. "You been missing since right after you finished your Froot Loops this morning."

Martin shrugged. "So? Why you worried about where I been?" He tossed a nearby pillow at his curious brother's head. As he sat back once again, a thick wad of cash fell from the pocket of his sweatpants, and

Martin set it beside him. The eyes of all of his friends widened immediately.

"Yo, where the fuck you get that from?" Sammy asked.

Martin grinned at his brother slyly. He had known the money would
impress his boys. He was thrilled about his newfound wealth. "I made all
that today," he said, proudly. "I'm hustling for A.J. now."

"You selling crack?" Chauncey asked, incredulously. To him that was
impressive, to say the least. Selling drugs took guts, it took heart.

Marquis barraged him with questions. "Word? How that work? How
much you get to keep? You gotta stand on the block and shit?"

Martin explained the particulars. He filled them in on how A.J. had
approached him, and had asked if he wanted to get down with his team.
Martin and his family were struggling. Their moms was on welfare, the
money was slow, and he was tired of being the kid that never had shit. All
Marquis heard was that Martin had made all that money—that whole
big knot of cash—in one day. That was all the time it took to get all that
paper. Martin got to keep thirty dollars of every one hundred dollars he
made. At thirteen years old, those numbers didn't sound too bad.

Marquis had just found out that his father was a crackhead. The man
who had once been his hero was no more. He couldn't go to his mother
for the things he wanted, the material things he felt he had to have. He
saw his mother struggling, working double shifts at the home for the
mentally retarded to keep them afloat, while his father was slipping. He
would never dream of burdening her further with any frivolous requests
for sneakers or clothes. But Marquis wasn't used to having to do without.
He was accustomed to having the best. Instantly, he knew what he had
to do.

12

GRINDING

Marquis got on his grind. He started spending all of his time in the streets. He went to school, but as soon as the last bell rang, he was on the block. And the money came pouring in. He tried at first to keep his activities hidden from his mother. So for that reason he kept his school attendance up, and he tucked his money in his underwear drawer. But it wasn't long before he reasoned that he was getting more money standing on the block than he ever would sitting in a classroom. Still, he kept balancing his junior high school education and his education on the block.

Marquis took his part of the block and worked it like his forty acres. The cold New York winters never deterred him from getting that money. He would throw on three or four layers of clothes and a skully and stand outside all night long. The money came like clockwork, the fiends desperate for a steady supplier. Unlike his peers, who turned their pagers off at midnight to get a good night's sleep, Marquis's business was open all night, like a true hustler. His pager was never off, and custys beeped him day and night. Ingrid was often working nights, and this allowed thirteen-year-old Marquis to come and go as much as he needed to in order to chase a sale. He would get up out of his bed if a fiend paged him. He'd throw his clothes on over his pajamas and go out and get that paper. He never turned down an opportunity to make money. He was consistent and, for the most part, likable. He had a no-nonsense way about him that made it hard for the fiends to approach him wrongly. But at the same time, he was a friendly and funny dude, which made it hard for the other young hustlers to hate him. A.J. certainly took notice of this young protégé, who wasn't afraid of hard work. Marquis's enemies were outnumbered by his friends. And to A.J. it seemed that he was a natural-born hustler.

Then came Marquis's friend Jamari. Jamari lived in the Mariner's Harbor projects not far from where Marquis and his crew lived. Jamari went to school with them, and often hung around wanting to be down. Marquis was the only one who was really willing to give the unknown boy a chance. And he was further drawn to Jamari when he found out that the boy's mother was a crackhead. Marquis could identify, although he imagined that it must be different when the fiend was your *mother*. Many nights Jamari didn't go home, since there was seldom anything to eat there anyway. Ingrid fed him a meal on many occasions, as Jamari became Marquis's good friend. And by the time they finished the eighth grade, Jamari was practically living with Marquis. He spent the night more often than not. Ingrid didn't complain, and Marquis unselfishly shared what he had with this kid, who he felt he had so much in common with. They became like brothers with different mothers.

When he first started coming around, Jamari was a sheep among wolves. He dressed like a cornball, and Marquis had to show him how to rock his jeans, how to wear his hat and lace his sneakers. Jamari soaked it all up, and was an eager student. He admired Marquis, and wanted to be more like him—more accepted by both the girls in the hood and the niggas on the block.

Up until the age of fourteen, all the boys had been known by their given names. There was Marquis Graham, and then there was Jamari, Martin, his brother Sammy, and Chauncey. Upon entering high school, the boys abandoned their bikes and occasional football games, and began to come up in the game among the local hustlers. They adopted names comparable to those of their older counterparts. They were searching for themselves, and searching for new identities, trying to carve a niche in the broken society in which they dwelled. Sammy was now known as Smitty; Chauncey shed his given name for Chance. Only Martin and

Marquis had opted not to alter their personas at first. But in all the boys, a transition was underway that would mold them from this point forward.

Marquis didn't make the decision to change his name spontaneously. Instead, shedding his given name was a metaphorical peeling off of old layers, of old scars. He had a special love for his mother, this woman who somehow managed to hold it all together despite the anarchy around her. Marquis had seen his mother weather countless storms, had witnessed her strength and her grace firsthand. He was proud that she was his mother, and he wanted to pay homage to all the love and guidance she'd given him over the years. So he started calling himself by his mother's maiden name—Bourne—only he altered the spelling for good measure. He no longer wanted to think of himself as his father's son, his father's heir apparent. It was his mother who had shown him how to fix a flat on his bicycle. It was his mother who listened when he told her about the fights he had gotten into with other boys around the way. His mother had been the one who held him down, had his back, and was there for him. There had been too many nights—too many days—when all he had was his mother. And all she had was her son.

Born had begun to change in his father's absence. He was longing for the relationship between a father and a son that is so vital in every young man's life. His father had ignited a fire in him that he'd then allowed to be extinguished. A hunger dwelled within Born for the power and honor he'd witnessed his father having before the crack had come into play. He was hungry for money and respect. And now that his dad was around less and less, it became obvious that the streets would be the place he'd turn to to fill the void left by his father.

Marquis was different now, but his mother flat-out refused to call him Born. Ingrid thought it was stupid to walk around calling yourself something other than your legal name, regardless of his reasons for doing so. She was the only one who continued to call him Marquis, and he didn't protest. It would have been pointless to argue with her about it. But she recognized that the transition from impressionable youngster to ruthless hustler was under way in her son.

Ingrid Graham was Born's favorite girl in the world, and all of her friends thought it was precious that her son loved her as unabashedly as he did. In his eyes, his mother was smarter and more perceptive than the average woman. So it should never have surprised him when his mother uncovered what he thought was a well-kept secret. His father was smoking now more than ever. Leo was home whenever he was broke, and out getting high whenever he got money. Ingrid still hadn't tried to talk to her son about what was happening in their family, because she didn't even know where to begin. Born spent less time at home and more time on the grind.

He and his boys had a tight crew going, and eventually they got their hands on some guns. Trouble was, they were all about sixteen or seventeen, and everybody was still living at home with their moms. Born was the only one whose mother didn't snoop around his room. Ingrid was never that type. She left his shit alone as long as he left her shit alone. So it was agreed that Born would hold everybody's guns at his house, and each day everyone would come to him and pick up their piece.

This setup worked for a while. Every day the crew would come to the crib and get their artillery, and then they would hit the block and get money. By now their crew was notorious. It was common knowledge that the 55 Holland boys would rob, steal, shoot . . . whatever! It was all about money to them. They had a legacy already. Known for resorting to collecting hood ransoms from rival crews (they would kidnap a rival hustler who had a little paper and hold him till they got five or six grand for his safe return), it became clear that they were not above *any* means of getting money.

Then Martin began to play the role of a stick-up kid. He was successful most often, because when a victim took one look in his evil eyes, no one dared to challenge him. They simply handed over their valuables and prayed that he let them leave with their lives. He robbed old ladies, young girls, hustlers from other neighborhoods—anybody who had what he wanted. Soon the rest of the crew had caught on, and together they pulled off robbery after robbery. But, this successful track record came to a halt when Martin and the rest of the crew tried to rob two younger hustlers from the Harbor projects named Junior and DonDon.

Martin, Born, Smitty, and Chance were all in on this robbery. Junior and DonDon talked a lot of shit and did a lot of bragging about what they had, and about the money they made. There had been bad blood between Born's crew and Junior and DonDon for a long time. Their crews often sold to the same customers, and stepped on each other's toes, on each other's turf. This was one crime that was more personal than anything else. So the four of them cornered Junior and DonDon in the lobby of a building in the Harbor projects, and demanded it all—their jewelry, money, sneakers, and all that.

"Gimme all yo shit, nigga. Punk ass! Go 'head and give me a reason to shoot you!" Martin barked.

Born, Smitty, and Chance all had their guns pointed at both Junior and DonDon. Junior stared at Martin over the barrel of his .45. "Fuck you," Junior said, disrespecting the robbery. He didn't think the cowards had the heart to shoot them. "Y'all ain't ready to use them guns. Stop playing."

Martin shook his head. "You sure about that?" he asked.

Junior looked as if he might change his mind. But Martin decided it was too late for that. He fired, hitting Junior dead in the head. Then he turned his gun on DonDon.

"Oh, shit!" DonDon reached for his own gun, figuring he might as well go out shooting. He was considerably outnumbered, but he shot it out anyway. Born opened four holes in him before DonDon could fire twice. The 55 Holland niggas walked away with every item of value that Junior and DonDon had put their lives on the line for. When all was said and done, DonDon was in a wheelchair and Junior was dead.

Word on the street spread that the 55 Holland niggas were behind the robbery of Junior and DonDon. The hood was all abuzz with speculation, and still, Born underestimated his moms, and thought she was clueless about what he was doing.

Then one morning, Born was asleep in his room. Leo wasn't there that day, and it was just Born and his mother at home. It was early—about eight o'clock in the morning. Ingrid came in and frantically woke her son up. She shook Born awake, and said, "Marquis, get up! The cops are outside in front of the building, and they're coming upstairs. You need to get them guns up out of here!"

"What?" Born was shocked, because he had no idea that she knew about those guns. He didn't have time to question it, though. He jumped out of bed and took the bag from underneath his bed. "How you know they're coming up here? They could be going to somebody else's apartment."

Ingrid grabbed the bag and frowned at her son. "Boy, you know damn well your ass is hot right now," she said. She ran to her next-door neighbor's apartment, and tapped eagerly on the door. The woman let Ingrid in, and after a brief explanation she hid the bag way in the back of her closet. Ingrid knew that the cops had her son and his crew on their radar.

Born had thought his mother was too lame to notice, but he had underestimated how well his father had taught his wife to pay attention. She had known all along what Born was up to. She had heard what the streets were saying about him, and she had long ago noticed that her son was deep in the game. Ingrid had been expecting the cops to come looking for him sooner or later. She would address it in her own way, but the issue at hand was more pressing than all that. She had to save him from going to jail.

Once back inside their apartment, Ingrid and Marquis nervously awaited the inevitable. They didn't need to wait too long. The cops came banging at their door no more than five minutes later. They came in, eight of them in full riot gear. "Get on the floor and place your hands behind your head!" they barked at Born. Ingrid was also subjected to scrutiny, as the cops made her stand with her hands behind her head. They ransacked the apartment, searching every room and looking in every crevice. But thanks to his mother, when they searched Born's room they didn't find those guns.

But they did find some of Junior's jewelry, and a few bags of weed. "Looks like we got you," one of the cops sneered at him. Born didn't panic. They brought him in for questioning, along with Smitty, Martin, and Chance. But none of them talked, and the cops had no way of proving that the rope chain and pinkie ring had belonged to Junior. Nothing was found that could connect the 55 crew to the crime committed.

Still, Born was shocked. His mother had never been the type to snoop. Or so he thought. But she had known what he'd been doing all along. After that, Born started wondering how much else she knew. And he stopped underestimating Ingrid Graham. But he kept getting in trouble. He and his crew were brought in for questioning in connection with attempted murders, assaults, home invasions, and drug dealing. It got to the point that whenever someone got shot or assaulted, the police questioned one or all of the 55 Holland niggas. Born was constantly in trouble. It wasn't long before the state got involved, and they put him in a group home all the way out in Queens.

He was in the group home for a year or so before he got kicked out for fighting. Fighting was part of survival of the fittest in a group home environment. The fight hadn't even been Born's fault, but they sent him to juvenile detention. He was always in some kind of group home or detention center in his early teens, and his mother always held him down. She made sure he had sheets, towels, clothes, tapes, whatever. Ingrid was sick without her son at home, and she knew that part of his "I don't give a fuck" attitude stemmed from the pain he was feeling over the departure of his father.

Being away from home was not the deterrent that the state of New York hoped it would be. In fact, in a lot of ways it prepared Born for jail. It was while he spent time at a juvenile detention center in the Bronx that Born witnessed the crack epidemic in a way that he never had before. Fiends lined up by the dozens to buy crack from one man. Born had never witnessed such extreme poverty and addiction until then. But it also showed him the potential for profit the drug game held. He watched bum-ass niggas make miraculous come-ups just by serving the fiends, who would give *anything* to get high. By the time he returned home after his stint in the group home, it was no secret to Ingrid that the respectable young man she knew as Marquis was also a ruthless thug known in the streets as Born. He was a fearless young man with nothing to lose and the world to gain. Born had arrogance that people either hated or loved, and he didn't care about anything. Born was a wild one, and the streets grew to revere him.

While doing his stint in the Bronx group home, he was allowed to come back to home to Staten Island from time to time. He would put in work on the block every time he was home. A counselor at that group home named Shakim noticed that whenever Born went home for a while, he would come back with all kinds of clothes, sneakers, coats, all kinds of shit. Born had a six-hundred-dollar blue Polo sweater that everyone knew was pricey. He was always styling, and everyone took notice. Shakim had read up Born's rap sheet, and he knew his whole story. So he would look at all the pricey new clothes and expensive jewelry that Born had each time he came back, and he'd shake his head.

"Damn! You out there slingin' them golden grams, huh?" Shakim asked Born. "It ain't hard to tell what you're out there doing." He knew what Born was doing. Shakim noticed that Born's eyes were always bloodshot and lazy. He knew that Born was smoking weed and that he was hustling. He decided to try to get through to the boy's mother as a last-ditch effort to save the young man.

Shakim had a conversation with Ingrid that didn't go as well as he had planned. "Your son has too many expensive things. I know that you send him some of it. But he gets plenty on his own. He's drawing attention to himself. And he's sending the wrong message to the other group home residents. These kids are supposed to be turning their lives around. But your son is making it look so much more enticing on the other side of life."

"Uh-huh," Ingrid said. She acted like she had no idea what Born was up to. "Everything that Marquis has, I've given to him. I'm his only source of income." But she wasn't. Born was doing it all by himself. She told Shakim, "I *work*. I can buy things for my son if I want, can't I?"

But Shakim knew the deal. After his conversation with Ingrid, Shakim told Born that he still had a lot to learn as a "hustler." "What you're doing is so obvious," he said. "Because for the past six weeks you haven't even been going to pick up the allowance the group home gives you. You don't need that money, so you keep forgetting to go get it."

Born stood there feeling like a fool for being so obvious. Shakim was right about all of his suspicions. It was no real secret what Born was doing out there. The system did nothing to deter him.

His father was fucked-up by that time. Leo was a full-blown crack addict, and to add to the problem, his health was deteriorating. His heart was failing; he was in a wheelchair. He was messed up. During one of Born's visits home, Leo had a talk with his son.

"I want to talk to you about something. Sit down," Leo instructed. Born did as he was told. "I see you getting real caught up in them streets. I see you. But you're too smart to be out there in the streets like me."

Born laughed, snidely. "Why? You don't think you're a good example?"

Leo ignored his son's sarcasm. "What are you hustling for? Your mother gets you whatever you want. I get you whatever you want. What are your hustling *for*?"

Born shrugged. True, Ingrid took him to shop at Macy's. He had Guess jeans. But she couldn't afford to buy him five pairs of Guess jeans like she once did. She could only get him two or three pairs. Born wanted a pair for each day of the week. And his mother was already working too hard in order to provide for his expensive tastes. He did what he did so that he wouldn't ever have to do without. He did it for status.

Leo knew that. And he pressed the issue further. "You ain't making no real money out there, Marquis. Get your act together and fly straight." Born agreed with him. He wasn't making no real money out there at the time. But he swore to himself that when he came home he would do the shit right and stop hustling backward. He didn't heed his father's warnings, figuring that Leo was just tired of seeing Born hustle the right way, unlike Leo had done.

Leo could tell that Born wasn't going to change. "Well, if you insist on being hardheaded, the least you can do is keep some bail money handy. Always have bail money, so you ain't gotta depend on nobody else."

Born nodded. But on the inside he winced. That was the advice a father gave his youngest son about being a hustler. Always have bail money ready. When Born came home he got right back on his grind.

Born had a steady girlfriend during this time. Her name was Simone, and they had met at a party thrown by one of his friends. Simone was a pretty girl with a Coke bottle figure. She was the first girl to get Born to let his guard down completely. She had his nose wide open. They were teenage sweethearts, and Born had shared all of himself with her. During the days when Born was in and out of group homes and in and out of trouble, Simone had been a breath of fresh air. She lived in Park Hill, and she was fly as hell. Whenever she stepped on the scene, niggas took notice, and Born was proud to have her as his girl. He had opened up to her about the pain of his childhood, and he shared his money with her. Born took her shopping, bought her jewelry, kept her laced in all the hottest clothes. Simone had been given every luxury imaginable, and Born had given her his heart.

It wasn't until he came back home to Staten Island for good that he found out that, in his absence, Simone had been fucking everybody in the projects. She and her friend Tanya were bosom buddies, and from what he heard, the two of them were both being scandalous. Not long after he came home for good, Born vowed revenge. And he got that revenge when he fucked Simone's friend Tanya, and then told her all about it. Simone was devastated and hurt, and her friendship with Tanya immediately ended. The two girls never spoke to each other again, and Simone was so distraught that she came to his mother's house in tears. Ingrid talked to the girl, and told her that she had gotten what her hand called for. When Born was hurt, he tended to hurt people back. But when Simone was gone, Born's mother had scolded him, and she told him that he was dead wrong for playing two friends against each other. Born didn't listen, though. He vowed to never give a bitch his heart again.

The money started piling up. Born began helping his moms with the bills, paying the rent, buying clothes and jewelry for himself, and feeling important for the first time. He began to have the acclaim that he had always thirsted for, and it felt pretty good.

The part that bothered him was that he couldn't help wondering if his father was proud of him. Part of him was angry with himself for even caring about Leo Graham and whether or not he had managed to make him proud. The man was a failure himself, as far as Born was concerned. But strangely, Born still longed for his father's approval, his attention. He wanted his father to be proud. But he would never admit that.

Born started trying to make bigger moves. He wanted more than just a little bit of money. He wanted tons of it, and he wasn't afraid to make moves without his crew behind him. When he found out that niggas had dough, he found a way to get dough with them, or he would take it from them instead. Jamari was with him all the way; Born's novice, watching and learning. For Born, it was nice being a role model to somebody. He knew he had more going for him than the average hustler in the hood. He was his father's child, and that had given him a front-row seat to the mechanics of the drug game. Being the son of a man like Leo—an Original Gangsta whose name rang bells—had clearly prepared Born for his turn on the throne. And now that Leo had fallen, it was almost as if Born had picked up the torch and was determined to run with it. He would not lose. And Jamari seemed to recognize that as well. He seemed to look up to Born. And Born took that seriously, knowing that having power meant having followers who would do anything you needed. He figured that someone like Jamari might come in handy someday.

Born was the man. He had big rings, jewelry, chains, the whole nine. He was on top of the world. Shopping sprees every weekend, sneakers for every outfit, and jewelry galore. He was caked up. When he went shopping he often took Jamari with him, just to have company going to the mall. He would buy Jamari sneakers, too, and Born put him on. He gave Jamari an identity and taught him all the bylaws of the hustler's manual. Soon Jamari had all kinds of cute girls on his arm, and he was beginning to forge an identity of his own in the streets. Through Born, Jamari gained access to all the components necessary for success in the game: the drugs, the guns, the jewelry, the women. Jamari was learning from the best.

Born's mother wasn't happy about the direction her son's life was headed in. She felt helpless and angry that her husband's lifestyle had influenced Born and his career choice. Many times she argued with Leo. She told him that it was his fault that Marquis was hustling, that Leo was to blame for the path her son had taken in life. Some nights Ingrid looked at her husband, and somewhere deep within her, she felt contempt toward him. She was disgusted, because he had influenced her only child to follow the same path as the father he adored.

But there had also been many nights when she'd questioned *herself* for not taking a bigger stand against Marquis selling drugs. She had watched him slowly find his way into the game, and couldn't pretend that she hadn't known from the beginning that Marquis was in the game. Born had always had a unique relationship with his mother. Their lines of communication were wide open. Sure, she had told him not to do it. She reminded him that she was working hard to give him all of the things he had—all of the Bally's footwear, Coogi sweaters, and the goose-down leathers. She even tried harder to give him *everything* he wanted, as a deterrent to the streets. Whatever Marquis asked for, he got. Whatever he wanted, she made sure she found a way to get it for him. But the harder she had to work to provide all of these things for Born, the more determined he became to get so much money that his moms never had to work that hard again.

Born already had twice the amount of nice things his friends had. In fact, Jamari used to wear his coats, his clothes, even his sneakers. And Born didn't worry about the clothes his friend borrowed, since he had plenty more where that had come from. The problem with Born was that he was accustomed to having all the finery that Leo had introduced him to. And now that Leo was unable to provide these things as readily, Born was sick of watching his mother work her fingers to the bone to try and keep it all going. He used to notice that Ingrid fell asleep still wearing her uniform when she got home from work. How she could barely keep her eyes open at the dinner table. On the weekends, Ingrid would be so tired from working all week that she would sleep well into the afternoon. She was exhausting herself in a futile attempt to change the direction in which her son's life was headed. Despite her pleas, he immersed himself deeper in the drug game.

Whenever she canvassed the house in search of dirty clothes to wash, she would find small baggies in Marquis's room. She knew that these baggies were used for packaging drugs. Suddenly there was an awful lot of money in the pockets of his jeans and coats. She saw the signs, knew the truth. Eventually his activities were no longer something he could hide.

She heard all the stories about his fights, his run-ins with rival crews. And in her heart she knew that he was rebelling against the addiction his father was battling. His fury in the streets was synonymous with his fury toward his father. Ingrid felt helpless to stop him, and was terrified that he would wind up dead in the cold-hearted streets where he was holding court. Then, when he was fifteen years old, Born was arrested in the lobby of her building. They caught him with five bags of weed in his pocket. Lucky for him, his cracks were upstairs at the time, so that's all they found. They arrested him for the weed, and they took his jewelry as evidence. When he got out, Born went and bought two more chains to replace the ones they had taken from him. It seemed impossible to stop him, and Ingrid feared she would lose her only child to the streets he couldn't leave alone.

Leo was on a mission half the time, as Born started coming home with larger and larger amounts of money. Born began offering it to his mother to help with the rent, the bills, to buy food. At first Ingrid refused to take it. She didn't want his drug money, because she didn't condone his drug dealing. But it got harder and harder for her to turn the money down. Ingrid honestly needed the help that Born was offering to her. It got to the point where she couldn't turn it down anymore. But she made it clear to him that she wasn't happy about it. She told him that she didn't want him hustling, but she knew that there was nothing she could do to stop him. Instead she told him to be careful. To watch his back, and to stay on point. But now, as Marquis went from the wide-eyed young man she'd had the pleasure of raising to a full-blown hustler determined to pick up where his father had left off, Ingrid wished she had somehow forced him to stop altogether. For the sake of her own conscience.

13

THE BIG PAYBACK

1988

At sixteen years old, Born didn't give a fuck anymore. He and his boys were a team, still hustling crack in Arlington, and also in the Harbor projects, for A.J. and his crew. To Born, the money was good, and the streets were a familiar venue, and he was on the come up. He was seeing less of his father these days. Leo was a shell of the man he once was, and Born was ashamed of what he'd become. Despite his feelings of disappointment in his father, Born never told Leo how he felt. At the end of the day, Born still had some respect for him. He was still his father, regardless of his shortcomings. Born, and his father's other children, had been left to fend for themselves now. All of his older siblings had reached adulthood, and they'd given up their hopes that Leo would get his act together. In fact, some were just as strung out as Leo. They'd accepted that their father was no longer the respected and powerful man he once was. And now Born was beginning to accept it as well. He had dropped out of high school, and was hustling harder than ever.

It was a cold, early Sunday morning in January. Born was once again the only hustler outside, cloaked in layers of clothes to shield him from the freezing temperatures. A pair of long johns, a sweatshirt, and a hoodie were all tucked inside of his Carhart jacket. His hands were snug inside his gloves as he scanned the block for fiends on the prowl. He didn't have to wait long. A scrawny, half-dressed white woman with stringy brown hair made her way up Holland Avenue. Priscilla. He recognized her, and remembered the last time he had seen her—in a crack house with her four-year-old daughter. She had no shame, and Born's heart went out to her child. He felt bad for all the kids of crack addicts, who are forced to watch in silence as their parents commit suicide with every hit of the pipe. Born watched her as she emerged from one of several smoke houses sprinkled throughout the surrounding blocks. She walked swiftly toward Born, and smiled in anticipation as she bought twenty dollars' worth from him. "There's money in there," she said, nodding toward the crack house she'd just left. "You should go up in there and see who wants something." Born had been to the spot on a few occasions, and was familiar with it. He knew that the fiends smoked their shit there, zoned out, and commiserated.

Making his way to the rundown house, Born saw a little boy sitting outside of the house on the steps. The boy looked young—no older than seven—and he shivered in his dirty, cheap jacket as he sat on the steps in the cold morning air. Born noticed the expression on the youngster's face, and he shook his head. The kid looked dirty, his clothes were dingy, and his skin ashy. He looked bored and lost, as he sat there on the steps of the crack house. Probably not his first visit to such an establishment, Born guessed. But he wasn't there to play social worker. He stepped past the youngster and inside the house, where he was greeted by the sight of junkies in various stages of euphoria. A few came right over, recognizing their pusher, and bought from Born.

He didn't notice right away the older man in the back of the room, with a flimsy black wool coat pulled carelessly around his tall, lanky frame. After serving the last of the users who had crowded around him when he entered the spot, Born scanned the room for any other customers before he left. He saw the man standing idly in the back, and gazing apprehensively at Born. It was then that Born realized the crackhead staring back at him was his own father.

A rage burned deep within Born, as he stood looking at his father, the light of the early morning peeking through the house's dingy windows.

Leo turned to walk away before his son could confirm his recognition. But Born called after him, "Don't walk away, Pop." Leo stopped in his tracks. "I got that," Born said. "You can get it from me."

The words cut Leo like a knife, his worst fears realized. His son had seen him at his worst, strung out as he was. It was the lowest point in his life. Born walked toward his father, tromping across the wood floors in his Timberland construction boots, and closing the distance between them easily. Now, face-to-face, the two generations stared back at one another, their unspoken conversation so intense. Leo's eyes held so many apologies, so many things he wished he had the words to explain to his baby boy. Born's eyes held disappointment, the loss of all respect, and the anger of a man-child abandoned too soon by his father. Born extended his right hand to reveal the crack vial in his palm. He watched his father trying not to grab it, fighting the urge to seize the rock in his son's hand. Leo didn't want to buy crack from his son. But damn, he wanted that high!

Born watched his father's inner battle, growing all the more disgusted as the seconds elapsed. Leo couldn't look his son in the eye anymore, and instead stared at the drug in his outstretched hand. "Take it." Born's voice was flat and unfeeling. "Here."

Leo, still hesitant, didn't budge. "What's the problem?" Born's face held a cynical grin; the sad clown, smiling despite the pain he really felt inside. "You're gonna give your money to *somebody* out here. It might as well be me."

Leo felt lower than low. He pulled his last ten dollars from his pocket and handed it to his youngest child. Born took it and placed the crack into his father's old, wrinkled hand, a hand that had once seemed so strong, so powerful, now looked bony and cold. He watched his father struggle, trying to find something to say. And Born let him squirm, let him cringe at the discomfort of the situation. Leo was frustrated, and not knowing what else to say, he asked, "Does your mother know you're out here selling this shit?"

Born laughed. "What, you gonna tell on me, Pop? Go 'head. Tell her. So, I can tell her that you're out here smoking crack. Go 'head!" He laughed once more, right in his father's face. Leo, realizing there was nothing he could say in his own defense, turned and began to walk away. His son's laughter echoed in his ears.

"Just another fiend, man," Born muttered to himself. "That nigga's just another fiend."

Born walked out of the crack house, leaving his father to get high with his fellow addicts. Born shook his head as he made his way back down the steps and past the little boy who still sat out front. This time, the kid looked directly at Born. He could see a vacant expression in the young boy's eyes, and it broke his heart. Born felt like he was looking in the mirror at his own self as a child, wondering why crack had to infiltrate his family. Although Born had never had to sit around crack houses and watch his father's addiction on that level, still he could identify with the child sitting before him. He knew how it felt to feel neglected by a parent who makes you feel like drugs are more important to them than you are. He felt guilty knowing that he was contributing to the habit of whoever this kid's parent was. But Born quickly dismissed the feeling, telling himself that if he didn't supply the fiends with drugs, some other hustler would gladly do it. Still, he felt the pain in the eyes of the little boy as he walked away, making his way up the block.

The look in the kid's eyes haunted him so much that without a second thought Born walked to the bodega on the corner. He ordered a breakfast sandwich—sausage, egg, and cheese on a roll—and got a pint of Tropicana orange juice from the freezer. He looked behind the counter and directed the store owner to fill up a brown paper bag with all the candy kids adore—Jolly Ranchers, Now & Laters, taffy, gum, Skittles, Tootsie Rolls, jellyfish, Blow Pops, the works. Then Born walked back to the house where his father was surely getting high by now. He approached the steps and saw the young boy sitting there still. He walked up on him and asked, "Yo, shorty, what's your name?"

The boy looked at Born suspiciously for a moment. He had been raised in the streets, and knew better than to converse with too many strangers. He looked Born over from head to toe. Then he answered, "Kevin."

Born nodded his head. "Okay, Kevin. Here." He handed him the bag with the breakfast sandwich, and watched as the child hungrily searched through its contents. A smile spread across his face, and he looked up at Born.

"Thanks," he said.

Born smiled at the shorty. "You're welcome." He watched him devour the breakfast sandwich as if it was his first meal in days. It broke Born's heart, and he reached into his jacket pocket and pulled out the brown paper bag filled with candy. The child's eyes lit up at the sight of another bag of goodies, and Born laughed. Despite the little boy's obvious upbringing in the streets, he couldn't conceal his enthusiasm at the sight of all that candy. "Yo," Born said. "Don't eat all this at one time. It's enough in there to last you a little minute." He handed Kevin the bag of candy and watched as a huge smile spread across his face.

Kevin was thrilled. "Thanks, man!"

Born patted the kid on his nappy head, and smiled. He wanted to say something, but had no idea what to say. Finally, he found the words. "You keep your head up, shorty. It'll get better. Trust me." Born winked at little Kevin, whose mouth was filled to capacity with food, and he walked away.

Unbeknownst to Born, Leo had watched the whole thing from inside the crack house. He stared out the window watching his son's exchange with the little boy, and his heart sank. He saw the pity in Born's eyes as he looked down at the child. Born's demeanor toward the child had said, "I understand."

Leo looked at the crack pipe in his hand, and felt like shit. He got choked up for a minute, and then he grabbed the crack in his palm a little tighter. It was time to numb the pain. Time to escape reality for a little while. He got high, thinking the entire time about his son and how he had disappointed him. It was one of the saddest days of his life.

Yet Leo was so far gone that after that first time Born sold crack to his father, Leo came back to Born when the opportunity arose. Born preferred it that way, in all honesty. Crackheads are not well respected in the streets. Born hated to think of anyone talking down to his father, or humiliating him. He was never his father's primary source for the drug. But if Leo was in need and he ran into Born, he got his crack from him. The relationship between father and son had taken a twisted turn. They'd gone from being a larger-than-life father and his adoring son to an addict and his dealer. And Ingrid seemed blind to all of it.

Born and Martin had been hustling for A.J., taking the deal of thirty dollars off of every hundred they made. Together he and Martin held down a drug spot on the first floor in their building. When people saw them coming, they usually had different reactions to the two friends. When folks saw Born, they saw Miss Ingrid's son, the respectful young man who was in the streets, but also was not the type you had to watch your back around out of fear of being stabbed in it. But Martin had a reputation for being a bully. Many people saw him as a loudmouthed menace, when in fact he was just a guy who liked to get drunk and start shit. That was just the way Martin was. But he was Born's man, and they made a lot of money together. The two had been such good friends from the time they'd been small boys that an unspoken trust had developed between them. They were doing their thing, and bringing in lots of money. And they were doing it quietly.

It was no secret that drugs were being sold on the borough's north shore. The police were focused on the projects. The Mariner's Harbor projects were within walking distance from where Born and his crew lived. Arlington Terrace wasn't the projects. It was a nice, working-class community. The grounds consisted of a cluster of several buildings and a small park, with five-bedroom town houses sprinkled around the perimeter. Hardly the place you'd expect to find a drug empire being run on such a grand scale. Born and his boys flew under the radar virtually undetected, and slept on by their counterparts in the Harbor projects. The money piled up, and things were looking up. But they began to want more money, more of a cut from what they were selling.

A.J., however, wouldn't budge. He figured these youngsters should be glad that somebody was giving them a shot at all, and he let them know their percentage wasn't negotiable.

"Y'all niggas are asking for too much," A.J. said. Born and his crew had asked for a sixty-forty split. "I wish I could work witchu, you know what I'm saying? But, y'all lil niggas set the bar too high. Y'all want to get a promotion before you even had a chance to really prove yourselves."

"How you figure we haven't proved ourselves?" Born asked, his face twisted in a grimace. "We been bringing you more money as a crew than all your other workers combined. We might be young, but we ain't stupid. We can do the math, A.J. The proof is in the numbers."

A.J. shook his head. "The numbers are good, but that's only because my product pretty much sells itself. I got y'all out here slanging top-of-the-line cocaine. The money is coming because the shit sells itself. You lil muthafuckas should be glad that I'm giving you a chance to see some real paper out here. You already got a good deal. Don't get greedy." A.J. waved his hand as if the meeting was concluded.

This didn't sit well with the young men, who were hungry for a bigger piece of the pie. They didn't bring up the subject with A.J. again, since he had made his position perfectly clear. But they didn't go away quietly either. When they were together, they often griped about A.J. Martin became the most vocal about his displeasure with the cut they were getting, and it wasn't long before Born agreed. They had had enough. If A.J. wasn't willing to give them what they wanted, they were going to take it. Fuck it.

Born and Martin went to A.J. one day and told him they had been robbed. Their story was bullshit. And in reality they had just kept the drugs and sold them on their own, using the money they made to put themselves on. They got themselves established without A.J., and then they put their whole crew on. Born, Martin, Jamari, Chance, and Smitty were a team. They chartered their own territory, and did their own thing. They were notorious for doing whatever it took to get money. Right before everyone's eyes, the crew from 55 Holland were the niggas running things in Arlington. They did whatever it took to get money, from shootings to robberies, from burglaries to crack sales. Martin emerged as the enforcer of the crew, having the heart to lay a nigga out without hesitation. Martin's reputation preceded him, and he was a legend in his own time.

At sixteen years old, Born had gotten himself an apartment of his own, separate from his mother. The apartment was downstairs on the second floor of the same building he'd grown up in. Ingrid didn't complain, since her son was living right downstairs. It made her feel better knowing that he was so close by. And he no longer kept his guns, his drugs, or any other incriminating evidence at his mother's place. He had his spot for that. The rent on the subleased apartment was cheap, especially with all the money he was bringing in. Born and the rest of the crew had stepped up their game. Now they no longer had to do many hand-to-hand sales. They employed workers for that, young dudes from around the way who were happy with the money they made from the block.

Things were going well. But Born could see the worry in his mother's eyes. Ingrid looked at her son with a gaze full of wistfulness. She saw what could have been. Her son, who in school had been so good at math, and such an intelligent student, was now just a drug dealer, albeit a successful one. To her he was so much more than that. But the intelligent, witty, and lovable young man she saw when she looked at Marquis was very different from the hardened young criminal folks saw in Born. Her coworkers would ask her about it. "Was that your son that got arrested last night?" or "Did Marquis know the guy that got arrested for killing that boy last week?"

Ingrid sat and conveyed her embarrassment to her sister, Betty, on the phone one night. Betty had moved down south in order to get away from her own wayward children and all of their problems. Ingrid envied her sometimes, wishing that she had the courage to walk away as easily as Betty had. As Ingrid shared her dismay with her sister, she had no idea that Born had overheard.

"I'm going to work, and my coworkers are questioning me about my son. They got the nerve to ask me, 'Was that Marquis that got arrested for that shooting? You know the one where the girl got wounded by that stray bullet? I read in the paper that they arrested four or five boys. And when I read that they arrested Marquis Graham, I said, "Ain't that Ingrid's son?" ' Then they wanna act surprised when I tell them that it was Marquis. I wanted to cuss all them muthafuckas out! But I didn't. The last thing I need to do is to give them a reason to fire me."

Betty sucked her teeth. "So, what did you tell them?" she asked.

Ingrid lit a cigarette, and exhaled the smoke. "I answered their questions calmly, even though I wanted to put them nosy bitches in their places. I said that he was young and unruly, and very hardheaded. But I know he ain't shoot that girl. I left it at that. Nobody questioned me any further. And I went on about my day as if everything was gonna be fine." Ingrid took another drag. "But I ain't gonna lie to you, Betty. I'm scared."

"Scared about what?" Betty asked. "They ain't gon' fire you."

"I'm not worried about them firing me. I don't *want* to get fired, but that ain't what I'm worried about. I've always worked, always had a good reputation. But now Marquis is getting in more trouble, and Leo is . . ." Ingrid couldn't find the right word to use to describe her husband's current state. "I'm scared that I'm about to lose one of them."

Betty understood what her sister was feeling. "Ingrid, you need a break. That's what I think. You got too much going on right now. Marquis is giving you hell, and so is Leo. And still you run around working and letting everybody pile their problems on your shoulders."

"Ain't nobody piling their problems on my shoulders, Betty."

"*Everybody* is piling their problems on your shoulders, Ingrid. You've always been that type of person. Quick to help out a friend in need. You watch people's kids, and drive people to doctor appointments. Everybody loves you. And sometimes they take you for granted. You need to come and move to Virginia with me. Don't nobody ask me for shit, 'cuz they know they ain't getting shit." Betty wasn't lying. She was the type to put a person in their place, like it or not. Betty had no problem saying "no," and meaning it.

"I can't leave New York now," Ingrid said, with a sigh. She would have loved to get away, and move to where life was simpler, with Betty. But she would have felt like she was giving up on her husband, and giving up on her son. "I need to be here right now. But I need these two to stop shining a spotlight on our family. I think I deserve to be able to walk out of here every day with my head held high."

Born had listened to his mother's conversation, feeling guilty for all the embarrassment he had caused her. He made a decision to try to avoid bringing trouble to his mother's doorstep. It was important to Born, now that he was older, that no criminal activity be traced to him at his mother's house. He never wanted to cast her in an unfavorable light or put her in any kind of jeopardy for the choices he'd made.

But that didn't stop Ingrid from worrying about him. Born was out there one night in 1991, getting his hustle on. He had been outside all that evening with his boys, getting money and supervising their workers, handling business, with their drugs and guns stashed in nearby garbage cans and mailboxes. Things had changed drastically. On this night his mother was sitting in her darkened bedroom looking out her window. Leo was asleep beside her, and she was watching for signs of her son. She worried more and more about Marquis, because she knew that he was living dangerously.

14

POWER MOVES

Born decided to go upstairs to see his mother at around one o'clock in the morning. He knew she would be up, because he knew his mother was a night owl, and it was a Saturday night. As he approached his building, he saw movement out of the corner of his eye. Ingrid saw it all unfold as she watched in horror in the dark from her bedroom window.

A.J. hopped out of his Explorer with his gun drawn. Born turned, and he saw A.J. and heard the shots ring out in the night at the same time. A.J. stood with bullets flying from his .45, and the handful of people nearby ran for cover. Born pulled his nine, and shot back, the two guns sounding like a twisted symphony in the cold winter air. Born ran into the building, hearing his mother's cries echoing in his ears. He wouldn't run to her apartment for fear of bringing a gun battle to his mother's doorstep. He ran for the staircase and heard tires screeching outside. Not knowing if anyone was pursuing him inside the building, he ran up the stairs two and three at a time, his heart beating a mile a minute. He was sweating and panting, pushing himself up the flight of stairs. By the time he made it, breathlessly, to his drug spot on the second floor, Martin was already there with the door flung open. Born grabbed his .380. Martin was already strapped, and they ran back downstairs without any conversation between them. When they got to the lobby, the whole crew was there: Smitty, Chance, and several other young soldiers from the hood came downstairs, everyone strapped with artillery. The building emptied out, everyone pouring into the night, prepared for war.

Ingrid called out from her bedroom window. *"Marquis!"* Her voice was that of a mother pleading for the life of her son. The desperation could be heard as she screamed her son's name into the stillness that lingered after the gunfire. Born looked up into his mother's eyes, and his look spoke volumes. His expression told her that he was a man on a mission, that he would not stop until he had A.J.'s head. Ingrid cried out again. "Marquis, please!" But her son didn't listen. Instead, he kept pressing forward into the darkness with his crew behind him. Ingrid sat in the window, frozen, with tears falling from her eyes. She didn't bother to turn to see if Leo was awake. Her husband had to have heard her voice as it pierced the silence in the apartment. But Leo said nothing, and Ingrid never turned to look at him. It didn't matter. She knew that he lived with the guilt of knowing that he was to blame for Born being the hellraiser that he was. With her heart in her throat, Ingrid stared out the window, praying repeatedly for her son.

The 55 Holland crew piled into vehicles. Born jumped into the passenger seat of Martin's hooptie. Smitty and Chance jumped in the back. The car behind them contained even more firepower. Born was enraged about the close call he'd just survived. "I'ma kill that muthafucka!" He kept seeing A.J.'s face as his gun sparked in Born's direction. "That's my word."

Martin was eerily silent. His brow was firmly set, and he looked like he was just as thirsty for A.J.'s blood as his friend was. They drove around frantically, in search of A.J. They were determined to lay the nigga down that night, and be done with the beef between them. They circled every hood in Staten Island in search of A.J.'s truck, or for any sign of the coward.

"Don't worry," Chance said from the backseat. "We're gonna get that nigga. He gotta come out sometime."

Finally, they returned to Arlington, and that's when Martin spotted A.J.'s truck parked near one of the town houses. He parked his car, and turned off the engine and headlights so as not to be detected. They were a considerable distance away from where A.J.'s truck was parked, and they figured A.J. was already inside one of the town houses.

"That nigga gotta be in one of them. We could split up and see which one it is, and bring his ass out in the open." Chance looked at the row of town houses, figuring it shouldn't take them long to find him. But as they approached, Martin could see that A.J. was in the Explorer with two other men. "Born!" he whispered anxiously. "That nigga's still in the truck!"

Born looked at Martin, and then at the truck to see for himself. But without any warning, Martin set it off all by himself. He ran toward the truck, guns blazing.

A.J. stepped out of the car, as did two other men in black, and the bullets flew back and forth for several minutes. A town house began to empty out, with more of A.J.'s crew spilling outside with guns drawn. Chance, Smitty, and the rest of their boys all ran for cover, still firing. With only a few trees and parked cars between them, A.J.'s crew and Born's crew shot it out.

The hood grows eerily silent whenever shots are fired. Suddenly, all sound seems to cease besides the sound of the shots echoing in the night. Born heard each and every bullet that was fired. Some came closer than others. Still, he fired back, anxious to kill the man who had shot at him. "Come on out, A.J.!" he yelled, as he fired a barrage of bullets and then stopped to reload. The whole time, Born thought about his mother. He heard her pleading voice in his head calling out to him, begging him not to go out there. He knew she was probably upstairs hearing the gunfire, and praying that it wasn't her son who would be lying in a body bag by the end of the night. Born continued shooting at A.J. and his crew, and dodging the bullets that were flying in his direction. He was determined that his mother would not be bent over his casket, heartbroken. Not this time. On this night it would have to be someone else's mother playing that role.

Born stepped out from behind the car he had positioned himself behind. He took clear aim at A.J. and let off a hail of bullets before ducking back into his fortress, and then emerging again with more gunshots. Finally, one of Born's shots hit its mark, and A.J. was caught in the chest. This was the moment in time when Born's legacy was cemented. He was the man that had finally brought A.J. to his knees. As A.J. fell to the ground, he was hit twice more in the shoulder and leg, both by Martin's bullets. Quickly Born retreated with his cronies in tow, as sirens could at last be heard in the distance. Born and his boys got out of there, and as they ran it appeared that all of them were accounted for. For a minute it seemed that none of them were harmed in the melee.

Born ran backward, still firing at the few members of A.J.'s crew who had not yet retreated. He could see that A.J. wasn't moving, and he caught sight of Martin making his escape. Born took flight as well; he headed for the safety of his mother's apartment.

When Born got to his mother's apartment, Ingrid was standing in her open doorway, waiting for him. He came up the stairs and saw her familiar brown face looking so relieved, so very grateful to see her only child still standing. She ran to him and hugged him so tightly. "Thank God!" she said, over and over. "Thank God, Marquis!"

She ushered him inside, and then she clung to him, hugging her son as if she never wanted to let him go. "I'm alright!" Born reassured her. "I'm okay, Ma." Ingrid cried, and was only comforted by the fact that it had not been her child—not this time. It was not her child sprawled outside, his hot blood spilling on the cold concrete. Born would never forget the feeling he had on that February evening. The life he lived made him feel cold inside. Another emotional wall was erected within him. He'd felt hopeless, and he was never really the same after that night. He truly didn't expect to survive to see his seventeenth birthday. And he didn't even give a fuck.

But when the shooting had stopped, and everyone had scattered, screams had come from the front of the bar on the corner. Bobby, a young cat who always hung around Born and his crew, was shaking on the sidewalk with three holes in his chest. His was a death that was so undeserving. Bobby had been what was known in the streets as a "sometime hustler." He didn't do it all the time, wasn't in it for the long haul.

But he would hustle for Born and them if he wanted some money to take a chick out, or if he was going somewhere and needed to buy something. He wasn't a bully, nor was he a typical hoodlum. He was a guy who was well liked by everyone. This was the last young man anybody wanted to see go down.

In Born's opinion, Bobby was a decent guy whose hand didn't call for what he got. If such a horrible death could befall Bobby, Born could only imagine what life had in store for him. Born stopped being scared of death after that. He started feeling like it was inevitable, that it was a part of life. It's not that he wanted to die. But he wasn't afraid to put his life on the line to get ahead. He made bigger moves, without always worrying about the consequences. He really didn't care anymore. He started stepping on other people's toes. He was stealing customers and making sales on other people's turf. Born didn't give a fuck, and he dared niggas to say something to him. A.J. didn't die from his wounds. But he didn't cooperate with the police investigation, and his boys held him down while he recuperated. Born and his crew robbed A.J.'s drug spots as often as they could after that. They had no fear, no reservations about going after a hustler who was older than them. A.J. was older, but they were more ruthless. Plus, his crew was weak, and there were too many loose links in his chain. He had made too many enemies, and there were too many people for him to watch all at once. Born was mad that he hadn't killed him. He sure had tried. He wanted A.J. dead, and he wouldn't be satisfied until he was.

A.J. remained hidden for a long while after he was released from the hospital. He was embarrassed more than anything. He had allowed a crew of youngsters who *he* had brought into the game knock him off his own throne. Born and his crew were well respected after they put A.J. on temporary life support. A.J., on the other hand, had lost his swagger. It wasn't until the weather got warm and spring came into bloom that A.J. showed his face in the hood once again. And it wasn't long after that that A.J. was killed. A lone shooter gunned him down outside of a club called the Island Room, and the case went unsolved. There weren't many people who didn't suspect that the 55 Holland niggas had had something to do with it. But no one was ever charged. Their reign at the top had officially begun.

15

BOYS TO MEN

As the boys became men, things started to change. Born began to realize that he was pulling most of the weight in their operation. It was he who got out there early and stayed late. He was the one making contact with the gunrunners and the loan sharks, forming connections to those that sold weight. Like a singing group that comes into the music industry on some all for one and one for all shit. Once the lead singer realizes *his* name is the one that everyone remembers, it becomes obvious that the rest of the group is obsolete. The same was true of Born and the 55 Holland crew. Eventually, as the young men grew older and their egos clashed, the crew was starting to dismantle amid angry words and intense confrontations.

Born was ready to branch out on his own, and to stop dealing with the deadweight of his cronies. The last straw came when he found himself sitting alone on the block one winter night, wondering why the rest of his boys weren't out there with him. The workers had gone home for the night, but Born knew that the fiends never sleep. There was so much money to be had. Crackheads galore came to him to cop that night, and Born couldn't help wondering how much money they were missing out on simply because he was the only one smart enough to hustle even when Jack Frost was out. That's when it dawned on him that he was dealing with guys who didn't want to put in the work necessary to achieve the type of success he wanted. He was dealing with dudes who were too lazy to ball till they fall.

Born told his crew that he was ready to branch off on his own. "I'm done with this crew shit," he said. "I love y'all niggas, but business ain't right between us. I'm the one out here taking chances, stepping on toes, and putting my freedom at risk with the moves I'm making. We gon' always be boys, you know what I'm saying? But I gotta get on my own and do me from now on."

Martin wasn't happy about it at all. His facial expression turned sinister as he listened to his lifelong friend defecting from his camp. "Fuck kinda bullshit is you talking?" Martin growled. "Ain't nobody doing they own thing. This is a fuckin' team, you hear what I'm saying? Ain't no 'I' in team, nigga. We came in this shit together. That's how it's gonna stay."

Smitty also had his reservations about just letting him walk away without question. "How you gonna leave us behind, Born? So you made some connections, and now you wanna use that shit for your own personal gain, and fuck us? That's how it is?"

Born shook his head. "I ain't leaving nobody behind. All I'm saying is that I got a plan. Y'all don't seem like you wanna listen to my plan or come along with me. I'm out here day and night, hustling my ass off. Y'all muthafuckas is sitting up in the house getting high and fucking mad bitches. That's all good. But there's a time for that. We supposed to get money first and celebrate later. I'm tired of trying to convince y'all niggas that there's too much dough out there for us to get lazy now."

"So now we're lazy!" Smitty said, frowning.

Born laughed. "I expected you to side with your brother—"

"This ain't got nothing to do with me agreeing with my brother. This shit is about keeping the crew together. We're supposed to be a team," he reminded Born.

Chance chimed in. "You're being selfish, Born."

"How am I being selfish?" Born couldn't believe they were acting like a bunch of fucking kids.

"You know that we depend on you for certain shit," Chance explained. "Martin is the muscle. Me and Smitty, we do a lot of the fieldwork. We got our own positions to play. But you're the brains behind a lot of what we do. So if you leave, you're taking away a vital part of our success by leaving."

Born respected Chance's honesty. Martin wasn't as diplomatic.

"You *can't* leave," he said, emphatically. "Period. I'm not gonna stand for that shit. I will rob you *every single day* if you leave the crew, nigga. I mean that shit. Every time I see you, I'ma take what you got, and that's my word." Martin glared at Born, daring him to challenge him.

Born stood there with a grin on his face, listening to his childhood friend tell him that he was gonna rob him every day rather than watch him get money by himself. Martin's words infuriated Born, because he felt that not only was he being challenged in front of their whole crew, but Martin was ignoring the fact that no one else was pulling their weight the way that Born was. "I'm not worried about that," Born said. He wasn't intimidated by Martin's role as the "muscle" of the crew. Born had plenty of muscle of his own. Besides his broad chest and muscular build, Born had two guns in his waistband as Martin made his threat. It was winter time at one o'clock in the morning. No one was around but the four of them. If he wanted to, Born could have made Martin a memory for threatening him in that way. But knowing that his friend was emotional at the moment, Born kept his cool. "I want to be fair to everybody," he said. "I'm willing to leave with nothing. Absolutely nothing: no drugs, no money. I just want *out*."

Chance understood where Born was coming from, although Smitty and Martin didn't understand at all. "It sounds like you got your mind made up. I mean, we can't make you stay with the crew. I think that would be the honorable decision for you to make. We all came from the grain together. This ain't how it's supposed to be. But I can understand where you're coming from. I'm not gonna beg you to stay."

Born's mind was made up anyway. He nodded, and stood waiting for the reactions of his other two friends. Martin felt betrayed, as did Smitty. But there was really nothing they could do to stop him.

Martin looked at Born disapprovingly. "Aiight," he said. "You wanna get money by yourself? Then fuck you, nigga!" Martin slinked off, with Smitty following close behind him. Chance gave Born a pound and left also. And that's how it ended. Born left them with all the drugs, all the cash. He started over with only three guns, some money in the stash, and good connections in his favor.

Born somehow managed to remain on speaking terms with his crew. But things were never quite the same, particularly between him and Martin. It wasn't easy for Born to be at odds with his boys. It wasn't an easy transition. And he found that it was much different being out there all on his own. The success or failure of his next moves would be entirely up to him. Born utilized the connections he had made during his years on the grind, and a very valuable connection he had made years earlier while he had been living in a group home in the Bronx.

Zion Williams was one of the few group home residents that Born had socialized with. In fact, he had become friends with Zion completely by accident. Zion's mother had died when he was a very small child, and he had kept certain mementos that reminded him of her. He kept these things underneath his mattress—a hairpin, a Bible, and a gold necklace with a cross on it that she had worn everyday when she was alive. One day, Zion had taken out the gold necklace and stared at it for what seemed like hours. It was his mother's birthday, and that was always a sad day for the young man, who still missed her tremendously. During the course of this day, Zion kept his mother's necklace in his pocket, and somewhere along the line it fell out. He was distraught, and searched the whole facility for his keepsake. But he couldn't find it, and Zion was furious. He wondered if someone had stolen it, and if that was the case he would surely never see it again. But it was Born who had found it stuck up under the seat cushion on the couch in the lounge. He thought about keeping it, selling it, or whatever. But Born was making so much money that the 14-karat gold trinket wouldn't have made a dent in his pockets. He knew that the sentimental value it possessed for Zion was priceless.

Born found Zion moping in the library. "Zion, I heard you was looking for this," he said. "I found it in the lounge." He held up the necklace, and Zion's face lit up.

"Yo!" he said, excited. "Thanks." Zion was grateful beyond words. He knew that if any of the other guys had found it, it would have been a

memory. This act of honesty endeared Born to Zion, and the two became friends. It would prove to be a priceless connection for Born, as he
maneuvered his way up the ladder in the game.

Word on the street was that Zion was knee-deep in the crack game.
When Born got in touch with Zion to let him know that he was working
solo now and needed to get on, Zion put Born in touch with a guy
named Dorian from Brooklyn. Dorian was the nigga to see, since his
prices were unbeatable. He was selling cook-up for a mere seventeen
grand a brick. Born got his money together and started doing business
with Dorian. Within three weeks of his departure from his childhood
crew, Born had gone from hustling hand-to-hand to selling weight all by
himself.

The highlight came for Born on the day he walked into his mom's
apartment and handed her a big Hefty bag. His father was fucked up for
real by then. He was in and out of the hospital, and constantly ill. And
when he was home, he was in a wheelchair, and Ingrid had to do damn
near everything for him. Born knew that it was hard on his mother, seeing her husband turn into a shell of the man he once was. And Born
wanted to do whatever he could to see her smile again.

Born went by to see his mother one Sunday morning. He walked in,
and she was in the kitchen washing the breakfast dishes. Born sat down
with the big garbage bag on the floor in front of him, and talked to her
while she washed the dishes. "What's up, Ma?" Born asked her, smiling.

Ingrid loved seeing Marquis smile. His dimples were a rare sight, since
her son seldom smiled. And when she did get to see them it made him
look like her little boy all over again. Not the grown-ass man he had become. "Nothing much," she answered. "I'm not looking forward to work
tomorrow. The weekends always go by so fast, and before you know it,
it's Monday all over again, and I gotta go right back to work. I can't wait
to retire."

Born smiled at this, and nodded his understanding. "How's Pop?"

Leo was asleep in the bedroom, and judging from the way Ingrid
rolled her eyes at the mention of his name, he was still up to no good.
"He'd be alright if he left that shit alone," Ingrid said. She couldn't be-

lieve that her once strong and respected husband had been reduced to an ailing drug addict. "But he's okay, I guess."

Born shook his head, and changed the subject. "So what you making for dinner tonight?"

Ingrid smiled. No matter how bad things seemed, Marquis never lost his appetite. "Fried chicken and macaroni and cheese," she said. Born rubbed his hands together in anticipation. They discussed Ingrid's desire to retire. She had been working ever since she came to New York at the age of seventeen. Ingrid was tired, and eager to be able to sit back without having to report for her shift at the home. She wanted to enjoy what was left of her life.

When she was done with the dishes, Born rose to leave. Ingrid frowned. "I thought you were staying for dinner," she protested.

Born shook his head. "Put a plate up for me. I'll come and get it later. I got some running around to do." He gave her the bag. "This is for you," he said. "Wait until I'm gone before you open it."

Ingrid looked at him suspiciously. "What's in this bag, Marquis? You know I don't want you leaving no bullshit over here—"

"Ma, it ain't nothing like that. Just wait till I leave." Born kissed his mother, and gave her a big bear hug, and he left.

Ingrid waited until Born left her house. She dragged the Hefty bag into her living room, and sat down to open it. The bag was doubled and knotted at the top, so it took her a little while. When she did, Ingrid covered her mouth and gasped. She was shocked! She could never have guessed that when she opened that bag she would find thirty thousand dollars in small bills. Ingrid had not seen that much cash at once since Leo had fallen out of hustling. She picked up a handful of twenties and shook back the tears that formed in her eyes. Her son had saved the day once again.

Ingrid called her son. She didn't ask where he'd gotten all that money. She obviously knew. "Marquis, I don't know what to say. How did you know how bad I needed this money?" Ingrid had long been over-whelmed with bills and debt and just trying to maintain, while Leo was destroying himself. Ingrid was never one to wear her problems on her sleeve, preferring to suffer in silence and pray about it. But, Born knew she needed money.

"Ma, just 'cuz you never complain don't mean I'm blind to what's going on. I know that all the bills are backed up. I see them laying on your dresser whenever I come over there. Your car is always breaking down. I know you can use that dough. Use whatever you need, but try and save some of it for a rainy day."

Ingrid gripped the phone tightly, feeling gratitude beyond measure wash over her. "Thank you, Marquis," she said. "So much." Ingrid hung up the phone after speaking to her son, and she never breathed a word to Leo about that dough. That became another one of her and Born's little secrets. That day had been one of the proudest moments in Born's life. The money wasn't enough to retire on. But Born figured that money would allow Ingrid to do something nice for herself for a change. She was the type to always look out for other people, never giving the same attention to her own wants and needs. Born was on the come up. Giving his mother that money had symbolized his rise to power, and signaled that she could depend on her son and no longer have to work like a slave. He felt like a man. More of a man than his own father.

Born began to see how far he'd come from being a shorty in the game to a grown man doing big business on a very grand scale. Born was selling weight. He was on top of the world, and still climbing.

There was some animosity between Born and Martin at the beginning of his departure. Smitty and Chance continued talking to Born, although their conversations were a lot more strained. Jamari was still cool, because it had been Born who invited him into their crew in the first place. It seemed that a line had been drawn in the sand, and Born was curious to see who would stand on his side when all was said and done. But it would be the death of his father that brought it all full circle.

Leo's health was going further and further downhill. He was legally blind, and one of his legs was amputated as a result of untreated diabetes. Day after day Born went back to his childhood home, and he watched his father die. Leo's last few conversations with his son were lighthearted reflections on how fun-loving and carefree Born had been as a child, compared to the ferociously determined man that stood today. Leo admired his son and the man he had become, and in his own way he told this to Born. Yet by the time he drew his last breath in the fall of 1992, there was still so much that Leo had never said to his son. He had never said that he was sorry for his failure as a father, never said that he wished he could have been stronger. Born was left with a hole in his heart and no way to fill it.

Before he died, Leo had lain in an induced coma after his body was ravaged by a massive heart attack. All the years of drug use had physically consumed him. All the years of neglecting his health and never visiting a doctor had caught up with him. With the respirator connected to his mouth, and his eyes closed, Leo looked like a man at death's door. But still he was holding on. On that day, though, his vital signs had been unstable. The doctors didn't sound optimistic, and Ingrid had warned Born that he should make peace with his father. She seemed to sense that the end was near for her husband. Born refused to think like that, though. He refused to believe that his father would die on him. He walked close to his father's bedside, and leaned in close to his father's ear.

"Yo." Born had felt awkward talking to his father while he was still unresponsive. He wondered if Leo could even hear him. But he said what he had come to say. "Yo. You better not give up. I hope you can hear me." Born looked down at his father's face. He saw all the years of fast living and wild ways all over his face. He remembered the way he used to look before his downfall. He saw the scars on his father's face from all of his notorious brawls. The way his mouth hung open, obstructed by tubes, reminded Born of seeing his father after he'd gone on a cocaine binge, sleeping for days with his mouth hanging open just this way. He missed him already.

"Don't give up, Pop." Ignoring the urge to cry, he turned and walked away. Born went home, went back to his block. He went about his routine, still checking in with his mother regarding his father's condition. But two days after his visit, Born's father died.

16

THE END OF AN ERA

Born was strong for his mother, knowing that she had lost more than just her husband. Ingrid Graham had lost her mentor, her friend, and her first love. It was such a sad sight to see her walking through life with no Leo to care for. There would be no light in her eyes for a long, long time. During this grieving process, Born wanted to be a rock for his moms to lean on, and yet his own pain was so raw. She made the funeral arrangements, and he helped her out with whatever money she needed. He thought he had summoned up the strength to attend the funeral, and he prepared himself for it as best he could. But when the day arrived, he found himself sitting in the church beside his mother, unable to look at his father's body lying prone in the coffin.

The church was packed to capacity, with all of Staten Island seeming to fill the sanctuary. Everybody knew Leo, yet many of them were meeting Ingrid for the first time. Nobody really knew her, despite the fact that the whole world knew Leo Graham. Ingrid had always been a private woman, an exact opposite of the man she loved so dearly. She had lived her life outside of the spotlight, content with Leo being the center of attention. Leo had loved to live his life that way—with all eyes on him. But Ingrid was cut from a different cloth. She preferred to be demure, and stand in the shadows. It was one of the reasons Leo loved her as he'd never loved another woman.

Born listened as the preacher spoke, and had to laugh to himself at the irony. Leo had lived his life with his middle finger in the air. He didn't give a damn about law, religion, or any type of protocol. The man had as many enemies as he had friends, and Born sat there smiling as he thought of all the times his father had been shot at, stabbed, and cussed out. All the drama of living his life in the fast lane. Leonard Graham had lived his life according to his own whims and by his own standards. But in this, his last appearance before all mankind, Leonard was being eulogized by a man of God, a preacher who denounced the very things his father stood for. Born grinned, knowing that his father was truly one of a kind. He would miss the smooth old man, even with all his faults.

Born looked around the church, and was caught off guard when he saw his boys sprinkled throughout the congregation. First he spotted Chance sitting in the third row. Then he saw Smitty and Jamari sitting two rows from the back. He listened as the preacher asked if anyone cared to share any remarks about the deceased. He sat there as several of his half siblings and his father's friends stood up and talked about Leo. Born held his mother's hand while he listened to story after story about the life and times of Leo Graham. Some moments were lighthearted, and the crowd would laugh as they reminisced over his father. Finally, he saw Martin make his way up to the microphone. The two of them still hadn't fully made amends after Born's departure from the crew. Born was still hurt that Martin had threatened to rob him every day, and he was surprised to see him there. He watched in stunned silence as his childhood friend cleared his throat, and glanced over at Born. Then Martin turned to Leo's body lying still and at peace, and he smiled.

Martin looked at the crowd. "I sat here, and I listened to all of y'all talking about Leo Graham and all his funny stories. I grew up with his son Born, and I know Leo could be funny sometimes, because he sure made me laugh over the years. But I wanted to say something kinda serious about the dude." Unaccustomed to speaking in public, Martin folded the funeral program in his hand and toyed with it awkwardly. "He had his struggles, you know what I'm saying? He wasn't perfect. But he was a good man. He made a good impression on a lot of people, even with his problems. I always hung out at my man Born's crib when we were kids. His house was the best place to go after school. He had all the video games, he was the first one in our building with a VCR, and his moms used to let us play our music real loud."

Everybody laughed at his honesty. "But to me, the best part of going to Born's crib was getting to see Leo up close and personal. When we were kids, Leo was like a superhero to us. Kinda like Superman or the Incredible Hulk. I ain't have no dad at my house, and neither did most of us. So when we saw Leo come through the hood, it was like all of us got excited. This was all of our dads. He had . . . like . . . a way about him that only old gangstas have." Martin was grinning as if he could still see Leo gliding down the block with his old-school bop. "Leo used to always come around and talk to Born. He would tell him how to be successful in life and what to do, what not to do. But since I was always on the scene, Leo used to tell me a lot, too. He taught me some real lessons when I was a shorty, at a time when there wasn't nobody else really trying to teach me nothing. I was always hardheaded. I used to give my moms a hard time and try to be the man all the time. But whenever I saw Leo, he would pull my coat and tell me to get my act together. I used to really admire the guy, so I took what he said to heart, and I respected him. But then, he got sick." Martin looked over at Ingrid and Born sitting hand-in-hand in the front row, and he knew that they understood exactly what he meant. "And you could say what you want about the dude, but he was still the same Leo to me. He never lost his swagger. And I never stopped looking at him as a hero, neither. I guess sometimes heroes just don't live forever. And sometimes they make mistakes in life, just like the rest of us. I know that he was a father figure to a lot of us kids growing up. And I'm gonna miss him a whole lot." Martin dabbed at his eyes, with the back of his tightly balled fist, and then he cleared his throat. He looked at Born and his mother once more. "You can call me if you need anything at all, and I got y'all." And just like that, Martin took his seat in the congregation, and reclaimed his spot in Born's heart. It almost moved him to tears. From that day forward, in business Born was still on his own. But despite the fact that they made money separately, they all looked out for one another the same as they always had. And Born knew that his friends were true. Especially Martin.

The funeral commenced, and when he finally stood at his father's side and looked down at his cold body, lying stiff in his casket, Born felt lost. He shook his head, feeling his father had died too young, certainly too soon. "You gave up." Born said it, hoping that somehow his father could hear him now. "You quit on me."

He turned and took his mother by the hand, and only inwardly did he mourn the loss of his hero. At the funeral Born wouldn't allow himself the satisfaction of crying. He was strong for his mother, and the sad little boy inside of him went uncomforted once more.

17

EXCUSE ME, MISS

The streets never sleep, and so Born was back on the block within days of burying his father. It was his way of doing what he had set out to do. He wanted to pick up the torch that Leo had dropped, and Born was determined to win. He wanted to do it for his father, and he hoped to be the man that his father had been unable to be. But he hit a speed bump along the way.

Born was arrested for possession of a controlled substance two months after his father's death. He had been caught with about an ounce of weed, and he was eager to get out of jail on bail before his mother found out that he'd been arrested. Born didn't want to further complicate things, and stress her out more than she already was, so Born called Jamari to get the five thousand dollars that he needed to get out.

Jamari was the only one from his childhood crew that Born still did business with. Martin, Chance, and Smitty were still doing their thing separately. Jamari was the only one still working with him, because Born had taken him under his wing from the start. Everything Jamari learned about the hood he learned from Born. The first time he held the cold steel of a biscuit, Born had placed it in his hands. Jamari had risen in the game, and ultimately gained respect in the hood because of the circles Born had opened up to him.

Just days before his arrest, Born had given Jamari more work to sell, and Born knew that Jamari had the money. Their cash flowed steadily, and Born kept on top of it all. So when Born called for bail money, Jamari told him that he would be there that day to get him out. "Don't worry about nothing, Born. I got you."

Born waited all day for Jamari to come and bail him out. As the hours passed, Born became more and more furious. When the guards loaded him on the prison bus for his trip to Rikers Island, after no one had shown up in court to bail him out, Born was livid. He called Jamari as soon as he got to Rikers, and Jamari didn't answer the phone. Finally, Born was forced to call his mother.

"Ma," Born said, feeling like a complete loser for having to burden his mother with this shit now. "I got locked up, and I need bail. Can you come and get me?"

Ingrid sighed. She wanted nothing more than for Marquis to get out of the game altogether, and to stay out of it. "Yeah," she said. "I'll be there to get you."

Ingrid came down and bailed her son out the next day, and he hated that she had more to worry about now. He went looking for Jamari as soon as she got him out.

When he found his friend, Born was irate. He confronted Jamari on the block in the Harbor projects, and was tempted to kill him on the spot. Born charged across the courtyard headed in Jamari's direction. Jamari spotted Born, and he was visibly nervous. On the inside, Jamari was telling himself that Born was just a man. He told himself that he had nothing to fear. But outwardly, it was obvious to Born that Jamari was scared to death. He shifted his weight uneasily from one foot to the other. And when Born finally stood in front of him, Jamari couldn't seem to stand still.

"Where's my money at, nigga?" Born cut right to the chase. He stood tall, and his commanding presence clearly intimidated Jamari.

Jamari's voice faltered. "Born, let me tell you what happened," he began. "I was on my way to bail you out. I was driving down the block in New Brighton."

"What block?" Born barked.

"Jersey Street, right there in front of the projects," Jamari clarified. "I got pulled over by the police. I didn't even do nothing wrong, but they snatched me out of the car and searched me. While they had me up against the gate, searching me, they searched the car, too. But they didn't find shit. I wasn't dirty that day, so they had no reason to pull me over in the first place. After they finished fucking with me, they let me get back inside my car. So I waited till the cops pulled off, and I went on my way. But when I got to the court, the bail money that I had stashed in the glove compartment was missing. The cops must have stole the money, Born, 'cuz I had left the glove compartment unlocked. I didn't want to contact you until I managed to make the money back somehow." Jamari wasn't sure that Born was buying his story, and as he gave his explanation, he never looked Born directly in the eye.

Born was speechless when he heard his friend's account. Jamari's tale made Born's blood boil. Born had made his living in the streets, where it was imperative that he learn how to read people's emotions. Often body language spoke louder than verbal conversations. And Jamari's body language signaled that there was larceny in his heart. He fidgeted nervously, and his voice trembled.

Born stared at Jamari for a long time after hearing his story. "Jamari, do you think I'm a fool?" he asked at last.

Jamari shook his head, no. "Nah, Born. I know you ain't no fool—"

"You think I'm naïve?"

"Nah, Born."

"So you know that I see through you right now, then?"

Jamari didn't bother to answer the rhetorical question, and stared back at Born in silence.

"You must have forgot that I told that same bullshit story to A.J. when I wanted to do my own thing. Me and my niggas lied about being robbed, and we kept the product for ourselves. Remember that? So I know your story is bullshit."

"Nah, Born. It ain't even like that. I swear on my mother's life I didn't take that money from you. I ain't lying to you, Born."

Born looked at him in disbelief. He knew in his heart that Jamari was full of shit. But he had no proof. And having just buried his father, and having just been released from jail, Born didn't have it in him to go crazy. He thought about his mother and how upset she would be if he found himself deeper in trouble for fucking Jamari up. So Born did the next best thing. He cut him off, and counted his dough as a loss. But not before letting Jamari know that he saw through his story. "Jamari," he said calmly. "I know you betrayed me. I know you took my dough, and your story about the cops is a lie. You can swear on anybody you want. But no matter how much you deny it, you know the truth, and I know it, too. You fucked up." Seeing Jamari looking nervous enough to wet his pants, Born laughed. "It's all good, li'l homie. I ain't gonna hurt you. Just give me back all my work and get the fuck out my face."

"Born, I ain't never take nothing from you," Jamari protested.

But Born was done talking. He snatched Jamari up by the collar of his shirt and pulled his face within inches of his own. "Give my shit back, and walk away before I change my mind," he snarled.

Jamari dug nervously through his pockets and handed Born the crack he still had left to sell. Born took it, turned his back on his former friend, and walked away. Born never dealt with him again after that. Their friendship was a thing of the past. Even though they no longer crossed paths like they used to, Born was still bitter about what he perceived as being kicked when he was down. It was a feeling he didn't like one bit.

But Born had more important things to focus on: mainly, his rise to prominence on the block, and how he had begun to blossom into a full-fledged baller right in front of everyone's eyes. He was now driving a black 1994 Mercedes Benz E320 convertible and living in an exclusive luxury building among wealthy neighbors. He had all that a man with power would want. Except a woman to share it with.

Up to that point in his life, Born had loved only one girl. His teenage love, Simone, had succeeded in wounding Born's pride and breaking his heart, and after that he never let chicks get too close to him. His attitude after that always was, "What's in it for me?" He wasn't looking to fall in love ever again. He said that he would never give his heart to anyone else.

There were scores of women in Born's life. Most of them were merely sex toys for Born, but there were a couple who had managed to hold his interests even when they weren't fucking. He had dated one young lady who was a real fly girl. Chanel was from Queens, and she came to see Born at his mother's house in Staten Island. When she came to see him she was wearing all kinds of jewelry—big rope chains, bamboo earrings, name rings, and all kinds of gold adorned her body. Born brought her around, figuring that all the neighborhood homies would be impressed with his stylish new shorty.

As soon as he brought her to the hood, Martin had sized her up. He noticed that she was one of those light-skinned girls who thought her shit didn't stink. He also noticed the pricey jewelry that seemed to adorn every inch of her body. Martin pulled Born to the side and said, "Yo, Born. We gonna rob that bitch." He smiled at Born, and Born cracked up laughing, assuming that his friend was joking around.

"Let me rock her in the hood for a little while first," Born said, in jest. "Don't rob shorty yet," he joked. They laughed among themselves, and then went their separate ways. Days went by, and then Chanel called to tell Born that she was coming to see him again. He was glad, because her sex was out of this world. So he called his boys and explained why he'd be out of the loop for the day, and he took a shower in anticipation of her arrival.

When she got to his crib, he opened the door and saw her standing there looking naked, with absolutely no jewelry on whatsoever. Chanel was in tears, and she couldn't even speak at first. As soon as he saw her like that, he shook his head. He already knew what had happened.

"Yo, some niggas robbed me in the lobby," she said. She was shaken and crying as he ushered her into the apartment. "Three big niggas with guns."

Born shook his head, knowing that Martin, Smitty, and Chance were behind it. He listened as she went on and on about her traumatic experience. "They even took my nose ring!" She was distraught, and Born fought the urge to laugh. "Is this what it's like in your hood?" she asked, with her face frowned up. "This is the type of shit that goes on out here?" Chanel's tears had turned into tears of rage.

Born grinned at her prissy ass. *Anybody* could get it out here," he said. "Niggas is hungry, and you come through all shining like that." Born's expression was cold and unsympathetic. He shook his head in dismay, called her a cab, and sent her home. As soon as she left, he went to find his friends. As he walked through the lobby, he noticed that the lightbulbs had been shattered, and the building's entranceway was darker than ever. They had set shorty up real good. He walked outside in search of his crew, and he found them in the back of his building.

Born approached them and shook his head. "I thought I just asked y'all niggas not to rob the bitch."

All three of his friends broke out in laughter, and Born laughed also, as they all gave each other a pound. "I told y'all to let me rock her in the hood for a little while, and what do y'all niggas do? You rob the bitch the very next time I bring her ass out here!" He was still smiling, and his boys knew that he wasn't really mad. "Aiight, lemme see. What did y'all muthafuckas get?" He sat there in back of his mother's building and split up the loot with his boys. This was typical of his nonchalance toward women and his lack of feeling when it came to them.

All that changed on the day that he met Jada Ford.

He saw her standing in front of the group home in Mariner's Harbor, and was instantly mesmerized by the unfamiliar beauty. Born made it his business to know any and everybody within the borough where he did most of his dirt. Many a hustler had fallen by not recognizing the subtlest changes around them. So when he saw Jada standing there, he wondered who she was and why he'd never seen her before. He drove around the block a few times, trying to catch another glimpse of her. On his third time around the block, he saw her walking, and he had to follow her. Her ass was amazing, and her walk was mean! Born was further intrigued when his attempts to holler at her were immediately shot down. Born wasn't accustomed to being rejected. He was the man, and women usually fell at his feet. But Jada was hesitant. And she was beautiful. It made him that much more determined to see what she was all about.

When he finally convinced her to go to lunch with him, he wondered what would become of them after this initial encounter. He sat across from her at a table in the back corner of the diner. He thought her eyes were so alive, almost like they were dancing, as she looked around the place, taking in the decor. Born wondered where she was from, so he asked her.

"Brooklyn," Jada answered, directly. "Where you from?"

"I'm from here—from Staten Island." The waitress arrived to take their orders. Born ordered a sandwich. Jada followed his lead and ordered the same. When the waitress was gone, Born looked once more at Jada. "What part of Brooklyn?"

Jada smiled at Born's not-so-subtle questioning. "Flatbush."

"So what you doing out here today? You came to visit your man or somethin'?"

Jada smirked. "My sister lives out here, and I'm waiting for her to get home." She wondered why Born seemed to look at her so intensely. His eyes made her feel see-through.

"So your sister lives in the group home over there?"

"You ask an awful lot of questions."

"I'm sorry. I just want to make conversation—"

"So then ask me what my favorite color is. Ask me what's my sign." Jada was edgy.

Born liked a challenge. Jada definitely seemed to fit the bill. But he sensed that she was only *acting* tough. He could tell that she was vulnerable somewhere deep down inside, and he was curious about it. "Okay, Jada. What's your favorite color? Huh? What's your sign? You got any pets? You got any kids? You got a man?"

Jada couldn't help laughing. She liked his style for some reason. "Now that's more like it," she said. "I like yellow."

"Yellow?"

"Yes, yellow. I'm a Cancer. I don't have any pets, no kids, no man, nothing." Jada finished her response just as their food arrived. "Now it's your turn. Answer those same questions," she said. She unfolded her napkin and placed it in her lap, still well mannered, despite her otherwise unrefined existence.

Born said grace before he ate, which impressed Jada. That was the last thing she expected him to do. Then he shoveled a mouthful of French fries into his mouth and proceeded to talk. Jada tried not to look at his chewed-up food as she enjoyed her own. "I don't really have a favorite color," Born said. "I know it definitely ain't yellow."

Jada pretended to be offended as he poked fun at her color preference. "Shut up," she said, laughing.

He thought about the answer to the other questions. "I'm a Pisces. I don't have no kids or none of that shit, either." He bit into his sandwich. "I got some sharks in a tank in my living room, though. I don't know if that counts as pets." He continued gulping down his sandwich as if it was his last meal.

Jada sat, staring at his poor manners. She knew he had some money, judging from the car, the jewelry, and simply his style. But he had very little class. He talked with his mouth full, food flying this way and that. Finally, Jada said, "You don't get out much, huh?"

Born wiped his mouth with his napkin, and absorbed the sarcastic remark. He knew he was eating with reckless abandon. "I apologize if I'm being rude. I don't get to sit down and eat too often," he explained. "Sitting down like this ain't something I get to do every day. Most of the time, I eat on the go."

Jada nodded. "So then I feel special. I feel like you took time out of your *busy* schedule to sit down and eat lunch with li'l old me." Her voice was flat and insincere.

He nodded in agreement. "I think you're being sarcastic. But that's alright."

Jada laughed. "But you need to chew with your mouth closed, you know?" Jada demonstrated, biting into her own sandwich and chewing neatly, with an encouraging grin on her face.

Born shrugged his shoulders as Jada offered her tutorial. "This is how I eat, pretty girl. You'll learn to love it," Born said. "So why you don't have a man? A pretty young lady like yourself, cute little body, nice conversation. Why are you all alone in Staten Island looking for your sister?"

Jada shrugged. "I guess I'm not alone now, right?" She was beginning to wonder if this might lead to something. Born seemed like a likable guy.

Born grinned and took a sip of his soda. He watched Jada chew her food, watched her wipe her mouth with her napkin and sit back. "Nah, you ain't alone right now," he agreed. He caught himself staring at her pretty eyes once more. He couldn't help it.

Born knew that he wanted to spend more time with her than this simple meal. "You should come chill with me at my crib . . ."

"See? That's where I knew this was going." Jada took another bite of her sandwich, and then reached for her pocketbook. She was instantly turned off. Here she was thinking that Born had potential, and all he wanted was some ass. Born grabbed her hand before she could get to it.

"Nah. I'm just saying—"

"Saying what? Nigga, I'm from the streets—"

"You from the streets?" Born was grinning, patronizing her.

"Yeah. That's right. I'm from the streets, so I recognize bullshit. You pulled up in your Benz, took me to a cute little lunch, flashed your jewels, asked your questions. Now you want something in return, and I ain't with that." She made another grab for her purse, but Born pulled it toward him, and smiled at her, tauntingly.

"So you from the streets, huh, little girl? You recognize bullshit? Wow." Born looked as if he was stunned by her allegations, but he was still smiling. Despite her anger, she couldn't help falling in love with his dimples. Born kept smiling, tickled by the fact that Jada had been so quick to take offense. "I wasn't trying to serve you no bullshit. I was just offering you somewhere comfortable to hang out at while you wait for your sister. That's all. But, I see you're extra defensive, so I apologize." His grin turned somewhat sinister. "But why'd you automatically assume I wanted some ass? I didn't think you were that type."

Jada looked at the food on her plate, seemingly convicted.

Born continued. "Plus, I would hope that if you *were* that type of girl, you would charge me more than a six-dollar sandwich. 'Cause you look like you're worth way more than that."

"Okay, so give me my bag. Let me pay for what I ate."

"I ain't done yet." Born was amused by Jada's anger. "Neither are you! You didn't even finish your food. Stop actin' like that." Jada scowled at him as he held his hands up in surrender. "You should have told me you was from the streets. Then I woulda been prepared to deal with you." Born's remark was dripping with sarcasm, and Jada was irked by it.

"Don't be mad that I can see through your game," she said. "I know a little bit about a lot. Just remember that."

"Tell me what you know about, little girl."

"First of all," she said, sitting up in her seat. "I ain't no damn little girl. I'm twenty years old. Second of all, I know about a lot more than some young nigga from Staten Island such as yourself." Satisfied that she had put him in his place, Jada continued munching on her lunch. This dude had no idea what she knew about. She'd been in the streets for years, been to jail and back. The nerve of him to question what she had seen or been exposed to in her lifetime!

"Okay. You said all that, and what? You still ain't tell me what you know about. What? What you seen a couple of dice games, some niggas smoking weed? What?" Born resumed eating and talking with his mouth full. "What makes you so gangsta?"

Jada folded her arms across her chest. "I been out in the streets most of my life, so I've seen all kinds of shit. You name it. I've been in crack houses, seen niggas get shot and stabbed. I know about dirty old men, about silly young men. I know about grimy women and trifling hos, and I know all about your type." Jada thought about the men she'd come across working with Kelly and Mr. Charlie. She really had seen more than she wished she had, and she didn't think Born could be much different. Men were men. She didn't really care how Born received what she was saying. She had nothing to hide from anyone. She was clean, and she wanted to stay that way.

"How long you been on your own?" he asked her.

"Since I was born."

Born shook his head, and continued to eat his sandwich. Another black girl lost. He'd heard it all before. After successfully gulping down more than half of it, and swigging about a third of his soda, he sat back and looked at Jada. She chewed her own food, and then she sat daintily sipping her Coke through a straw. "I'm from the streets, too," Born said.

"I've been a lot of places, seen a lot of things. I ain't no slouch. You can trust me on that. And I can see that you ain't no slouch, either."

Jada smiled, grateful that he could tell she was no lame, that she was no easy mark. "Okay, well then, I guess we have something in common." She pulled out a cigarette and lit it. "What do you do?"

Born gazed at her blankly. "I do a little bit." Born watched Jada's parted lips as she exhaled smoke from the Newport. "Why don't you come hang out with me, and I'll show you what I'm all about."

Jada was tempted, but still hesitant. "Why should I trust that you won't do something crazy if I go with you?"

Born's smile was so sexy that it seemed like it could melt an iceberg. "I wouldn't hurt you. You can trust that. But if you don't want to, it's alright." He looked around the diner. "Plus, I don't know if I can trust you. You might be an undercover." Born said it with a smile, doubting that she could really be a cop.

Jada twisted her mouth contrarily. "I'm offended. I can't stand the police. That's one thing you don't have to worry about." After her stint in prison, Jada had no love for cops of any kind.

"See? We have something else in common. I can't stand the police, neither. Look at all the things we have in common." He smiled again. "So why you don't wanna talk about your sister? I'm saying, I never saw you around here before. You look good, so I would remember seeing you before. And now you pop up on the scene all sexy and tough at the same time. What's your story?" He looked at her as if he knew more than he ought to.

Jada wondered why his straightforwardness made her feel comfortable rather than repulsed. She didn't like nosy people. But somehow, Born came across as genuinely interested, not prying. Without thinking about it, she answered him. "Me and my sister moved to Staten Island a little while ago. We moved out here from Brooklyn because they put my sister in a group home out here. My mom and my sister don't speak, so I just came to see her by myself. Okay?"

Born nodded. "Okay. I understand now. Do you think she'll mind if I steal your time for a few hours?"

Jada grinned slightly. "I'm not sure. Where did you plan on taking me?"

"Well, we had some lunch. Now let's go see a movie."

Jada thought it over. She wondered whether she should trust this handsome stranger, or if she should just go back and wait for Ava. She sat staring at her empty plate for several minutes before she looked up and saw Born staring at her.

"So, you coming with me or what?" he asked.

Jada shrugged. "I'll roll with you for a little while. Just let me leave a note for my sister so that she knows I'm out here."

Born nodded, agreeing. "You can give her my pager number and tell her to beep me when she gets home and I'll bring you back to where she lives." Jada watched Born summon the waitress and request the check. She liked his take-charge demeanor. She felt strangely drawn to his over-confident nature. While Born settled the bill, Jada quickly scribbled a note to her sister.

Ava, I came to see you. I'm still in Staten Island. When you get back, page me at this number, and I'll come back. (917) 555-1045. I can't wait to see you.

Jada

They left the diner, and drove back to Ava's group home. Jada went inside and dropped off the note, and came back to Born, who was waiting patiently in the car. He drove off, through the Harbor, and on down Richmond Terrace. As they passed West Brighton—Jada's old neighborhood—she stole a glance at her past. She wondered if her mother was still sitting in her apartment with the television turned off, pretending that she wasn't home. She wondered if Mr. Charlie was still as conniving as he used to be. Jada was determined to never go back to rock bottom, where she'd been before.

Born noticed that Jada was quiet. He figured she was lost in thought, and he didn't interrupt that. Instead, he continued to steal glances at her as he drove. Jada didn't look at Born. She continued looking out the window, a list of questions forming in her mind. Who was this guy? Why did he want to spend time with her? What would happen next?

At the same time, Born was wondering as well, wondering why he was so intrigued by this pretty girl he'd never seen before. Wondering what it was about her that made him want to break her guard down. He drove down Forest Avenue, close to the lustrous green lawn sprawled across Clove Lake Park. He turned into the parking lot of a small brick apartment building nestled discreetly between a doctor's office and a set of homes. Once the car was parked, Born looked at Jada and said simply, "This is where I live." He got out of the car, and Jada followed in silence.

They entered the quiet lobby, and Born bypassed the locks and security codes. Then they walked down a carpeted hallway to a small elevator, which they boarded. Born pressed five and they rode in silence until the doors opened up. Before they exited, Jada stopped Born, and she stood holding the elevator doors open. "Why did you bring me here?" she asked him. Jada figured he wanted some ass, and she wanted him to lay his cards on the table before they went any further.

He shrugged. "I thought you wanted to watch a movie. This is where I live, so I thought we could watch a movie here. I don't go to movie theaters and shit like that." Born looked at Jada's face, noticed the guarded expression on it. He sighed. "You seem like you have trouble trusting people," he said. "You jumped to the wrong conclusion when we ate lunch today, and you made me feel like I was putting pressure on you when I wasn't. I tried to ask about your family, and you jumped down my throat. So I figured that bringing you here, where I live, would make you see that I don't have nothing to hide. You can trust me."

"Trust is earned. I learned that much from the streets."

Born smirked. Here she was with this "from the streets" shit again. This girl sounding like she really thought she knew something about the streets. He knew she was still somewhat naïve, simply because he could see it in her eyes. But for reasons that Born had yet to understand, he was interested in this particular young lady, more so than the countless others he spent time with. This one, he knew somehow, was special. "So let me give you a reason to trust me by inviting you into my home. This is where I lay my head. It don't get no more trustworthy than that."

Jada stood for another few moments, thinking. Then she stepped aside and allowed Born to walk past her, off the elevator and down the hallway to the last door. He turned the key in apartment 530, and they entered his domain.

Jada looked around at the brown sofa, the plain glass tables, and the simple lamps. The place was littered with CDs, the table was covered with them. "Wow, you need to hire a maid." Jada frowned at the clothes on the floor, and the boxes of new sneakers scattered throughout the room. She looked at the larger-than-life speakers with food wrappers and empty bottles perched on top.

Born shook his head in dismay. "You just never have nothing nice to say, huh?"

"How old are you?" Jada asked, out of the blue.

"I'm twenty-three. Why? What's that got to do with anything?"

She smiled, shyly. "I think it's impressive that you have your own place in such a nice building and you're such a young man. That was a nice thing to say, wasn't it?" she asked.

Born nodded, agreeing. And then he smiled at her. There were those dimples again. "Yeah, that was nice," he admitted. "Make yourself at home."

Jada did, sitting beside him on the sofa. She saw the huge television set that seemed to take up half of the living room. She saw the piles of VHS tapes lined up at the bottom of the entertainment center, and figured she could have her pick of what she wanted to watch. She decided to make conversation first. "So, can I ask you some questions?"

"Go 'head," he said. "I told you I ain't got nothing to hide."

Jada sat back, and crossed her legs. "What's your real name, Born?"

"Marquis Lamont Graham."

"Damn, you gave me your whole government name, huh?" She smiled. "What do you do for a living?"

His smile began to fade somewhat. "I don't work."

Jada was smiling now, since they both knew he was a hustler. "Okay. You don't work. So what do you do?"

Born shrugged. "I'm just surviving, you know what I'm saying?" He tried to act like he wasn't uncomfortable with her line of questioning. But he really was.

"Born, when did you get involved in selling—"

"Don't ask no more questions." Born sat back, his long legs spread wide apart. "I showed you all there is to see about me. You know more than you should already. So now it's your turn. Tell me what you're all about. I'm listening."

"That depends on what it is you wanna know."

Born shrugged his shoulders. "Start with telling me about your sister. Why's she in a group home?"

Jada looked at Born. He was asking tough questions now. She swallowed hard, lit up a cigarette, and told Born about all the drama—Ava's suicide attempt, the accident that killed J.D., and about the move from Brooklyn to Staten Island. When she was done, she sat back and looked at Born, trying to gauge his reaction. Born's expression was blank as he watched her try to read him. She continued. "So we moved out here to be closer to Ava, and I been staying in touch with my sister ever since." She sat back, feeling she had tidily summed up the less seedy aspects of the past several years of her life. Sure, she'd left out a lot of the story. But she had answered his question. Born wasn't so easily satisfied.

"So where do you live now? With your moms?"

Jada looked at Born, long and hard. "No. I don't live with my mother."

"So who do you live with? You live by yourself?"

Jada shook her head. Then she shrugged her shoulders. "I live with a friend of mine. She has a place of her own. But I'm only gonna be there until I get on my feet and get a job and everything."

Born listened to Jada. He had seen a dozen other girls just like her: young, pretty, lost, and searching for something. He wondered once again what it was about Jada that seemed so different from the others. He thought she had potential, though he hardly even knew her. "So you're twenty, you live with your friend, and you don't have a man?" Born nodded. "But what's the *whole* story?" He watched Jada's eyes flutter his way.

Jada didn't know what to make of this question. Born couldn't be a mind reader, but she wondered how he sensed that there was so much more to her story than the abridged version she'd just given him. She found herself wanting to tell him, and she couldn't figure out why. But just then, Born's pager began to vibrate, and an unknown number appeared. He dialed the number, held a brief conversation, and handed Jada the phone. It was Ava. And after assuring her sister that she was fine, that she was on her way to see her, Jada hung up. Strangely, she was disappointed that she wouldn't be able to finish her conversation with Born. She asked Born if they could continue it some other time. "I like talking to you," she said.

He grinned, because he had also enjoyed their conversation, and found Jada easy to talk to. He found her to be a kindred spirit, someone whose life had seen plenty of ups and downs, just as his had. Born and Jada gathered their things, and he dropped her off at Ava's group home. On the way their conversation was easier. Born told Jada that he understood how it was to have concern for a family member's well being, as Jada seemed to be concerned for Ava. He told Jada that he admired her for coming to see her sister. Jada thanked him as he pulled up outside the group home. She let him know that she was grateful that he had been such a gentleman. He gave her his pager number. And this time, he didn't worry that she might not call.

TWO OF A KIND

18

BONNIE AND CLYDE

Born picked Jada up from Shante's place on Steuben Street one day in August 1995. Jada had paged him from a pay phone at the corner store. He called the unfamiliar number right back, and was glad to hear her voice when she answered it. Ever since their initial encounter, he had waited patiently for this very phone call. Jada hoped that he would be free that day, since Shante's boyfriend was back at her apartment. Jada needed to get out and do something to occupy her time. But Ava was going to take her SATs that day, and Jada had no money to occupy herself while Shante and her man played house. Born was glad that Jada had paged him, since almost a week had passed since their first unexpected date. He suggested that he come and get her, so that they could watch the movie they never got to watch the first time around. He pulled up in his Benz just as she came outside.

Jada walked over to the car, wearing a red T-shirt and some Guess jeans. Born saw potential in her. She was so pretty that he was eager to see what she would look like all dressed up, with her hair done professionally and wearing some jewelry. He noticed that she wore no earrings, no jewelry of any sort. She was plain, and still stunning, as she climbed inside his ride.

"Hello," she said.

Born grinned. "Wassup, pretty girl? You ready to pick up where we left off?"

Jada grinned right back. "Yup. Let's go."

Born drove off, and headed for his place. He was curious to find out which movie Jada had brought to watch on his large-screen TV. So he asked her. "You said you were gonna bring the movie. So let me see what you got."

Jada pulled a movie out of her bag and showed it to him. Born looked at the movie in her hands, then looked at her as if she was crazy. He looked back at the movie, hoping his eyes were deceiving him. Then he looked at her again. "You're kidding, right? You want me to watch *Grease*?"

Jada laughed. "Yes, I want you to watch *Grease* with me. I love this movie." Jada knew Born would be reluctant to watch a movie about two white kids falling in love in the 1950s. But it was Jada's favorite movie.

"Why do you love that movie?" His face was contorted, as if he was really puzzled by this.

She laughed again. "*Grease* is about two people from opposite sides of the tracks who fall in love. And in the end, they're both willing to change so that they can be together. That's a beautiful story, right?" She smiled.

Born sighed, exasperated. "Next time, I'm picking the movie." Jada laughed, and sang along quietly with the Anita Baker song playing on the radio. He glanced at her from time to time as he drove, still amazed by her beautiful facial features and her glowing light brown skin. She seemed a little less edgy than she was the first time. "I don't think me and you are from opposite sides of the tracks, though." He said it as he turned down Forest Avenue.

Jada looked at him. "No? You think you come from the same type of shit as me?"

He nodded. "I know I do. You told me that your sister was in trouble, and she tried to kill herself. You said you been on your own since sixteen, been through all kinds of shit, seen all kinds of shit. So that says it all right there. I've been through my share of bullshit, too." He looked at her as they stopped at a red light. "I think we have more in common than you think."

Jada shrugged her shoulders. "Maybe we're not from opposite sides of the tracks," she said. "But you can still enjoy *Grease*."

Born laughed as he turned into his building's parking lot and found his usual space. He parked his beloved automobile, and then he and Jada headed for his place. When they got inside the lobby, Born pressed the button for the elevator, and looked at Jada from head to toe. She noticed his scrutiny, and she frowned. "Don't do that," she said.

He smiled, innocently. "Don't do what?"

"Don't look at women like that. We don't like it." Jada boarded the elevator when the doors opened. Born followed her, his eyes glued to her ass.

"How did I look at you?" he asked. "I didn't mean no harm."

Jada rolled her eyes, though she wasn't really as annoyed as she pretended to be. "You know what look I'm talking about. Men have a way of looking at a woman and making her feel naked. Don't do that, please."

The elevator doors opened, and Born smiled facetiously. "So, you don't like being naked?" he asked.

Jada shook her head and laughed at his joke as she followed him down the hallway to his apartment. She found it in the same condition as the last time she'd been there, except this time there was a razor blade, a plate, and a digital scale sitting on the table. She quickly surmised what he had been doing before he came to pick her up. Finding a comfortable place on his couch, Jada sat while Born went to the kitchen to retrieve snacks for the movie. He came back and placed the popcorn, pretzels, potato chips, two glasses, and a two-liter bottle of soda on the table. Born sat close beside Jada and looked at her. But this time when he looked at her, Jada didn't feel like he was undressing her with his eyes.

His eyes looked serious. They seemed intense. Again, she wondered why he looked at her like that.

"I like you," he said. "I don't know what it is about you, but I like you." Jada held his gaze, feeling her pulse quicken, strangely. Born nodded his head. "I must like you a whole lot, because I can't believe that I'm about to watch *Grease*."

Jada laughed. The ice had been broken. Born stood up and put the tape into the VCR, and then sat back down on the sofa. For the next couple of hours he found himself enjoying the antics of the crew from Rydell High. Jada knew the words to all of the songs, and Born watched her enjoy the movie. When it was over, Born went to the kitchen and got a beer out of the refrigerator. He offered Jada one, and she accepted. Plopping down beside her, he handed her the Heineken, and took a long swig of his own.

"See? That wasn't so bad, right?" Jada asked. "I could tell you liked the movie, so don't try to front like you didn't."

Born smiled, showing the dimples Jada loved so much. His pager went off, and Born glanced at it. Recognizing the number, he quickly grabbed the phone, and had a very animated conversation as Jada listened.

"What the fuck! Yo, why y'all niggas ain't call me as soon as you got the shit?"

Jada listened closely.

"So who got it now? Yo Mike! Don't let them niggas give my shit to nobody else! I told them that I wanted first crack at it. Aiight!" Born hung up the phone and rubbed his head, as if the conversation had stressed him out.

"What's the matter?" Jada asked. "You want to call it a night? I can come back another time."

Born shook his head. The last thing he wanted was for their time together to end so soon. He grabbed his car keys off of the table. "Nah, I don't want to call it a night. Can you wait here for me for a little while?"

Jada looked around the cluttered apartment and felt uncomfortable at the thought of being in his place by herself, although she was flattered that he trusted her to stay there alone. "Can't I come with you?" she asked. "Where do you have to go?"

Born looked at her as if he was trying to figure out if he should bring her along. "I gotta drop off something to my boys."

Jada nodded and stood up. "I'll come with you, then," she said. "How bad could it be?"

They proceeded downstairs and hopped back into Born's car. He drove to York Avenue, where he turned and pulled up in front of a run-down shanty with boards on its windows. Jada looked at him inquisitively, and he smiled. "You said you're from the streets, right? So come on. This shouldn't be nothing."

Jada climbed out of the car and followed Born to the run-down house. He didn't climb the collapsing steps. Instead, he led her through the knee-high grass to a side door. He knocked on the door five times in quick succession, paused, and then knocked twice more. Then the door swung open, and Born entered the seemingly abandoned house. Jada was right behind him.

They walked into what looked to Jada like a dark dungeon. Born greeted two young men who stood silently by the heavy door just inside the entrance. Both of these guys met Born with a warm reception, and neither one said a word to Jada. After talking to Born and indulging in a brief conversation, they separated to allow passage to him and his guest. Both of the young soldiers took in Jada's neatly voluptuous appearance, but neither spoke to her directly. Born offered no introduction as he ushered Jada past them, and into the confines of the darkened house. She saw more young men who looked to be about Born's age sitting around on old battered sofas spread throughout the spacious front room. There was money stacked on a table that had one of its legs missing, and Jada knew immediately that these men were up to some type of illegal activity. They stood and greeted Born when he walked in, each of them receiving him with enthusiasm and smiles.

Born seemed to fit right in among these strangers, and Jada felt like an outsider in their midst. After a lengthy exchange with the fellas, Born introduced Jada to the room. "This is Jada, everybody. Get used to her face. You'll be seeing it a lot more often from now on."

Jada didn't know what to make of Born's comment, so she simply smiled awkwardly, and waved at all of them. "What's up, everybody?" she said.

One of them—a tall, light-skinned brother with slanted eyes and a thin mustache—stood up and put both of his hands in the pockets of his jeans. Born turned to Jada and said, "I'll be right back. Wait out here for a minute." Born and the light-skinned man walked down a short hallway and into an adjoining room. They shut the door behind them, and Jada was left standing in a room with five men she didn't know. All kinds of thoughts ran through her mind, and she wondered if this was a setup. Would they gang-rape her? And if they did, who would believe her? She didn't know Born from a hole in the wall. And like a stupid little schoolgirl, she had followed him into an abandoned house full of young thugs. She tried not to panic.

"So, Jada, how long you been Born's girl?" one baby-faced stranger asked her.

She shrugged her shoulders, and shook off her paranoia. "I wouldn't say I'm his girl. I just met him. He seems like a nice guy, though."

The guy laughed and slapped his cohort playfully on the arm. "I knew this nigga couldn't have a girl this fine." The cohort didn't laugh, but only shook his head at his friend's theatrics.

"So you met him on some hustling shit, or what?" This clown was irritating Jada with his questions. He walked over to her. "You know, real recognize real, so I can tell you got a little hood in you." He sized her up, lustfully.

"Nah." Jada shook her head, chewing her gum. "You don't know me, so you couldn't possibly know what I got in me."

The baby-faced clown grinned at Jada and fiddled with the toothpick in his mouth. "I like you, shorty. Word up. Got a little spunk to ya. That's kinda nice. You got a sister or something, 'cause I'm trying to make it happen?"

"Nigga, if you don't get out her face, I'll embarrass you in here." Born emerged, carrying a large dark blue duffel bag, with the light-skinned man right beside him. The expression on his face was dead serious. "Don't get fucked up, Jamari." Born looked at Jada, and his gaze softened a little. "Jada, don't talk to strangers, baby girl."

Jamari looked at Born and held his hands up, defensively. "I was just playing, son. I was only messing with shorty."

Born stared Jamari down, and the light-skinned guy he had gone to the back room with stepped in to break the tension. "Yo, Born, holla at me later on." He gave Born a pound, and steered him toward the door. Jamari stood there, as if he had no idea why Born was upset. Jada watched Born gather his composure and turn away from Jamari. She said nothing as Born said his good-byes to all the men in the room. She followed Born to the door, and the young soldiers held it open. They left without any further conversation, and climbed back into Born's car. He was silent, and she couldn't tell whether or not he was still upset about his confrontation with the guy inside the house. Jada didn't question it, and she buckled her seat belt. When he drove away, Jada turned to him, and asked, "What's in the bag?"

Born looked at her sideways, and then nodded toward the bag sitting on the backseat. "Tools."

"What are all those tools for?" Jada sat wide-eyed, staring at the large gym bag filled to capacity with something heavy.

Born shrugged. "A couple of them are for me and my niggas. But most of them shits is for sale, knawmean?"

She looked at him, knowing full well what kinds of tools were contained in that gym bag. Guns. Jada sat, wondering who this man was and if it was safe to be with him after all. He seemed to read her mind, and he said, reassuringly, "Don't worry. You didn't give me a reason to hurt you yet. You don't have to get nervous."

Jada smiled, uneasily. "So what if I was a cop?" she asked. "What if I whipped out my badge right now?"

Born looked at her, then turned his attention back to the road. "You ain't a cop," he said. "But if you were, I would kill you. It's that simple."

Jada believed him. But strangely, she wasn't afraid. She looked at him again, and said, "So you're a gunrunner? Is that all?"

Born glanced at her out of the corner of his eye. "I do a little bit of this and a little bit of that."

Jada's gaze remained fixed on Born's face. "You sell drugs, Born?"

He looked at her, then returned his focus to the road ahead. "Drugs sell themselves," he said. Then he turned up the radio, and no further conversation took place until they pulled up in front of 55 Holland Avenue.

Born got out of the car and greeted a young man dressed in an oversized black T-shirt and jeans standing at the side of the building. Born reached inside the car, and passed the bag to the young stranger, with only small talk between them. He climbed back into the car, and the stranger headed back into the building. Jada took it all in, and sat silently as Born drove away.

He pulled up in front of a row of town houses, and got out of the car once more. "Come on," he said.

Jada followed him as he headed through a courtyard to an area where residents milled around and kids played tag. A tall, older black man, who looked old enough to be Born's father, headed toward them, walking with a very determined stride. Born broke out in laughter.

"Look at you, Moe Black! Where you goin', nigga? 'Cause you walkin' tall and looking straight!" Even old Moe Black had to laugh at Born's sarcasm. Moe was usually as high as a kite, so for Born to see him looking so sober was surprising. "Only thing missing is a big stick, Black. Walk tall and carry a big muthafuckin' stick!" Black, still laughing, gave Born five. Jada laughed at Born's sense of humor. He explained to Jada that Moe Black was once one of his father's cronies. "My father loved this nigga like a brother. So Black is like family to me."

As if on cue, Black chimed in, "Yo, I need one, Born. But I'm a little short."

"How you short now and you owe me from last time, too?" Born asked, in amazement.

"I know—"

"What do you know?"

"Yo, Born, I ain't got it, man. I'm waiting for my wife to get back from bingo. She ain't home yet."

"Every time you get ready to give me my money, your wife ain't get home yet."

"I'ma have your money."

"When?"

"Probably Sunday."

"*Probably* Sunday?"

"Sunday, man. I'll give it to you at the NA meeting they have in your mother's building."

Born roared in laughter and looked at Jada. "You hear this shit? He gonna pay me for drugs at the Narcotics Anonymous meeting!" Born was in hysterics. Jada laughed uneasily, as well as at the irony in the situation. Inside, she cried for that old man, knowing how thirsty he was for a hit of that pipe. She knew all too well what that was like. Moe Black, meanwhile, waved off Born's mockery and pressed for what he needed. "Come on, Born."

"How much you got now?"

Black rummaged through his pockets, and came out with a bunch of bills and some change. "Seven dollars and ninety cents."

Born shook his head. "Seven dollars and ninety cents." His tone was very matter-of-fact. He looked at Jada once more. "See what I go through?" Jada smiled outwardly, but if Born had taken a moment to look closer, he may have seen the torment in her eyes. Jada remembered feeling what that fiend was feeling. Remembered what it was like when she just *needed* that high.

Born's mind was playing tricks on him. As he looked at Moe Black, he saw his father. Black had been a very good friend of Leo's, and Born saw the similarities between them. It seemed as though history was almost repeating itself, except now it wasn't Leo Graham playing the part of the fiend. It was Moe Black, his right-hand man. Born always looked out for Black for that very reason. Even if Black didn't have all the money, as was the case this evening, Born still gave him what he needed. He had love for Moe Black. He had a soft spot for this man who reminded him of his father. He made the exchange with Black and walked away with Jada by his side. She wondered what she should make of all that she was witnessing.

Before she could give it much thought, they approached a bench, where two guys were sitting beside a very masculine-looking girl. Born greeted every one of them with a pound, and then introduced Jada once again.

"Jada, this is my nigga Smitty." Born pointed to a stocky brown-skinned brother with a Woolrich jacket on. "This is my man Martin." Jada greeted the lanky, ruthless-looking man with a permanent scowl on his face. "And this is Pat. She works with them."

Jada said hello to everyone, and listened as Born filled them in on the new package he'd picked up. "I gave the shit to Chance, and he's bringing them upstairs to the spot. I made sure y'all got everything you paid for. Plus, I threw a li'l somethin' extra in there for you, knawmean? Let me know if somebody else needs that, or whatever, and I'll get it to you. Ain't nobody else out here gonna give niggas shit that clean for prices that low. So fuck with me." Born talked to them for a few more brief minutes, and then he and Jada made their way back to his car. Born opened the passenger door for her, and held it until she climbed inside. Then he got into the car and drove off, glancing at Jada. They reached a stop sign.

"So, now what?" Born asked. "Cat got your tongue?"

"No. I'm just trying to digest all this, that's all."

Born laughed. "But I thought you was gangsta. You're from the streets. What's the problem?"

Jada scowled. "I never said I was a criminal. I just said that I was from the streets." She stared out of her passenger-side window. "You can drop me back off at my friend's house now."

"I can," Born said it warmly. "But I don't want to. Not yet."

Jada continued staring out of the window, wondering why she was wasting her time with this guy. She had thought he might be someone she'd want to get to know. But suddenly he was starting to seem as if he expected her to be in awe of his lifestyle. Jada found some things about Born that she admired—his take-charge demeanor, and his style overall. But she was also starting to see him as a cruel and ruthless hustler. The truth was that the encounter between Born and the crackhead earlier had reminded Jada of what she had once been. Suddenly her mind was flooded with memories of all the times she had begged a dealer to give it to her, even though she was short. All the times she'd been laughed at and demeaned for the sake of getting high. These were memories that Jada could do without. And now she couldn't seem to block them out.

He said, "You act like you scared or something."

She shrugged him off, and stared out the window. "You act like I'm supposed to be impressed because you hustle. That's not impressive."

Born didn't like how that sounded. He frowned. "I'm not trying to impress you, sweetheart. I told your stankin' ass you could stay at my apartment while I ran out to handle my business." Jada's remark had ignited a fuse that blew Born's temper out of proportion. "You're acting like I brought you to show you what I'm workin' with. You should have never asked to come if you was scared to see how I'm living."

Jada twisted her neck in the way that only a black girl can, and looked at Born through narrowed eyes. "What the fuck you mean my 'stankin' ass,' nigga? You don't know me like that."

"And you don't know me like that for you to be saying that I'm trying to impress you. I don't try to impress nobody. Just remember that."

Jada continued staring at Born like he had totally lost his mind. "Yeah," she said, nodding. "Drop me off back at my friend's house." She folded her arms across her chest, and watched the road ahead. "Now!"

Born chuckled, sarcastically. "I already told you that I'm not dropping you off yet. Just be easy."

"You can't kidnap me and make me stay in your car!" Jada was pissed.

Born screeched to a halt in the middle of Richmond Terrace. Cars behind them blasted their horns and grinded to a stop behind him. He turned to Jada. "You can get out now if you want to. I'm not kidnapping you, little girl. Go 'head. Get out right here."

Jada looked at the angry drivers as they passed Born's Benz. He continued to sit there idling, as he awaited her decision. "Fine!" She folded her arms across her chest, and sat back. Born laughed at the little brat beside him, and he drove her back to his place.

They rode in silence all the way, and when they arrived, Jada got out and slammed the passenger door. She headed toward the building and waited as Born unlocked the fortress that was his lobby. Once inside, they boarded the elevator and the tension was thick. As the doors closed, Jada stood with her back to the wall, still scowling, and Born pressed every button calmly. Then he stepped over to her, towering over her. His presence consumed the small space in which they stood. With their faces only inches apart, Born smiled at her. *Those damn dimples!* she thought. And then he kissed her, their tongues rhythmically dancing and their bodies so close he could feel her heartbeat. Floor by floor, they continued to kiss. At times it was soft, and at other moments passionate. But Jada had never been kissed like that in all her life. Born's kiss was almost better than sex. By the time they arrived at his apartment door, they had made up. They both knew it would be a good night after all.

When they got inside his place, he turned on his radio, and music filled the room through his Bose speakers. Born led her by the hand toward his bedroom, but Jada pulled back. "No," she said. "Not yet. It's too soon for that."

Born respected her reluctance, and instead he led her to the couch. She sat beside him, her mind reeling with all the things she was feeling. But the most dominant was a sense of guilt. Jada felt that if Born knew her for who she really was, he might not want to be with her at all. He kissed her so perfectly, and she wanted to have him fill her every void. But this wasn't right. It wasn't real. She swallowed the lump in her throat, and looked at him. "I think we should get to know each other better, Born." She said it, and watched his expression. It didn't change, and so she continued. "I think there's some things that I should tell you about who I really am before we go any further."

Now she had his undivided attention. He sat upright as Jada took a deep breath.

"You might want to put me out when I finish telling you the story," she said, laughing uneasily, because she was feeling really nervous about what his reaction would be to her past addiction. "I like you, Born. I want to see if there could be something between us. But first I have to be honest with you about who I am and who I used to be."

"Okay," he said, sitting back and getting comfortable. "I'm listening."

Jada started at the beginning, and she bared her soul to Born. She started with her home life, and how her mother had chosen a man over her children. She continued, telling him about their move to Staten Island, and then about meeting Mr. Charlie. She went on to how she'd started smoking woolahs, then straight crack, and eventually hit rock bottom. Every sordid detail was laid out. Jada held nothing back. And to her, it felt like stepping off a cliff, hoping that your parachute actually opened. All she knew for sure was that the truth should come from her before Born had the misfortune of hearing it from someone else.

Listening to Jada, Born felt like he was on an emotional roller coaster. The woman beside him was pretty, she was sexy, and she was smart. But she was a former crackhead, and that was something that Born hadn't expected. It was a turnoff. She told Born everything about her life on the streets, about the way Mr. Charlie had treated her, both good and bad. Born listened to Jada's story in astonishment. These things had happened before he'd met her, yet he still felt disappointed by the revelations. She had been a true fiend. She had sold her body. She was weak like his father had been, and that was something Born couldn't easily get past.

Born looked at Jada, who sat back at the end of her story, awaiting his response. He felt a sense of disappointment about Jada's past, but he was hesitant to let her know that.

"So you don't smoke no more?" he asked. "You don't get tempted now?"

Jada shook her head vigorously. "No. Not at all. I'm clean now, and I'm never using that shit again!" The look on her face was so sincere. "You don't understand," she said. "That drug had me doing all kinds of shit that if I think about it now it makes me sick. I was selling my body, stealing, selling drugs, doing whatever I had to do to get it. Now that I look back at how low I stooped, I don't ever, ever want to go back there again."

She looked at Born, trying to read his face. He looked at her, staring into her eyes so hard that she thought he was looking for something specific.

"Yo, I respect your honesty, for real," he said. "It takes a strong person to be up front and honest about some shit like that. I appreciate you telling me all of this yourself."

Jada waited for him to say more, but he didn't. The truth was that Born didn't know what to say, what to feel, or how to take what she had said. He was somewhat disappointed, knowing that she had been a fiend. But he did admire her for having the strength to kick her habit. Born thought about his father's battle with addiction. He knew it took strength to fight it, and he admired her for doing what Leo Graham had failed to do.

Jada sat there, the suspense killing her. "So, do you want me to get out now?"

Born had a tough time understanding why he was so intrigued by Jada. Part of him thought, perhaps she was best kept at a distance because of her past. But she reminded him of a child that wasn't fully strong enough. He saw potential in her, and wanted to teach her how to be strong. Jada wasn't like most of the chicks he'd dealt with. He'd had prettier girlfriends, all types of jump-offs, some more lovely than the next. But there was something different about her that he couldn't quite put his finger on. So while he doubted that he could ever wife her, he sincerely wanted to be her friend.

Born shook his head. "Nah," he said. "Not at all." He reached for her hand, and she gave it to him. "Thanks for telling me the truth. In my business, honesty is hard to come by. You showed me that you got a lot of heart. And I really respect you for that."

Jada smiled. "Thanks."

Born stood up and turned off the radio. There would be no sex tonight. He put a movie in the VCR, and turned on the television. When he sat back down, they watched a bootleg copy of *The Fugitive* and enjoyed each other's company. By the end of the movie, Jada was asleep, with her head resting on Born's shoulder. He maneuvered himself into a more comfortable position, and grabbed the throw he kept on the sofa for nights when he fell asleep on it. He covered the two of them, and he held her all night, as she snored softly in his arms. It was the first time she spent the night with him, and Born figured that he just may have found an unexpected Bonnie to his Clyde.

19

THE FIRST TIME

Jada woke up the next morning, realizing that she had spent the whole night sleeping across Born. She looked around the cluttered living room, as light filtered through the windows. Born was still sleeping, with his head laid back across the couch. His arm hung loosely around Jada, as he slept with his mouth slightly opened, and adorable still. Jada wondered what he must think of her now. And she also wondered what would happen between them now that all the cards had been laid out.

She got up and went to the bathroom, finding it much cleaner than she had expected. He slept while she grabbed a clean washcloth from among a neat stack of blue ones on the side of the tub, and took a quick shower. She had to put the same clothes back on, but she stuck her panties in her pocket for when she got back to Shante's house. Feeling better afterward, Jada looked at her reflection in the mirror. She felt clean both inside and out. She felt renewed, and had no regrets about being candid with Born. She wondered what would happen next.

Jada emerged from the bathroom to find Born waking up. He smiled, seeing her come out of the bathroom and sit next to him on the sofa.

"Good morning, pretty girl," he said. He sat up and looked around. "You can feel free to make breakfast or whatever." He said it with a sly smile on his face. "I got eggs and all that kind of shit in the kitchen."

Jada looked at him. She started to say something slick, but instead she smiled back at him. She was happy that he still wanted her company after hearing the truth about who she was. She stood up and asked, "Well then, how do you like your eggs?"

After she scrambled the eggs and threw together some grits and some sausage, Jada and Born shared another meal together.

He brought her back to Shante's house, so that she could change her clothes. And when she was done, he was right downstairs waiting for her. They spent the day together, with her watching him wheel and deal, and him feeling her out, trying to see if she was worth his time. Born made Jada laugh, and she made him think. The two of them shared interesting conversations and formed an easy friendship.

Every day they spent time together, and their bond grew stronger. Born liked the fact that Jada wasn't afraid to disagree with him. They had their share of arguments and debates. And Born liked that she didn't back down. He knew that he was a good-looking guy, but he was real enough to know that he was no Adonis. Yet once his money had started piling up, chicks in the hood had started tossing so much pussy his way that he turned a lot of it down. Jada didn't seem overly impressed by his status, his money. She had been hesitant to give him the time of day at first. And, in some strange way, that endeared her to him. It made him feel like—after surviving the trauma of addiction—she was picky about who she spent time with, and he felt somehow privileged that she had chosen to spend time with him.

But he didn't lie to her and tell her that he was willing to give her more than what she was already getting. He liked Jada. She was, in a lot of ways, his very best friend. But he wasn't yet able to come to terms with her past as a crackhead and a ho. He didn't want to lead her on and tell her otherwise. One day, after sharing a heartfelt conversation about Jada missing her father as a little girl, and a bottle of Bacardi, Jada had told Born that she loved him. She insisted that even though she knew she was kinda tipsy, she really did love him. Born refused to say it back to her, because at that point in time it wasn't the truth. He explained that he cared about her a lot. But he didn't love her. Not yet. And he didn't want to lie to her. Born told her that he wanted to be unlike all the men in her past. He didn't want to disappoint her or manipulate her in any way. He wanted to make her stronger and wiser. He wanted to see her succeed.

Born was brutally honest with her. If her outfit looked cheap or unattractive, he told her that. If she made a stupid decision or failed to think a situation through clearly, he told her so. So when she professed her love for him, Born didn't do the same. Instead, he told her that he appreciated her love and would never take it for granted. But to him, Jada was like his little homie.

He wanted to teach her to be tougher, smarter, and more successful than she ever thought she could be. He saw the potential in her to be a great woman, and he liked Jada's style. She was pretty, yet she wasn't stuck up. He had taken her to project buildings with pissy elevators, mice, and water bugs in the flooded basements, and with all other kinds of undesirable conditions. He took her with him when he went to meet fiends and users. He also took her with him to nice restaurants, to hang with his boys, and to parties. She blended in, regardless of the surroundings. She had the ability to be classy or street, depending on the circumstances, and Born loved that about her. The girl had an edge to her that intoxicated him without question.

Born admired the honest way she had revealed all the parts of her troubled past. Her truthfulness made him want to open up to her about his own past. He began to share with her parts of himself that he hadn't shared with anyone else. He explained his father's addiction to crack, his love for his mother, and the history of his life in the streets. He talked all about Leo's crack use, his fall from grace, and Born's subsequent entry into the game. But for the first time he talked about how watching his father fall apart had made him *feel*. He had never told anyone how hurt he was that his father—his hero—had quit being his idol and become a crackhead. He told her that even after all this time, he still missed his father.

He had never shared so much of himself with any chick. Or with anyone at all, for that matter. Born knew a lot of interesting people from all walks of life. But he had never met anyone who stimulated his mind the way that Jada did. Their conversations were some of the best he'd ever had. And it wasn't until he found her that he realized how profound the absence of stimulating conversation had been in his life. He felt that Jada made him a better man. She gave him good advice, listened to his dreams, and kept his secrets. He felt an unmistakable connection with her. For once in his life, he opened up completely to someone, and he told Jada what was in his heart.

Their conversations always flowed well. They began to grow closer, and to trust one another. Then, on a blustery night in February 1996, their relationship changed. The physical tension between them had become so intense that it couldn't be ignored. Jada was looking scrumptious in a tight black sweater and tight black pants. They were in his car driving to his place on their way from a card game at his boy Smitty's new place. He looked at the shape of her body, and he wanted to know what she looked like underneath those clothes. He couldn't help but want to take things a step further.

At a red light, Born leaned closer to Jada. She looked happily surprised by this gesture, and she smiled as Born moved closer and kissed her. Jada kissed him back, and she didn't protest as his hands wandered slowly over her body. The car behind them honked to let them know that the light was now green, and Born drove on, hungry for her like he couldn't explain.

When they reached his apartment, they went at each other in the dark like neither had anticipated. He walked in after her, tall and stocky, with heavy footsteps in his Timberland boots. She loved the sight of him walking through the door like that. It made her pulse race, and she got a rush watching him move. They clung together, kissing and touching, all the while whispering, "Damn!" and "Come here."

Soon they were in the stillness of his bedroom. Born led her to the comfort of his king-size Sealy, covered in crisp white bedding. She began to take off her sweater, when to her surprise, Born stood and flipped on the lamp at his bedside. Jada frowned, and immediately stopped undressing. "Turn off the lights," she asked, softly.

Born shook his head. "Nah. I wanna see you, baby girl."

Born sat, waiting for her to take off her clothes. Jada's eyes pleaded. "Born, I don't feel comfortable—"

"You should," he said. "You're a beautiful girl. You have a beautiful body. Why you so scared to let it be seen? Let me see you."

Jada didn't budge. Born stood and took off his T-shirt. He stripped out of his jeans and took off his boxers. And there he stood, naked except for a do-rag and a pair of sweat socks. He stood, fully exposed, with his chubby eight-inch penis standing at half mast. Jada was understandably distracted as Born walked toward her. He walked over to her calmly, wearing a grin that seemed simultaneously sexy and arrogant, and began to undress her. He took off her top. A large scar was visible in the middle of her breasts, where her bra was unable to camouflage it. Born traced his finger across the upraised two-inch scar.

The reality of the situation came raining down around him. This woman for whom he cared so much was a former crackhead. This scar, this damage, had been done to her as a result of selling her body. Born looked into her eyes and saw her fear of rejection. He continued to undress her. Jada stood there nervously, feeling more vulnerable than ever before.

Born unhooked her bra. He stared at her and he saw all of her—all the damage that living as a crack whore had done to her physically. Jada felt like the last of her secrets had been exposed, and she stepped out of her pants and pulled off her panties. Now she stood completely naked in the presence of the one person whose opinion mattered more than anything else. Born was seeing her naked for the first time, and he recoiled somewhat, as she had known he would. The scars from her knife fight with Kelly were visible, and the damage clearly evident. Jada was mortified, but at the same time somehow relieved. At least now Born would see her for who she really was. The moment was silently awkward. Then Born reached for her, and suddenly stopped. To Jada, it seemed almost as if she could read his mind. She figured he was thinking that he had made a mistake, that he didn't want her after all. But to her surprise, he pulled her toward him and cradled her in his arms.

He held her close to him in silence, and she tried not to cry. She shook her head again, more for the purpose of fighting back tears now. She felt so vulnerable. Born could feel her discomfort, and he held her to him. He hugged her close, and kissed her lips, his arms wrapped tightly around her small frame. His silent embrace spoke so clearly to her, and Jada clung to him. She felt so safe in that moment, so protected. He led her to the bed and laid her down. When she closed her eyes, he told her, "Look at me."

Jada opened her eyes, and looked into his. There she saw acceptance and understanding. She saw someone who didn't judge her, and it made her want to cry. Born touched her so firmly, and so intensely, that she couldn't help moaning. He kissed her body, even the scar that she hated so much. Then he put on a condom and made love to her as no man ever had. He told her again and again that she was his pretty girl, that she felt so good. She watched him touch her like she had never been touched, and kiss her in places that made her insides scream. For Jada, even though she'd had sex with many men, with Born she experienced intimacy for the very first time. It felt like redemption. Born connected with something deep inside of her. As they lay rocking to a rhythm all their own, it seemed as if theirs was an unmatched synchronicity. Jada responded to him, felt beautiful with him. And they filled each other's voids after all.

Afterward, Born reached over and grabbed a small bottle of Hennessy that was still sitting on the nightstand from the night before. Taking a swig, he exhaled deeply and looked at Jada lying beneath his snowy white sheets, and puffing silently on a cigarette. Her silhouette was perfect under the thin material, and all of her curves were amazing. But beneath that sheet, Born had seen the truth.

Jada looked into his beautiful eyes. She looked at his thick, sexy lips, and recalled what those lips had done to her battered body only moments before. She relaxed.

Born playfully nudged her chin with his fist. "No matter what happens," he said. "Promise me we'll always be friends."

Jada wasn't sure how to react to that. Was "friends" all that he wanted to be? Was he already regretting having sex with her? "I promise, I'll always be your friend."

Born smiled at her. "I'll always be yours, too," he said. "Friends till the end." He lay there, trying to keep things in perspective. Sex didn't necessarily have to change anything, he reasoned. They could still be best friends. But despite his efforts to convince himself that friendship was enough, he couldn't help but feel for the tarnished young woman he lay beside.

She slept in his arms that night, in his bed, with their legs laced together. Born watched her sleep, wondering how she had managed to soften his hardened heart when it came to drug addiction. He thought about his father. He thought about how disappointed he had been in Leo when he was alive and getting high. Born wondered why he was now considering a relationship with someone going through the same struggle. But there was something different about Jada. She had sworn to him that she was finished with drugs. She only smoked cigarettes now, and drank only socially. The truth was, he loved her company, and he loved *her*— period. He didn't know how he'd let it happen. He never wanted to love her. She wasn't the type of woman he wanted to give his heart to. But he couldn't help it. She completed him. They made love again when the sun came up.

Her fingertips had lightly brushed the skin on Born's face on that cold February morning as he woke her up. His mustache and goatee had been stubbly to the touch, and she loved it—she thought he was the closest thing to perfect. Born's eyes searched hers with an intensity that made her heartbeat quicken. It seemed like he was looking beyond her dark brown eyes and peering right into her soul. She felt vulnerable with him staring into her eyes that way. She was afraid of what he might see there. But she felt silly for feeling like that. The night before she had made love to Born for the first time. She had exposed herself to him, body and soul, and there was nothing to hide anymore. Jada wondered if she should break the silence that had fallen between them. Searching her mind for something to say, she continued to caress his face. But it would be Born who broke the silence, though not as romantically as she may have hoped.

"Don't ever hurt me, Jada." He said it without a smile on his face, just a serious look, and an even tone in his voice. "I let you in. Don't make me regret that."

Jada looked away, unsure how to respond. She shook her head, her eyes locked on Born's bare chest. "I won't hurt you," she said, firmly. "I would never do that."

He kept staring at her, though she no longer met his gaze. He was wondering how she had managed to penetrate his emotional fortress. The tainted creature before him had managed to melt his heart. "You can't look me in my eyes," he said.

Jada frowned and looked directly at Born, determined now to show him that she could. "That's not true. I look you in your eyes all the time."

"But not for long," he said. "You always turn away, like it makes you uncomfortable."

Jada shrugged her shoulders, and stared back at Born. "Maybe it does a little bit. Because I'm afraid you won't like what you see."

Born smiled, ever so slightly, and kissed her softly. "I love you," he said.

Silence fell between them for several profound moments. A broad smile spread across Jada's face, and she battled the urge to pinch herself. What he'd said to her was like a dream come true, and it felt to her, at that moment, like those words coming from that man were exactly what she'd been waiting for her whole life. "I love you, too." She felt like the happiest woman alive.

Jada was by his side and in his bed from that day on. She was his baby girl, his weakness. And she adored the ground he walked on.

She moved into his place, and they were official. Jada became Born's other half. She traveled in and out of state with him. She rode shotgun when he went to make deliveries. When they went out to parties or concerts, Jada held his gun for him, since bouncers rarely searched the women. She even watched him bag up his drugs on occasion, and he watched her like a hawk. He was waiting for her to slip up, putting her face-to-face with the drug that had had her twisted not so long ago. He was testing her to see what her reaction would be when she saw it. And Jada passed the test. She was committed to staying clean, and he was so proud. He had almost *expected* her to slip up, but she never did, and that impressed him. Born wasn't one to trust easily. His trust came in layers. He had trusted his father, his friend Jamari, and trusted Simone. More often than not, he had been let down. So he didn't trust Jada easily. Women had burned him before, and he was slow to let his guard down fully at first. But little by little he began to let Jada chip away at his doubts. He put all his faith in her, and she was determined he never regret it.

Jada was by his side step by step. She was earning Born's trust and stealing his heart as she helped him put together an empire that niggas would try to duplicate for a long time to come. Born introduced Jada to his mother, and Ingrid prepared dinner for them when they came over to her house. Jada felt special when Ingrid told her that she was the first young lady Born had brought home to meet her since he'd moved out years ago. Knowing that Miss Ingrid was the most important woman in Born's life, Jada knew it was a big deal that he had introduced them. She knew that she was officially "in."

On the way home that night, Jada looked over at Born as he drove. When he met her gaze, she smiled at him. "Thank you for trusting me, Born. I know that's not easy for you. But you trust me, and you love me. That means so much to me, baby. It really does."

Born smiled at her. "I do love you and trust you," he said. "And I believe that you won't make me regret that. I really feel that you won't let me down. I'll bet the house on that."

Jada was so happy to hear him say those words. She was fiercely determined not to ever make him regret the confidence that he had in her. Night after night they made crazy love, and plotted how together they would take over the world one block at a time. It was the sweetest thing, the love they shared, the dreams they had. And for once they found contentment in each other's arms.

20

PARTNERS IN CRIME

Bitches hated on Jada hard for being with Born. They would look at her all greasy, and roll their eyes at her when she and Born walked into a room together. He was that nigga around the way, so all the broads wanted him for themselves. Even Shante. She would tell Jada things, and warn her not to trust Born. She made Jada think that he was lying to her, that he had other girls. Shante kept telling her, "Don't think that you're his one and only. Remember, Jada, trust no one." And at first, Jada doubted him. She brought a lot of what Shante told her back to Born. And he made Jada see her friend for what she was. Shante was still smoking crack, still boosting, and she was hating. She had a man, but he was hustling backward. The nigga sold weed, but he smoked blunts like they were cigarettes. So seeing Jada with Born—who was taking her on shopping sprees and trips, and keeping her looking fabulous—made Shante sick. After a while, Born didn't want Jada hanging with Shante anymore. He didn't want her around someone that jealous and that was still smoking. In fact, she was the person Jada had *started* smoking crack with. Born convinced Jada that Shante wasn't a real friend. So she let go of that friendship. She stopped calling Shante, and Shante stopped calling her.

Jada didn't have other friends. It was just her sister, Ava, and no one else. By then Ava was attending the University of Pennsylvania, and she was on the right track. Jada spent all her time with Born, and they became partners in crime.

Born was still connected to Dorian, the guy from Brooklyn. He was dealing costly fish scale in assorted quantities. He also sold cheaper cook-up cocaine and did business with small-time hustlers as well. Dorian had been in the game for years, and in all that time he had never seen anyone hustle the way Born did. The kid was relentless. Born was never short with money, and often came back to re-up long before Dorian thought he would. He had never seen the young hustler with a crew, or with any henchmen. He worked alone, and Born was making lots of money—and bringing Dorian big money in return. They began to form a mutual admiration for one another's style. Then a situation arose that intensified that sentiment.

Dorian found out that there was a plot to set Born up. Another hustler from Staten Island was talking too much, and news in Dorian's circle had traveled faster than the speed of light. Dorian heard from more than one reliable source that a hustler named Celly from Stapleton was after Born's spot. Celly was trying to lock down the island with his wholesale coke and heroin trade. But Born was making it hard, with the top spenders in the game spending their money with him instead. Celly couldn't beat his prices. So rather than find a way to compete, he wanted to take the competition out of the game.

Dorian liked Born, and admired him, because he reminded him of himself when he first got into the game. He saw the hunger in Born's hustle. Born seemed like an example of how to play the game rather than to allow the game to play you. He was never in the police's radar, and never unfair to those he did business with. He got his money, and kept it moving. But what Dorian admired most about Born was the fact that he worked alone. He stood firmly on his own two feet, with no crew behind him. Born knew when to be loud, and when to be low-key, and Dorian liked what he saw in the young hustler. Celly, on the other hand, was a hater and a rat bastard. One of Dorian's boys had been locked up with Celly, and told him that the nigga was snitching. Nothing was worse than a snitch to Dorian. He and Celly had no love between them, only business. And even the business Celly brought to Dorian was sporadic. He didn't cop from Dorian nearly as much as Born did. Celly only *talked* big. So it was a pleasure for Dorian to alert Born to what was about to go down.

He discussed the situation with Born, telling him to watch his back. Born didn't take such things just at face value. For all he knew, Dorian could be throwing shit in the game, just to get rid of a thorn in his own side. So Born did his homework. He put his ear to the street, and sure enough, he was able to confirm it. In a borough where all the hoods combined would equal only half of Brooklyn, news traveled easily. Born was grateful to Dorian for possibly saving his life. He had been the first to tell him what was brewing, and no one knew when Celly was planning to strike.

Two weeks later Celly was executed in his kitchen, along with his uncle and his brother. Never one to pay someone else to do his dirty work, Born had pulled the trigger himself, and he did it discreetly. He simply ambushed Celly's little sister as she came home from school. He snuck up behind her, and made her open the door. Once they gained access to Celly's house using her key, Born held the ten-year-old girl at gunpoint until her brother finally came home. Celly, his uncle, and his brother were met with immediate gunfire, and may never even have known who caused it. Born left Celly's little sister tied to a bench in Tompkins Square Park. By the time the police found her, she was too petrified to tell them about the man who had killed her brother and uncles. Their bodies weren't discovered until the stench from the decomposition drew the neighbors' attention. It was a crime that rocked the borough, and one that made niggas think twice about what they said. Everybody knew that Celly had loose lips. He never cared what he said about anybody. Though many suspected that Born had been behind Celly's murder, the dead man had far too many enemies for anyone to know for sure. From that point on, Dorian and Born had a great business relationship, as well as a blossoming friendship. Dorian remained professional. But he had a soft spot for the thoroughbred he saw in Born.

Usually when they did business Born came by himself. He had been buying weight from Dorian, and cutting some of it down into twenty- and fifty-dollar quantities, while the rest he sold in ounces. But now Born wanted to discuss something else. He wanted to change the game, and he felt that he had a proposition that Dorian would be unable to refuse. Born invited Dorian to bring his wifey, Sunny, along to dinner with him and Jada. Dorian accepted, figuring that whatever Born had on his mind might be interesting. He gladly brought Sunny along to balance out the equation.

Dorian told Sunny that one of his "clients" wanted to come and meet with him. Never one to divulge too much information to Sunny at once, he explained that the client was bringing a female friend with him, and that she should get dressed and put on her finest shit. He was taking her out for a night on the town. Sunny understood that this meant that the men would discuss business while she was expected to keep the female entertained. This would probably be a close working relationship between Dorian and this other party, because bringing wifeys into the equation always signaled that big business was being conducted: Dorian bringing Sunny along on business was a sign that this client was welcome in his cipher. She couldn't wait to see who it was.

When they arrived at Calalou's, the best West Indian restaurant in Manhattan, Sunny was surprised to see that Born was the client Dorian had been talking about. She had seen Born on only a handful of occasions. He seemed serious and no-nonsense. He was polite and not nearly as gutter as some of the others she'd seen. But her opinion didn't matter much. If Dorian was meeting with him, he must be alright.

Sunny walked in wearing a cream-colored Gaultier dress with beaded Lauboutin sandals. Her short, light-brown hair was cut perfectly and slicked back off her softly made-up face. Her haircut was edgy, a look one could only pull off if she were as stunning as Sunny. She looked like she belonged on a runway. Dorian looked just as regal. But that would have been the case regardless of what he wore. Dorian was a tall and well-toned, brown-skinned brother. He had a neat mustache and goatee that accented his juicy lips. His eyebrows were thick and dark, his nose in perfect proportion. Dorian was clearly older than Sunny. But they made an amazing couple. He was dapper in a tan pair of slacks, Stacey Adams footwear, and a simple, brown button-up shirt.

He spotted Born sitting at a table in the back with his lady, and he led Sunny toward them.

Sunny would always remember the first time she saw Jada. There was something about her that she liked instantly. Jada was a stunning brown-skinned beauty with a delicate smile. She wore her hair upswept, accented by bangs cut to precise perfection. She wore a shimmering silk bronze-colored halter top paired with sexy tight jeans. Instinctively, Sunny looked at Jada's shoes as she and Born stood to greet them, and saw that she wore a pair of Gucci slingbacks. Nice. Sunny had the meanest shoe game in town, and she could see that Jada's wasn't bad, either. She took in the Gucci alligator bag that sat on the table beside Jada, and Sunny concluded that Born was keeping his girlfriend well appointed. Sunny didn't hate at all, because she knew that no one in the room had more money than Dorian did. Born himself was decked out in a pair of baggy black jeans, Wallabies, and a crisp white linen shirt. Born never really dressed up, and even though the venue this evening was an upscale restaurant, he still kept it somewhat gangsta. Sunny was a fashionista, so seeing Jada laid out so impeccably made her warm up to her immediately. They exchanged smiles and a handshake as they were introduced, and then they sat and began their evening.

"So, what y'all feel like eating tonight?" Dorian asked, in his heavy baritone. Sunny put her elbows on the table and clasped her hands together under her chin as she waited for the answer.

Born sat back and looked at Jada as if he wasn't really sure what he wanted. Jada shook her head, smiling. "I want to apologize up front for how my baby eats in public!" She scowled at Born, and he laughed. His lack of table manners had not changed.

Dorian laughed as well, and looked at Jada. "Okay, I can tell that you and Sunny got a lot in common," he said. "She stays on my case about shit like that." Looking at Sunny, Dorian grinned, and said, "While we're issuing warnings, let me tell you right now that Sunny don't know how to bite her tongue," he said. "I keep reminding her that everything you think don't need to be spoken. But she don't hear me. So let me apologize now for whatever comes out of her pretty little mouth."

Sunny rolled her eyes at Dorian, and then looked at Born. "So I guess *we're* the ones with the fuckin' problems, huh, Born?"

Born laughed, and said, "Yeah, I see they put all our business on Front Street as soon as we sat down."

"I mean, my ass had *barely* hit the seat before they got started!" Sunny was laughing, and Dorian held his hands up, and said, "I rest my case."

Sunny waved her hand at Dorian, playfully. Then she turned her attention back to their dinner companions. "How long have y'all been together, Jada?"

Jada smiled at the exchange. She could tell that she was going to like Sunny and her no-holds-barred personality. "Just a few months," she said. "How about you two? How long has it been?"

At this question, Sunny smiled. Her face was lovely, and smiling only made it lovelier. "Nine years," she said. "I started out with this dude when I was seventeen years old. I'm the reason he's the big success he is now!"

Dorian laughed. "Yeah right!" Sunny also laughed, as he nudged her playfully. "You're the reason my blood pressure is high."

Born and Jada laughed, and the waitress came over and took their orders. Jada, true to form, followed her man's lead and ordered the same as Born—chicken roti on that particular evening. Dorian ordered jerk chicken. Sunny ordered a lobster. Secretly, Jada was intrigued by Sunny's choice of lobster, since Jada loved to eat it, but didn't know how to eat one publicly. She had eaten lobster at home, using all kinds of things to crack the shell. But in a fancy restaurant like this one, she wondered how Sunny would eat it. Jada was still becoming accustomed to living the good life, and she could tell that Sunny was already acclimated to it. The waitress took their drink orders, and was gone. Bob Marley crooned from the speakers, and the candlelight flickered from every table throughout the cozy restaurant. The place had an elegant decor, and all the patrons were dressed up, out for an evening with friends. The small talk lingered for a short while.

Eventually, the men began to discuss business in hushed tones, with Born outlining his plan to take over a larger chunk of Staten Island's drug trade. Born saw weaknesses in every crew on Staten Island's north shore, and he had already conquered his share of turf in that section of the borough. He wanted to branch out to the south shore, which was where the white people lived. That was where the money was, and Born was eager to get his hands on some fish scale in order to tap into the wealthier clientele. All he needed from Dorian was a good price, and exclusivity. He wanted Dorian to agree to make Born his sole Staten Island connection, so that Born could really begin his planned takeover of the borough's cocaine trade. That's what this meeting was about.

Born was already consistently moving large quantities. He had started out buying bricks of plain cook-up cocaine from Dorian at the low price of seventeen grand per brick. Born had made a lot of money this way, breaking it down and easily quadrupling his profit by selling it retail. He had two workers who split the day into two shifts—day and night. One hustled crack from sunrise to sunset and the other did the opposite. With their help, he was already making a killing on the streets of Shaolin. Now he wanted to diversify his drug sales from strictly retail dimes and twenties to wholesale as well, selling grams and ounces of cocaine to other dealers. If Dorian agreed to deal with him exclusively, in no time Born could be Staten Island's only kingpin. Soon he would have a better product than the competition, and he could really shut 'em down. By dealing with keys of fish scale Born was set to go from being a low-level hustler to a big-timer.

Dorian could see that the young man was ready to step his game up. Born was one of the few who were making big moves in Staten Island, and he had brought Dorian a lot of business already. The other dealers Dorian did business with in Staten Island weren't nearly as consistent as Born. It wouldn't be much of a loss at all for him to give Born the exclusivity he wanted. Dorian smiled at the young playa with as much heart as Dorian had had himself at that age. Now Born was about to get his hands on the goods, and his operation would take place on a much grander scale from this point forward. Dorian felt it could prove to be a mutually beneficial arrangement. Born mapped out his plan, explaining that for every key he got from Dorian, he would wholesale five hundred grams of it to other dealers, and retail five hundred grams of it, selling it in small quantities to the fiends. If the young hustler could continue to move as many bricks as he was moving, it would have been enough for Dorian. But here he was with a proposal to move even more! By tapping into this market, the white folks with the money to purchase large amounts, Born was setting a goal for himself of shutting down the borough and being on top at last. He was prepared to go block by block and get a bigger piece of the pie, while Dorian was determined not to take a loss.

Finally, after weighing the pros and cons of the situation, Dorian offered Born what he felt was an excellent price for the keys he needed: twenty-five thousand per brick. Born was pleased, and they shook on it. If this worked out, they could both be very wealthy men in a very short period of time.

Born wasn't excessively flashy, which Dorian admired. Jada, too, seemed like the type who wouldn't go looking for trouble. But Dorian could also tell by how well she got along with Sunny that Jada could probably brawl with the best of them if it came down to it. Sunny was not the type to get along with fake, phony, stuck-up bitches. And she sat there beside him, having a passionate conversation with Jada. Both men secretly felt that the closer the women they loved became, the better the chances of them continuing their lucrative business deal. The two men got along well, since Born had brought in a ton of money for Dorian in the time they'd been dealing with each other. Sunny and Jada becoming friends would only be an asset to their working relationship.

The women made small talk, discussing the latest entertainment industry gossip, and fashion. Jada listened, interested, as Sunny described a trip she and Dorian had taken to St. Bart's in the Caribbean. By the time the food arrived, the women were fast friends, and both Dorian and Born seemed pleased.

Everyone began to dig in. Born said a prayer before his meal, and dug in wholeheartedly. He didn't change around anybody, and Dorian and Sunny were no exception. Jada didn't even bother him about it, as he talked with his mouth full and didn't use his napkin often enough. She was too busy intently watching Sunny easily crack the lobster's shell using a small silver utensil that the waitress had given her, to reveal the most succulent, delicious-looking lobster Jada had ever seen. Sunny saw Jada coveting her food, and she broke off a piece and put it on Jada's plate. "Try it. You're staring so hard, I'm scared I might choke on it."

Jada laughed, and wondered why she liked this girl. Sunny looked like she belonged onstage, but what a mouth she had! Jada liked her straightforwardness, and by the end of the night, the ladies were arranging to meet for lunch the following weekend.

Jada thought Sunny exuded sophistication. She seemed like a woman who was used to having the finer things in life, and who would settle for nothing less than the best. Sunny liked Jada's style as well, and thought she was perfectly suited for Born. The two looked so cute together. They finished each other's sentences, and they looked at each other like there was nobody in the room but the two of them.

By that point in their relationship, Sunny and Dorian had lost that lovey-dovey feeling that exists in new relationships. She gave Dorian pussy when he gave her presents. They were still in love. But it wasn't like it had been when they were younger and just starting out. In the beginning, Dorian wasn't dealing with all of the pressure to stay on top. He used to pay attention to Sunny, and he spent just about every waking moment with her. But after a while he was always busy, always working. Still, they loved each other. But it wasn't fun and exciting anymore, as it appeared to still be for Jada and Born.

At the end of the night, the couples parted ways, and Jada and Born left the restaurant and went home to a night of straight sexual recklessness. They had a lot to celebrate. Born's rise to prominence was all but guaranteed now that his deal with Dorian had been finalized. After downing a whole bottle of Moët together, Born made her scream until the sun came up, and Jada wondered how she would be able to face the neighbors. It was the best time in their lives; they were so completely happy.

That weekend, Sunny called Jada and asked if she wanted to go shopping. Dorian was having a big party, and Born and Jada were invited to attend. This was the type of invitation one does not turn down, and Jada had no idea what she would wear. So Sunny's suggestion of a shopping spree was perfect, and Jada prepared to go find something fabulous to wear.

Sunny and Jada perused the racks in Saks, searching for white dresses. Dorian had finally taken Sunny's advice, and was throwing himself a birthday party. The theme was all white, and both women were determined to shine on the arms of the men they loved. It was May, and spring was in the air. They were both excited about what would definitely be Brooklyn's party of the season.

Sunny held up a silk charmeuse pleated dress. "Try this on," she said, and then turned back to the racks. Jada looked confused. Sunny looked around, sarcastically. "What the hell you looking at? Can't I help a sister out?"

Jada smiled, and snatched the outfit. "I don't think it's gonna look right. I can tell you that right now." Jada was always self-conscious about her scars being visible with a plunging neckline, and the garment Sunny had given her had very little fabric. But the fabric felt divine in Jada's hands.

"Just trust me, and try it on," Sunny coached. "I can see you in that. You need to show off a little more skin, girl!"

Jada looked again at Sunny's outfit that day, and could see how she might think Jada was overdressed. Sunny had on a pair of denim short shorts, which drew attention to the thickness of her thighs, coupled with a baby T and a pair of espadrilles. Her hair was pulled off her face. Jada smiled skeptically, and went to the dressing room, where she removed her jeans and tank top to try on the dress. She held up the dress that Sunny had given her, and looked at it. It was not the type of look that Jada would have gone for on her own, since she didn't want her scars to show. But she decided to try it on to see if Sunny was on to something. She pulled the silken fabric over her head and fastened the clasp at the nape of her neck. To her surprise, as flimsy as the dress was, it covered all her imperfections. She swirled around and noticed the way the fabric shimmered in the lighting of the dressing room. She smoothed the dress down over her butt and looked at her reflection in the mirror. The dress fell midthigh on her curvaceous frame. Looking at her reflection in the mirror, she couldn't believe her eyes. She looked absolutely breathtaking in the dress, and she turned sideways to get a better view. She loved it. The bottom of the dress hung sexily over her thighs and showed off her gorgeous skin tone. The top was awe-inspiring with its elaborate neckline, and Jada couldn't believe her eyes. She was momentarily entranced, until Sunny rudely banged on the dressing room door.

"Come on!" she yelled. "Stop stalling, and let me see. The shit can't be that bad."

Jada smiled, and pulled the dressing room door open. She stood in front of Sunny, and the other women milling around, and everyone gasped. Sunny smiled widely. "See? I told you this was the one. Stick with me, kid!" She punched Jada on the arm playfully. "You look *mahvelous!*"

Jada frowned, slightly unsure. "It's so short!" She turned and looked at the way the pleats accentuated her ass, falling only slightly below it.

Sunny laughed. "That's the point," she said.

A white woman with a classy short red haircut was standing close by. She looked at Jada, and agreed with Sunny. "Honey, with a body like that you should be wearing something even shorter." The woman winked and gave a thumbs-up, and Sunny smiled, approvingly. Sunny handed Jada a pair of white lace Manolo pumps, which Jada's petite feet slid into easily. She looked in the mirror and loved her look from head to toe. She felt like a star. Jada glanced at the price tag hanging from the dress, and shook her head. Sunny saw the look of alarm on Jada's face and patted her reassuringly. "Don't be afraid to spend the money they make," Sunny said. Jada looked at her. "You have to learn to enjoy the fruits of their labor, because otherwise, what's the point? You only live once."

Sunny pulled her own garments off the rack and went into the dressing room to try them on. Jada looked at her reflection in the mirror once more. She loved the outfit, and knew that Born's chin would hit the floor when he saw her in it. She thought to herself that Sunny had a point. You only live once.

The ladies purchased their pricey outfits, paying cash and loving the shocked looks on the faces of the white cashiers as they did so. As they left the store, Jada wondered what Born would think if she told him that she had just bought a five-hundred-dollar pair of shoes and a seven-hundred-dollar dress for one night. But then she thought about the thousands of dollars he spent on his beloved car and his own clothes and sneakers. Jada decided that like Sunny, she would feel no guilt.

Next Sunny and Jada went uptown to get their hair done. Sunny introduced Jada to her stylist—a man named Rae—who was so openly gay and unashamed of it that Jada loved him instantly. After much convincing, Jada added weave extensions to her already long hair, giving it extra volume and length for a much fuller, sexier look. Her hair hung in loose, curly, chocolate waves, and she loved it. Sunny had her short hair washed and the ends trimmed, and then blown straight. She added shoulder-length extensions, and had her eyelashes professionally enhanced. Her lashes were long and dramatic, drawing attention to her sexy eyes. Afterward, they went to lunch. And as they enjoyed their pizza, they got to know each other without their lovers being present.

"So, are you ready for all the pressure Born's gonna be under now?" Sunny asked.

Jada wasn't sure where that comment came from, as she ate her pizza. She didn't know how much Dorian had shared with Sunny about his arrangement with Born. She only knew what Born had told her. And she wondered if he would want her discussing his dealings with Sunny. But Jada thought about how encouraging Born had been when she told her that Sunny had invited her to lunch. He thought she needed friends, and Sunny was the perfect candidate. Jada chose her words carefully.

"I'm ready for whatever happens," she said. "I have to take what comes and just continue to play my position. I love Born, so that's all there is to it."

Sunny nodded. "Good answer, good answer." She said it with a hint of sarcasm, and she smiled. "I hear you. All I know is that it gets hard sometimes. It gets lonely at the top. Trust me."

Sunny's words sounded prophetic, and Jada nodded. She thought that maybe it wouldn't be perfect everyday. But at least the love between her and Born would get her through the bad days. Sunny turned the conversation in a new direction.

"Listen, Jada. Tonight is gonna be a big deal. All the biggest players in BK are gonna be there. But then all the gold-digging bitches will be there, too. We have got to be fierce tonight! There's no way I can have any of them broads outshining me at my man's party. Plus, I know his baby's mama will be there, and I want her to be sick when she sees me sitting next to Dorian looking gorgeous."

Jada frowned. She swallowed her food and took a sip of her soda. "I thought you've been with Dorian since you were seventeen," Jada said. "How does he have a baby with someone else?"

Sunny smirked, since Jada had obviously been paying attention. She liked that. "Dorian has always crept around from time to time. He's a good-looking man with a lot of money. Bitches throw themselves at Dorian, and I know that. One bitch caught him out there and had his son. It's okay, because he doesn't love her. He flaunts me in her face, and always makes it clear that I'm his number one. But the bitch is still like dirt under my nails. And tonight, I plan to make her squirm."

Jada smiled, and finished her meal. She had no idea just how true to her word Sunny would be.

21

PARTY OVER HERE

That night when Jada got home Born was already dressed for the party. Never one to get all *GQ* and dressed up, Born still looked good in a white Phat Farm shirt and matching shorts. He wore crisp white Nikes on his feet as he sat on the sofa. He greeted Jada, and told her that her hair looked nice. He couldn't stop staring at her at first, and his smile let her know that she looked as sexy as she felt. Then he resumed counting money, as he'd been doing when she arrived. Taking advantage of his distraction, Jada took all her bags with her and went to take a bath.

She pinned her hair up and ran the bathwater as hot as it could get. She enjoyed the solitude of the steamy bathroom as she luxuriated in the hot water. She washed up, then got out, dried off, and smoothed cocoa butter oil into her skin. Jada applied her makeup in the mirror with precision, and was pleased with the results. She slipped into a pair of sheer panties, and then slid her dress out of the garment bag hanging on the bathroom door. She took out her hair clip and fixed her hair, loving the way she looked. She slid her feet into the most beautiful shoes in the world, and emerged in search of her perfume.

Born saw her and immediately lost count. Jada looked absolutely breathtaking, as she stood there in front of him. He stood up, looked her over once more, and shook his head from side to side. "Goddamn! You look . . . goddamn!"

Jada smiled shyly, and turned around so that he could see her assets.

He smiled, and nodded his approval. Then he pulled her close, and kissed her and said, "You gonna fuck around and get pregnant wearing a dress like that around me."

Jada beamed at the thought of being pregnant with Born's baby. She could tell that he meant what he said, because he couldn't keep his hands to himself. He was feeling her all up under her little dress, and Jada giggled at his touch. "Come on, now," she purred, trying to resist the irresistible Born. "I have to finish getting ready."

Born looked at her, thinking she looked perfect. "You're ready now."

Jada shook her head, but he wouldn't let her loose. She was still giggling and trying to resist the urge to give in to what he was doing. Born grinned at her as he unbuckled his belt, all the while fiddling around in her panties. Jada couldn't control her giggles, because she couldn't believe Born really couldn't keep his hands off her! She could tell she wasn't going to get the chance to put on the finishing touches of her outfit. Born pulled her over to the wall and pressed her back against it. Jada stopped giggling but continued smiling at Born. He was grinning back at her as he pulled her leg up and propped it on his arm. Right there, standing against the living room wall, he put himself inside her, and Jada was in ecstasy. She clung to Born as he moved in and out, and her smile was replaced by a look of pure passion. He loved that look, her facial expressions when he hit it. He loved the way she responded to him, and he could tell that she was on the verge of a big one.

Jada looked helpless, almost coming, but not quite there yet. Born watched her, and he sexed her not too hard and not too soft.

"Say it," he demanded, smiling at her provocatively.

Jada was breathless. "I'm cummin'," she said in a passionate whisper. "I'm cummin', daddy."

He watched her face contort in pleasure, and once she exploded, so did he. Jada held on to him as she caught her breath.

He looked in her eyes and smiled. "I told you you were ready," he said. He pulled himself away from her, gently putting her leg back down.

Jada stood against the wall, out of breath and smiling from the thrill of the quickie. She walked into the bathroom to wash herself, and Born was hot on her trail. She said, "Damn, I must really look good in this dress."

Born laughed as they both stood in the bathroom cleaning up the pretty mess they'd made. "You just don't know," he said. "You look good enough to eat."

Jada smiled. "Bon appétit!" she joked.

Born laughed. "Sunny helped you pick that out?" he asked. "Took you to get your hair done and all that?"

"Yeah. She has good taste, as you can see. But wait until you see what *she's* wearing tonight." Jada shook her hand like it was hot, smiling naughtily, and Born shook his head.

He had mixed emotions about the influence that Sunny was having on Jada. True, she looked beautiful tonight. But Born was concerned that Sunny might encourage Jada to go too far. Born loved Jada, and he knew how impressionable she was. He didn't want Sunny, or anyone else, to get her caught up in a lifestyle that didn't suit her. "You look nice, Jada," he said. "But don't start dressing too—"

Jada cut him off with a kiss. "I'm not Sunny," she said. "I'm not gonna start dressing as sexy as she does *all* the time. Just tonight." Jada winked at him. "But, I like her. I think she might become a friend of mine." Jada looked Born in his eyes, trying to discern whether or not he approved. "Is that okay with you? I mean, do you mind, really?" Jada's question was sincere.

Born looked into those same pretty eyes that he'd been so mesmerized by the day they met. He was happy that Jada had found a chick she liked. She didn't have a lot of friends, since Shante was old news and Ava was away at school. Jada spent most of her time either with Born or home alone. Sunny might turn out to be exactly what Jada needed. And it didn't hurt that she was Dorian's wifey. He kissed her on the nose. "You be friends with whoever you want, baby girl. If you like Sunny, you hang out with Sunny." He looked at her seriously. "But don't lose yourself around nobody. Don't change. This is the Jada I love."

Jada looked at Born, understanding his warning and the hidden message. She understood his concern for what she might do when he wasn't around. Jada shook her head, and she said, "I'm not going back to where I was before for nobody or nothing in this world. You have my word on that."

He slapped her playfully on the ass, and smiled at her. She turned and looked at her reflection in the mirror. She touched up her lipstick, and put on her diamond hoop earrings, and the diamond tennis bracelet Born had given her. She turned back to face him. He was smiling in awe of her. "Damn, baby girl."

Jada smiled, grabbed her small clutch, and pulled him toward the door. "Let's get to the party before I get pregnant."

Born laughed as she led him out the door.

He was amazed that he was on the verge of walking into Dorian's party—the crème de la crème of events—with a woman as fine as Jada on his arm. On the way there, he thought about how far he'd come. He thought about his boys, and about how they would probably never get the opportunity to rub elbows with hustlers of Dorian's caliber. He was a major player now, with more money in the streets than he'd ever had before. Born realized that leaving his old crew behind had been one of his smartest moves to date. Because now he was on his way to an exclusive event filled with VIPs while his niggas were still holding down the block.

When they arrived at the brownstone tucked among the homes of some of the borough's premier black families, the party was already in full swing. This wasn't Dorian's house, but one an "associate" had let him use for the event. The music could be heard outdoors, as the partygoers reveled and danced. Born parked his car and escorted Jada past men who couldn't help but stare at her. Her legs glowed as she stepped in her sexy heels past all of them. But their stares didn't offend Born. He knew that she was beautiful, and he smiled because she was all his.

At the door, two tall burly brothers stood in silence. Born stepped forward and spoke into one man's ear. At once the man nodded to his partner, and the two parted, allowing Born and Jada to pass. They went inside, and scanned the room for the guest of honor. The crowd was all dressed in white, and everyone had put on their very finest. It was a magnificent scene. Sexy waitresses worked the room wearing short white cocktail dresses and little else. They served Cristal from flutes they balanced on trays. Born and Jada both grabbed a glass as they made their way through the crowd, swaying to the sound of Biggie's "Who Shot Ya."

They found Dorian standing in a sea of men in white. He saw Born and his face lit up, as he ushered him and Jada into his circle of friends. There were introductions galore, and Jada tried to remember names and faces. They made themselves comfortable, Born sitting on the sofa beside Dorian and Jada perched on the arm of the sofa next to Born. They sipped champagne and listened to the music, as Dorian and Born talked and laughed. Jada listened quietly as Dorian told Born who various individuals were throughout the room. She could tell that these were important people. She scanned the crowd, checking out the other women in the room and what they were wearing. She saw some cute dresses, a few nice pairs of shoes. Jada was admiring all the beautiful people in designer clothes. But she was surprised to see a couple of the women looking at her in a nasty way, as if they were jealous. She didn't know if it was because she was with Born or if it was because she looked as stunning as she did. But she didn't care. She smiled at them, as if to say, "Hate, bitches."

Then Dorian pointed across the room with a huge smile on his face. "And there is the person everybody *really* came to see." Dorian watched proudly as Sunny walked in wearing a long, white, crocheted Roberto Cavalli dress with peek-a-boo holes throughout. Strips of fabric beneath the stitching concealed her breasts, but the dress left little else to the imagination. Her entire back was out, and it showed off her midriff. The dress clung to the top of her large ass for dear life. Every eye in the room was on that dress. It was a lovely accessory for her perfect body, and Dorian beamed with pride. Sunny's eyelashes fluttered long and false, but absolutely lovely on her pretty face. From a distance, she looked like an angel.

"This is her night," he said, as she walked over to them. "I'm just the man lucky enough to be by her side." Dorian literally couldn't take his eyes off of her, as Sunny walked over to their corner, stopping along the way to greet a few partygoers. When she finally made her way to the group, everyone greeted Sunny enthusiastically. Sunny kissed Dorian long and deep, and then she wiped her lipstick off his mouth.

Jada was sitting next to Born with her golden legs crossed, and she watched Born's reaction. He, like every other heterosexual man in the room, looked at Sunny from head to toe. But then, without looking directly at Jada, he reached over and took her hand in his. She smiled, comforted by Born's show of affection as she took in Sunny's flawless appearance. "Hey, diva. You look good!" Jada smiled from ear to ear.

Sunny returned the gesture, and took Jada by the hand. "Thanks, girl. You, too. Now, come with me so I can show you off a little. Born wants to keep you all to himself tonight, but I'm not having it!" Born nodded and watched as Jada followed Sunny through the crowd.

Sunny led Jada through the throngs of people, stopping along the way to introduce her to a couple of them. All the while they felt the heat from the stares of some of the women scattered throughout the party. Sunny seemed immune to it all. She was used to bullshit like that. She led Jada to another large room, where people sat around on leather sofas mingling and laughing. They stopped in that room and danced for a while, drawing the attention of everyone in the room. There were lots of beautiful women at the party, but Sunny and Jada were the belles of the ball. After about an hour, Sunny led Jada upstairs to the section of the house that was off-limits to most of the guests. Only Dorian and his immediate circle were up there. Born was with them, and Sunny led Jada into the VIP section of the party.

The smell of weed smoke wafted throughout the whole top floor. Jada saw Born pass a blunt to Dorian, and Dorian took it and inhaled. Born breathed out the smoke as Jada caught his eye and walked over with Sunny in tow. Sunny walked right up to Dorian and took the blunt from his hands. She puffed on it deeply, and Dorian shook his head, jokingly.

Born pulled Jada onto his lap, and she looked into his bloodshot eyes. He smiled at her, and kissed her softly on the lips. "Wassup, pretty girl? You having fun?"

Jada smiled back at Born, who looked as high as a kite. She had only seen him smoke weed on two occasions, and she knew that he was twisted. She nodded. "Yeah. But not as much fun as you."

Sunny passed her the blunt. "Here, girl," she said.

Jada looked at the blunt in Sunny's outstretched hand, and then looked at Born. Her expression was a puzzled one as she looked to him for direction. She hadn't done drugs of any kind since she left rehab, and she didn't know whether to take the blunt or not. He sensed this, and nodded his approval. *It's just weed*, he thought to himself. *How bad could it be?* "Go ahead," he said. "I got you."

Jada puffed on the cigar filled with haze, and slowly felt her mind grow fuzzy. They passed it back and forth between the four of them until it was gone. Then Sunny took Jada by the hand once more, leaving Dorian and Born to twist another one. She led Jada back downstairs, and they rejoined the party, feeling great.

Sunny sipped her champagne and looked at Jada.

"The bitch right there in the white leather dress is Dorian's son's mother." Sunny pointed her chin discreetly at a short, slim, dark-skinned black woman standing with a group of four other females. Jada looked at the woman without being too obvious, as she sipped her drink. She saw that the woman was very pretty, with a smooth chocolate complexion and a fabulous short haircut. She looked in Sunny and Jada's direction, and she whispered to her friends. Soon all the women were looking at them. Sunny noticed, and she raised her glass as if proposing a toast. Dorian's ex returned the gesture, but the look on her face said something totally different. Sunny smiled, and said through clenched teeth, "Yeah. That's the ho." She turned to Jada. "Her name is Raquel. She's the worst excuse for a woman. Always trying to use her son as leverage against Dorian." Sunny shook her head. "She can't get over the fact that I'm the one he wants, and not her. Granted, he cheated on me with her." Sunny rolled her eyes, obviously annoyed by the fact. "But that shit wasn't nothing. She just got lucky and got pregnant. But the bitch found out the hard way that he didn't want her like that. Now, whenever she can she tries to get Dorian to pay attention to her. But she uses their little boy as a pawn." Jada could tell that Sunny had hate in her heart for the pretty young woman standing across the room.

Jada nodded. "Well, they must get along pretty good, since she came to his party." To her, it sounded like Dorian was having his cake and eating it, too.

Sunny rolled her eyes. "Please! She only came so that she can try and front to her friends. She knows that Dorian is that nigga, and she likes to act like she's somebody because he's her son's father. But that don't make her nobody. I can't stand that bitch."

Sunny drained her glass and placed it on a nearby table before she and Jada left that room and went into another part of the large house. The deejay played Jay Z's "Ain't No Nigga," and soon everybody in the place was dancing. Sunny and Jada two-stepped in their sexy dresses, getting the attention of all the men standing nearby. Some of the women were so jealous that it was evident by the looks on their faces. None of them dared say a word, though. The men all paused, but none approached Sunny, since they knew that she was Dorian's wifey, and flirting with her would mean beef with D and his crew. No one wanted that. But Jada was someone they hadn't seen before. And she was looking sexy as hell, swaying to the beat. She felt all eyes on her, and Jada wasn't the least bit uncomfortable. She kept right on dancing and enjoying herself, feeling a buzz from the mix of marijuana and champagne. She felt arms encircle her waist, and she tensed up, figuring that some nigga must have gotten carried away. Somebody must have grown tired of watching and decided to try and dance with her. She turned around, prepared to nicely decline the dance, but found Born standing there.

Jada smiled, and put her arms around his neck and danced with her man. Born looked at her and smiled back, knowing that he was the envy of just about every man in the room at that moment. "You missed me?" she asked.

Born didn't tell her how he'd noticed all the men staring at her body as she danced. He didn't tell her about the whispers he'd heard throughout the party about "that bad bitch that Sunny is walking around with." But he smiled instead, and said, "Yeah. I did."

Jada kissed him, and was oblivious to all the other people at the party. To Jada, it was just her and her man.

Meanwhile, Sunny wandered off to find Dorian. She went back into the room where Raquel and her friends were lingering. Dorian was in there, in a corner talking with a few of his boys. Sunny stopped to talk to a girl named Olivia, whose brother Lamin and Dorian had done business together, and over the years they had formed a close working relationship. They were often guests at each other's parties, and his sister Olivia was a girl Sunny considered a friend. Sunny didn't have many friends, and it wasn't a term that she threw around loosely. She knew many people, but she had very few friends. Olivia's brother Lamin was doing big things in the music industry, parlaying his street money into legitimate money. This was precisely what Sunny was trying to persuade Dorian to do. She wished he would listen, but Dorian knew one thing and one thing only: the game.

Olivia was telling Sunny something about a music video shoot, and Sunny's ears perked up at the idea of lights, cameras, and attention. Sunny had always loved the spotlight, and craved it, but she had never pursued a career in entertainment. Her looks were exotic enough to model or act, but Sunny had never tried to do either of those things. Her mother was Puerto Rican and her father was black. And unlike most of her peers, Sunny's parents were still happily married and living a cozy working, middle-class lifestyle. Sunny was the baby of the family, and the only girl. She had two older brothers who had hovered over her until Dorian came through and shut them down.

Dorian was five years older than her, and a hustler through and through. When she met him, she was seventeen years old and stunning. He met her one day when he was shopping in Brooklyn's Kings Plaza mall. She was at the jewelry counter looking at a bracelet, and he came up from behind and swept her off her feet. Dorian was tall and had a very commanding presence. His walk was heavy, his voice almost hypnotic. Dorian impressed Sunny and her family with his wealth and his status. Knowing that she was so much younger, and that her family was overprotective, Dorian wined and dined Sunny. He lavished her with gifts and lavished her family as well. And he courted her with respect. On her eighteenth birthday, he slept with her for the first time. She had been with him ever since, by his side through thick and thin. The elder of her brothers worked for Dorian now, and it was a family affair. She was happy with him, but always wondered what she could do to get her own money, her own acclaim. So as Olivia filled her in on the details of the upcoming video shoot, Sunny hung on her every word. That is, until she saw Raquel heading toward Dorian.

Born and Jada entered the room just as Raquel approached Dorian's side. The deejay switched to reggae, and the crowd began to couple off. Born pulled Jada close and danced with her. Sunny looked over Olivia's shoulder and saw Raquel standing in front of Dorian, grinding her ass on him. Sunny calmly excused herself from Olivia and walked across the room. Jada was still tipsy, and loving the feeling of swaying to the music with Born. She was oblivious. But Born saw what was about to go down, and he watched it all unfold.

Raquel was obviously drunk, and Dorian stood still as she gyrated in front of him. He had a smile on his face, and his boys standing close by had smirks on their faces at this display. Raquel was tossing that ass at Dorian, making him stand back and take notice. Everybody was watching. But then they saw Sunny approach. Everyone knew that Sunny was Dorian's lady. And everyone knew that Sunny was no joke. Sunny was glamorous and sexy, but no one should be fooled. She would pull out her earrings and bust somebody's ass in a heartbeat. Raquel continued grinding on Dorian, until Sunny came and stood right in Raquel's face. The two women stood eye to eye, and everybody waited to see what would happen.

Raquel stood and looked at Sunny. She stopped dancing and smiled at her, innocently. "What's the matter, Sunny? It's only a dance."

"Step aside." Sunny said it calmly. "Before you get embarrassed in here."

Raquel's friends walked over and waited to see what would happen next. They stood with their arms folded across their chests, as if they were ready to defend their girl at the drop of a dime. Sunny's friend

Olivia walked over and stood behind her with an expression on her face that showed she wasn't playing. Olivia was no joke either, and Sunny knew she was always strapped and would have her back. Sunny stood with her hands on her hips, and Raquel laughed.

"Sunny, you can't tell me who I can dance with. This is my son's father, sweetheart. If I want to dance with him, I'm gonna do that. You shouldn't be so insecure." Raquel laughed again, and continued winding her hips seductively in front of Dorian.

Seeing that this was about to escalate, Dorian slipped away from her and stood close to Sunny. He kissed her on the cheek, trying to diffuse the situation. He saw everyone looking at the three of them, and he didn't want there to be a big scene. Sunny didn't flip. She took Dorian's hand and began to wind in front of him with so much seduction that he was visibly shocked. Sunny had his undivided attention as she slowly twisted and wound her hips erotically. And her body looked way better than Raquel's as she moved in slow motion. Her movements were so seductive that she looked like a professional exotic dancer as she moved. Every single eye in the room was on Sunny, as she danced for her man. It seemed like this was a private moment, and she was performing for his sole pleasure. Dorian smiled, with a woody in his pants. Sunny smiled back, with her hands in the air and her hips moving like a belly dancer, while Raquel boiled on the sidelines.

Jada grinned, as she watched Sunny's performance and the look on Raquel's face. Everyone had expected Sunny to hit the woman, but instead she was making her look stupid. The grin on Dorian's face said it all, as he watched his princess dance for him. Raquel's friends came close and whispered to her with their eyes glued on Sunny. Sunny took note of all of it, and continued to hold Dorian's gaze. He came closer to her and put his hands on her big ass as they danced. It appeared that there was no other woman in the room but Sunny, as Dorian danced with her. Raquel fumed in silence until the deejay finally switched back to rap music. Sunny kissed Dorian deeply and he held her close. She looked at Raquel, who was still standing nearby scowling, and she walked over to her.

"Raquel, you don't need to remind me that he's your son's father. I know that. In fact, little Dorian, Jr., is like my own child. When he's over our house, I treat him like the little prince that he is. And he loves me." Sunny's smile was antagonistic, and she could tell that she was getting to Raquel. Raquel's own cynical smile had long ago faded from her face and had been replaced by an angry scowl, her lips set in a firm line. Sunny knew she had her furious. "So this ain't about little D.J. This is about you coming in here laying your ass on my man. Don't get fucked up."

Raquel twisted her neck in typical black girl fashion. "Bitch, who's gonna fuck me up?" Raquel was drunk, and it showed in her delivery. She was loud, and all heads turned to them once more. Her words were slurred, and she was leaning a little past six. "Sunny, ain't nobody scared of you!"

Without any further warning, Sunny backslapped Raquel so hard that she fell backward, and stumbled over a stool behind her. She tumbled onto the floor with so much force that her dress tore. Raquel heard all the laughter and gasping from the crowd around her, and she quickly sprang to her feet. Her girlfriends rushed in to help her get up. Dorian grabbed Raquel by the arm and blocked Sunny from going after her again. But Sunny was finished. She hadn't even broken a sweat, and she stood there smiling at Raquel. "You don't have to be scared in order to get hurt. Remember that." Sunny ignored Raquel's cussing and yelling, and she looked at Dorian and said, "Send her home now."

Sunny turned around and started to walk away. But then she turned back to Raquel, who was still cussing at her, and said, "Oh, and one more thing, bitch. You're not woman enough to make me feel insecure. You're a ho. You fucked around on Dorian. That's why he left you. That's why he fucked your girl CeCe over there while you were pregnant." Sunny nodded toward one of Raquel's friends behind her.

The look on Raquel's face was priceless, as her drunken gaze fell from her friend to Dorian and back again. It was obvious that this information was new to Raquel, and she looked betrayed. Everyone wondered if Sunny was making it up. Would Sunny stay with Dorian knowing that he had not only fucked around on her with Raquel, but also with Raquel's friend? Everybody wondered. But the look on Dorian's face suggested it was factual. Raquel looked like she wanted to be sick. Sunny walked away with Olivia, and found Jada and Born along the way. They all laughed together, as Dorian escorted drunken Raquel outside.

Born shook his head and laughed as Sunny and Jada cackled over the episode that had just unfolded. "Yo, you played her," Born said, as Sunny shook with laughter. "She was heated."

Sunny shrugged her shoulders. "She shouldn't fuck with me, then."

Dorian put Raquel and her crew in a car with one of his boys and sent her home. She was furious, and he knew she would be a headache later on. But right now he was focused on Sunny. He loved her style, loved the fact that she wouldn't hesitate to pimp slap a bitch even in a dress as sexy as the one she was wearing. He considered himself lucky to have Sunny, and he was grateful that she had stuck around even after he got Raquel pregnant. Sunny owned his heart, regardless of the other women he may have spent time with. When Sunny found out that he had cheated on her with Raquel, she was devastated. Money or no money, she had been prepared to leave him.

When she was pregnant, Raquel had made a point of showing up on Dorian's doorstep with her belly bulging, demanding that Sunny hear her out. Sunny was distraught, and she left Dorian's house and moved back in with her parents. But Dorian went over there every day and begged her to hear him out. When she finally agreed, he sat her down and told her the complete truth. He admitted cheating on Sunny, just for the thrill of new pussy. He told her that during the time he was sleeping with her, Raquel was secretly messing around with someone else. So when she popped up pregnant, he was skeptical at first. He told Sunny that he wasn't even sure it was his baby. He would wait, he said, until the child was born, and have a blood test done. If it was his child, he would care for him or her. But it was over with Raquel. He swore to Sunny. She wasn't trying to hear Dorian, though. Sunny refused to take him back.

Dorian was so upset with Raquel for blowing up his spot that he seduced her gullible friend for the fun of it. He had even been so disrespectful as to hold phone conversations with Raquel while her friend CeCe was giving him head. CeCe had no problem playing her so-called friend by fucking her baby's daddy behind her back. She was happy to be the object of Dorian's desire for once. For him, it was his payback. Raquel had cost him the love of his life. When Dorian, Jr., was born, Dorian got a blood test to prove paternity. But none was needed. D.J. was a darker-skinned version of his father. It was no question.

To win Sunny back, Dorian came clean and told Sunny all about his escapades. He even told her about CeCe to illustrate just how little respect he had for Raquel, let alone love. Eventually his persistence paid off, and Sunny took him back. Dorian considered himself blessed. She was the type of woman that you only come across once in life, if you're lucky enough. Never had he met a woman who he could be completely real with. Sunny, in turn, respected Dorian's honesty and how he took care of her. She wasn't about to let another bitch have her spot, even if it meant that she had to accept Dorian's philandering ways.

He walked over to Sunny and looked at her with a big smile plastered on his face, as Born and Jada looked on. "Why you had to send that girl sailing across the floor like that?" Everyone erupted in laughter at Raquel's expense, and Sunny shrugged her shoulders.

"Tell her to stop trying me. You would think she'd have learned her lesson by now." This was certainly not the first confrontation between Sunny and Raquel. It would likely not be their last, either.

Dorian held Sunny's waist, and shook his head. "Listen, I got some friends of mine who just got here, and I want to introduce Born to them. You stay out of trouble." He looked at Sunny and Jada and back again. Both women smiled innocently, and nodded. Dorian and Born both laughed as they walked away. Jada and Sunny talked over drinks and recounted what had just happened. It was the beginning of a beautiful friendship.

The party went on without further incident. Everyone danced and drank and enjoyed themselves until the wee hours of the morning. It had been a good night for business, and Born had been introduced to quite a lot of valuable connections thanks to Dorian. All night, Born drank his usual Hennessy, and by 3:00 A.M., he was twisted. But true to form he maintained his composure enough to stand straight and walk right. Jada took the keys, grateful for the chance to drive Born's precious Benz. The two of them walked hand-in-hand toward the door, where Sunny stood beside Dorian saying good night to all their guests. Not many were left. It was late, and few remained, as the deejay packed up and prepared to leave. They bid the guest of honor farewell, wishing Dorian a happy birthday.

Sunny walked Jada to the end of the walkway, promising to call her later in the week. Sunny looked at Born, who was evidently tipsy, and smiled. "I'm glad y'all had a good time." Jada laughed, and they turned to leave.

As they made it to Born's car, parked across the street from the brownstone, Jada noticed a black Lexus pull up slowly in front of the house. Sunny's back was turned as she sauntered slowly back toward the house, where Dorian stood in the doorway. It seemed like Sunny's feet were hurting after a long night, judging from how she was walking. Suddenly, the Lexus screeched to a halt and gunfire rang out through the passenger side window. The silence of the prestigious upper-crust neighborhood was shattered by the sound of bullets being fired.

Strangely, Sunny seemed to be the target, and she took off running like a trained sprinter—heels and all. She ran toward the house, as the shooter fired more rounds into the night sky. The person shooting was yelling, and Jada only half heard what they said, as she watched Dorian run toward Sunny to shield her.

"You fuckin' *bitch*! You thought that shit was over? You ain't gotta be *scared* to get hurt, right?" The shooter let off two more shots. The sound of tires screeching filled the night.

Raquel? Jada was in shock, and Born was instantly sober. Born jumped out of the car and pulled his gun, just as the Lexus sped away.

Sunny had managed to make it to the front door and into Dorian's arms. Jada and Born ran back toward the brownstone to see if she had been hit, and as they reached the doorway they saw Dorian's men finally coming to shut shit down. Their guns were drawn as they ushered Born and Jada back inside.

The deejay was hiding behind one of the sofas. The ten or fifteen guests still lingering were traumatized as well. But Dorian's only concern was Sunny, and ensuring that she was unharmed by the hail of bullets.

Sunny was shaking and crying, and her tough-girl image was momentarily forgotten. She was vulnerable and scared, and Dorian comforted her, gently. "Shhh," he told her as he held her in his arms. "Okay." He consoled her, as the room remained otherwise silent.

"That bitch was trying to kill me," Sunny cried.

"I'll take care of it, Sunny. She was shooting straight up in the air, she wasn't aiming at you—"

"Fuck that shit, D!" Sunny stood, fists balled at her side, ready to fight. Her hair was tousled, her mascara was running, and her dress revealed more than it was supposed to. Sunny's anger was obvious, as her voice echoed off the brownstone walls. "What are you, fuckin' defending her?!" Sunny was outraged.

"I ain't defending nobody, Sunny! I'm gonna handle it. She's fuckin' buggin'." Dorian was obviously frustrated.

"That's your damn fault! You never should have let her come here. The bitch tried to kill me!" Sunny yelled.

Dorian tried to embrace her, and she stepped away from him. Everyone in the room felt like they were witnessing a private moment that they shouldn't be watching. But no one knew what to say or whether to get involved. Sunny was in tears. "I hate you!" she yelled, sobbing.

Born nudged Jada. "Take her upstairs to calm down."

Dorian turned and looked at Jada, as if he thought this was a good idea, and Jada stepped forward.

Sunny held up her hand. "I don't want to stay here. I want to get the fuck out of this house."

Dorian shook his head. "Not yet. Listen to me—"

"Fuck that, Dorian!"

Jada stepped forward. "Sunny." She looked into the frightened eyes of her newfound friend. "Come pull yourself together before you leave."

Sunny began to cry once again, realizing that she must look like shit in front of all these people. That was a tragedy in and of itself, because Sunny made it a point to *always* look her very best. She couldn't believe that Raquel was crazy enough to shoot at her, and she was furious. She was embarrassed.

Jada took her hand, and led her reluctantly up the stairs. They went in to a large marble-tiled bathroom, and Sunny sat on the toilet and cried her eyes out. Jada comforted her from a distance, handing her tissues and telling her that she understood how shaken Sunny was. Jada waited until Sunny was calm enough to talk, after several minutes. Finally, Sunny began to make sense.

"The bitch hates me. She hates me because Dorian doesn't want her. He made his choice. It's not enough that she has the kid. She has to flaunt it in my face because she knows I can't have any." Sunny cried more as she said this, and Jada's heart broke for the poor woman. She had no idea that Sunny was unable to have children.

"I'm sorry," she said. "How many times did you try to have a baby?"

Sunny sniffled. "I've been pregnant twice, and both times I lost the baby in my fourth month. Both boys." Sunny's eyes welled up again. "I have trouble holding the pregnancy into the second trimester. And I want a baby. I want to have his baby so bad." Sunny looked in the air, wistfully. "It would make everything perfect. But I can't give him that. And she can."

Jada listened sympathetically. "How old is his son?"

"He's three. And he's so adorable." Sunny smiled at the thought of Dorian's son, and her love for him was obvious. "I love D.J. But she rubs it in my face that he's not my son. She reminds me every chance she gets. After I lost the second baby, she came over and brought me baby clothes. I had just come home from the hospital after having the miscarriage. The bitch came by our house and gave me clothes for the baby, telling me that she figured she'd give them to me anyway, in case I wanted to try again. I wanted to kill that bitch."

Jada shook her head, finding it hard to imagine having to deal with a woman who could be so cruel and so crazy. "Well, she's insane. She's just jealous of you, and that's the only thing she knows will hurt you. Don't let her see you sweat."

Sunny sighed. "I don't want to let her have the satisfaction of knowing that it bothers me so much. I try to act like it's no big deal. But now she fuckin' shot at me, and I'm supposed to just keep being with Dorian? What kind of shit is that for me to have to deal with?"

Jada didn't know what to say. She didn't want to bad-mouth Dorian, yet she knew that if a bitch was shooting at her over a man, she would be gone. It sounded to Jada as if Dorian was having his way with both women. But she didn't say that. Instead she said, "You know he loves you. He obviously doesn't love her. Keep your head, and go home with Dorian so he can handle this. He has to take care of it, because he told you he would. Just wait and see what he does."

Jada handed Sunny a wet paper towel, and Sunny pulled herself to her feet and wiped the makeup off her face. Looking at their reflections in the mirror, Sunny smiled at Jada. "Thank you. I owe you for this."

"Nah. You don't owe me nothing. That's what friends are for." Jada smiled, and the two of them headed downstairs.

Dorian waited at the bottom of the stairs trying to read the expression on Sunny's face. Jada, meanwhile, made eye contact with Born, and her eyes looked sad. He watched her make her descent, wondering if she had been able to calm Sunny down. Dorian took Sunny by the hand and pulled her toward him gently. She didn't resist, and he kissed her lightly.

"She won't get away with this, Sunny. I promise, okay? Trust me." Dorian looked for Sunny's acknowledgment, but none came as she stared back at him blankly.

Born took Jada by the hand, and they quietly made their exit, anxious to get home after what had been a night they wouldn't forget.

22

BIRDS OF A FEATHER

Summer 1996

Dorian and Born did big business together, and their cash flow increased steadily as time went by. Born started his takeover of Shaolin's slums, as well as of its cul-de-sacs. He made deliveries all over the borough, and he had smoke houses set up in three sections of the island as well.

His childhood crew began to crumble into even smaller pieces. Martin was arrested for attempted murder after a robbery went wrong. His victim survived four gunshot wounds, and was prepared to testify. Martin copped a plea, rather than take it to trial unnecessarily. It broke Born's heart to learn that his boy was forced to serve a sentence of eight to ten years in prison. But Martin had lived his life with recklessness, and he was paying a heavy penalty. Born made sure he sent his boy money every chance he got, and wrote him letters to keep his spirits up. He knew that Martin was sick about being so far from home.

Born, meanwhile, was getting money like never before, and he was still unafraid of stepping on other people's toes. He had a spot in Stapleton, and that was lucrative for him. But Born wanted work in Park Hill as well. He went to see what was what, and he rode through there in his Benz one Friday night. He wasn't disappointed. All of Targee Street was lined with young workers grinding, trying to make a dollar out of fifteen cents.

Born pulled up at the gas station, and went inside the PLO store, an establishment nicknamed as such because it was run by Palestinian men. Born got a bottled water and came back outside. He noticed a young high-school-age kid standing nearby, and surmised that he was working for somebody. He came to this conclusion by sizing up the young man's sneakers, his lack of jewelry, and the late hour at which he stood alone on the block. Born had done his homework about Park Hill's drug scene, so he had an idea of who was getting money with whom. Born sipped his water and walked closer to the kid.

"A, yo," Born called out. The kid turned in his direction. "How much you getting standing out here for niggas?"

"What?" The young stranger looked at Born like he was crazy. "Yo, I don't know you." Born shrugged. "I just asked you a question," he said. "I already know you probably working for either Roy or Wizz. I know who's getting money in the hill." Born could tell by the look on the kid's face that he was on the right track, so he continued. "Anyway, what they giving you? Thirty off a hundred?"

Knowing this wasn't a bad deal that he was getting, the kid confidently nodded his head. "Yup. You can't beat that shit."

Born smirked. "Yes, I can. Fuck with me, instead, and I'll give you forty off every hundred. Plus, I can make sure you get more custys dealing with me. It's dead as a muthafucka out here tonight. And it's too cold to be standing out here for nothing."

Born saw the look on the young man's face, and he waited for his response. "What's your name?" the kid asked.

"Born." He handed the light-skinned kid a piece of paper with his cell phone number on it. "Call me when you're ready to start getting paid."

"Aiight." The kid took the number, looking around to make sure that Wizz wasn't lurking anywhere. He was definitely going to call this guy to see if he was serious. He'd seen Born before, at parties in the borough. Staten Island was so small that parties were like minireunions. You saw the same faces, the same people. And Born's face was one that this kid had seen before. He tucked the number in his pocket, and watched Born turn to walk back to his Benz.

"Yo," the kid called after him, just as he got to his car door and opened it. Born turned around.

"My name is Tommy."

Born nodded, and climbed inside his ride. Tommy called him a week later, and he was working for Born from then on. Things seemed to be going well, and Born was glad to be tapping into a whole new set of customers in the hill. Months went by, and he had a nice thing going with his small empire. He saw a familiar number on his pager one day, and he called it back. This call wasn't at all what he expected.

"Somebody paged me from this number," Born said.

"Yo, who this?" the caller asked.

Born laughed. "Who did you page?" The nerve of this nigga, whoever he was, to be asking who he was.

"Okay. I see you got your tough-guy stance right now. No problem, I'll get right to the point. I don't like niggas stealing food off my plate, Born. I wanna talk to you, next time you come to Park Hill."

"Who is this?" Born asked, intrigued that someone would be bold enough to call him like this.

"This that nigga Wizz. You know who I am. I wanna holla at you about your hiring practices."

Born smirked. "Okay. So where you want me to come check you at?"

The caller chuckled. "I'll come to you. Don't worry."

The line went dead, and Born found himself laughing at the audacity of Wizz to approach him like this. He wasn't worried about it, though. Wizz was a mean-faced bully from Park Hill who felt like no one should be allowed to get money out there except him. Born wasn't the type to let anyone tell him where he could get money. So he hung up the phone and didn't change one thing that he was doing. He kept his operation running, kept Jada smiling, and he stayed on his job. But when he went to Park Hill on a Friday night to see Tommy, things took a dramatic turn. As soon as he arrived, he saw Tommy. He pulled up alongside him, and Tommy looked at Born, blankly.

"Yo, Born, Wizz wanna talk to you." He stood with his hands in his pockets, and Born could tell that Tommy was shaken.

Born smirked, slightly, and scanned the block with his eyes. This character Wizz had the nerve to send for him. Who did this guy think he was? "Where he at?"

Tommy nodded toward the building he was standing in front of. "Upstairs at Nicole's house."

"Aiight." Born double-parked his car, and headed to the apartment inside of building number 185. Tommy stayed there on the third floor with his sister, Nicole. Born knocked on the apartment door, and waited for her to answer it. He was no stranger to this apartment, since he always went there to collect his dough after the cash rolled in around the first and fifteenth of every month. But when Tommy's sister came to the door on this day, Born should have been able to tell by the look on her face that something was amiss. The young lady looked visibly nervous, and she didn't look him directly in the eyes. She told Born that Wizz was in the kitchen, and Born went toward where she pointed.

When he entered the kitchen, he saw Wizz seated at the table with Roy and three other goons. There was a shotgun placed precariously on the table, and Wizz sat, his eyes focused on Born with a deadly stare. His eyes were narrowed, and his expression was no-nonsense. Instinctively, Born reached for his gun on his hip.

"Unh, unh, unh," Wizz warned. "Don't do that. I just wanna talk to you." He put his hands up to show that they were empty, and he held Born's gaze.

Born stood there, knowing that he could get to his gun if he went for it. But he was outnumbered, and he stood his ground waiting to see what would happen. He appreciated the intimidation factors they tried to utilize, and laughed on the inside.

"Come on, Born." Wizz had a sinister smile on his face. "You know you can't get no money out here. This is me and Roy out here. You can't come stealing our workers and thinking everything is okay." He shook his head. "You must really want war. You coming out here, snatching up our customers with cheaper prices than ours, stealing our employees with better percentages. That shit ain't right. That's not good for business. We don't come out to where you live and set up shop, steal your workers. Show us the same respect."

Born stood with the slightest grin on his face. He was nervous, quiet as he kept it. Wizz had him cornered, and Born was alone. But he stood defiantly, saying nothing.

"I hope you understand this shit ain't personal. It's not that we don't like you, knawmean? Not that we don't admire what you're trying to do. We see you making big moves, locking shit down. But not out here. This here is ours. And I'm only gonna tell you this once."

The shotgun still lay menacingly in front of him, so Born bit his tongue. "Aiight."

Wizz nodded. "Good. I knew you seemed like a smart guy. Now get on outta here. Thanks for coming by."

Born considered reaching for his gun once more, but thought better of it. Wizz had the upper hand this time. But even though he hadn't expected the situation to unfold like it had, Born had known that this moment would come eventually. It took a lot of attitude, and a lot of character, to go to a neighborhood and set up shop, with no crew behind you. Born had known it was just a matter of time before somebody got up the courage to challenge him face-to-face. With Wizz laughing at him as he turned his back, Born walked cautiously from the apartment and got back inside his car. Tommy was nowhere in sight by then.

Born went home that night, and he was visibly distracted. Jada could tell that he was stressed-out about something, but she had no idea what it was. He didn't talk about it, but inside he was furious that Wizz had confronted him like he had. Born wondered if the hood had forgotten who he was—whose son he was, and what that meant.

As angry as he was, Born knew that he couldn't single-handedly go to war with a whole neighborhood. He called Dorian and explained the situation, telling him that he wasn't going to just roll over and play dead while Wizz got all the Park Hill clientele. Dorian listened closely as Born explained what had happened, and his outrage about it. Dorian advised his friend to lay low, and to stay out of Park Hill for the time being. He had a plan that would take care of Wizz and his crew, and get Born the turf he wanted so badly.

The summer passed, with Wizz continuing to lock down the hill, and being the neighborhood bully. The whole time Born was putting a plan in motion with Dorian's help, planting seeds that would bloom sooner than Wizz ever expected. All season long, Born put in double the hours, double the work to build himself up with Dorian's guidance. It took a lot of work, a lot of grinding to get what he wanted, and he found himself spending less time with Jada and more time in the streets. While they had once been inseparable, Born was now busily setting up his empire and leaving Jada to find her own stimulation. Dorian was becoming his mentor. Born was a young twenty-four-year-old, and Dorian a more mature thirty-year-old who had been there and done that. He took Born under his wing, and showed him how to shut shit down.

It was the last day in July when Born rode slowly through the streets of Park Hill, with Dorian riding shotgun. They found Wizz in front of 141 Park Hill Avenue, standing with his man Roy, Tommy, and another, unidentified, goon. Born rolled down his window and summoned Wizz over to the car with a smile.

Wizz sidled over, looking menacing as usual, and said, "What up? How can I help you today?"

Born grinned like the Cheshire cat. "Yo, Wizz, it's good to see you, man. Listen." Wizz looked at Dorian and then back, as Born continued speaking. "We let you have a nice little run out here, son. You've had months to get money. We stepped back and let you have your time. After all, this is your hood, knawmean?" Born watched the expression on Wizz's face change to one of utter bewilderment. "Anyway, your run is over. I'm setting up shop again, effective immediately. And whoever want it can get it. You feel me? This time I got my own niggas out here. You can keep your workers and your crew. We shutting shit down, so you can either get on board or step aside."

"You must be fuckin' crazy," Wizz hissed. He looked at Born, then at Dorian, his hand resting threateningly on the gun in his waistband. But Wizz didn't pull his gun. He knew who Dorian was, and his reputation preceded him. Wizz knew that to pull his gun would be a death sentence.

Dorian looked Wizz in his evil eyes. Dorian's demeanor was intimidating. He exuded power. As he spoke, he knew that Wizz could tell that he wasn't one to be fucked with. "Call it crazy if you want, but check it. We here, and we ain't leaving. You came at my nigga Born with shotguns on the table and shit. I heard all about it. Now I'm sure you know who *I* am. If not, you can learn the hard way. However you want it. But it's a wrap for y'all. You gave him a warning. That's cool. We're giving you the same courtesy. You've been warned." Dorian turned away from Wizz, signaling that the conversation was over.

Born pulled off, leaving Wizz fuming in his wake. Their takeover of the hill was underway. Already they had secured five apartments in various buildings on Bowen Street, Vanderbilt Avenue, and Park Hill Avenue. Each apartment had tenants who had the appearance of normalcy. One was occupied by an older man in his fifties. No one ever suspected that this nice, quiet older man with no wife or kids was actually Dorian's uncle Butch. His apartment was where Born's crew packaged their work. Two of the apartments housed what appeared to be working couples who drove sensible cars. These couples were actually Dorian's peoples, planted there to keep their ears to the street and store the crew's arsenal. These couples' real day job was hustling fish scale to the wealthy cokeheads in the surrounding areas of Rosebank and Grymes Hill, and anywhere else on the borough's south shore that it called for. The last two apartments were drug spots occupied by workers. Out of these apartments they sold crack to local fiends, moving large quantities of product on a consistent basis. In addition to these, Born had young hustlers in training working the block, both on Targee Street and on Broad Street in Stapleton. Within a month, not only was Born successfully locking Park Hill down, but several of Wizz's own workers—including Tommy—were now working for Born.

Setting up shop on this level had been very costly for Born. Everyone had to be paid, and the rents on all the apartments had to be paid, plus payments under the table for the housing assistants who had helped him get the apartments. But it was money well spent, as Born's operation began to thrive. To add insult to injury, Wizz's right-hand man, Roy, was found shot in the head execution style, his body slumped over the steering wheel of his Camry. The police and the newspapers chalked it up as another career criminal and societal bully gunned down. Not only had Wizz lost a good friend, but he was being taken over by an outsider. Wizz was beyond devastated, as he watched his enemies rise to power before his very eyes.

Dorian and Born became neighborhood fixtures in Park Hill. On any given day you could see one or both of them at the area barbershops, stores, and street corners shooting the breeze with the locals. They became well-liked and embraced by many of the people in the area. They gained a valuable asset in the storeowners on the block. They used the PLO store as a front for their own shady dealings, and it brought them close to three thousand dollars a night. They kicked a small percentage of it back to the Palestinians, and all was well. Everybody made money.

Wizz was so disgusted by what was happening that he actually contemplated snitching on Born and his niggas. He hated seeing this son of a bitch get money in his hood. But Wizz couldn't bring himself to drop a dime on anybody, no matter how hard it was to watch Born prosper. With Dorian's help, Born was reigning supreme in Wizz's own backyard, and he was sick about it. His pockets grew leaner by the day, as he refused to work with Born. Wizz was reduced to being the dealer all the fiends went to only when they couldn't get a hold of any of Born's workers. Wizz was their last resort, and he was bitter about his reduction in status in his own hood.

In October, Born's friend Smitty threw a party at a club called Gutta on Bay Street in Staten Island. Born decided to bring Jada along with him to show support for his friend, and he invited Dorian and Sunny to come along as well. Lately, Jada had been nagging him about spending time with her, and he wanted to keep her content. Dorian brought Sunny along for that same reason. They got there and found a line outside the obviously jam-packed club. Smitty stood outside, and walked over to Born and Dorian as they stepped up on the scene with their ladies on their arms.

"What's poppin', my nigga?" Smitty greeted Born with a ghetto hand-shake and spoke to Dorian as well. Sunny and Jada walked ahead of their men, going into the club and passing the line at the door. They ignored the stares and glares they got from those with the misfortune of having to wait on the long line, and went inside to get their party on. Both ladies looked divine. Sunny wore painted-on Dolce and Gabbana jeans, a Dolce top, and Gucci wedge-heeled sandals. Jada was more modest in her DSquared jeans, fitted midriff-baring T-shirt, and some funky heels she found in the East Village. It wasn't all about the clothes they wore: All the ice dripping from the fingers, wrists, and delicate necks of these two women was also hard to miss.

Born and Dorian leaned against the wall, talking to Smitty. Dorian complimented Smitty on what would obviously be a successful event, judging from the cars pulling up and the crowd partying noisily inside. As the men talked, an SUV pulled up curbside with Chance and one of his boys, named Sly. Born cracked up laughing, as Chance rolled down the power windows on his Pathfinder.

"Wow, ain't this some shit? A shooter and an armed robber riding around together!"

Everybody laughed, including Chance and Sly, knowing that Born's description of them was sadly accurate. They parked their truck, and all the men proceeded into the party.

The place was packed, and Born and Dorian spotted Sunny and Jada at the bar. They were toasting something, and seemed to be enjoying themselves. Born tapped Dorian and pointed toward a table near the back exit, and they made their way toward it. Sitting down, they ordered a bottle of Moët and sat back, taking in the scene. The deejay played Method Man's "Bring the Pain," and Sunny and Jada made their way to the dance floor. Despite the fact that the crowd was large, very few people were dancing. As Sunny and Jada danced, they noticed several girls giving them the evil eye, as if dancing was against the law in Staten Island. Noticing this, Dorian questioned Born.

"Is this what it's like all the time at parties out here? Everybody just stands around and looks at each other?"

Born looked around the room at all the brothers standing against the wall with drinks in their hands. Few of the men were dancing at all, and there were only a handful of women on the dance floor. The rest of the women stood around looking each other up and down and scowling at the few chicks who had the audacity to dance at a party! Dorian had never seen anything like it. He noticed that Sunny and Jada got the majority of the evil stares, since the two of them were relatively unknown throughout the borough, and both were pretty women. It seemed that the other women at the party spent most of their time staring at them with contempt, rather than enjoying themselves.

Born nodded his head. "Yup. It's like they get dressed up and come out to stare at each other." Born shook his head. "The only reason I came to this shit is because it's Smitty's party."

Dorian sipped his drink as he watched Sunny and Jada disappear into the crowd, obviously tired of being ogled by all the females surrounding the dance floor. He saw that Born was staring intently at someone or something across the room. Dorian followed Born's gaze and saw Wizz standing close to the deejay booth. He was talking to someone who Dorian didn't recognize. "There go your man, Wizz," Dorian said.

But Born didn't hear him. He was enraged. He saw Wizz standing and talking to Jamari, of all people, and he shook his head in disgust. Born was livid. He had known that he was supposed to kill Jamari for stealing from him so many years ago. He knew that Jamari had stolen the money that he said the cops had taken from him. But Born hadn't bodied him. Instead, he had let Jamari live, figuring that he would fall apart without Born to hold him together. But now, there was Jamari shooting the breeze with the competition. Born felt absolutely betrayed. Dorian brought Born out of his trance.

"Yo, Born!" Dorian laughed. "You really don't like that muthafucka, huh?"

Born looked at Dorian. "Nah, I don't like neither one of them niggas." Born explained his history with Jamari, from how Born had welcomed him into his crew and given him the tools of the trade, to Jamari's betrayal and the five-thousand-dollar loss Born was forced to take. Dorian frowned as Born finished the story.

"If you let that nigga get away with it, he's gonna cross you again," Dorian warned Born.

"I ain't gonna give that nigga a chance to get close enough to cross me. Fuck that muthafucka!" Born's face looked so serious. "That shit is just too perfect. Two fuckin' rat bastards making friends." Born shook his head at the irony of his two archenemies crossing paths.

He had no idea what a powerful alliance was being formed before his very eyes.

Meanwhile, Sunny looked around the club, feeling like she was on display. Every female in the room was shooting daggers at her, and the men undressed her with their eyes. Even the men who had women by their sides were staring lustfully at her and Jada. She couldn't take it anymore. "Jada, this shit is whack!" Sunny shook her head. "These bitches are tryin' to make me beat somebody's ass. If one more ho looks at me like she wants it, I'm gonna fuck her up." Sunny said this loud enough for all in close proximity to hear her. "Let's take a break from this shit." Sunny pulled Jada toward the ladies' room, and they waited patiently on the long line. After several minutes of waiting on the unmoving line, Sunny glanced around, subtly checking out the scene. Suddenly she took Jada by the hand, and pulled her into the men's room, which had no line and was completely unoccupied.

"See, this is where I come when I gotta piss and I can't wait for the women's bathroom to empty out. The men's bathroom is always empty."

Jada nodded, looking around. "And their shit is cleaner, too!" The two of them went into separate stalls and handled their business. Sunny emerged first, and when Jada came out two minutes later, her chin hit the floor.

Sunny stood at the sink, having just washed her hands. She had a small pocket-sized mirror on the counter, with a long white line of cocaine lying across it. Sunny held one nostril and snorted the line of coke through the other, looking up at Jada's reflection in the mirror when she was done. Sunny smiled at the look on Jada's face as she stared longingly at the cocaine, and then looked at Sunny in shock.

Sunny could tell by the look on Jada's face that she wanted some. Jada all but salivated at the sight of the cocaine, and she instinctively looked around for Born, half expecting him to walk into the men's bathroom at any moment. Sunny saw Jada look around, and she smiled once more. "Girl, relax. Ain't nobody coming in here. I locked the door." She saw her friend stare at the white line again, saw the look of pure longing on her face. Jada's eyes were focused on the powder diamonds lying invitingly across the surface of the mirror. She saw the little crystals in it, looking like tiny shards of glass, and she knew that this was the good shit. "Look at you fiendin'," she said, jokingly. "I can tell by the look on your face that you indulge. Help yourself."

Jada felt a tug-of-war in her heart. She considered telling Sunny that she was a recovering addict. She considered saying no, and just leaving the bathroom. But standing there in front of the drug unsupervised by Born for the first time since she left rehab, Jada wanted nothing more than to feel the euphoria that cocaine brought her. She salivated at the thought of experiencing that feeling again. She looked at Sunny, and her friend smiled, encouragingly. Jada told herself that this wasn't crack. She could control *this* urge, she reasoned. The high wouldn't be as noticeable. This was something she could handle. This would be different. She could keep this a secret. As if reading her mind, Sunny said, "I won't tell Born as long as you don't tell Dorian."

Jada closed her eyes, sweat forming on her face, and swallowed hard. She looked at Sunny, and then at the line of white powder, and she inched closer to it. Standing directly in front of it, Jada's gaze was fixed. She leaned over, and snorted the rest of it, instantly feeling the effects. This was some good shit!

Jada stood up tall and straight when she was finished, and looked at her reflection in the mirror. Her pupils were dilated, and she felt a surge of energy. It was an amazing rush. Jada felt instantly at home. She felt alive again, and the euphoria was so familiar. It felt so perfect, just like old times. She relished the feeling, since it had been so long since she'd experienced the wonders of a cocaine high. Sunny smiled, just as zooted as her friend.

"Come on. Now the party will be way better!"

They emerged from the men's bathroom undetected and blended back into the crowd. They wandered toward the far side of the club, where there were more people dancing and enjoying themselves than standing around staring. There they danced, in a place all their own. For over an hour they danced and mingled with a handful of Born's friends from around the way. Chance noticed that Jada was a lot more talkative and energetic than usual, but he figured that was because she was drinking and enjoying herself. Sunny was her usual ball of energy, and they all hung out enjoying themselves, until Chance and his boys wandered off. Finding a table on the opposite side of the party from where Born and Dorian were holding court, Sunny and Jada sat and enjoyed the rush of their respective highs. And just as Sunny had predicted, the party was way more enjoyable for both of them.

After another half an hour or so, the feeling wore off, and Jada sat back, feeling like her old self again. Sunny snapped her fingers and sang along with Lil Kim. "Get money!" She looked over at Jada and smiled at her friend. Jada smiled back.

"I'm so glad I got a friend who parties," Sunny said. Jada caught her meaning of the term "parties," and smiled. "I always take a twenty or a fifty of Dorian's shit for myself. You don't steal bags from Born when he bags up?" Sunny asked, amazed.

Jada felt tremendous guilt then, at the mention of Born's name. Damn! She was instantly filled with regret. What had she done?

Jada shook her head. "I don't think I could bring myself to steal from Born." Her tone of voice was sad and filled with remorse.

Sunny pursed her lips. "Shiiiit! I don't consider it stealing. What's his is mine, you know what I'm saying?" She crossed her legs and continued snapping her fingers, dancing in her seat, clearly unfazed and not feeling the same guilty torment that Jada was enduring.

Jada looked around the party and saw some familiar faces from her days living in West Brighton. She spotted Phillip, a guy she had messed around with when she and Shante were being scandalous for crack money. She remembered fucking Phillip for ten dollars back then. Thinking of the fact that she'd just gotten high again, she cringed. Jada silently assured herself that she would never stoop that low again. She was in a loving relationship with a man she respected. She had money and status, and if she wanted to party with Sunny from time to time, she figured there was nothing wrong with that. She wasn't going to be a crackhead again. But looking over at Phillip, she recalled how that had been one low point that she had enjoyed one hundred percent. She pointed him out to Sunny.

"That nigga right there has a dick the size of Shaquille O'Neal's foot!" Sunny laughed and slapped Jada five in a congratulatory way.

"Wow. That shit must have been good," Sunny said, staring at the gangly, brown-skinned brother. "He ain't too cute, but that shit makes up for it."

"It sure does." Jada laughed, and nodded in agreement.

Suddenly there was a commotion on the dance floor. Sunny and Jada seemed to notice it first. Their senses were heightened after getting high. The crowd parted, and Sunny and Jada both stood on their seats trying to see what was going on. They caught sight of two guys fighting in the center of the crowd, as the bouncers rushed in to break it up.

Everything was at a standstill as the fight was broken up and the two individuals involved were thrown out. The music stopped, the lights came on, and the sound of people complaining and talking filled the club.

Everybody waited to see if the music would come back on, if the lights would go dim once more. But after ten minutes of nothing happening, Born and Dorian maneuvered their way through the throngs of people and came to Sunny and Jada's table.

"Let's get up outta here," Born said. "This shit is over." He shook his head in frustration. Parties in Staten Island always seemed to end in a fight that caused the whole party to be shut down. It was one of the many reasons why he rarely went out in his home borough. Usually Manhattan and Brooklyn were where he spent his downtime.

They all headed for the exit, past the envious stares of some partygo-ers. It sounded like a high school cafeteria in the club, filled with angry, drunk black people and no music to calm them down. He caught a glimpse of Jamari looking at him and Jada as they left, and Born scowled at him and kept on moving. Jamari couldn't help but stare at both the man he admired to the point of envy and the woman he wanted for him-self. Born held Jada at the small of her back, gently guiding her through the sea of people. As they made their way outside, Jada saw Phillip again, and Sunny saw him, too. They smiled at their private joke.

Born found Smitty outside, and he bid his friend farewell as they left. They all climbed inside Dorian's BMW, with Born sitting up front and the ladies lounging comfortably in the backseat. They pulled away from the club and drove down Bay Street toward the expressway. When they had driven close to five blocks, all the occupants in the vehicle were shocked to hear sirens directly behind them. Police in an NYPD van were behind them, signaling for them to stop. Dorian pulled the car over and wondered what was happening.

Sunny and Jada turned around in their seats and saw the police van pull up behind them. Four officers got out of the van with their guns drawn, and approached Dorian's car on either side. A separate squad car screeched to a halt behind the van, and Jada and Sunny sat nervously in the backseat. Both of them were already paranoid, and this only made it worse.

"Put your hands up!" the officer closest to the driver's side yelled, ner-vously. Dorian put his hands in the air, and looked at the cop, hoping he didn't have an itchy trigger finger. *"License and registration! Now!"*

Dorian looked at the white man in the uniform, and held his gaze. "Alright," he said, calmly. "I'm gonna roll the window down. Then, I'm gonna reach inside my pocket and hand you my wallet," he said. He slowly pressed the button, lowering the power windows, and handed the cop his license and registration.

"Who's car is this?" the cop asked, while his partner had his gun pointed at Born, sitting idly in the passenger seat. Two other cops stood by both Sunny and Jada's doors. Jada looked at the cop who stood next to her window, and he stared back at her with a fixed expression on his face. Born wasn't dirty, but Dorian was. He had several fifty-dollar bags of fish scale in his sock. He had brought it along to sell at the party, and now he hoped this was a routine traffic stop. But judging by the looks of the cops and their visible weapons, it didn't seem very routine. Sunny, meanwhile, sweated bullets, knowing that she had two bags of Dorian's drugs in her purse. If they found it, not only would she go to jail, but she would have a whole hell of a lot of explaining to do to Dorian.

"It's my car, officer," Dorian said, and knew that police hated nothing more than seeing black folks driving fancy cars legally.

"Where do you work?" the cop asked.

Dorian stared at the man, wanting so badly to say something smart, but knowing that doing so wouldn't be wise. "I'm a bricklayer," Dorian said. Born smirked at his friend's wit.

The cop looked at Dorian directly. His expression was blank. Jada was in the backseat, wondering why the cop outside her window was staring at her so intently. To her surprise, he opened her car door and ordered her out of the car.

"Miss, can you step outside of the vehicle, please?"

Jada looked around. "Me?"

"Yes, you. Step out of the car."

Born protested. "Why she gotta get out of the car? She ain't driving."

"Shut up!" the cop barked. *"Step out of the vehicle, ma'am!"*

Jada did as she was told, and got out of the car. The officer led her close to the trunk of the car, out of earshot of the other passengers. The other three cops kept their guns pointed at the remaining three occupants in the car. The squad car that had pulled up after the van emptied out, and two more white male officers approached.

"What's your name?"

"Jada Ford."

The cop looked toward the car, and then back at Jada, checking her out from head to toe. "You have any I.D.?"

She fumbled in her Gucci bag, and handed him her driver's license.

She wondered if this was payback for her getting high that night. Why had the cop singled her out?

"How do you know these men?" the cop asked, searching her eyes for signs of deception. Jada knew that she had to be convincing in order to prevent the situation from escalating. Jada shrugged, frowning. "They're friends of mine, officer. What's the problem?"

Ignoring her question, the red-haired cop probed further. "Where did you all go tonight? You seem pretty dressed up."

Jada looked at the three uniformed overseers before her, and she felt angry. But keeping her emotions in check, she said, "We went to a party."

"Where?"

"At a club on Bay Street."

"Which one?"

Jada hesitated, unsure. "Gutta."

"Where are you going now?"

"He was taking me home."

"Where do you live?"

"Brooklyn." Jada scanned all three of their pale faces. "Did something happen?"

The red-haired officer nodded. "There was an incident nearby, and we're investigating it." He looked at Jada, quizzically. "So, these guys were with you all night? You're vouching for them?"

Jada looked at the man, wondering what was really going on. "Yes, sir. They were with me all night, and I'll certainly vouch for them."

He handed her back her identification, and she followed him back to the car. He looked inside the car, where Dorian and Born sat with blank, expressionless faces. Sunny was chewing her gum innocently, her face almost angelic. "You can go," the cop said. "Thanks for your patience."

Dorian waited until the officers headed back to their cars before he pulled off. Everyone breathed a collective sigh of relief as he drove away.

Born looked at his baby girl. "What did they ask you?"

Jada shook her head. "All kinds of shit!" She recounted the mini-interrogation she'd just endured, and they all concluded that it was another case of racial profiling. Black people and nice cars were presumably a mismatch.

Dorian drove Born and Jada back to Born's apartment, and then he and Sunny went home to Brooklyn. Born noticed Jada seemed bothered by her encounter with the cops.

"Cat got your tongue?" Born asked.

Jada snapped out of her trance, her thoughts on the terrible regret she felt over getting high that night. She felt so guilty, almost like she owed Born an apology, even though he had no idea what she'd done. She shrugged. "Nope."

They got off the elevator and walked down the hallway to the place they called home. And the minute they got inside, Jada made love to Born with a passion unmatched. She went at him like a woman gone mad, blinded by her feelings of guilt and regret, channeling that energy into ferocious lovemaking. She sucked him eagerly, and sexed him wildly, and afterward she lay in his arms, drifting softly to sleep, still telling herself that she had everything under control.

23

LOOSE ENDS

December 1996

Sunny and Jada were high once again, sitting in the brand-new house on Westwood Avenue in Staten Island that Born had purchased. He was ecstatic that he was a homeowner before reaching his thirties, and he was happy to see Jada enjoying the decorating process so much. On this day Sunny had come over to help Jada hang her drapes and to find the perfect spot for all the artwork she'd bought to adorn the walls. But Born was out handling business as usual, and Dorian was off somewhere doing the same. So Sunny and Jada had seized the opportunity to test Dorian's newest batch of coke, some of which Sunny had swiped when her man wasn't looking. They snorted his new shipment of fish scale, and they weren't disappointed. Now they were insanely high, and euphoric.

Sunny and Jada's friendship was fast becoming a blur of white lines laid out like a feast before them. Getting high together was something the two of them did almost daily. Their friendship was strengthened by the secret addiction they both dealt with. Their conversation on this evening was a long one, since they were both in extremely talkative moods. They hadn't eaten a thing all day. And despite the fact that they had partied the night before until the wee hours of the morning, neither of them was sleepy.

Dorian and Born were working harder than ever, and spending more time away from the women who loved them. Dorian had taken Born under his wing as a protégé, and spent lots of time grooming him for the next level. And Born was an eager student, soaking up what Dorian taught him eagerly. So in the absence of the men they loved, Sunny and Jada had discovered the allure of New York City's nightlife, and more often than not, they were out in the clubs together. They threw on designer outfits and their most beautiful jewelry, and painted the town red, night after night. They got high together, sharing what Sunny managed to take from Dorian on a regular basis.

Jada's initial apprehension and regret over getting high appeared to be gone, and she indulged more and more often. Since he was with her less and less, Born didn't notice the fact that Jada was sliding back to her old self, inch by inch.

At first she only got high when she was with Sunny. That was more than enough, since she saw Sunny several times a week. Born would be gone, and Dorian would be MIA, and the women would snort themselves into utopia. But soon Jada was damn near fiendin' to see her friend, knowing that she came with goodies in her bag of tricks. Not only would they get high whenever they got a chance to be away from their men, but Sunny always gave her some to take home with her. Jada had been humble, and modest, and respectfully declined at first. But as time wore on, she had caved in. She would bring it home and hide it. When the morning came, and Born was asleep, Jada would go into the bathroom and snort. She'd shower, change, and snort some more. By the time she finished making Born a big breakfast, he would be waking up, and she would be sobering up. He was none the wiser.

But when she crashed, she would be overcome with the blues. She would think about her mother during these times, how unimportant she felt that she and Ava were to their mother. She thought about how her mother had thrown her out in the streets and never looked back. Jada felt guilty about how she had betrayed her mother, guilty for fucking Mr. Charlie. She also felt guilty for sneaking and using behind Born's back. She knew that he loved her, and that getting high again would be a deal breaker. When the pain of her past and the reality of her current state got to be too much for Jada, she would disappear and get high once more. Then she felt better. So much better. Born noticed her mood swings, that she would be happy and upbeat one minute, and irritable the next. He attributed this to PMS, and ignored her when she got like that. He figured she just needed to see more of him.

This day the women got zooted, and had an animated conversation about love. They were "up" in every sense of the word, as they hung the expensive curtains and decorated Jada's living room. They were fresh off a shopping spree, and they had some beautiful things to turn Jada's new house into a home.

"Shit, Sunny!" Jada was way more energetic than usual. "I can't believe I live in this house!" She looked around her, excited that Born was making moves on this level. The four-bedroom house in Randall Manor was everything Jada had ever hoped for. It had a full dining room, a huge living room, a patio, and a kitchen that was larger than any Jada could have dreamed of. The backyard was huge, and the thought of all the barbecues they'd have back there made Jada's heart race.

Sunny smiled. "This house is gorgeous, Jada. You two are gonna be so happy here." Sunny kept fixing her already perfect clothes.

Jada was swirling around in the middle of the floor, holding a plum-colored organza curtain panel. The fabric was exquisite, and Jada loved the feel of it. She finally stopped spinning, and was giddy from the dizziness she felt. She laughed and looked at Sunny. "We're two lucky bitches," she said. "We got some good men in our corner."

Sunny nodded, but her expression was uninspired. "Yeah, we are. But don't think shit is sweet, just because it looks that way."

"Well, it seems like Dorian loves you a whole lot, and he'll do whatever it takes to make you happy, am I wrong?" Jada was growing weary of Sunny's cryptic complaints about life as a hustler's wife.

Sunny shook her head no. "No. You're not wrong. Dorian does love me. I love him, too. But I never get to see him. Being his lady means spending most of my time alone. That's why he buys me nice things and beautiful homes. All I have, day in and day out, are all the things he buys me. He's hardly ever around." Sunny sniffed, a habit she picked up from snorting blow so much. She took the curtain out of Jada's hand, fearing that her friend would crumple the material before she got a chance to hang it up. "That shit gets hard after a while, and no amount of money can make up for that feeling. Hopefully, you never have to know what that's like."

Jada danced around to a song playing on the radio. She heard what Sunny was saying, but she was too happy to think about that now. Born was spending a lot of time away from her lately, but that was so that he could buy this house, the clothes, the cars. He was trying to keep Jada happy, and he was doing a great job. Sunny smiled, seeing her friend enjoy her high, for she, too, was feeling on top of the world. She liked Jada so much. It felt like she was her twin, who had been separated from her at birth, and she wanted to look out for her always. Sunny saw Jada as a little girl who thought she knew it all, but really had so very much to learn.

"You know Dorian swept me off my feet," Sunny said, her legs crossed and her foot bobbing steadily. She had a sly smile gracing her face. "He swept my whole family right the fuck off their feet, too."

Jada laughed, a little too loud, still being very extra. Sunny continued.

"I was seventeen when I met him. He was twenty-two. I loved him from the second I saw him. He was everything I wanted in a man. He was handsome, smart, funny. He had a nice car, his own place, and he dressed like a male model. He molded me into the woman he wanted me to be. He taught me how to live my life, how to think, how to make love to him and satisfy him. I became the perfect woman that he envisioned for himself. At first, it was me and him against the world, just like it is now for you and Born." Sunny looked at Jada, meaningfully. "Then I got pushed aside like yesterday's newspaper so that he could make even more money. Now I feel like we have all the money in the world, but I never see my baby anymore."

Jada finally sat down. She was out of breath from dancing and moving around. "But Dorian loves you so much, Sunny. You can tell he does. When he's around you—"

"Exactly!" Sunny interrupted. "*When* he's around. That's becoming less and less often nowadays." She listened to herself, and thought that she sounded ungrateful. "I mean, I really can't complain, you know what I'm saying? The man takes damn good care of me." Sunny lit a cigarette. "But, you know, I got some money of my own put away just in case."

"Just in case what?" Jada asked, naïvely.

Sunny looked at her as if she'd asked a stupid question. "Just in case the muthafucka leaves, Jada. What you think?" She shook her head at how green Jada was. "What if the nigga would have fallen in love with Raquel? What if he kicked me to the curb for her? Don't think for a second I don't have my 'just in case' money ready for something like that. You can't be too careful." Sunny looked at Jada seriously. "You better have some change put away for a rainy day, too." Sunny sounded like an older aunt, telling a young lady how to handle her new husband. "Always have your own, girl. I wish I would have went to modeling school, or went out to L.A. to try to get into acting. But I chose to be with Dorian because he took care of me. I was content to spend his money instead of making my own. He loved me, and he made me happy. Now I wish that this wasn't all *his* shit that he can take away from me whenever he wants to. Nothing is worse than getting used to living the high life, and then being forced to go back to nothing. I've seen many females in this game get fucked over by the men they loved. They thought shit was always gonna be sweet. And when it happened, they weren't prepared. They failed to plan. And when you fail to plan, you plan to fail."

Jada smiled at that. "So you got your plan all mapped out, huh?"

Sunny nodded. "Yup. I got my whole shit all figured out. I'm telling you, Jada. Look out for you first. You'll be sorry if you don't."

Jada realized that she had never thought about it this way. She still couldn't bring herself to believe that Born would ever leave her with nothing. Not Born. Not ever.

Sunny sighed. "But at the end of the day, whether it's my money or his money, Dorian treats me like a queen. I realize that I'm a lucky woman. He takes care of everything."

Jada looked at the ice on her fingers and at the expensive clothes Sunny wore, and nodded in agreement as Sunny continued.

"He takes care of all of us. He helped my parents keep their house when it was being foreclosed. Dorian paid for everything. He gave my brother a job working for him, and Reuben makes a lot of money with Dorian. My other brother, Ronny, he disagrees with the whole thing, and he always preaches about how Dorian is selling poison to people. But when his son—my nephew, Eddie—got arrested, it was Dorian's drug money that got him out of jail. He's bailed my family out of trouble on lots of occasions."

Jada thought about what Sunny said. "Do you feel obligated to him because he helped your family out as much as he did?"

Sunny looked at her. "I'm not sure it's that I feel obligated. I feel like I would do anything for him, because of all the things he's done for me." She paused. "I love him so much that sometimes it scares me, Jada."

Jada listened, understanding love that fierce and powerful. She loved Born with all her heart and soul, and there wasn't much that she wouldn't do for him.

Sunny smiled, a pained, injured smile. "Raquel doesn't know how much she gets to me."

Jada frowned. "How has she been acting since the party?"

Sunny told Jada how Dorian had confronted Raquel at the apartment in Park Slope he kept her in. He had nearly choked the life out of Raquel, and had smacked her around something terrible for shooting at Sunny. Raquel swore that she had only fired into the air, but Dorian didn't care. He wanted her to stay the hell away from Sunny from then on, and Raquel had been complying so far. She wasn't allowed to come near the house that he and Sunny shared. He picked his son up and dropped him off, and kept the two women as far apart as possible.

"She's putting on this act now." Sunny's face looked twisted, like she'd sucked on a lemon. "Lately, she's been sweet as pie. All she's doing is trying to win him over by being obedient. She hasn't argued with him since that night, and he argued with her every damn day before that." Sunny shook her head. "He thinks I'm overreacting. I told him that I know she ain't changed, because she be giving me these evil faces when he ain't looking. Then when I tell him about it, he says, 'The bitch ain't doing shit to you, Sunny!' He thinks I'm just exaggerating, or looking for something to be mad at. It gets to the point that sometimes I think I be hallucinating or paranoid. I wonder if it's the coke or what?"

Jada laughed, and reluctantly Sunny did, too. They finished hanging the curtains and had a drink or two to celebrate the new digs. When Born was still not home at eleven o'clock, they decided to hit the club. Jada showered and changed into a pair of black jeans, a black cashmere turtleneck, and her brown Moschino fox fur jacket. She grabbed her new stiletto boots, and was ready to go. They headed to Brooklyn in Sunny's midnight blue Jaguar. When they arrived at the house on Bergen Street in Cobble Hill, Jada entered Sunny's home and sat downstairs in the living room while Sunny went upstairs and got dressed to go out. Jada watched *In Living Color* while Sunny took a steamy shower in her luxurious bathroom. She emerged in a pair of D&G jeans, a tight cream-colored sweater with matching boots, and the most beautiful fur that Jada had ever seen.

"Oh my God!" Jada yelled. "When did you get that coat? What kind of fur is that?" Jada stared at the beautiful fur jacket with a leather-looking material around the sleeve cuffs and the borders.

Sunny spun around to show Jada the detail. The waist-length jacket was the centerpiece of the whole outfit, accentuated by Sunny's short, slicked-back hair and very little makeup. She wore gold feather earrings and a black coral choker on a gold chain. It looked incredible. "It's a lynx with crocodile around the edges. Dorian bought it for me when we went up to Canada last January. The shit cost twenty grand! I've been waiting for the perfect night to wear it. Girl, I thought Dorian would take me out to show me off in it. Please! If I keep waiting for that, I'll be fifty before I get to wear this jacket." Jada saw the hurt Sunny felt behind that statement, but her friend quickly brushed it off. "I can't wait to see them bitches at the club tonight hating on us. We're both fabulous tonight!"

They knew they looked good as they left and drove to The Coco Lounge, one of Brooklyn's best gathering places for the ghetto fabulous. After they arrived, and had parked the car, every man on the scene turned to look at the two stunning ladies strutting through in all their finery.

"Hey, sweet thang. Come let me holla at ya for a minute."

"Look at all that ass in them jeans."

"Yo, shorty!"

"Hey, light skin!"

"Excuse me, can I talk to you for a minute?"

"Can I walk with y'all?"

By the time they made it to the velvet rope, and Sunny had slithered up to the guy at the door, it seemed every eye was focused on them. Sunny approached the tall black man standing guard, and asked for P.J., the nigga who ran the joint, and who also happened to be one of Dorian's peoples. A trio of sisters with long weaves and too-tight outfits started mouthing off.

"Yo, who the fuck is they? Salt and Pepa?" The three of them, and some of the other people waiting on line, laughed at Sunny and Jada's expense.

Sunny turned toward the heifer, and frowned. "You're a hater, bitch. Don't be mad 'cause you ain't got no clout." Sunny blew a bubble with the gum in her mouth, and rolled her eyes.

The pudgy, brown-skinned one with the worst weave got all puffed up. "Yo, you better stop trying to be fuckin' cute—"

"I ain't gotta try, ho. Some of us get the shit naturally." Sunny looked her up and down for emphasis. Just as the exchange was about to escalate, Sunny felt a tap on her arm, and P.J. ushered her and Jada inside. P.J. was the best—the top party promoter and club owner in town. He always rolled out the welcome mat for Sunny on the strength of who Dorian was. Sunny loved the VIP treatment he always extended to her.

They strolled inside, and took in the atmosphere. It was a playa's ball in the truest sense of the word. It seemed that every baller in Brooklyn was on the scene, and everywhere they looked they saw minks, foxes, leathers, silk, and expensive drinks. The music was bumping, as Jada led Sunny toward the bar. Before she could make it to an empty stool, a tall light-skinned man with freckles offered to buy Jada a drink. She declined, and didn't pause. Sunny was also swatting men away, as they walked to the bar with B.I.G.'s "Juicy" blaring from the speakers. They made themselves comfortable at the bar, ordered drinks, and enjoyed the music.

Sunny's eyes scanned the room, and she saw several of Dorian's friends. This meant that she was being watched, but also that she was safe. None of Dorian's boys would let any harm come to Sunny. Over the years she'd played the role of Supreme Wifey to the fullest. Whenever one of his soldiers or family members needed to lay low, Sunny happily accommodated them in their home, never complaining about the unexpected houseguests. She delivered money and picked up packages for Dorian when he couldn't do it himself, and she was treated with the same respect her man received. She was always strapped, and conducted herself like Dorian's better half. She was cocky and gorgeous, loyal and grimy if necessary. All of them protected her just out of genuine love for the type of chick she was.

Jada sat on the stool, sipping her Hennessy and looking around. She spotted Raquel at a table in the back with a couple of her friends. Jada chuckled to herself, noticing that Raquel's friend CeCe—the one who had slept with Dorian—wasn't around anymore. She pointed Raquel's presence out to Sunny discreetly.

Sunny scowled, and turned her back. She sipped her drink, and talked with a couple of girls she knew. She introduced Jada to all of them, and once again, Jada tried to keep all the names straight. Once they were done with their drinks, both of them were ready to leave. Sunny didn't like the fact that all of Dorian's crew seemed to be on the scene, waiting to report any missteps or stumbles. And she hated that Raquel was there, too. The thought of being in the same room as Dorian's baby's mama made her skin crawl.

"Let's go to Elite. This place is tired." As they made their way out the door, Raquel followed them outside and tapped Sunny on the shoulder to get her attention. Sunny spun around, looking resplendent in her lynx jacket, and faced her archnemesis.

Raquel grinned. She knew that Sunny was slipping. There had been a time when Dorian acted like no one was good enough compared to

Sunny. But lately Dorian had been giving Raquel more attention, coming by for sex more often, making her feel like there was hope for them after all. She looked at Sunny, and said, "Do you know why Dorian keeps coming back to me for pussy?"

Raquel's friends laughed at her audaciousness. Jada's eyes widened, and she waited to see what Sunny would say or do. Raquel didn't wait for an answer.

"Because you don't ride him like a *buck* the way I do." Raquel stood there waiting for Sunny to flip, trying to provoke her. Raquel's friends snickered behind her, and Jada wondered if she'd have to fight alongside Sunny if shit hit the fan.

Sunny blinked, took a step back, and looked at the bitch before her. "Then keep riding him how he likes it," Sunny said, calmly. She nodded her head. "I'll keep riding his bank account."

Sunny walked away from Raquel, and Raquel laughed. She knew that Sunny didn't believe her, and she was fine with that. The truth would be revealed soon enough. "Okay!" she called after Sunny. "Remember that you told me that."

Sunny kept on walking, and Jada was right beside her. But then one of Raquel's friends said, "Oh, and what's-your-name, tell Born to stop playing and call me. I want to see if what they say about men with big feet is true. That nigga is fine!"

Jada stopped walking. She stood in place, then turned around suddenly and charged at the bitch who had said it. Sunny was stunned, and she scrambled after Jada. But by the time she got there, Jada had jumped on the shorter girl, and was tearing her up. Raquel and her whole clique set it off on Jada, pulling out razors and jumping her, pummeling her. Jada was outnumbered, and getting fucked up. All Sunny could think about was her lynx and crocodile jacket. Fighting was not an option in this outfit. She pulled out her 9mm and aimed at the nearest bitch.

"Back the fuck up!" Sunny meant business, and all of them backed down. Raquel wasn't so drunk anymore with a gun in her face. Jada got on her feet, her fur jacket completely destroyed. Sunny brushed Jada off with one hand, and held the girls at bay with the gun in the other. P.J. came out of the club, and saw Sunny with her heat drawn.

"Yo, what the fuck is goin' on out here?" he asked, shaking his head. There was always some shit between these two!

"Yo, P.J., let me get up outta here." Sunny eyed Raquel meanly. She wanted to get to her car, and get home to her man. That was all.

P.J. nodded his head. "Go ahead, Sunny. I got you."

Sunny put her gun away, and led Jada off, while P.J. stood there watching Raquel and her crew to make sure they didn't do anything crazy. Sunny got Jada inside the truck, and let her have it. "What kinda shit was that, Jada?"

"You heard what she said about Born! I don't let bitches talk to me like that, Sunny."

Sunny shook her head. "But look at my outfit tonight, ma." Sunny looked at Jada as if she was crazy, "*Bitch,* I got on fuckin' three-inch heels! You don't start fighting four Brooklyn bitches when I'm in a twenty-thousand-dollar coat and fuckin' stilettos!"

Jada stared at Sunny, dumbfounded. And then she burst out laughing. Sunny laughed, too, at the absurdity of what they'd just done. Jada apologized. "I'm sorry, Sunny. I didn't think, I just reacted. She the type of bitch that'll make me go back to jail. I don't play when it comes to my man. I don't need bitches like that checking for him. Now she knows without a doubt that Born is off-limits."

Sunny shook her head. "Please! Now all she knows is that Born's bitch is *crazy* and she got one less mink jacket from getting a BK-style ass whooping." Sunny looked at Jada sideways.

Jada shoved Sunny playfully in the arm, pretending to be offended. They laughed and headed home, with another night to reminisce over in the years to come.

24

ULTERIOR MOTIVES

Months passed, and then Jada got a surprise. She got a letter from Ava. It was spring break at U Penn, and she wanted to come back to New York for the vacation. She wanted to know if she could stay with Jada and Born, since they'd recently purchased the new house. Jada was, at first, excited. This would be the first time that she and Ava would have a chance to hang out and catch up since Jada's release from rehab and Ava's going away to college. But then paranoia set in, and Jada worried that Sunny might let slip around her unknowing sister that they got high on occasion. This was still Jada's little secret, and she worried that she would be exposed. She planned to bring Ava along on her excursions with Sunny, to show her off in their inner circle. But suddenly she wasn't so sure that Sunny wouldn't let their secret cat out of the bag.

Ava also had another revelation enclosed within her letter. She had reunited with their mother via letters they had written to one another when Ava was away at college. Ava had been the one who had initiated the correspondence, by writing a letter to her mother on the advice of her group home counselor, Mrs. Lopez. Jada was shocked. She thought that Edna's refusal to defend Ava against J.D. would be unforgivable. Jada was also still bitter with her mother for her own reasons—mainly for throwing her out, and for turning a blind eye while Jada was strung out on crack. Jada felt envious that Edna had responded to the letter Ava had written her while she'd ignored Jada's letter to her mother while she was in rehab. Once again, Jada felt rejected.

Not only had Ava made amends with their mother, and forgiven her for the situation with J.D. that had led to Ava's suicide attempt, but she was going to church with Edna on Easter Sunday. Ava invited Jada to come along, and Jada respectfully declined. She still didn't want to reconcile with their mother, who Jada felt was heartless and selfish. Jada wasn't ready to let bygones be bygones. Not yet. She wondered how Ava was able to forgive their mother. Jada hadn't forgotten that she and her sister had been forced to endure the horror of J.D. while Edna had sat idly by and done nothing. How could that be forgiven? Jada chalked it up to yet another situation where poor, gullible Ava was falling prey to some monster. She could forgive Edna all she wanted. Jada refused to do the same.

Even though she didn't understand Ava's willingness to reconnect with their mother, she was still thrilled about seeing Ava again. Jada fixed up one of the guest rooms for her sister's arrival, and she anxiously awaited the day Ava would be back in her midst. When at last the day arrived, Born went with Jada to the train station to pick her sister up. Penn Station was packed, and they stood among hundreds of people looking for their soon-to-be houseguest. Born only knew that she was Jada's little sister, whom he had never met. But when Ava stepped off the train, and Jada took off running toward her, Born's jaw went slack with surprise. Ava was even more beautiful than her sister. Her hair was naturally long and hung down to the middle of her back, bone straight. Her eyebrows were arched to perfection, with eyes just as encompassing as her sister's. She was clearly Jada's sibling, but she had a more exotic beauty than her sister possessed. Born was secretly smitten.

Jada excitedly introduced Born to Ava, and they all greeted one another and proceeded to the parking lot. Ava was all smiles, as she took in her sister's sexy outfit and pricey clothes. Born kept silent as the two women talked nonstop from the terminal to the parking lot. Once inside the car, Jada decided she was hungry, and Ava was also starved after her trip. They drove through midtown until they found a Popeye's chicken spot. The ladies asked Born what he wanted, and then went inside to get their food. They had been in there for close to ten minutes when Ava came out alone. She climbed into the backseat, and began explaining before Born had a chance to question anything.

"Jada wanted the Cajun fries, and it's gonna take them ten more minutes to make them," she said. She opened up her bag of food and reached in for a drumstick before pausing. "Is it alright if I eat in your car? This is really nice, by the way."

Born smiled. "Yeah. Thanks. Go 'head and eat. I don't mind." He wouldn't have denied her much, as pretty as she was. He felt guilty for his feelings, since he was in love with her older sister. But, *damn,* she was so pretty.

Ava bit into her chicken. "So, I guess you're excited about your new house, huh?" she asked. "I can't wait to see it."

Born watched her through the rearview mirror as she daintily chewed her food with her mouth closed, just like Jada. He caught himself staring, and he diverted his gaze and looked out the window at New York City, as alive as ever. "Yeah. Jada fixed it up real nice, too. Sunny helped her do it. It's real cozy, and all that. You can make yourself at home, you know? How long are you staying?"

Ava shrugged. "I have two weeks to do what I want. I might stay with you guys for the whole time, or I might go visit my mother for a while."

Born was surprised by this, since Jada hadn't told him that her sister and mother had reconciled. He was under the impression that Edna was estranged from both of her daughters. He frowned, and Ava noticed.

"I know. She did a lot to hurt me and my sister. But I think, in a way, we did a lot to hurt her, too." Ava paused, wondering how much Born knew about her sister's past; about the drugs. She didn't want to reveal too much. "I know that when we were little, Mommy fucked up. She put us in danger, she compromised our safety for her own selfish reasons. That shit nearly cost me my life. But me and Jada kinda turned our backs on her, and left her by herself. There's so much about our mother that I didn't know, and Jada won't listen. Anyway, my moms got saved, and she's all into church now. So I found it in my heart to forgive her. I think Jada should try to do the same thing. But she's stubborn, and she's still mad. I understand. But I want her to try to forgive Mommy, too."

Born nodded. "Yeah. I understand Jada feeling like she does, though. She thinks her moms left her out there when she needed her. It's hard to forgive your parents sometimes."

Ava wondered if he was speaking from experience. She looked at him, noticing for the first time how Born seldom smiled, but his eyes were still so soft. Jada came back to the car with her bag of goodies, and off they went to Staten Island.

The conversation along the way consisted mostly of the sisters catching up on what was going on in one another's lives. Born kept his eyes on the road ahead, and contributed his two cents to the conversation when it was needed. He couldn't believe that the gorgeous young lady in the backseat had once tried to end her life. What a waste that would have been, he thought. It was hard to keep his eyes off of her. To Ava, Born seemed like a nice enough guy, and he showed affection toward her sister. Even when Jada started nagging Born about getting the toilet in their master bathroom fixed, he took it like a champ, and said all the right things to get her to shut the fuck up. Ava was impressed. She was happy that Jada had found someone who was as low-key and mature as Born seemed to be.

Once they arrived, Jada got Ava situated in her guest room. Ava was anxious to meet Sunny, whom she'd heard so much about. They changed clothes, and got ready to meet her in Manhattan for dinner and drinks. Dressed to impress, they headed for BeeBee's Soul Food on Forty-ninth Street. When they got there, Sunny was already seated with a glass of chardonnay in front of her. She stood to greet Jada and her gorgeous sister as they came near.

"Oh my God, you're even prettier than Jada!" Sunny hugged Ava before they were even formally introduced. She was high, though she was managing to maintain her composure, for the most part. Jada smiled, recognizing that her friend was high. But Ava was oblivious, thinking Sunny was just excited and outgoing.

Jada laughed, and pretended to be offended. "Thanks, bitch."

Ava was laughing, as Sunny finally released her. Jada shook her head, smiling. "Anyway, Ava, this is Sunny as you can see."

Sunny sat back down, and the sisters joined her. Jada and Ava ordered their drinks, and Ava took in the ambiance of the restaurant until their drinks arrived. Sunny looked at Ava, with her long hair and chiseled face, and smiled. "So, you're Jada's sister, home from college, and you want to have fun, right?"

Ava grinned, as if Sunny had read her mind. "Exactly!"

Jada shook her head, wondering if Ava was prepared for Sunny's version of fun. "Tell Sunny what you do for fun at college, Ava."

Ava shrugged. "Go to the movies, read, exercise, or watch TV. Either that or mess around with the few guys worth being bothered with." She sipped her Bacardi and Coke.

Sunny waved her hand, dismissively. "We ain't doin' *none* of that shit!" Ava almost spit out her drink from laughter. "That don't sound like fun at all!" Sunny frowned.

Ava shook her head. "I don't have much fun out there. It's all work, and very little play. That's why I couldn't wait to come back to New York." She looked at Sunny. "Jada kept telling me how much fun you are, and I wanted to see for myself. You two go to clubs all the time, from what she tells me. I'm surprised the men in your life don't complain."

Jada waved her off. "Please. Born is so busy himself that he probably don't even notice that I'm in the clubs that much."

Ava looked doubtful. "What about you, Sunny? Do you have a man? Does he mind you going out all the time?"

Sunny grinned slyly at the pretty young girl. "My baby likes for me to go out and be seen. I make him look good."

Ava laughed. She could tell that Sunny was a handful. She held her glass up in a toast. "To spring break!"

Jada and Sunny leaned forward and clinked glasses with Ava to celebrate her quest for fun in the city. They ordered, Sunny opting for only a salad, while the sisters went all out with soul food entrées.

Sunny looked at Jada and her sister, and saw two very different people.

One—Jada—was a street savvy sex kitten with an edge to her, courtesy of her status as a baller's bitch. Jada had style, and a way about her that made her seem tough and in control. Sunny suspected that there was one hell of a story behind her good friend. In Ava, she saw a young lady with unmistakable beauty who seemed to have an innocence about her that Jada didn't possess. Sunny's first impression of Ava was that she was a little naïve, and was quite amazed by how well her older sister had done for herself.

Over dinner the ladies conversed about the things ladies love: clothes, shoes, and men. It was the last topic that caused the conversation to take an interesting shift.

Sunny had just finished a tirade, something about men not being shit. "So, speaking of men," Ava began. "It has to be nice having men who are so powerful and so wealthy. But do they complain that you two don't do anything all day?"

Silence.

Jada wondered where the hell that remark had come from. "I do something all day, Ava. It's a job taking care of the house, and making sure Born's happy when he comes home. Don't you think so?" Jada looked at Sunny.

Sunny looked bored with Ava. "I don't think Dorian cares whether or not I do something all day. He loves me. Have you ever been in love, Ava?"

Ava considered the question. "Yeah. Well, I thought I was at the time. But that's irrelevant."

Sunny rolled her eyes again.

Ava figured that Sunny wasn't enjoying her use of big words like *irrelevant*. She tried to dumb down her lingo for her audience. "All I'm saying is, your lifestyle seems really nice. It looks and sounds real glamorous. But I think it's so much better to get your own, to pursue academics or learn a trade until you make your own money. That's all I'm saying."

Jada shook her head as if Ava had it all wrong. "So you think we're lazy?"

Sunny's eyes narrowed. She was five seconds from being turned off by Jada's little sister.

Ava shook her head. "Nah. I'm not saying that at all. That's what makes you happy. But for me, I think it would be weird. No disrespect, but it seems like y'all get dressed up and go to parties out of sheer boredom. And that would drive me crazy—"

Sunny held up her hand as if she wanted Ava to stop talking. "Enough," Sunny said in a low voice. She sighed, heavily. "You have a lot to learn, Ava. Let me teach you. First of all it *seems* to be an enchanting lifestyle because it is. To me it's like waking up in a fairy tale every day. I have the man that I want, the house that we earned together, and the fruits of his labor and mine to show for it. If I wanted to do for myself, I could. And I will. When I'm ready. But for now, it works for me just fine the way it is." Sunny smiled, and her previously icy demeanor melted to reveal a soft, beautiful face. "I'm gonna show you what I mean. By the time you leave to go back to your Ivy League campus, you're gonna see that it can be nice to live the way the other half lives every now and then."

Ava looked skeptical, and Jada smiled in anticipation.

For the next four nights, the three of them partied at all of New York's hot spots. Sunny took joy in letting Ava wear some of the outfits that Sunny herself felt were old, even though they weren't. These were the clothes she felt she could only be seen in once a year, at most. Ava filled them all out beautifully, and everywhere the ladies went they turned heads and stopped traffic. Ava, being the youngest and the most unfamiliar face in Jada and Sunny's circle of friends and associates, was the center of attention most often. She soaked it all up humbly, truly enjoying her sister's company, and having fun getting to know Sunny. She drank very little at first. But by the second and third evenings, Ava was drinking more, and more. She was tipsy by the time they got home most nights, and Jada loved seeing her let loose for once. Ava was having fun, and she almost dreaded having to go back to school eventually. It had been so long since Ava had lived a life of excess. Her drinking and weed-smoking days were long behind her. Watching Jada battle crack addiction had been a huge wake-up call for Ava. But now, soaking up her sister's extravagant lifestyle, Ava was beginning to see what she'd been missing.

Jada and Sunny managed to get high without Ava knowing what was going on. One of them would chill with Ava on the dance floor or at the bar, while the other went to the bathroom and got high. Ava was letting her hair down, meeting men, and enjoying the lifestyle of the rich and ghetto fabulous.

By day four, the ladies had been partying like crazy, nonstop. Ava was amazed that she found it hard to keep up with her sister, who was older than her by two years! She wondered where the hell Jada got all that energy. It seemed like she never slept. She never got tired. And Sunny, being the social butterfly that she was, knew all kinds of people from all walks of life. They hadn't stood on line at one event the entire time. Night after night they walked through the velvet ropes with all eyes on them.

One night, as they came in exhausted, Jada staggered upstairs to crash in her king-size bed. Born wasn't home yet, and without undressing, she climbed into bed and passed out in a comalike sleep. Ava went to her own room, and gathered her pajamas. Then she headed for the guest bathroom downstairs to take a shower. She washed her hair, cleansed her body, and shut the water off when she was done. The house was quiet as she stepped out of the shower into the cool air, letting her body dry naturally as she wrapped her hair up in a towel like a turban.

Meanwhile, Born had come home, tired from a long night spent chilling with Dorian, and making moves as usual. He had been hanging with Dorian and his crew more than ever, and soaking up the crazy lives they lived. Dorian had many women, aside from Sunny. Each one was more beautiful than the next. Most of the guys in their crew cheated on their women, since pussy was something so readily available to hustlers of their caliber. Born kept quiet about it, and didn't knock them for what they chose to do. But the love he had for Jada prevented him from stepping out on her. He was faithful to her, loved her completely, and didn't indulge in the infidelities that Dorian did. The allure of cheating, and sex with dozens of women, had long ago dissipated for Born, and he was happy with the love he shared with Jada alone.

He went upstairs, and saw that Jada was knocked out, still fully dressed. Hanging his jacket on the doorknob, he went into the master bathroom off of their bedroom to take a piss—only to find that the toilet wasn't working, yet again. He cursed himself for not listening to Jada when she told him to get the damn toilet fixed in that bathroom. Always the master procrastinator, Born had kept putting it off. He made a mental note to call the plumber later that day. He quietly walked downstairs, walking lightly so as not to wake Ava, whose guest room was on the first floor. Reaching the bathroom door, he turned the knob and walked in. Then his chin hit the floor.

Ava stood there naked, with her back turned. Her ass was the closest thing to perfect he'd ever seen. It was beautiful. He stood dumbfounded and motionless, as she turned around and saw him standing there. She was startled seeing him, and she jumped. She gasped, and saw the stunned expression on Born's face. But neither of them moved, despite the alarm that was evident in their facial expressions. Her C-cup breasts stood out, with her brown nipples rock hard from the draft of the open door. His gaze fell to her bush, her soft hair so neatly trimmed down there.

Born stared a little too long, his mouth hanging open in shock. Ava's body was superb, so delicate and perfectly proportioned. Ava had no idea why she felt no urge to cover herself, as she stood before her sister's man in the nude. She wasn't drunk, but she sure as hell wasn't sober, and in her tipsy state of mind, she chose not to cover herself. She could tell that Born didn't mind. She was clearly surprised, as evidenced by the look on her face, and yet she hadn't screamed or cried out. Strangely, she found herself comfortable with Born looking at her this way. Jada had no idea how lucky she was to have a man as fine as him. Slowly, Born shut the door, and left her standing there. Not a word was spoken between them.

Born closed his eyes and leaned against the wall for support. Damn! The girl had a body like a Coke bottle. With his dick harder than a brick wall, he headed upstairs to Jada, planning to wake her ass up. He needed to bust a nut terribly. To his dismay, he couldn't wake her from her sleep, and he tried everything he could to arouse his sleeping beauty. Jada was gone, and for a moment he contemplated taking it while she was asleep. But he couldn't bring himself to do that, feeling it wasn't worth it if she wasn't into it. He was reduced to jerking off beside her. He tried to get the image of Ava's body out of his mind, as he masturbated. But it was her name that fell softly from his lips in an impassioned whisper as he came in torrents. He cleaned himself up, dreading the next day when he would have to tell Jada what had happened. He knew she wouldn't like it one bit.

Ava woke up first thing the next morning, and went to the kitchen to fix herself some juice to get the dryness out of her mouth. Her body was dehydrated from the previous night's alcohol consumption, and she felt like hell. She entered the kitchen to find Born sitting at the table in a wife beater and sweatpants, eating a bowl of Rice Krispies.

Ava quickly contemplated going back to her room. But Born greeted her, as he slurped his cereal. "Good morning," he said. "Come here for a second. I want to apologize for last night."

Ava smiled awkwardly, opened the refrigerator, and reached for some much needed water. She gulped down the Poland Spring, as Born watched the muscles in her neck expand and contract as she swallowed. He turned away in time to avoid detection, and Ava sat down across from him at the table.

"Don't tell Jada about it," Ava advised. "It'll be weird if she knows you saw me like that." Ava looked at Born, wondering if he could tell that she wanted him. She wondered if last night he could tell from the look on her face, even though she knew it was wrong.

Born was relieved that Ava wouldn't tell about last night, knowing that Jada would have been unhappy, to say the least. He nodded. In his head he was thinking about how much he would love to see Ava naked again. He quickly changed the subject. "I guess y'all had fun last night," he said. "My baby is still up there sleeping."

Ava rolled her eyes. "They took me to Nipsy's. It was crazy in there. People of all cultures come in there, dressed all kinds of ways. We felt like the only normal ones there. But everybody was dancing, and having fun, so we did, too. Sunny knows everybody, so we went around and met lots of people. Then we went to breakfast, and came home after that. I don't think I could keep up with those two night after night."

Born looked at Ava's face, realizing that she spoke so differently from her sister. She sounded like she was seeing a different world, and he wasn't sure if she liked what she saw. "So, you're tired of all the parties and all that?"

"Born, I can do this for a week with no problem. But not every day. This is okay for Jada, because she likes living in the fast lane. That's not really where I feel most comfortable."

Born looked at Ava for signs of things she wasn't telling him. He wondered if she had seen Jada stray from him in any way. Lately, Jada had seemed distant, almost cold when Born came around. He noticed her having mood swings more often, and being antsy. He wondered if it had anything to do with men she met while she partied with Sunny. He hoped not, and gave Jada the benefit of the doubt. He knew that she loved him. He wanted to trust her.

"You don't party all the time out in Pennsylvania? You don't go to Philly to party every now and then?"

Ava nodded. "Yeah. I party sometimes. But not every night like Jada and Sunny. I don't see how they keep going. I'm tipsy after two or three drinks. But not those two. They're like Energizer Bunnies."

Born laughed, still slurping at his cereal. Ava looked at him, watched him enjoy his cereal as she drank her water. She noticed the way his brown eyes looked even brighter when he smiled. She watched his lips as he chewed, and then cleared her throat and looked away when he caught her staring.

Born smiled. Was shorty checking out his lips? He wondered, but decided to play it off. He was flattered at the thought of her finding him attractive, since she looked like an angel. "I guess you think I eat like a pig, too, huh? Jada gets on my case all the time about how I eat like a slave."

Ava laughed, relieved that he seemed to ignore the fact that his sexy mouth entranced her. "Nah, it's all good." She started to get up, and Born stopped her.

"Yo, you ready for my party tonight?" he asked. "I know you're sick of all the parties and the fast lane, as you put it. But this one you can't miss. Dorian's throwing it for me to celebrate my birthday. He's having the shit on one of those cruise ships that goes around New York Harbor all night. It's gonna be crazy."

Ava vigorously nodded her head. Born tried not to look at her breasts in her white tank top. Instead, he focused his gaze on her face, equally as tantalizing. "I'm excited, because Sunny makes it sound like the party of the year. I just don't know what I'm gonna wear."

Born nodded. "Don't worry. I think Jada and Sunny will hook you up. They got clothes that ain't even in style yet."

Ava laughed, and got up from the table. She smiled at Born, the sexual tension between them thick enough to slice. "I'll see you tonight," she said.

Born watched her ass as she walked away, then finished his cereal, and hit the streets.

By around noon, Jada was still sleeping. Ava finally went in and managed to rouse her sister. She shook Jada awake, whining that Born wasn't home, so she should get up and entertain her sister. After several minutes, Jada got out of bed, and went to take a much needed shower, still dressed in last night's clothes. She felt like hell. The aftereffects of her cocaine binge and ridiculous alcohol consumption from the previous day were worse than ever before. She washed up in the hot shower, then got out and wrapped an oversized towel around her small frame. She walked out of the bathroom, and into her adjoining bedroom. She pulled the small bag of blow out of her makeup bag, and spread the shimmering powder out in front of her on a sterling silver tray atop her dresser. She bent over, ready to snort the white line, shaking in anticipation. But before she could properly snort, her bedroom door swung open, and Jada's heart froze in her chest. She trembled, terrified that Born had busted her red-handed. Instead, Ava walked in with a cup of coffee in her hand.

"I thought you could use some help waking up . . ." Ava stopped speaking when she saw what her sister was doing.

Jada looked around for something to cover it all up with, but it was too late. The damage had been done, and Ava had seen what her sister was up to. She barged into the room, outraged.

"Oh my *God*!" Ava shrieked.

"Ava, calm down." Jada was pleading with her. She didn't want Born to come home unexpectedly, and hear them yelling.

"Calm down?!?"

"Yes! Stop yelling so loud in here."

"What the fuck is wrong with you, Jada? You're still using cocaine?"

"Ava, it ain't that serious—"

"What the fuck do you mean, 'it ain't that serious,' Jada?" Ava was still yelling. "Is that why you keep getting nosebleeds and acting all strange half the time?"

"Ava, come on!" Jada just wanted her sister to disappear at that moment.

"You're still getting high?" Ava's eyes were fixed on her sister; the disappointment in them was clearly evident.

Jada was speechless. She stood there staring at her sister in silence. She had nothing to say in her own defense, because no excuse would have been good enough.

"What about Born?" Ava asked. "Does he know?"

Jada shook her head no, and hung it in shame. Jada's head was swimming with regret. She was crying, her gaze and her tone of voice pleading. "Just stay out of it. I got this shit under control."

"I'm gonna tell him," Ava said, calmly.

Jada's head snapped back, and she was suddenly volatile. She stepped closer to Ava, her towel clinging to her small frame. "Okay, now wait a fuckin' minute. You need to mind your business!"

"You are my business! You're my sister."

"Well, Born is not your business, Ava."

"Well, if he loves you he will get you help—"

Jada was dead serious. "Don't bring him into this. You let me worry about Born."

Ava shook her head. "Well, don't you think this would hurt him, Jada? Don't you think it would kill him to know that you're throwing your life away while he's trying to fill your life with happiness? How could you do this to him? Shit, you got a good man here!" Ava was so angry, and so sincere that her body language exhibited this. She talked animatedly to her sister, knowing that Born would leave her if he knew what she was doing. "Look at the house he got you living in. All your diamonds and furs, and all the things he does to keep you happy. And you repay him by getting high behind his back?"

Jada walked closer to her sister. "You find your own man, Ava. You worry about them niggas up at college and keep Born's name out your mouth! I'm not hurting him as long as he doesn't know. Don't stand in my face, in my house, and threaten to tell on me. He's my man. Not yours! And I'll worry about how he feels and what he needs to know about me."

Ava shook her head. "He needs to know that you're a cokehead, Jada. You got this man walking around thinking that you're perfect. He loves you. A blind man could see that. But you're sneaking behind his back, and you're playing him. You might as well be cheating on him, Jada."

Jada's jaw was firmly set. She was as mad as hell. "Fuck you, Ava! Okay? Don't stand there and judge me. You probably want him for yourself! Coming in here with your little fancy education, looking down your nose at me because I live a different lifestyle. It kills you to see that I'm happy without you—that I'm happy without fuckin' Mommy. Well, I *am* happy. I don't need you or her. I'm a big girl, you understand? Don't come into my life, wishing it was yours, and then have the nerve to try and turn my man against me because you're jealous that you can't have him!"

Jada was out of breath after her tirade, and she stood with her chest heaving. Ava stood back and stared at her sister. She let her words linger, allowing the pain of what she'd said resonate. Ava shook her head, placed the cup of coffee on the dresser, and walked out of Jada's bedroom. Ava was destroyed.

She walked downstairs to the guest room, and began to gather and slowly pack her things. Ava wondered what hurt more—the pain of realizing that her sister was still using drugs, or the truth of what she'd said about Ava being envious. The love Born felt toward Jada was plain to see. Ava knew that he would be destroyed to find out that Jada had slipped. So why had she really threatened to tell him? She wasn't so sure what her own true motives were. For the past few days Ava had felt herself growing more and more envious of Jada's lifestyle: the money, the status, the man. She had to admit that she was a little jealous. Born looked so good, and he seemed like such a good man, and Ava knew in her heart that if she had a man like that she would never hurt him. She knew that, feeling the way she did about Born, it was clearly time for her to leave this house and let Jada live her life. Ava was feeling things for her sister's man that she had no business feeling, and now Jada's secret indulgence had been exposed, and she didn't want her sister's help. Ava packed, called a cab, and went to her mother's house in West Brighton. Jada cried her eyes out in the privacy of her bedroom.

When Born arrived home, looking forward to his birthday party, he was surprised to see Jada looking upset. He asked her where Ava was, and he noticed that Jada started crying at the mere mention of her sister's name. Jada told him that they had had an argument about Ava reconciling with their mother, and it had ended badly. She explained that Ava had left, and that she assumed that her sister was going to stay with her mother for the remainder of her vacation. Born couldn't help feeling disappointed that he wouldn't see Ava again. He couldn't deny that he had been looking forward to seeing her at his party, that he wanted to spend time with her that night. But he felt guilty for feeling that way, and quickly brushed those feelings aside. He wondered if Ava's real reason for leaving was the incident from the previous night. She had said not to tell Jada that he'd seen her naked, so why would she leave so suddenly? He assumed that Ava had said some pretty painful things to his baby girl, since Jada's eyes were puffy from crying, and it seemed she'd gotten a

nosebleed from all the stress. He told her he loved her, assured her that
he was all she needed and that he wasn't going anywhere, and he got her
to smile. Jada masked her torment within, and got dressed to help her
man celebrate his birthday.

That night was one of the longest of Jada's life. Not only had Ava left
her house after discovering her secret, but Born was here celebrating his
birthday on a splendid ship in the middle of the water, surrounded by all
the people he thought knew and loved him. His mother was there, several of his boys from back in the day, and all the friends he'd made during his meteoric rise. And by his side was Jada, the one woman he loved
and adored. She was all that he ever wanted in a woman, and she knew
that it was all a lie. She wasn't the person he thought he knew. She was a
cokehead, as Ava had told her she was. She was a liar, and a drug addict,
and she didn't deserve this man who loved her so much. Jada was inwardly distraught but outwardly stunning, as she made the rounds with
Born. He paraded her around, as proud as a peacock for being with her.
She looked amazing in her black Gucci dress and shoes, with her hair
done in a neat ponytail. Jada felt like the party would never end. All she
wanted was to find a way to fix the mess she made, and to try and right
her wrongs before the next person who discovered her secret was Born.

25

BLINDFOLDS

Sunny was excited about tonight. It was the night of Born's party aboard the cruise ship, and she was overseeing the minutest of details. She got her manicure and pedicure done, and her outfit pressed and delivered. Her hair was styled to perfection, and she felt great. The whole affair had been Sunny's brainchild. She wanted an excuse to celebrate, another reason to party. She used Born's birthday as an excuse to throw a big gathering aboard a ship that circled New York Harbor. Sunny was bored. She was sick of the day-in and day-out cycle of parties and bullshit. So she put her all into the planning of Born's party. Of course, she enlisted Jada's help. Born was, after all, *her* man. But Sunny made sure her preferences were made clear when it came to the decor, the meals, and the liquor. The party was a gift from Dorian, and Sunny felt that she was playing her position as wifey by ensuring that Dorian's reputation for throwing an amazing party remained intact. She saw that every detail was attended to. Jada's job was to let her know Born's favorite color, his favorite dessert, and his ring size. Dorian had a nice surprise in store for Born.

Sunny arranged to rent the entire top level of the vessel for Born's birthday party. She knew the party was going to be fabulous. But she had ulterior motives this evening. She wanted to show Ava that the lifestyle she and Jada were living was indeed glamorous and enticing. She wanted Ava to see that this life was a good life, if you make it that way. It seemed to Sunny that Ava thought she was above her sister. Dorian had taught her how to read people well. And she could tell that Ava loved her sister. The bond between them was obvious. But it also seemed like Ava believed that since she'd done the right thing— graduated with honors, gone on to college—she was somehow more deserving than her sister. More worthy of the finer things in life. Sunny saw that Ava was intrigued by how her sister lived. But she could also see that she disapproved. In Sunny's opinion, Jada was doing alright for herself. Shit, they both were. Sunny and Jada had expensive homes, clothes, cars, and jewels. What more could one ask for? She wanted to show Ava the family atmosphere among them. Maybe then she'd feel differently.

Sunny heard the phone ringing just as she was contemplating going upstairs to take a hit. She walked to the living room and picked up the cordless handset. "Hello?" she answered, as she headed for the stairs.

"Wassup, Sunny?" Raquel's voice resounded in her ear.

"Dorian's not here." Sunny prepared to hang up the phone.

"I know. 'Cuz he's here." Raquel sounded like she was laughing at her.

Sunny stopped climbing the stairs, holding on to the rail for support. She kept her voice nonchalant, and said, "What kind of desperate shit are you pulling now, Raquel?"

"You told me to keep riding Dorian," Raquel reminded her. "And I've been doing just that. I've been riding him, sucking him, fucking him—"

"Whatever!" Sunny laughed, as if this was all bullshit. "He don't want you, bitch."

Raquel laughed last, and hers was sinister as she cackled in Sunny's ear. "Oh, yes he does. He's supposed to be in VA now, right? I know what he told you. Check inside the zipper in his duffel bag when he comes home. He loves to see me in these."

The line went dead, as Raquel hung up the phone. Sunny was furious, and distraught. Raquel must be crazy. She sat there on the stairs leading to her bedroom, leading to her drugs. She paused, wondering where Dorian really was. After all, they were hosting a party in less than an hour, and he was supposed to be driving home from Virginia, just as

Raquel had said. He *was* driving home from VA, she told herself. Dorian wouldn't mess with Raquel again after all they'd been through.

Sunny felt a tear roll down her cheek. And she wondered who she was kidding. She looked around her at all the things she and Dorian had, all the things they shared: the photos, the memories, the furniture, the paint on the walls. It was all theirs. It was what they had built. She had the appearance of love, and of protection. But where was Dorian? Where was he every night when she was getting high with her friends, and spending money like time? All the years of women—Raquel and others—and she had stayed. She stayed, and she got high to ease the pain.

She was angry, and she was hurt. It was probably true. Raquel had probably been fucking him all along. Sunny cried, realizing that she got high so much to escape that truth. But she'd known it all along. Part of her was not at all surprised by what she had been told. She turned and ran up the stairs, and into her bedroom. She looked around, and grabbed her red Coach bag. She pulled out her stash, and laid her escape route out for herself once more. But looking in her dresser mirror at her own reflection, Sunny saw herself so clearly. She paused. She looked at the sadness in her eyes. The pain. She saw herself as she truly was, and she shook her head in despair, and held on to the dresser for support.

She had to stop running from the truth. Sunny saw herself, really, as the beautiful bombshell who still didn't think she was good enough. She was the swan who still looked in the mirror and saw an ugly duckling. Every time Dorian cheated on her, Sunny's self-esteem plummeted another notch. She reasoned that he must be cheating because she was unable to give him children. She was flawed, she thought, and Dorian wanted what she couldn't provide for him. It made her feel inadequate, and she had tried so hard to be his all in all. She wanted Dorian to see her, and to want nothing more.

Sunny took her hit, and proceeded to pack her belongings wildly. She ravaged their bedroom, bathroom, and linen closet as she prepared her exit. She was out of there! She knocked over vases and picture frames, perfume bottles and jewelry boxes. Tearing a path to her luggage, she proceeded to toss all of her things into suitcases. Fuck the party! Fuck Dorian, and all of it! Sunny was fed up.

Dorian finally arrived, at the very height of Sunny's frenzy. As soon as she heard him come in the front door, she came charging down the stairs, and pounced on him. Knowing that Sunny was a live wire, at first he thought she was happy to see him. It was the night of Born's birthday party, after all, and he knew that Sunny loved to party. But instead of embracing him, Sunny snatched his duffel bag from his hand, zipped it open, and reached into its inside pocket. She dug around for a second, and then pulled out a piece of pink fabric. Holding it up, she looked at him, heartbroken. Dorian was confused. Realizing what it was, he tried to grab it back. But Sunny held it at bay. He knew right away that Raquel had set him up. That little bitch!

Dorian stood calmly, looking around at the path of destruction that had been laid throughout his home. He looked at Sunny as she screamed at him, so close to his face that he could smell her Newport-tainted breath. *"I hate you!"*

She ran up the stairs to resume packing her things. Her suspicions had been confirmed, and she was fed up. Dorian was furious with himself. He knew that he was slipping. He knew that Raquel was open. He knew she hated Sunny, that the two of them were in a competition for his love. But to Dorian, there was no competition. His heart belonged to Sunny. He had love for Raquel as the mother of his son. And yeah, he played himself from time to time and hit it. But only because of the sense of entitlement he felt with her. She was his baby's mama, so in his mind that gave him carte blanche to fuck her when he saw fit. Raquel was good in bed. But at the end of the day, she was just a plaything he found hard to resist.

Raquel was cut off completely when she shot at Sunny at his party. Dorian had refused to see her, and forbid her from coming near him or Sunny. Raquel had followed all his rules, and didn't bother him. She had been civil toward him when it came to discussing their son. But otherwise it had seemed that she was ready to move on. But then she had gotten herself a new man. When Dorian found out that Raquel was fucking with some nine-to-five nigga who her friend had introduced her to, he was upset. He was at her house picking up D.J. one night when Mr. Legit came to take her out. Dorian had just put D.J. in the car when he saw the guy pull up in his Audi, and ring the bell. Dorian walked back toward the house, and was at the man's side just as Raquel opened the door.

"Who the fuck is this?" he had demanded, looking at Raquel while pointing at her date.

Raquel looked surprised, but she explained that his name was Jason and he was taking her out. Dorian shook his head, and looked at the lame beside him. "You ain't taking her nowhere, my man. Beat it before I lose my temper."

Jason looked at Raquel, expecting her to protest. She didn't. Not wanting a fight with the intimidating character before him, Raquel's date turned and got back in his car, and drove off. Raquel was furious. She had argued with Dorian for over an hour, telling him that he couldn't ban her from his life and then forbid her from having one of her own. Dorian, honestly, didn't understand why he felt so territorial when it came to her. But he wasn't ready to let some other man play father to his son. Against his better judgment, he started fucking with her again. His only condition was that she had to agree to be discreet and keep it from Sunny. Raquel had been complying with that rule for months, and giving him top of the line head to boot. He had spent the past two evenings sitting back in his favorite seat in her living room, with her on all fours on the floor before him—all while a porno played on her big TV. Dorian had felt like a king, as Raquel had devoured his manhood like a hungry cat. With her ass seductively posed in the air for him to see, she would stare into his eyes as she pleasured him. The look in her eyes said, "I adore you." "I'll do whatever you want." He was caught up, and he had let his guard down. And now Raquel had exposed that vulnerability.

On this day Raquel had sexed him so perfectly that Dorian had fallen asleep afterward, right there in his favorite chair. He had only meant to close his eyes for a second, but that second had lasted hours, and Raquel had let him sleep. She never even bothered to awaken him, knowing that this was the night of Born's party and that Sunny would be waiting. Raquel was no longer allowed to attend events that Sunny attended, so she was more than happy to let him rest comfortably. Obviously, she had slipped the panties he liked so much into his bag. He had fucked up, and he knew it.

He climbed the stairs, and surveyed the damage that Sunny had done to their home in her fury. Sunny was angrily packing her things, and Dorian stood in the doorway of their bedroom watching her.

"Here I am trying to have a party, and show Ava that this shit is love. That this shit is sweet. But it's all fake, Dorian! All this shit is fake! You're fuckin' *'I love you's'* are fake, *you're* fake!" Sunny was irate. "The bitch fuckin' shot at me! She shot at me, Dorian! She terrorizes me with the fact that I can't have your kids, and you're still fucking her! You heartless bastard! *I fuckin' hate you!!"*

Dorian calmly stepped over the clothes and bags, shoes and boxes strewn across the floor. He sat in the leather armchair near the window, and lit a half blunt that sat idly in the ashtray on the small table close by. He puffed the marijuana smoke as Sunny ranted and raved, as she packed her things, with tears cascading down her face. She was furious that he sat there so calmly, because she was seriously leaving. Even though she dreaded going back to her mother, who would surely urge her to work it out. After all, Dorian financed their lifestyles. Their whole family had too much invested for her to walk away. She had no idea where she would go. But she had money, and that's all she needed. She was leaving Dorian for good this time.

Dorian exhaled, and the smoke filled the room. He watched Sunny struggle to zip her overstuffed suitcase. "I know you've been stealing from me," he said. "And I didn't leave *you.*" He puffed some more. Sunny turned around and looked at him, the shock evident on her face. Dorian took another toke, and continued. "I've always known about it. Why do you think I started leaving more money than usual laying around? I used to ask you to count my money for me, when I had already counted it. Just to see what you would do. I was testing you. 'Cuz I always gave to you." Dorian's tone was calm and very relaxed, as he continued to smoke. "Whatever you wanted. Trips, clothes, cars, parties, whatever you wanted. I do for your family. But I know women always want more. They can't resist temptation. So eventually, things changed, and you slipped. Eighty-seven hundred dollars on the dresser became eighty-five hundred dollars when I woke up. I was gonna leave you then. But I watched and waited to see what you would do. I wanted to see what you would buy that I wasn't already giving you."

Sunny stood still, tears streaming down her face, hanging on his every word. She was stunned by what she was hearing.

"I watched you. But you didn't use the money you took to buy anything. You started stashing it. I saw you hiding money. You would put it in a box of shoes at the bottom of your closet."

Sunny smirked, amused at how well Sherlock had known her all along.

"You had a shoebox with a pair of pink high heels inside. But inside the toe of the shoes, you used to hide money. I knew all about it. You had a lot of it, too. When you filled up that box, you started using another one at the bottom of your closet. At first I thought you was trying to play me. But you just kept stacking dough. I saw that all you really wanted was to be able to feel like you had your own. You were so independent, and you always hated having to come to me and ask for money. I *always* noticed that. I would tell you, 'Sunny, you and your family can come to me for *whatever* you need.' And your family came to me. They came with no problem. But not you. You didn't like feeling like you were getting a handout. So you stole to make yourself feel like it was something you earned. But even what you took was used for me or for us, for the house. Sometimes just for you, but I didn't mind. I loved you. I understood you." Dorian paused, and lit the blunt that had burned out as he talked. He inhaled, exhaled, and stared into Sunny's eyes across the room. "But then my *work* started to come up short."

Sunny held her breath, her heart racing like a horse in her chest.

"I always told you stories about my dealings with these customers of mine. I always warned you not to go that route, because of what I've seen. I told you that muthafuckas will make it sound appealing and fun, but that shit is no joke. Cocaine is nothing to fuck with. I once saw a fiend take a hit, and then she just broke out running and screaming at the top of her lungs. It was funny, and me and you laughed about it when I told you. But that shit ain't really funny. What I'm selling here is the devil, just in powder form. This shit is poison. And I warned you that that fiend who ran off like she was possessed was no different from the bitches you see at parties looking gorgeous, and are still in the bathroom getting high. It looks like they're maintaining. But that's just an illusion. There's always a story behind all that bullshit. It looks fun and enticing, but that shit is the worst. And you said you understood, princess. *I told you!* I told you about all your friends who were models and actresses, and all that other shit. They're the worst ones. Most of them bitches are high all the time. You thought I wanted to hold you back. You acted like I didn't want you to have your own spotlight. But I was only trying to keep you from getting too close to the fire."

He put his blunt down, and walked silently toward her. Sunny could barely look him in his eyes.

"When my work started coming up short, I thought I was buggin' at first. Figured I counted wrong. But the first time, it was one missing. The next time, it was three. Whoa, wait a minute. I knew I didn't count wrong. So I watched you one time. You thought I was distracted with D.J. when he came over. He was little then, and you came upstairs to find some movie he wanted to watch. You thought I was downstairs with him, but I crept up the stairs and watched you. You came in here, and you went in my stash, and you took one. Then you went in the bathroom." Dorian shook his head, still disturbed by that memory. The first time he knew for sure that Sunny was using. "I knew. I didn't confront you, because I didn't know what to say about it. I was already in love with you, and I felt responsible. I felt like it was *my* fault, because of the life I lived, and how I exposed you to the shit."

Sunny saw Dorian's eyes getting misty. He had never seemed so hurt in all the years she'd known him. And she was ashamed that she was the one who had disappointed him so much. She continued to cry.

He took her chin in his hand and tilted her face toward him. Dorian looked at her, piercingly. "When I found you, you were my little ghetto princess. I showed you this life . . . I *gave* you this life. You didn't know about this lifestyle until I introduced you to it. I thought I didn't really have a right to say nothin' to you because of how I was living. I saw that you were maintaining. You didn't seem to be so far gone. I watched you even closer after that, and I would leave shit in your path to see if you would bite the bait. You did, and I never said *shit*." Dorian shook his head in regret. "But I never left you. Didn't stop fuckin' with you. Over and over again, you stole from me. You still steal from me. But I love you, and I *never* left. And now you're gonna leave me, baby girl? We both got things about us we need to change. But how you gonna stand in a glass house and throw stones at me, when you have your own reasons to be sorry?" Dorian gripped her chin more firmly.

Sunny was in full tears now. There were no words, because she was at a loss. What could she say? Dorian knew the truth.

He saw the terror in her eyes—fear mixed with regret—and he let go of her face. He looked in her eyes. "I still love you, Sunny. But now, your shit is out of control. Now, you're *always* high. You're high right now. You can't control it no more. And as much as I hate to admit it, you need help now."

He wiped her eyes. And he felt himself almost want to cry. But Dorian wasn't the crying type. He manned up, and bit his lip to stop it from shaking. "I feel responsible, because I knew, and I didn't stop you. I didn't have the heart to stop you—"

Sunny had the hiccups from all her waterworks. She hadn't said a word so far, and she felt the need to try to explain. "It's not your fault, D. I got myself on this shit. I was just . . ."

"I know how it happens. I seen the shit a million times. But as long as you seemed to be in control, I was giving it to you, on the low. I might as well have been putting it in your hand. And then when you started being high *every* day, I couldn't stand seeing you so twisted all the time. I couldn't stand to be around you. I couldn't watch you like that— destroying yourself. But I loved you so much that I never had the heart to walk away from you."

Sunny wiped her eyes and looked up sadly at Dorian. "So is that why you're still fuckin' with Raquel? Because you think I got a problem?"

Dorian hugged Sunny. "You do have a problem," he said. He kissed her on the forehead, and took a step back from her. "And yeah, that's part of it. But I can't place all the blame on you. I made a big mistake. I was fuckin' with Raquel; I won't insult your intelligence and deny it. I was fuckin' her. But only because I could. And I'm sorry for that. I let her weaken me. But I still don't love her. You're still my angel, Sunny. You're still my heart. Even with you using that shit, and stealing my dough . . . I got it bad for you, ma. I can't walk away from you. And I'm telling you now I ain't letting you walk away from me." He looked like he meant it, and Sunny was so happy to hear him say it. She didn't want him to let her leave. She wanted him to make it all right. Dorian pulled her into his arms. "But you gotta stop. You gotta get this under control."

Sunny nodded, clinging to Dorian for dear life. "I will. I'm gonna stop, I swear."

He rocked her in his arms, told her that he still loved her, and pulled her toward their bed. Dorian undressed her slowly, and made love to her for the first time in months. They did it right there on the bed on top of all the clothes she had thrown across it in her haste to leave. They were blind to all the scattered debris, and for the moment they were above their problems. It seemed like they had rediscovered each other, and they loved one another with a passion that took their breath away. Drenched in sweat, and drained, they lay together afterward, knowing without saying it that this was a new beginning for them. They had finally stopped ignoring the truth.

As they lay there together, Sunny finally admitted that she needed help. Dorian promised her, swore to her, that he would be by her side every step of the way. He was finished with Raquel. He swore on his life.

They dressed for the party, and drove there holding hands in the car. When Born arrived with Jada on his arm, the party went wild. He and Jada looked great together—she in a skintight black Gucci dress, and Born in black denim jeans and a black button-up and black Timbs. Both of them were dripping in diamonds so clear and large that they gleamed in the moonlight. Born walked in smiling, and stayed that way the whole night. The music was a blend of all the decades in which Born had lived. Starting in the seventies and going all the way through to the nineties, the deejay kept the party going. They had a huge birthday cake with Born's picture on it, and everyone on board the beautiful ship sang happy birthday to him. When the singing and toasting died down, and the deejay brought it to the present-day with B.I.G., Kim, Foxy, and the Wu, Dorian pulled Born aside. He brought him down to one of the lower decks, and into a room way in the cut.

When Dorian turned the knob and Born entered the room behind him, he was confused by what he saw. At the table sat all of Dorian's crew: his two brothers, Sunny's brother who worked with him, Zion—the man who had introduced him to Dorian in the first place—and all his cohorts. Around this table sat the inner circle. The trusted few. The only people with whom Dorian really broke bread. In all, there were eight men who joined Dorian around the table. Powerful men. All of them had proven themselves trustworthy and sincere. Every one of them was his family.

But what made this all the more intriguing to Born was that every man's wifey was present also. The women sat around the table, each woman beside her man. Born noticed Sunny standing and smiling near the head of the table, and Jada was beside her. Dorian handed Born a box wrapped in black paper with a white bow on it.

Born smiled. "What's goin' on?"

Dorian smiled back. "Everyone in this room is part of the Family. The men you see seated around this table are my partners, guys who I do business with. But they're also the niggas I would go to war with, no questions asked. There's an attorney, Grant Keys, who works for the D.A.'s office in Brooklyn." Dorian motioned toward a very well-dressed and conservative-looking man seated next to Zion. "He can get you a bail hearing in the middle of the night if you need it. My nigga has judges in his pocket who he can call on if we need it. He can also let you know when a case is stacked against you, or what loopholes you can use to get out of some shit. Zion, as you know, is a bricklayer like us. But he's also making legitimate money in the music industry, with his production company. He knows a lot of people on both sides of the law, and you never know when you might need his resources." Dorian went all around the table, introducing each man and explaining his role in their organization. Born was fascinated.

"This is my crew," Dorian explained. "These women are their other halves; therefore, they're also part of my crew. There's a lot of power in this room. You read about some of us in the *Daily News,* and you hear about some of us on the street. We come from the same grit, and we made something out of nothing. We may not always use the same tactics to get money, but we get it nonetheless. And we stick together. We make things happen for each other. But there's a couple things you should know before I go any further. First of all, I don't welcome nobody into my crew I don't trust." Dorian counted off with his fingers. "Second, I don't fuck with niggas who don't get money . . . and I mean *all* the money." Laughter trickled throughout the room.

Dorian grinned at his friend, who reminded him of his younger self. "And third, I don't like a nigga who can't be humble. Some niggas let their hunger for power overshadow their loyalty to their friends. They get larceny in their hearts, and there's no larceny in our crew. Now, over the past few years, I've trusted you with a lot of money. There's been situations where I showed you that you can trust me as well, and that I have your back as long as you got mine." Dorian nodded his head for emphasis. Born remembered the situations Dorian was referring to as well, particularly when Celly had plotted to set him up. He was grateful for all that Dorian had done for him. "And I know that you're a humble man, and you're loyal. So this is for you." Everyone waited patiently as Dorian motioned for Born to open up his present.

Born tore open the wrapping, and opened the box to reveal a large platinum ring with a very distinctive design. The face was covered in diamonds so large they glistened. Dorian explained. "This ain't just a birthday present. It's your medallion. You're part of the crew now. We don't draw attention to ourselves with big chains with symbols, or have a special handshake. We don't dress up in all kinds of colors, or none of that. We wear our rings, and these are our medallions. There's only nine other rings like that one, and every man in this room has one of those rings. If you need something, there's someone in this room who can make it happen for you. And you will be called on to make shit happen for some of us at times, too. We do our shit quietly, and we wear our medallions proudly. So, here's yours, my nigga. Welcome to the Family." Born was moved beyond words at this gesture, and Jada stood smiling proudly. Born put on his ring, and gave Dorian a handshake and a hug as applause filled the room. Sunny raised her champagne glass in a toast, and everyone in the room returned the gesture. They toasted to Born, the newest member of the crew, and everyone sipped their champagne in unison.

It was a beautiful moment, and one that Born would never forget. Jada walked over and hugged him. He smiled at her, and thought she looked more beautiful than ever as she smiled back at that moment. She showed him her own "medallion"—a smaller, feminine version of Born's ring that she wore on her right ring finger. He smiled, knowing without being told that the women getting rings was all Sunny's idea.

Dorian and Born spoke privately after the crew's meeting. "Born, I want to let you know that I'm taking some time off to focus my attention on Sunny. She found out that I was fuckin' Raquel, and I almost lost her." Dorian shook his head at how close he had come to losing Sunny. "I gotta do what I can to make shit right, so I'm asking you to step up to the plate. I need you to be my eyes in the back of my head, so to speak. Take the reins and hold me down."

Born nodded, and assured Dorian that he had his back. "I got you, man. You know that."

Dorian looked at Born. He raised one eyebrow, and looked at his young apprentice intently. "I want to offer you some advice. And listen carefully to what I'm saying." Dorian placed one hand on Born's shoulder, and looked him square in the eyes. "Don't let your business get in the way of your relationship. Keep your eye on Jada. Pay attention to her. Make sure she's keeping her nose clean."

Born nodded his head, figuring that Dorian was advising him to make sure he didn't neglect Jada the way he had neglected Sunny. He didn't catch the hidden meaning in Dorian's warning. Birds of a feather tended to flock together. And although Sunny had never told him outright that Jada was using cocaine, Dorian figured that she probably was. She and Sunny spent most of their time together. And Sunny spent most of her time getting high. Two plus two equals four. He hoped that Born would heed his warning. The two men went off to find the women they loved, and rejoined the party.

All evening Dorian kept Sunny close to him. Jada didn't seem to mind the fact that they didn't slip away to get high like they usually did. She was distracted, anyway. Jada clung to Born for most of the night, explaining Ava's absence as due to illness when people asked. She looked like she was quietly playing her position with a smile on her face that night. But in truth, she had so much on her mind. Jada didn't tell Sunny about Ava discovering her secret, and she suffered that night, once again, in silence.

26

BLOWN AWAY

Sunny was reclaiming her love affair with Dorian. She made up her mind that night that she was going to kick her habit. She had a great man who had her back, and she felt she could face anything. Anything in the world.

Days turned into weeks, and weeks into months, as Sunny and Dorian began to piece her back together. She stopped partying, and Dorian let Born handle most of the business. What they needed to focus their attention on was their relationship, and they both recognized that. They still had love between them, and a relationship worth salvaging. So, they began to do just that. Every day, Sunny was tempted. Dorian did his best to fill the void that getting high had left, by substituting it with love. He told Sunny he was proud of her. That she was beautiful, and that she looked like an angel. She *was* his angel. Every day was a clean slate, he told her. And every day he told her that he was proud of her. That she was stronger than that poison. Sunny took it one day at a time, and before she knew it, it had been two months since Dorian had revealed that he knew the truth of her addiction. Sunny hadn't taken a single hit. She was so proud of herself. And now, to make things even better, she found out that she was pregnant. Sunny had gone to her doctor, complaining that she was throwing up violently. She thought it might have been withdrawal from the drugs. But the doctor confirmed what she had secretly known in her heart. She was pregnant.

She couldn't wait to tell Dorian. She got home after her early morning appointment and waited. She knew that Dorian would be home before noon to check on her. Sunny was in the kitchen making him breakfast for when he returned from his early run to handle business. He walked in, looking just as he had when she first met him. This was one of the two faces of her baby. When he was being Dorian the distinguished businessman, he was always well dressed, in expensive clothes, jewels, and footwear. But when he was being D the ruthless hustler, he wore the uniform of the streets. He entered wearing Timbs, dark jeans, and a hoodie. The hood was pulled low on his head, concealing his face somewhat. He stomped in, with his sexy and confident stride, and Sunny was ecstatic. Unlike the old days, she didn't concern herself with where he'd been. She was beginning to trust Dorian so much more. He no longer went to pick D.J. up personally from Raquel's house. He would send one of his soldiers to do it, telling Raquel to have him ready in time for someone to come and get his son. He had no phone conversations with Raquel unless Sunny was there, and the phone was on a speaker. He wasn't taking any chances. He loved Sunny that much. And since their confrontation, she had changed back to the woman he had fallen in love with. She was sexy again, not moody. She was his princess once more, and Raquel wasn't going to have the opportunity to ruin that again. He was grateful for the new start he and Sunny had been blessed with. Dorian nurtured her slowly back to the normalcy of being clean.

He couldn't take his eyes off of her. And then he couldn't keep his hands off of her. Their lovemaking was intense, just like it had been in the beginning, and Dorian and Sunny found themselves hungering for each other like never before.

Dorian came home and smelled the scent of breakfast wafting through his home. Sunny was cooking! He walked into the kitchen, and saw a sight for sore eyes. Sunny was as naked as a newborn child, except for a white apron tied around her slim waist. She looked delicious. He smiled wide, and took the hood off his head. Dorian walked over and covered her mouth with his, as the turkey bacon sizzled on the stove. He tossed her small body up on the countertop, and put himself between her legs.

He didn't enter her immediately. Instead, he rubbed his dick against her warmness, and teased her as he kissed her. Sunny sucked on Dorian's lips as she kissed him, and then she felt him inside of her. He held her bare ass in the palms of his hands, and stroked her with such perfection that she called out his name. Sunny moved with him, and they were one, as they breathed heavily, thrusting. Dorian sucked her neck, ever so softly, and held her so perfectly. She loved the way he handled her, and he loved the way she responded to him. Dorian didn't stop until the last bit of his seed was spent. He stared into her face, still standing between her legs, as she sat atop the counter. Then he kissed her again, softly. Sunny took Dorian's face in her delicate hands.

"I'm pregnant again."

Dorian smiled from ear to ear. But he could hear the fear in her voice. He kissed her lips, long and firm. He took off the apron tied around her nude body, and he kissed her belly. It was flat against his face, and he kissed it again for good measure. He looked at her abs, wondering how small his child was at that moment, loving the fact that his seed was growing inside of her womb.

"Hold tight, little one," he said to his unborn child. "I want to meet you in nine months. I want to see your beautiful mother holding you in her arms. So be strong." He stood back up, and faced Sunny. She threw her arms around his neck, and hugged him tightly to her. She kissed his face, his neck, and hugged him, elatedly crying. She had never been happier in all her life.

Sunny stayed drug free. She was adamant that this baby would live. This one would survive. She did everything right, getting the proper rest and eating the proper food. She took all the vitamins, went to every appointment, and prayed every single day. Sunny's crazy lifestyle was replaced by a calm one, and Dorian was at home with her every night, happily awaiting the completion of their family.

Jada, meanwhile, was at a crossroads. She no longer had what Sunny stole from Dorian to get her high. She had to find her own cocaine. She had a serious habit by now, and an expensive one, but no money. So now she had a problem. She had never listened to Sunny and saved for a rainy day, though this wasn't the kind of rainy day Sunny had been talking about. Besides, anyone she bought it from would surely tell Born, and then Jada's secret would be exposed. She had no choice. She started stealing from Born.

She knew that he kept meticulous count of the drugs he kept at home. He still counted and recounted his money and his drugs before going to sleep at night. After dealing with an addict all his life—his father—he knew that the temptation never leaves. Born was too smart for her to go that route. She couldn't take it from him outright. She found another way. Jada stole the keys to Born's stash house in Park Hill, made a copy for herself, and replaced them without him noticing.

Jada began to head to Park Hill every day. She would park nearby, and wait until she saw the workers leave to make deliveries. Once they were gone, she would go inside and take the drugs she needed. She was careful not to take too many at one time. She didn't want to set off any alarms. She was now doing the one thing that she had sworn she'd never do. She was stealing from the one man who had ever truly loved her. She kept getting high to get away from the feeling in the pit of her stomach when she came down.

Jada still spoke to Sunny, but not nearly as frequently. Sunny was pregnant, and Jada was happy for her. At least when she was high, she was happy for Sunny. When Jada wasn't high, she would depress herself by dwelling on the fact that she wasn't the one starting a family and getting her act together. Sunny was getting help, and Jada was falling deeper into her addiction.

By her fourth month of pregnancy, Sunny was nervous. This was the point at which she usually miscarried. But this time, it was different. She didn't have any trouble holding this baby, and her doctor told her that everything was pointing toward this being a successful pregnancy. Sunny was relieved, and Dorian was over the moon with excitement and joy. He'd seen a change in her. He knew that having the baby made it easier for her to stay clean. He liked her like this, and Dorian was determined to spend the rest of his days happy with his princess. He was oblivious to Raquel, silently seething on the sidelines.

Raquel believed that Dorian had tossed her aside because Sunny had forced him to. She didn't see that it had been her own actions that had made him leave her. It was her own fault that the man no longer had words for her, no more sex for her. Raquel was consumed with jealousy and hatred toward Sunny, and she couldn't control her rage. She followed Sunny and Dorian when they went out, watched them when they had no idea that she was anywhere around. She was obsessed, and her son, D.J., was caught in the middle of it all.

Whenever he came back from spending time with his father, Raquel questioned him, and dug for information about what was going on in Sunny and Dorian's home. D.J. loved Sunny, and was excited by the idea of having a little brother or sister. When he spoke about his excitement to his mother, Raquel got so angry that she yelled at him.

"I don't want to hear that shit!" she screamed. *"Fuck Sunny!"* Her voice bellowed, and D.J. stepped back, afraid. He was only four years old, and he was frightened by seeing his mother unraveling as she was. Raquel threw the brush in her hand, and it shattered the lamp on her living room table. She was enraged by this, and she cursed crazily to herself as she stormed out of the room. Raquel was out of control. "I hate that *bitch*! I fuckin' hate her!"

D.J. ran to his room and shut the door. He couldn't wait until his father sent for him, so that he could get away from his mother. Even at his young age, he could tell that she was slowly losing her mind.

On the day of Sunny's baby shower, during the eighth month of her pregnancy, Sunny was concerned that she looked like a monster. Her perfectly shaped nose had spread out, and now looked like she had Michael Jackson's original nose on her round face. She felt fat and unattractive, and she couldn't figure out what to wear to make herself look like the Sunny everyone knew and loved. There wouldn't be a sexy dress on Sunny at this party! She was in her walk-in closet trying to find a suitable outfit, when Dorian walked in, beaming with pride.

He looked at her soft, light legs as she stood with only a shirt and panties on. Sunny thought she'd lost her sex appeal, but Dorian found her to be more beautiful than ever. He loved her more than he ever had before, and was praying for a girl with Sunny's face and Dorian's mentality. He wanted their daughter to be the perfect blend of the two of them.

"What are you doin' in there?" he asked, smiling, as he watched Sunny dig through all her maternity clothes to find the perfect outfit for the occasion. "No matter what you put on, you're still gonna be the prettiest girl in the place, so what's the problem?"

Sunny turned around and smiled. "I don't want to look fat," she said, laughing. She rubbed her big round belly for emphasis.

Dorian walked over and kissed her bulging tummy. "You don't look fat, princess. You look pregnant. And I'm so fuckin' proud that you're pregnant with my baby." He kissed her on her soft lips, and slapped her playfully on the ass.

She smiled. "You say all the right things."

Dorian pulled out a blue denim maternity dress, and held it up. "Why don't you wear this? It's sexy." It was anything but. Sexy would never be a real term used to describe that dress. He grinned, playfully, and Sunny snatched the dress from him.

"You play too much." She held it up, and looked at it. "You think I should wear it?" It was a knee-length denim dress that hugged her pregnant belly, and it fell just below her knees. She liked it.

He nodded. "Yup. Put that on, baby. That's what Daddy wants to see you in today."

Dorian walked downstairs, leaving Sunny to get dressed. Sunny's mother, Marisol, along with Jada, Sunny's friend Olivia, and about four other women from the crew were all downstairs, decorating the house with pastel-colored streamers, balloons, and signs. Olivia laid out favors shaped like baby rattles with soft green ribbons attached. Jada hung a sign over Sunny's shower chair that said CONGRATULATIONS in big lettering. Marisol was in the kitchen with the other women making all sorts of food for the occasion—Spanish and soul food dishes. Dorian felt like an outcast in a house full of women. He went back upstairs and found Sunny preparing to get into the shower. He snuck up from behind and put his hands on her breasts, startling her.

She spun around, and slapped him, jokingly. "What are you trying to do, scare me to death?"

Dorian silenced her with a kiss, and then scooped her up in his arms and laid her on the bed. She giggled, as he ran to lock their bedroom door, and then began to take his clothes off. "We can't have sex with my mother right downstairs, Dorian!" Sunny protested weakly, as he undressed her.

He smiled a naughty smile. "Why not? It ain't like she don't know that we be doin' it."

Sunny giggled. "But she's here!"

"So?" He kissed her to silence any further protests. Coming up for air at last, he said, "She won't hear you. I promise."

Dorian smothered her in kisses, and made love to Sunny slowly. He kissed her from head to toe, and he handled her body so delicately. Never in her life had Sunny felt love like this. She forgot about all the guests arriving downstairs, and which outfit she would wear. She was in harmony with the man she loved, and it was heaven.

When they both lay breathless, staring into each other's eyes, Dorian shook his head. "I'm a lucky man," he said. "You know, the first time I saw you I didn't think you'd even talk to me. You're so beautiful, and I figured niggas tried to holla at you all the time. So when I stepped to you I was half expecting you to shut me down. But you didn't. I remember being so happy when I walked away with your phone number. I felt like God was smiling on me. And even with all the problems we've had, I still feel like he smiled on me the day that I met you. That day in the mall, I think I was meant to meet you. I was waiting for you, Sunny. This relationship, this baby . . . it's all that I need. I'm completely happy now. I really love you."

Sunny smiled, her cheeks pudgy and cute in her pregnant state. She whispered, "I really love you, too, Dorian."

He lightly pinched her nose, and grinned. "You better get downstairs and explain all this to your mother. I'm gonna tell her how you seduced me."

Sunny swatted at Dorian, and he ducked playfully. He sat up and helped her roll up out of bed. Then she got dressed, while he went downstairs to see who had arrived. The first face he saw was Born's, and he smiled. He was happy to see him, and greeted him as he came down the stairs.

Born was already chewing. "Yo, they got the fuckin' arroz con pollo up in there, D. That authentic Puerto Rican shit, too. Not that other bullshit Jada be—"

"Keep talking, and you won't eat at home for months," Jada remarked snidely, as she walked up on him. She batted her eyelashes. "Wassup, Dorian?"

Dorian laughed at the two of them, and said, "Jada, girl, I know you can burn. I don't know what your boy over here is talking about."

Jada chuckled and walked away, scowling at Born. He looked at Dorian and said, with his mouth full of food, "How you gonna sell me out like that?"

Dorian laughed at him, and they followed Jada into the spacious kitchen. Sunny's mother was still cooking. She cut her eyes at Dorian, and set her lips tightly. Dorian didn't have to ask what was wrong with her, because it wasn't long before she spoke her mind. "While you two are up there *getting it on,* and shit, Dorian"—her Nuyorican accent was priceless—"you got people out there waiting to eat. Wash your hands, and bring some of this food out there for everybody." She rolled her eyes, and grabbed a dish towel. She wound it up, and playfully swatted him on his back.

Dorian tried to mask the grin on his face, until Born said, "Nasty ass!"

Jada, Marisol, and all the other family members moving about the kitchen laughed at Dorian's expense. Dorian shook his head, and grabbed a platter of fried chicken and brought it out to the living room. He looked around and saw that his two brothers had arrived with their wives. He walked over and greeted them with hugs and smiles. Sunny's two brothers had also come, along with her father, Dale, and several of Sunny's friends. The doorbell was ringing steadily. One of Sunny's friends greeted guests at the door, and hung up their coats. It was January 1998, and the temperature had plummeted to twenty-eight degrees. The door-check girl hung up one fur, leather, or shearling after another. Dorian knew that this was only the beginning of the onslaught of guests he was expecting. They were going to pour out the world to Dorian, Sunny, and their baby. His happiness was beyond measure. Born followed him, and pulled him to the side.

"Yo, I'm not staying for long, D. I ain't sitting up in here with all these women with all them presents to open." Born pointed to the dining room table already loaded with boxes large and small.

Dorian frowned. "You think I'm sitting in here for all that gift opening and shit? Hell no! I'm gonna open up *the crew's* gifts with her. Now, the rest of that shit? Hell, no. I got the men set up in the basement with the game on. The bar is downstairs, so you know that's where I'll be."

Born thought about the big pool table in Dorian's basement, and immediately nodded. "Oh, aiight. That's more like it."

Sunny came into the living room amid gasps and smiles. Everyone complimented her on how stunning she was. Knowing how vain Sunny was, no one mentioned her spreading nose and her pudgy face. She still looked radiant. Those who were close to her knew that she had struggled to have a child, and they were thrilled for her and Dorian. She had a glow that was unmistakable, and Dorian was all over her. He came up behind Sunny, his hands encircling her wide waistline. He rubbed her stomach, and Sunny smiled happily. Cameras flashed across the room. Everyone began snapping pictures. It was a Kodak moment, for sure.

"When are you two getting married?" somebody called out.

Dorian smiled at the idea, and looked at Sunny. "As soon as she has this baby, and the diva can fit into some tight-ass dress, we're gonna do it," Dorian announced. Everyone reacted with shouts and applause at this announcement. Sunny proudly flashed the huge ring on her left hand for emphasis.

Born stood beside Jada, and nudged her when he heard this. "Make sure you catch the bouquet at their wedding," he said. " 'Cuz we're next."

Jada smiled, and her eyes twinkled at the thought of being Born's wife. He kissed her, and for a moment she forgot all about her addiction and her secrets. Everything was going to be alright, she told herself. Everybody was used to hearing the doorbell by then, with guests arriving every few minutes like clockwork. But when the doorbell rang at that moment, it was like a bell tolling for things to come.

Dorian and Sunny continued to take pictures, until he saw Olivia standing near the door with the girl who had been checking coats. It looked to Dorian like Olivia was upset, and was trying to avert a commotion by not allowing someone to enter the house. Olivia was in somebody's face, denying them access to the party. He saw who it was, and walked toward the door.

"Raquel, what's your problem? You know better than to come to my house. What do you want? D.J.'s with my mother," Dorian hissed at her, careful not to speak too loudly and alert Sunny.

Raquel looked at him like he had lost his entire mind. "What the fuck you mean, I know better than to come to your house, Dorian? I'm your son's muthafuckin' mother! I can come over here anytime I want, and—"

"Yo, *what* do you want, Raquel?" Dorian wanted her gone! He didn't want anything to upset Sunny in any way. Not when she'd come so far along in her pregnancy without complications.

"I came to drop off a gift, damn!" She chewed her gum, angrily.

"Where's it at?" Dorian looked around. He saw a box in Raquel's hand, but she had it behind her back.

"Let me in like everybody else." She looked him dead in his eyes. Her eyes looked different to Dorian, though. He remembered times when he'd looked into them and saw a woman who loved him. He had once seen someone who would do anything in the world to please him. Now he saw Raquel as someone who was tinkering on the thin line between love and obsession. She looked as though the love she was feeling for him had become dangerous. Like she thought nothing had changed between them when everything had changed. He dismissed the thought of

Raquel being obsessed with him, for the first time in his life ignoring his gut instinct.

He laughed at her, and turned his back. Born was walking his way, coming to tell him that Sunny wanted to take more pictures. Dorian looked at him and nodded toward Raquel. "Get the gift she brought, and get her outta here, please."

Born headed toward Raquel as Dorian headed back toward Sunny.

"D, come and take a picture with Sunny!" somebody yelled from the living room.

Raquel craned her neck to see inside the house. She caught a glimpse of Sunny, with her long brown hair flowing down her back. Born saw the expression on Raquel's face change from a frown to pure pain. She began to cry, and Born felt bad.

He said, "Don't cry, ma." Born looked in the air, as if to say, "Why me?" as Raquel became absolutely hysterical, crying. He saw her reach into her bag, and he thought she was probably fumbling around for a tissue. Her makeup ran all over her face, and she was still crying steadily. Born turned for a split second to look over his shoulder, and that second cost all of them dearly.

Raquel pulled out a black .32-caliber gun. She charged past Born unexpectedly, and he grabbed for her. But it was too late. In his momentary loss of focus, he had underestimated Raquel and the determination of a woman fed up.

Raquel ran into the house, with Sunny in her sights. She aimed at the pregnant beauty as she stood posing for a picture with Dorian kneeling before her, holding her belly. His head was resting against Sunny's womb, as he knelt on one knee. Cameras flashed as Raquel came charging in. Everyone's attention was captured then, and they all began to run for cover. By then Born had drawn his own gun, and not wanting to kill Dorian's son's mother, he shot Raquel in the leg. Raquel fell to the floor and raised her arm, still crying.

She aimed at Sunny's belly, and Dorian rushed toward Raquel to stop her. He stood to his feet, and as he rose, Raquel fired. The bullet hit Dorian directly in his Adam's apple, barely missing Sunny and her unborn child. Sunny's father grabbed her quickly out of the line of fire as Dorian fell to the floor, gurgling on his own blood.

Horrified, Raquel and Sunny both screamed from the bottom of their souls. Sunny tried desperately to get to Dorian, who lay on the floor in a bloody pool, but her father held her tightly and wouldn't let her move from where he had her shielded, between the wall and the china closet. If Raquel came for Sunny, she was going to have to shoot him first.

Raquel stood up uneasily, with the gun still pointed at any and everyone. She was clearly in pain from the shot to the leg she'd sustained. She let out a scream that sent chills up all their spines, and she cried. Raquel had never meant to hurt Dorian. She just wanted Sunny dead. Sunny and her baby. That was all she had wanted, to see them dead—not Dorian. She looked at Dorian, put the gun in her mouth, and then closed her eyes as she pulled the trigger.

The shot went off just as Sunny broke free and ran to Dorian's side. He lay on the floor, his eyes open, looking like he had so much to say. But no words were possible as the blood poured from his throat. Marisol came and held a towel up to the wound to try and stop the bleeding as Jada frantically dialed an ambulance. Born sat on the stairs with his gun in his hand. He couldn't believe what had just happened. He felt responsible. He had turned away from Raquel for the briefest moment, and this was all his fault.

"Get her outta here, please." That's all that Dorian had asked him to do, and now he lay dying on the floor. Born felt like shit. Sunny was hysterical.

Anarchy erupted in the house that had once been filled with so much joy. The setting that was supposed to be one of love, happiness, and the celebration of a new life had turned into a bloody den of death, as Raquel lay sprawled across the floor. Cradling the love of her life in her arms, Sunny cried harder and harder. "I love you, Dorian," she told him. "I love you, baby. Please don't die. Please, Dorian. Don't leave me, baby."

He wanted to tell her that he loved her, too. That she was his everything, and that he was sorry. But the bullet wound in his throat continued to gush. He stared into Sunny's eyes, and tried to convey his love for her that way. She looked so beautiful, even as she cried, he thought. Dorian breathed his last breath in Sunny's arms, looking into her eyes, and a part of her died, too. She wouldn't let go of him—not even when the paramedics and police finally arrived. She stayed there on the floor, cradling Dorian's lifeless body in her arms until her family pried her away. Dorian was dead, and she may as well have been dead, too.

27

TANGLED WEBS

Sunny was a wreck. She stood hollering at the casket, where Dorian lay stretched in an Armani suit and silk tie. It was a hustler's reunion, as every baller in Brooklyn, and several from the surrounding boroughs as well came to pay their respects to Dorian Douglas. The November wind whistled outside the church, as mourners poured in by the dozens. Diamonds sparkled, platinum gleamed, furs and leathers mingled as everyone put on their very finest to commemorate their friend. Whispers about his baby's crazy mother and the murder/suicide that had taken place at Sunny's baby shower filled the room, as Sunny all but fell out at the altar.

Sunny's mother and father stood on either side of her, as she broke down in gut-wrenching sobs at her beloved's side. Her belly swollen with their unborn child, she was on the verge of a complete breakdown. They led her reluctantly back to her seat, and the church nurses came over, fanning her and offering water. They wiped her forehead with damp cloths, and tried to calm her down. Her grief was shared by every woman in the room who had ever been in love, by every woman who had ever had a broken heart and a child to provide for all alone. Sunny was distraught.

Born sat with Jada by his side, and he wept. He felt so responsible, so guilty for taking his eyes off of Raquel. He hadn't known how crazy she was, how insanely in love with Dorian she had been. No one had expected her to try to kill Sunny and wind up killing Dorian instead. But Born still felt responsible. He felt that he had let his friend down. He remembered the times that Dorian had had his back. The situation with Celly, when Dorian had warned Born that he was about to be ambushed. The countless other times over the years when Dorian had watched out for him. And the one time Dorian had needed Born, he was unable to protect him. It was all too much for him to digest. Jada sat, gently rubbing Born's back and telling him that it was alright. He knew it wasn't, though. His best friend was gone, and he felt responsible. He felt terrible for Sunny and her baby, who would grow up without a father.

Born looked over at D.J., who sat crying in silence beside Dorian's mother, Gladys. D.J. looked completely lost and alone, with no mother or father to care for him. Born vowed to himself that he would always look after the boy. He felt that that was what Dorian would want him to do.

Born was so overcome with guilt and grief that he took off his medallion, and placed it in the casket with Dorian. Fuck it. It might as well be buried with him. Born was finished with the crew as far as he was concerned. He was unworthy of the honor Dorian had bestowed upon him when he'd given him that ring.

After the service and Dorian's burial at the cemetery, everyone gathered at Gladys's house for the funeral repast. Sunny sat in a corner with Jada all night, crying softly on her shoulder. Born couldn't face her, couldn't help breaking down whenever he talked to Sunny, who had lost the love of her life all because Born had slipped. He sat with his friend Zion and Dorian's brothers. He talked to D.J., and reassured the young boy that anything in the world he ever needed or wanted would be his if he called his uncle Born.

Sunny found Born sitting alone, gazing silently out of the window in a corner by himself. She walked up to him, with her eyes red and puffy from crying. "Born," she said. "I need to give this back to you." She held her hand open, and in it was Born's medallion. The ring was supposed to have been buried with Dorian, so Born was surprised to see it in Sunny's palm. He frowned and looked at her questioningly. Sunny answered what he hadn't even asked.

"I saw this laying beside him today, and I couldn't let you do that. Dorian would want you to keep this, and to rep for him, since he can't be here. The night he gave you this, he was so happy to have you on board. Don't play yourself and start feeling guilty or responsible in any way. The only one to blame for this is Raquel. And by now I hope she's burning in hell." Sunny's eyes filled with tears. It killed Born to see this woman, who was usually so tough and strong, now broken and destroyed by grief. She tried to compose herself, and said, "Take the ring, and don't ever let go of it. Consider it a little part of D for you to keep with you always."

Born heard the pain in Sunny's voice as she spoke. He took the ring from her, and placed it back on his finger. Sunny managed a weak smile. "Thank you," she said. "Dorian loved you. He really did."

Born hugged Sunny tightly, and wished that he could take away her pain somehow. Her pregnant belly was between them, as he held her, and she cried. He couldn't find any words to say to her. But his hug spoke volumes, as she cried on his shoulder.

By the time Born and Jada left Brooklyn that night, Born was convinced that life would never be the same for any of them. Dorian was gone, leaving Sunny behind, along with two fatherless children. Sunny was alone in the world, living with her family, because she couldn't walk into the house she had shared with Dorian without being overwhelmed by grief. Jada was feeling alone without her road dog Sunny, and she was forced to watch Born mourn his friend in silence, since Born wouldn't talk about it. Things were no longer as good as they had once been for their crew, and Born wondered what would happen next.

Zion put him in touch with another supplier, and Born managed to keep his hustle afloat. But he had lost the thrill that he had had with Dorian behind him. It wasn't the same anymore, and he began to consider getting out of the game for the first time since he had gotten into it.

However, there was a situation that required his attention more than the possibility of retirement. Jada was acting strange, and he couldn't figure out why. Jada called Sunny from time to time, and they would talk. But Sunny was in another place in her life. She didn't have time for anything but her baby, and Jada understood. She let Sunny mourn Dorian in solitude, and she spent most of her time at home, or with Born. She was depressed, though, and so was Born. He had lost his best friend. And Jada felt like she had lost hers, too. Jada understood her friend's grief, and gave her the space she needed to finish out her pregnancy in peace. Sunny was resting at her mother's house in Brooklyn, and wouldn't take visitors or phone calls. She was so depressed that her doctor ordered her on bed rest for the remainder of her pregnancy, and her family wanted to protect her. They kept her secluded, and they convinced Sunny to live. She had felt like dying when she lost Dorian. Sunny's family made her see that her baby was a gift from Dorian, her very last piece of him. She stayed in seclusion until she gave birth. From that point on, Sunny shut the world out, and it was all about her baby. Jada understood this. But she was alone now, with no one to keep her company, and a terrible secret that Born knew nothing about. Jada was an addict.

She started going out by herself, to the local clubs in Staten Island. Sometimes she met up with new friends she had met, and with some old pals like Shante. Born didn't like what he was seeing, and he wondered how long his relationship with her would last. They hardly had sex anymore, and Jada seemed distant, and somehow changed. He wondered if she was reacting to his depression over Dorian's death, or if she was lonely without Sunny and bored with nothing to do to keep her busy anymore. But whatever it was, he was starting to see Jada in a different light. A voice in his head warned him that it could be something far worse than what he hoped it was.

One day he brought her along with him when he went to Park Hill. He still had control of most of the drug trade out there, and he was in the area to check up on his crew. He took Jada with him to the stash house, and she waited in the living room while he talked to his man in the kitchen. Jada seemed jumpy, almost nervous, and Born couldn't figure out why. He didn't see her slip two crack vials into her pocket when his back was turned, and when they left she seemed a whole lot more relaxed. As they exited the building, they ran into Jamari and Wizz standing in the lobby smoking weed with a couple of local niggas. Born had almost forgotten about the allegiance the two of them had formed. He'd been so focused on getting money, mourning Dorian, and worrying about Jada, that he'd forgotten about these two clowns. He smirked as he escorted Jada past them and out of the building. Once outside, the two of them climbed into his car.

Born pulled off, and they headed home. But back in the building lobby, Jamari and Wizz watched him drive away, and exchanged glances. Both of them held a grudge against Born. Wizz was still resentful that Born had snatched his turf right out from underneath him. Now Dorian was dead, and Wizz felt the playing field was level now. He was ready to go to war with Born.

Jamari had stood in the lobby watching Born usher Jada to his car. He had once been Born's friend, had once wanted to be just like Born, to have the same respect and admiration that Born got in the hood. As he watched Born put his beautiful girlfriend in his car, Jamari was jealous. He stared at Jada's golden skin and pretty face. Her ass poking out of her BeBe jeans. He had lust in his eyes and jealousy in his heart, as he watched Born drive off with Jada. Wizz wanted war. But unbeknownst to Born, Jamari wanted Jada.

It was two days later, and she was back at it. Jada nervously hurried through the apartment toward the door. She knew that Chuck could come back at any minute. She turned the knob and sucked in her breath in shock when she saw a man standing there. He seemed startled by her reaction to him, and she apologized, realizing that he was only walking past the apartment on his way to the elevator.

"Excuse me," she said, apologetically. "You scared me a little." She was relieved that it wasn't Chuck or one of the other workers—or even worse, Born himself! She spent more and more time these days worrying about whether Born's eyes behind his back would catch her in the act. She found herself constantly looking in her rearview mirror when she was driving, fearful that she was being followed. Whenever she got high at home, she was constantly peeking out of the blinds and searching the house for imaginary hidden cameras. Jada was growing para-noid.

Jamari smiled at Jada. "I'm sorry about that. I never meant to scare you."

Jada was glad that she had on her shades, since she didn't want the stranger to recognize her. The elevator came, and they both boarded. The doors closed on them, and Jamari turned to Jada.

"You're Born's wife, right?"

Jada's eyes widened in horror. Who was this guy, and would he tell Born that he'd seen her there? How would she explain it? "Yeah," she said, simply.

Jamari nodded. "He's a very lucky man, knawmean? 'Cuz you're gorgeous."

Jada relaxed, hearing this. She smiled. Surely this man was no friend of Born's. All of his cohorts and henchmen would have known better than to speak to Jada this freely. They all knew that the penalty for crossing the line with Born's wifey was death. Jada thanked the stranger just as the doors opened to the lobby.

"Have a nice day," she said.

"You, too." Jamari watched her scurry toward her silver Acura, and drive off. He licked his lips in anticipation, and walked away.

And that was how she met him. He was just some guy waiting for the elevator. The next time Jada went back, she saw him again. He started flirting with her more and more, and it made Jada feel sexy. Not that she wasn't happy with Born. She was. And she never cheated on him. But everybody respected Born, and Jada was one hundred percent off-limits. No one would disrespect Born enough to say something slick to his wifey. So it felt good to meet somebody for a change who wasn't afraid to say, "I don't give a damn who her man is. She's fine!" Jada would talk to Jamari for a few minutes each time she ran into him. She should have figured out that he was watching her. That he knew what she was up to. But she was too focused on getting high. Jada had started to use crack again.

It was at a party in 1998 that Jada's mask was taken off. Jada was sweating like a runaway slave. She was on the dance floor at a local night-club, Prodigy, in Staten Island, dancing all her worries away. She was tired of feeling bad about her crack use. She enjoyed the rush, the surge through her body that she felt when she was high. She was dancing away the pain, and she didn't give a damn what song was playing or who was watching.

At the bar, Wizz elbowed his boy Jamari, and nodded toward the dance floor. "Ain't that your girl? That's Born's wifey. The one you're al-ways telling me is so fly, and all that shit. She high as hell right about now, nigga. Look at her." Wizz was in hysterics, doubled over with laughter, as he watched Jada's performance.

Jada was doing the running man, the cabbage patch, the tootsie roll, the wop, and the robot in consecutive order. She seemed to be on a trip all her own, as the deejay played Lil Kim's "Crush on You." She was dancing to a beat that no one heard but her. Shante, her old friend, was sitting at a table close to the dance floor with some of her girls. She laughed at Jada, too, and said to one of her friends sitting beside her, "She been buying us drinks all night, so don't y'all bitches let her see us laughing!" They all laughed, and slapped hands in agreement, with Jada deaf to their mockery of her.

Jamari shook his head, although he couldn't help but laugh as well. "That's a shame. You can't tell me that nigga don't know she smokin'. Why he don't get her some help, clean her up? She's a pretty girl."

Wizz blew him off. "Nigga, please. The bitch is a crackhead. She got no class to be out here, half dressed like that, doing all that jumping around." He looked at Jada as if she disgusted him. She wore a tight sweater with no bra, and a denim miniskirt. Her Jimmy Choo shoes were in her hands as she danced like she was at an audition for *Krush Groove*. "She's supposed to be his wifey, and he ain't taught her nothing. She's out here off point, spending all kinds of money, with all that mouth her man got, and all the enemies he done made. She lucky I don't snatch her stupid ass up and extort that nigga." Wizz talked big shit, as usual.

"All I'm saying is, she seems like she needs help. Born ain't got no time to see when somebody else needs help. Everything gotta always be about him. The nigga's so busy trying to be the man his father once was that he don't see his own shorty slippin'." Jamari stared at Jada making a complete ass of herself. "I used to look up to the nigga and shit, but then he had to act like I couldn't eat the same way he was eatin'. Like I couldn't floss like he was flossin'. He didn't want to share the wealth, 'cuz that nigga thinks he's somebody special." Jamari stared at Jada like she was the only one in the room. "He ain't fuckin' special. Nigga think shit is sweet. He ain't even gonna see me coming."

Wizz looked at Jamari and wondered if he knew how stupid he sounded. Wizz wanted to bring the war right to Born's doorstep, and go toe-to-toe for control of Park Hill. He hoped to ambush Born in Park Hill with his team of hitmen, and shoot it out once and for all. But Jamari kept talking about some plan he had. Some big thing that Born wasn't gonna see coming. Wizz shook his head, and knew that soon he would proceed with his own plan for war, rather than wait for Jamari's big plan to work out. They both laughed at Jada until she walked, breathlessly, from the dance floor, headed toward the bathroom.

Jamari stood and watched her disappear behind the bathroom door, understanding now why she was constantly sneaking into her man's drug lair. When he first noticed her waiting for Born's workers to leave before going inside the spot, Jamari thought she might be taking money from him, even entertained the thought that she was fucking one of his workers on the low. But now he knew. She was stealing crack, and Born must not know that she was smoking. Jamari knew Born well enough to know that he would never stand for Jada using drugs. This was Jamari's trump card.

Jada underestimated Staten Island's street buzz. Word traveled fast about her performance at the Prodigy, and it was Jamari who did the honor of bringing it to the man himself.

Jamari went to a card game that Chance was having. The setting was familiar territory for everyone—Chance's mom's house in Arlington. The whole crew was there, and to Born it felt like old times again. Jada didn't come with him this time. She was at home, sleeping so soundly that none of Born's efforts to wake her were successful. So tonight he'd gone solo to Chance's card game, and spent the evening talking shit and making money. But when Jamari arrived, Born stood to leave, and he passed Jamari on his way out. As usual, Jamari was all warm smiles and kind words to Born's face, asking how he was doing and sincerely seeming to care. Born answered Jamari, but looked at him as the has-been, as the wannabe that he was. Born kept his comments brief, and tried to pass his former friend by.

But Jamari called after him. "Yo, I saw your wifey up in Prodigy the other night. She looked like the Energizer Bunny in there, my nigga. She was dancing so hard and sweating so much, but she didn't care who was laughing. She was in her own little world. Knawmean?" Jamari grinned as he said it.

Born looked at him, wondering why every time he looked at Jamari all he saw was a snake. He looked at him like he was a piece of shit. He walked away without commenting on what Jamari had told him. But, as he left, Born replayed it over and over in his head. "She was in her own little world." Born had been told that Jada's car was being spotted more and more often in Park Hill. At first he worried that it might be another man. But hearing Jamari's words, Born's heart sank, and he wondered if she was getting high again. She couldn't be, he told himself, shoving the thought to the corners of his mind. But he didn't forget it.

Instead, he watched her. He picked up on all the things she did and said that were suspect. He took note of all the inconsistent behaviors, and began to piece together the puzzle. Dorian's words on the night of his birthday party rang in his ears constantly: *"Keep your eye on Jada. Pay attention to her. Make sure she's keeping her nose clean."*

Born's heart began to break ever so slowly, as the truth began to reveal itself. About three weeks later Born took Jada along with him on a trip to Park Hill. He said he had to pick up some money, and to handle some quick business, and then he would take her out for dinner. She was looking forward to it, since it had been a while since she had been in the mood to do something like this. She'd been more and more depressed, and Born had been spending more time away from home. Jada hoped that this would be like old times between them. She longed for life to return to how it had been in the beginning for them. She wanted to feel like she was the thing that was most important to Born, more important than the wealth and the status.

Inwardly, Born was tormented. He knew the truth in his heart, knew that she was using drugs again. He recognized the signs now, and he had retreated from her in order to spare himself the pain. They hadn't spent quality time together in a very long time.

She followed Born upstairs, to the same stash house that she was stealing from on a regular basis now. It felt awkward coming here with him, after all the times she'd been there stealing his work over the past several weeks. He opened the door, and she followed him inside. Chuck sat on the couch in the living room watching the large television. Born greeted Chuck and the other worker, Omar, who stood in the kitchen with a beer in his hand.

Born left Jada out front with his workers, while he went to the back room where his goods were kept. He stayed back there for close to ten minutes before emerging with his nostrils flaring. "Which one of y'all niggas is stealing from me?" his voice was booming, and Jada's heart paused momentarily.

She knew that she had been at the apartment earlier in the day, when she was supposed to be going to the nail salon. Jada had taken what Born was so obviously angry about. This time, instead of her usual one or two, she had been bold enough to take five cracks from the stash. She'd thought that it would be days before Born came here to check on his stash. She wanted to kick herself now for being so greedy and leaving such an obvious deficit.

"Which one of y'all niggas is skimming off the top?" Born looked enraged.

Chuck looked stunned, and nervous. He looked at his boy Omar, and hoped for both their sakes that he hadn't stolen from Born. Omar looked just as at a loss for words, and Born grew more agitated with each second that his questions went unanswered. He looked at Chuck, and drew his

.40 caliber. He pointed it at Chuck, and saw the fear in the young soldier's eyes. Chuck wasn't ready to die yet.

Chuck started begging for his life. "Yo, Born, I swear, man. I didn't take shit from you. I swear," Chuck said, nervously.

Born shook his head, unmoved. "Then who you had up in here with you?" Born swung the gun toward Omar, who trembled in fear. Born looked irate. "You stealing from me, Omar? Huh?"

Born's eyes were narrowed angrily, and Omar shook his head no, emphatically. "I just came back today from Delaware with Dorian's brothers. You know I wouldn't steal from you, Born."

Born listened to reason. Omar had been one of Dorian's most trusted soldiers long before he died. Omar's loyalty had been put to the test time and time again, and the young man had been proven trustworthy. Born knew deep down that Omar wouldn't steal from him. He turned his attention back to Chuck.

"So, you got some explaining to do, my nigga. I put you in charge of this spot. *You!* You're the only one that got keys to this muthafucka besides me! So I want you to tell me who been stealing my fuckin' work."

"Born—" Jada's voice was feeble, as she tried to intervene.

Born wasn't having it, though. He ignored her. "This is the third time I came through here unannounced and found shit missing. I know what I gave you, Chuck. And I know what you sold. So where the fuck is the rest of my work?"

Born's tone was even, the look in his eyes was menacing, and Chuck was scared to death. Jada stood in guilty silence, knowing that it was she who had stolen from her beloved. Not poor Chuck. But she didn't confess, or say anything in the young man's defense, for fear that she would be incriminating herself. She watched the events unfold in silence.

Born saw the pleading look in Chuck's eyes. The look that said, "I'm innocent. I really didn't do this." But something wasn't right, and Born was determined to get to the bottom of it, by any means necessary. He gun-butted Chuck dead in his jaw, and sent the young man's bloody spit flying from his mouth.

Jada screamed in shocked surprise, "Born, stop!"

Ignoring Jada's pleas, Born stood over Chuck, menacingly. "You think I'm fuckin' playin'?" Born advanced on the young hustler, mercilessly pummeling him with his gun.

Jada cried, tears streaming down her face, while Chuck cried out in pain as he was pistol whipped. She cried for Born to stop, but he was immune to her cries, and continued to beat Chuck savagely.

"Tell me you did it!" Born demanded. "Be a fuckin' man!"

Omar stood his ground, feeling genuinely sorry for his boy, Chuck. He knew that Chuck wouldn't steal from Born. But someone had, and Omar knew that there would be hell to pay. Omar said little in Chuck's defense, since he knew that Born was too powerful and too unpredictable to be questioned about the accuracy of his assumptions. Omar wondered how much had actually been stolen from the stash, since Born was beating Chuck as if he had taken his entire life savings. The beating got more and more vicious, with Chuck curled up in the fetal position to block Born's blows. He was whimpering in pain, and Born continued beating his ass. "Tell me you did it! Say that you took it!"

Finally, Omar spoke up over Jada's crying. "Yo, Born, man. That's enough. You're gonna kill the nigga."

Born didn't stop. He *couldn't* stop. He felt like a man possessed. He kept hitting Chuck with the gun, stomping him with his Timberland boots. He was like an animal uncaged, and he was no longer himself. Chuck spoke through his bloody mouth, "Yo, Born! I swear to *God*! I never stole from you."

Born kicked Chuck in his face. Somewhere deep in the recesses of his mind, Born knew that Jada had really been the one stealing from him. That was really why he was so angry. Her car was spotted in Park Hill more and more often. The only stash house that was being stolen from was this one. None of his other spots ever came up short. She was seen acting wild and out of her mind at a party. He knew in his heart of hearts that she was the culprit. That was his motivation for bringing her along on this visit to the hill. He didn't know *how* she had gotten to the stash. Maybe Chuck had known all along that she was taking the crack—maybe he was even giving it to her. If that was true, then he deserved this beating. And even if he wasn't giving it to her, Born reasoned that Chuck should have noticed the shortages sooner. He should have told Born that *somebody* was stealing the shit. He was convinced that somehow Chuck deserved this ass whipping. But Born really wanted to believe that, if she was indeed the guilty party, she wouldn't stand there and watch Chuck take such a brutal beating, knowing that she was the real thief among them. But Jada did not confess, and Born continued to fuck Chuck up. *"Tell me you did it!"* Born's voice was demanding, almost pleading. He was desperate, desperate to believe that Jada wouldn't do this to him.

Omar called Born out of his trance. "Born! The nigga might not be breathin' and shit, nigga. Hold up! *Born!"*

Finally Born stopped, and stood there panting, out of breath, with his chest heaving. Jada stood close by, with tears flowing like a river down her face. Born stared at Jada. She was traumatized, but Born held her gaze. His facial expression was filled with pain. Chuck was motionless, and Omar shook his head in pity.

"Yo, Born, get up outta here. I'll take care of this nigga. I'll get him to the hospital. Just get her outta here and lay low, my nigga." Omar's tone was calming, and Born knew he was right. He needed to get out of there before the cops came, and Chuck needed to get to a hospital. The poor guy needed immediate medical attention.

Born turned and snatched Jada roughly by the arm, and led her out of the apartment. They took the stairs two at a time, with Jada still in tears from the vicious scene she'd just seen play out. She was distraught, and Born's silence only fueled her state of panic. He drove away, eerily silent, his face was set in a deep scowl. Jada was shaken as they arrived back at their house, and they headed inside to the safety of home. Jada plopped down on the couch, crying both for her own indiscretions and for poor Chuck. She hoped the young man survived, because if not, she would die from the guilt. She closed her eyes, realizing that this had gotten way out of control. Born knew that someone was stealing. It was only a matter of time before her name got added to the list of suspects, and she knew she couldn't lie to him if he asked her. She began to panic, and wished she could call Sunny to tell her what was going on. But Sunny had problems of her own, and Jada had nowhere to turn.

Born went upstairs and changed his bloody clothes. Then he came back down and looked at Jada sitting sadly on the couch. He said nothing for a long time, staring at her as she sat sniffling on the sofa. Finally, he cleared his throat. "I'm going out," he said. "I'll be back late, so don't wait up."

Jada nodded, and Born left. She was actually glad that he left, since facing him was a difficult task with the amount of guilt she was feeling. She sat still for close to half an hour after Born left, sobbing and realizing that things were way out of hand. She had to get control of herself. After an hour Jada was itching to get rid of the guilty feeling she had inside, and she reached for her purse. She pulled out the crack vials she had stolen from Born, and held them in her hand. She marveled that such a tiny object had brought her such huge problems.

She went to the bathroom, shut the door, and got high. She sucked on the crack pipe and felt her head get light, felt her worries slip away. Piece by piece she felt the pain dissipate, and in its place came peace. By the time she was done smoking, all was right in the world, and she emerged from the bathroom feeling elated like never before.

She walked into the living room and put the radio on full blast. Appropriately, Toni Braxton was singing "You're Making Me High," and Jada sang along and danced offbeat. She was laughing at nothing in particular and just picking at her clothes like she saw a stain that was only visible to her. She thought she saw crack lying on the floor, and she panicked. The last thing she wanted was for Born to come home and find that. She bent down to pick it up, and she realized that it wasn't crack at all. It was only a tiny piece of white paper. She stayed down on the floor, picking at the carpet and hoping to discover small shards of cocaine hidden within the fibers of the carpet. She laughed to herself, though she had no idea what the joke was. She never heard Born come back into the house.

He stood in the living room entranceway staring at the woman he loved. Jada was crawling around on the carpet, laughing insanely to her-self, and oblivious to his presence. He watched her, his heart breaking slowly and painfully. The evidence was right before him that Jada had been using his drugs. He thought about Chuck, thought about the heart-less beating he had delivered to the innocent young man while Jada looked on and said nothing. Born wanted to die from guilt and regret. He had known, even as he begged Chuck to tell him that he had done it, who the guilty party really was. He knew that Chuck's refusal to admit it was a sign that the young man really wasn't lying. Born had wanted to believe that Jada wasn't capable of betraying him like this. She wouldn't hurt him like this. Especially because she knew how his father's drug use had affected him so deeply. He wanted to cry, but he held his emotions in check as he watched her crawl around the room, zooted. She turned, and saw him standing there. He could tell by the look on her face that she knew she had been caught.

Born stood in the doorway staring at her like she was an intruder in his home. Jada was twisted, as she stood to her feet. She was unmistak-ably high. She was fidgety, moving around, picking at the nonexistent lint on her clothes. But even in her state of mind she could tell that his gaze was scornful. She tried to straighten herself up, tried to appear like she wasn't high. But her attempt was pointless. Born recognized the signs; he knew the deal. Jada was so full of energy that she couldn't keep still. Born stared furiously at the stupid look on her face. He tried to look into her downcast eyes.

"Once a fiend, always a fiend, huh, Jada?" he asked her, rhetorically. "You still a crackhead, baby girl?" The expression on his face was one of pure hurt, pure pain.

She shook her head emphatically and attempted to spread what she hoped would be a seductive smile across her face. Instead, she twisted the corners of her lips into a wicked grin that sent Born's fury to new heights.

"You're so cute, baby. Come on, and let's go to bed." Jada's words were slurred, her vision slightly blurry. Born stood staring at her, still.

"Look at you." He shook his head again, and continued to look at her.

Jada was still twisting around, picking at all the lint visible only to her on her Guess jacket. He wanted to cry, but was too much of a man to ever let her see him vulnerable like that. He was too enraged to cry, and give her the satisfaction of seeing that he loved her that much. He was disgusted, and angry. Born kept his distance from her, because he knew that if he put his hands on her, he'd catch a case.

Jada stood there, high as ever, watching the man she loved look at her like she was a disease. That look was so familiar. He looked at her like she was filthy, like she was contaminated and disgusting. Jada had seen that look on the faces of countless men in her lifetime: Mr. Charlie, and all the men she'd fucked for Kelly. But never—*never*—on Born's face. And now there it was.

His voice was ice cold as Born frowned and said, "I shoulda known a nigga can't turn a ho into a housewife. All that talk about you cleaned yourself up, you turned over a new leaf—you was playing me all along." Born shook his head, distraught. "You're just another fuckin' fiend, Jada."

"Born, what are you talking about? I didn't do that—"

Born charged at her, and she instinctively shielded her face with her arms, and crouched into a defensive stance against the wall.

"Don't lie to me, you fuckin' bitch! I already know!" He was close enough to her face that she could feel his breath, and his rage. *"Stop fuckin' lying!"* He stood with his chest heaving and his adrenaline rushing. "You stole from me, Jada! You lied to me. You made a fuckin' fool out of me."

Jada began to cry, and the enormity of the situation became clear. Born knew that she'd been using crack, that she'd been stealing from him, that she had lied to him. It was over, and she wanted so badly to explain. "Born, please listen to me . . ."

But Born was done talking. And he was so close to crying that he had to get away from her. Born turned and walked out of the house, leaving Jada by herself, and slammed the door in his wake. The entire house shook from the force of him slamming the door. Jada was a mess. Still high, she slid down to the floor and couldn't stop hearing the sound of Born slamming the door in her head. He had slammed the door on their relationship as well, and it was enough to send her spiraling backward.

28

FALLEN ANGELS

Born went to his mother's house after finding Jada high. That was his home away from home, and the one place where he knew he could be himself completely. He felt so many emotions at once, and at the forefront of all of those was rage. He was so angry that he walked right past his mother, as she stood washing dishes in the kitchen, and into his old bedroom, where he locked the door and turned his radio up.

The room still looked the same as when he'd been a young man living in his mother's house. There was always one guest or another—cousins, uncles, and sometimes Born's own friends—who found it necessary to stay at his mother's house from time to time. She was always willing to help out a friend in need, and this was one of the many reasons people loved Ingrid Graham. She knocked on his bedroom door twice, and called Marquis by name. But when he ignored her, she walked back into the kitchen and allowed him to have time to himself. She knew her son. She didn't have to see his face to tell that something was wrong. Marquis would never walk into his mother's house without giving her a hug or a kiss or saying something slick. Ingrid resumed washing the dishes, and sang along to the Al Green song playing from her portable radio on the counter. She knew that when he calmed down enough to talk, he would come to her.

Born paced his room angrily. He was sick to his stomach, and felt like he might actually throw up. Jada was smoking again. He laughed at himself. How stupid and how blind he must have been not to notice! She was stealing from him. Born shook his head in amazement. He shook his head, because he had known all along. And that realization is what enraged him. Born punched the closet door in frustration, and didn't give any attention to his throbbing knuckles afterward. A large hole remained in the spot he had punched, and Born covered his face with his hands in exasperation. He was devastated.

Jada, his sweet baby girl. How could she do it? How long had she been doing it? Why did she do it? Why didn't he confront her sooner? The truth was, Born had noticed a change in Jada's behavior long ago. He had seen her moods change quickly. She would be sweet and sultry one moment, and then sad and withdrawn the next. In his head, he had wondered all along if she had gone back to cocaine. But his heart wouldn't let him believe she would hurt him like that, that she would throw away all that they had just so that she could suck on a glass dick. He couldn't believe that he had played the fool.

And *Jamari* knew. That meant that Wizz knew, too. In addition to all the emotions he was feeling, he was also terribly embarrassed. He wondered if everybody knew but him. He felt so stupid. They were probably laughing at what a fool he was, Born thought. He wiped the sweat from his forehead as he stood there, still wearing his jacket, and fuming. He just wanted the earth to swallow him up. He reached into his pocket, and pulled out a ten-dollar crack rock. He looked at it in the light of his familiar bedroom. Countless times he had bagged this shit up, sold it, gone out of town to move it, gone uptown to get it, and made a living in the trade of it. He thought about his father, then about Jada. This rock, this little pebble-sized piece of cocaine, had ruined the relationship he had with two people he had truly loved. It had taken his father's life, directly or indirectly. And now, Jada was in its crossfire. He felt a tear fall, and quickly wiped it away. He had to man up, now. It wasn't time for him to crumble. Born felt in his heart like the game was trying to beat him.

He had always felt as though his father had had the game *half* right. He could have been a big deal, his pops. Leo Graham was the man, and everybody either feared him or loved him. He wasn't what one would call a likable guy. He was a menace. But those he loved he took care of, and he had the game *almost* figured out. He thought he could beat it, thought he could conquer the golden rule of Hustling 101: You can't get high on the shit you're pushing. Leo thought he could handle it, and he was dead wrong. This rock Born held in his hand had beaten his father. Jada had thought she could play with fire without getting burned as well. She was stupid and weak, in Born's eyes at that moment. And to add insult to injury, she had stolen from him. He had given her an all-access pass to his life, his home, and his heart. He had allowed himself to trust her, and to believe in her. And she had repaid him by getting high and stealing from the one person who had ever loved her without boundaries. He still loved her, but he couldn't get past this, so it was time to let her go.

Born opened the door, and walked into the kitchen, looking for his mother. She wasn't there. He found her in the living room with her feet up, still listening to Al Green. She was reading a copy of *Essence* magazine while "I'm Still in Love with You" drifted from the radio's speakers. He loved coming home to the place where he'd spent his childhood. Ingrid still lived in the same apartment that she'd moved into when she came to New York from Georgia in the sixties. When she'd moved into Arlington Terrace, it was a high-rise development, where only the successful middle-class lived. It was a privilege to live there then. But as time went by and hardworking tenants had moved out, crime became commonplace. The exclusivity the development once boasted of was gone. And Arlington became as hood as any given project in Staten Island. But Ingrid had stayed through it all. She'd watched the neighborhood go from good to bad, and then from bad to worse. But she wasn't going anywhere.

His mother's presence gave him a comfort he couldn't explain. Few people in her apartment complex knew that his mother—one of the community's elders—was as well versed in the streets as she was. None of them knew that Ingrid had more money hidden in her humble apartment than some folks had in their life savings. Ingrid had money tucked in her kitchen, in her mattress, in a strongbox in her closet, and in a bevy of other places. But she also had money in the bank, a retirement plan, and insurance. She was a hustler, his moms, a smart woman who had watched and learned a lot over the years. And she was down for her son no matter what.

Born sat down in the chair that his father used to love. It was a black recliner that no one really sat in because it was old and worn. But Born sat there every time he came by. It had been his father's chair. The king's throne. He sat there now, with the crack vial in his hand, and looked at his mother. He laid it in the center of the coffee table, and Ingrid looked at her son as if he had lost his mind.

"What the hell is wrong with you, Marquis?" She looked over the rim of her glasses at him, like a schoolteacher would. "Why'd you bring that shit in my house?"

He looked at his mother, feeling completely hopeless. He wanted her to explain this shit to him. He needed her to tell him why this was happening to him. Why him? His voice cracked as he spoke. "What is it about that," he nodded toward the crack on the table, "that makes people hurt the ones they love?" His eyes were really searching hers for the answer.

Ingrid looked at her son, knowing that something serious had happened. She had heard his fist knock a hole in the closet, and she wondered what would prompt him to come into her house this enraged. And what was all this talk about crack?

Ingrid put her magazine down, and kept looking over the rim of her glasses at her son, her arms folded across her buxom chest. "What's on your mind, Marquis? What's the matter with you tonight?" She looked at his helpless expression, and was sincerely worried. Her son was a warrior. Never had she seen Marquis look this sick about a situation, not even at his own father's funeral. "Is this about Leo?"

Born shrugged his shoulders. "Is it? I don't know. It might be. It might be all about him in some strange way. It's like he's here all over again, and I feel let down all over again."

His mother looked confused. "What are you talking about, boy?"

"Ma!" Born didn't know why he was yelling at his mother. He

checked himself, and lowered his voice. "I gotta understand why this shit keeps fuckin' up my life."

His mother nodded, trying to help him out. "Well, first of all, stop cursing so much in here." She lit up a cigarette, and blew the smoke out. "Now start at the beginning. What happened tonight?"

Born looked at his mother, and she smiled softly, encouraging him to tell the story. This wasn't easy for him. Ingrid had only met Jada once, and she had seen the love in her son's eyes instantly. She could tell by the way he looked at Jada, and by how playful he was with her, that he was smitten. As long as Jada was OK with Marquis, she was okay with Ingrid. But now he had no idea how his mother would react to this news. "Jada's smoking that." He motioned toward the coffee table.

Ingrid looked at the crack on the table, and then she looked at her son. She shook her head, as if that would make what he'd just said untrue. No. This couldn't be happening, she prayed. Now she understood his anguish. First his father, and now his girlfriend. She shook her head in pity. Shock registered on her face. "Oh, my God, Marquis."

Born was so upset. "I found out tonight, but I think I kinda knew all along. I didn't want to believe it. But tonight I set a trap, and she walked right into it. She was stealing from me, and getting high behind my back. I can't believe it. But then, at the same time, I wonder how I didn't see it all along. I can't be with her no more, Ma. But my heart is broke, and I wanna just . . . hurt somebody. Word! I don't know what I'm supposed to do now. But I can't imagine me being with her another second. She's weak, and she's useless . . ."

"Now, wait a minute, Marquis," Ingrid scolded. "You can't be so quick to say who's weak and who's useless. You have to look at it both ways. If you think a crackhead is weak or useless, then you're saying that your father was weak and useless, and I'm not gonna let you sit in here and talk bad about your father."

Born let her have her say, because he hadn't meant to upset her. He didn't want to argue about what Leo was or wasn't. He wasn't there for that. He was there because he needed help with his shattered heart, which he held in fragments in his hands.

Ingrid continued. "You gotta get the cold out your own eye, before you go and tell somebody else they got some shit in theirs." Born started to protest her using the four-letter word, when she had just told him to stop cursing. But Ingrid cut him off. "I'm grown! I can curse as much as I want."

Born wanted to remind her that he was grown too, but he held his tongue. He shook his head in frustration, and let her have her say.

Ingrid continued. "Anyway, you're out here *selling* that mess, Marquis. You can't judge people for being weak and useless if you make your living off of those same people. That makes you a hypocrite. It makes you guilty of taking advantage of people who are weak and useless for your own personal gain. Think about it, Marquis. You felt so sad when your father died. You feel sad right now, knowing that Jada is using the same poison. But you're out there selling that poison to folks night and day. You're making sure somebody else's child, somebody else's husband, somebody else's friend remains weak and useless."

Born couldn't take it anymore. "You never complained before, Ma!" He was trying to be as delicate as possible. But it was getting hard to hear this lecture from the very person who had helped him spend so much of his drug money. "I know what you're saying is true, but—"

"I'm not sitting here and saying that I'm not guilty of my own sins. I know I didn't exactly demand that you stop doing what you were doing. That's something I regret to this day. But that's my point. All of us have sins. We all have our weaknesses. Don't judge people so harshly for theirs, because you'll be judged just as harshly for your own."

He nodded his head. He knew she was right. He had always seen his own ability to play the game as proof that he had it all figured out. He wasn't strung out on anything. In fact, Born had never used any drugs other than a little weed every now and then, a drink or two on occasion. He was on the right side of the game, as far as he was concerned. He was getting money, making moves. And he didn't look at it like he was preying on anybody's weakness. The money was out there. If he didn't go out and get it, someone else would. He saw no reason to feel guilty, when the crackheads made a choice to get high. That was his problem with Jada, with his father. They had both made a decision to get high, and they couldn't find the strength to stop getting high. Not even for his sake. Not even for the love he felt toward them.

"How long has she been using?" Ingrid asked. Born described Jada's history with drug abuse briefly to his mother, sparing her the grittiest details, about her selling her body. Ingrid sat back when he was done, and stared at him. Born wondered if his mother thought he was a fool. He guessed that Ingrid thought he had been dumb to get involved with a former addict in the first place. But she didn't think that at all. Ingrid was thinking about how she had also ignored the signs of Leo's drug use, how she had tried to block it out. She listened to Born tell her how he had thought Jada was really through with drugs when he met her. Ingrid remembered feeling that Leo could also be strong enough to let go, only to be let down again and again when he went right back to crack.

She thought back to when she had first realized that Leo was smoking. Finally, after several minutes of silence, she spoke. "Your father started using cocaine when you were little," she said. "Maybe eight or nine years old. I heard the rumors, saw the signs and all that shit. But I didn't want to know." Ingrid paused. "I knew that Leo was gettin' high. Him and his crew would come in here and get higher than the sky just about every night. I knew about that. I didn't fuss about it, because I knew that was part of Leo's package. He was maintaining. He had it under control. Leo was who he was, either love him or leave him. And I loved him." She sighed, and looked at her son, who was sitting and soaking up her every word, her body language, and all. Listening to her, he wondered how she had been able to love her husband despite his addiction. He knew he wouldn't be able to love Jada despite hers.

She looked at him. "Leo was a good man. He had good intentions. He loved you, Marquis. He really did. When he was doing good, we had the best of everything. His habit was something he seemed to have control of in the beginning. But when he started struggling, I could feel it. I felt like he wasn't telling me something. Something changed between us. Then the money started slowing up." Ingrid puffed her cigarette. "I always worked. Leo was into so many different hustles that we had to account for some legitimate money—some legal sources of income. So I always had a job. Plus, I always knew it was important to have my own. Even Leo stressed that to me. He always encouraged me to work, to have my rainy day money ready. And I listened. I kept me a job." Ingrid grinned, slightly. "I had to start hiding money, so that Leo wouldn't know what I had. He didn't steal from me. But if he knew there was money laying around, he would definitely want to smoke it up. And if I refused to give him the money, we would fight all night. So I hid it. I kept my own stash that he knew nothing about. Nobody knew about it. It wasn't much—just a couple of hundred dollars. But it was something for a rainy day that he didn't know about. That was always something I maintained." Ingrid thought to herself that this was yet another lesson that Leo had taught her. Life with Leo was one big lesson; he taught her how to drive, how to navigate the hood, and how to be his better half. He had also, unknowingly, taught her how to hide assets, and how to conceal money. He had been quite a teacher.

"Leo had a bad heart. He was getting a disability check on the first of every month, and he would always give me half of it up front. But then he was disappearing for a few days, until he smoked up the other half. All along, his disability check was steady, but for as long as I knew Leo, he was always coming through with extras, money always trickled in. But soon that stopped. That's when I had to pick up the pieces. I tried to keep you occupied so you wouldn't notice. But you started asking questions, and it got harder to hide. That let me know right away that something was causing him to lose his grip. He had never been so sloppy. I didn't admit it to myself at first, Marquis. At first, I convinced myself that it was another woman. I told myself that Leo was shacking up with some other bitch, that he was spending his money on someone else. But that wasn't it. Soon, I had to admit to myself that it was more than that. Leo got arrested for buying crack from an undercover when you were small. He did about eighteen months for that. I made excuses, told you he was down south with his family 'cause his uncle was sick. Just all kinds of lies."

Ingrid shook her head, wishing she had known how inevitable it was for Leo's promise to stay clean to come crashing down. "Leo came home, and went right back to his old ways. People saw him around the other buildings, looking a mess, spaced out. He wouldn't do his dirt in our building, because it would get right back to me. So he went to the other buildings to get his shit. I knew about it. I just kept on going. Just kept trying to keep it all together. For you."

Born listened to his mother. "How did you handle it?"

Ingrid shook her head, dismayed. "I didn't handle it at all. I ignored it. When Leo did come around, I would pretend I didn't know. I would act like everything was okay." Born watched his mother pause, appearing to fight back tears. "I was so impressed by your father, Marquis. He taught me so much. I learned more from him than from anybody else in my lifetime. He showed me how to read people, how to see through bullshit. I felt like he was the smartest man I had ever met, like he was invincible. I knew him so well that I could complete his sentences. I loved him. I watched him. So when he started slipping, I saw it right away. He thought he had his addiction under control, kept telling me it was alright. It was no big deal. And I wanted to believe that. I wanted to believe that he would pull himself together and get right back on track. He was still making money. But he was smoking it now. After a while, Leo was no longer respected like he used to be. But by then, I didn't have the heart to put him out, or to leave him. It got to the point where I really didn't care anymore. I was past all that." She stopped talking. Thoughts ran through her mind about how she would have done things differently if she could have. How she wished that she could have those days back once more, so that she could pull her husband back from the clutches of his addiction. Deep inside Ingrid wished she could have reached Leo before it was too late.

Born remembered his father being strung out. He remembered the point in time when Leo began to lose the respect of all the folks who once had bowed to him.

"We never really talked about all this before," Ingrid continued. "I guess it was so much a part of our life that we didn't address it at the time." She looked at her son, thought about the twists and turns his life had undergone after being exposed to all the activities within the four walls they called home. She wanted to help him deal with the devastating news he'd just found out about the woman he loved.

"You need to talk to her, Marquis. You need to find her some help—"

"Nah, Ma. She has to go! I can't be with her for one more night. I don't want to see her, I don't want her in my house—"

"You can't put the child out in the street!"

"Why not? She knew! She knew about Pop and how I felt about him using it. She swore she wouldn't use that shit again. Yo, she *stole* from me. She stood there and watched me beat a nigga's ass for stealing, when she knew all along it was her that stole from me!"

Ingrid shook her head, knowing there's no low too low for a crack addict.

Born shook his head, and stared at the floor. "I can't trust her. I got niggas laughing at me." Born sat and shook his head, in internal agony. He sat like that for a long while, and Ingrid searched for the right words to comfort him.

She sighed, bringing Born out of his reverie, and back to their conversation. "Ma, I'm so mad at her that if I see her, I might hurt her."

Ingrid nodded. She understood. But she also understood something else that her son seemed to be missing. "I know you're angry with Jada," Ingrid said. "But I think a big part of what you're feeling right now is anger toward your father that you never let go of." After she said it, her words hung in the air, resounding with truth.

Born shrugged his shoulders, as if to dismiss what she was saying. But as silence enveloped them, he thought about it, and realized that there might be some logic in Ingrid's statement. He looked at her, and he realized she was right. Born had never been good at talking about his emotions. Even now, with his own mother and the eyes of the world averted, he got choked up at the thought of discussing what he had kept bottled up for so long. Looking at his mother's calm eyes and warm expression, he was comforted. And he said, "I got a lot of questions for him, Ma. You know what I'm saying?"

Ingrid nodded, and Born pressed on. "I just been thinking about him a lot. Thinking about how he died, and all that. I miss him." Born looked away from his mother. "But I'm still a little mad at him, too." Having said that, he felt like a weight was lifted off of him for the first time. He wondered what it would feel like to unburden everything. "Word. I think a big part of me feels like he let us down. He gave up too easy. Gangstas don't go out like that."

Ingrid understood this. She knew that Born had been carrying around more pain and resentment than he should. Knowing that he was a proud young man, who liked to believe that he had everything under control, she had allowed him to try and shoulder that burden for as long as he was able. Now, she realized, he was ready to let her help him. She smiled, happy he was letting her do that. "Tell me what you haven't been saying," she said. "You gotta let this go, once and for all."

Born looked at his mother for a long time, unsure where to begin. Her round brown face was as familiar to him as his own voice. She had always been the yin to his father's yang, the other half of the whole. And now, just as it had always been, all they had was each other.

He began to talk to his mother—about everything. He told her how hurt he'd been watching his father kill himself with drugs. He talked about the pain he was feeling after finding out that Jada had succumbed to the same weakness. They talked for hours that afternoon. Hours that would normally have been spent going about the daily routine of life were instead spent putting a salve on old wounds that had been left on their own for too long. But perhaps most surprising to Born was the fact that he found himself getting a little choked up when some memories came flooding back. Seeing her son still too tough to cry broke her heart into a thousand pieces. When Leo died, Born had never shed a tear—not at the funeral, or in the days and months following it. He had found it impossible to cry for his dad. And even now, he didn't want to cry. But Ingrid and her son talked some more. They reminisced about the old times—both good and bad. And sitting there in his father's chair, talking to his favorite girl, Born cried for Leo Graham at last. And he faced the fact that, despite all the many roles he played in the lives of so many people, in reality, at his core Born was still just a scared little boy who missed his father.

Ingrid watched Born, understanding just what he was feeling. And she wished there was some way she could take all his pain away. She saw that her son's heart was broken, and knew he was finished with Jada. When they finished talking, and pulled themselves together, she tried to say something more in Jada's defense, but Born wouldn't hear it. He felt like he had been made to look like a clown, and he didn't like it. He wouldn't stand for it. Ingrid wasn't defending Jada's actions. But she knew that Born loved her. And she knew that Jada needed help. But looking at Born, she realized that he also needed help. Her heart broke for him, and she sighed. "What can I do to help you, Marquis?"

Born looked at his mother, and felt a little twinge of hope at last. She listened as he told her what he had in mind.

After talking with Ingrid for a little while longer, he left her house, knowing that he wasn't going home. He didn't want to see Jada. Not now, that's for sure. Born walked through the apartment complex, headed for his truck, parked in the lot. He felt like a whole ton had been lifted from his shoulders since his conversation with his mother. He missed Leo Graham, missed the man that he was before the drugs got ahold of him.

He climbed into his ride and sat back, the keys still in his hand and not in the ignition. He sat like that for a long time, once again thinking of his father and the days he'd smoked his life away. He started his car, and drove off down Richmond Terrace. His father's voice was as clear as a bell in his ears: *"Do what you can, young man,"* Leo used to always tell his son. It was a phrase that Born had never been able to forget, something his father always used to tell him. But he felt that Leo had never done all that he could have to be the father that Born had needed, the father that he still needed now. Born was sick of feeling the disappointment, sick of holding in his anger. Without thinking about it, he drove toward the expressway, and headed for the cemetery where Leo had been interred years prior. It was time for him to have a conversation with his father.

He pulled up outside of Frederick Douglass cemetery, and parked his car. The weather was unusually warm for a late March afternoon. The sky was clear, and a warm breeze blew, gently. He felt the sun on his face, and enjoyed it as he walked through the winding pathways of the cemetery toward Leo's final resting place. He looked around at some of the names on the other tombstones. He quickly calculated some of the ages. A woman, thirty-nine years old. A man, sixty-four. Another woman, fifty-two. A young boy, seventeen. Born wondered how many of these people had been drug addicts. How many of their families had suffered the way his had?

He approached Leo's grave slowly, staring at his father's name etched for eternity in cold stone. Coming here was always emotional for him. When he stood before his father's grave, he was never Born anymore. He was Marquis Graham, a young man at his father's side, wanting to grow up and be just like him. Whenever he came here, he was a child once more, standing in front of his parent, with so many unanswered questions.

He walked closer and stood there, directly in front of where his father lay. He read the inscription bearing the name Leonard Albert Graham and the words *Free at last*. How fitting, Born thought. He hoped his father was indeed free.

He closed his eyes and pictured his dad's face. He could see it clearly still. His dark hair and mustache. His smiling eyes and his keen nose. Born squatted and looked at the words again. Damn, he missed him. "Hey, Pop." He looked around and made sure no one was within earshot. "It's been a while since I came out here to talk to you. That's 'cause it's always so hard when I come to see you." Born looked away briefly, and continued.

"But I got some things to say. I'm feeling a kinda way about how you left us. I'm not talking about when you died, either. You left us long before that. I'm talking about that cocaine, you know what I'm sayin'? That's what made you leave. I gotta tell you I'm mad at you for that, man."

Born paused, and thought about how Leo went from riches to rags, and how he had left Born's mother to pick up the pieces. "You bailed out on us. You left us, and you knew how much we depended on you. You used to be *that nigga;* the one who everybody respected. That dude with the fly cars and all the money. The man that all the ladies fell in love with. The one that never took a loss, never got took. The infamous Leo Graham. That's who you were. But that cocaine got the best of you, Pop. That shit made you different. It changed you. And that ain't how it was supposed to be. You were supposed to be an old man right now talking to your son about how to survive. How to deal with having his heart broken. Nigga, you was supposed to be here giving me advice, helping me figure out what to do next. But you *ain't* here. You quit, Pop." Born had tears falling down his face, but he no longer looked around to see if anyone saw him. He didn't care.

"You quit. I told you that at your funeral. I meant that shit, too. Gangstas don't go out like that, man. They don't quit. You was supposed to fight that shit! You was supposed to beat that shit. But it beat you. And what about your wife? What about me?" Born wiped his eyes then, and bit his lower lip. "What about me?" Born cursed his father for what Leo had instilled in him. Leo had given him the blueprint for being a hustler, for being on top of his game. But he had not taught Born how to be a man. He had never taught him how to deal with a broken heart, the loss of a best friend, or the sting of humiliation. All he'd taught him was the game. But now Leo was nowhere around to guide Born out of it. And more than anything, that was what Born wanted at that moment. He wanted out. He wanted to let go of all the pain, the paranoia, the drama, the disappointment. But he had no idea how to do that.

He took a deep breath. Then another. He shook his head, overwhelmed by the flood of emotions. "I never got over that shit, Pop. I never really forgave you for leaving me all alone when I was too young to stand on my own. Ma needed you. She needed you more than you thought she did. She couldn't show me how to be a man. That was your job. But you was so far gone that you couldn't even see what was going on. I remember being a young shorty in the hood, and I was so glad that you were my dad. Everybody knew you. Everybody loved you. And you were *my* dad. That shit made me so proud. And then I remember years later seeing you and feeling embarrassed that you were my father."

Born's face was twisted into a grimace at the memory. "I remember being ashamed of you." He remembered feeling so let down. That feeling had never completely gone away. "But I *always* loved you, Pop. I always loved you. When I was a little boy, and you were the man, I loved you. And even when you was just another fiend standing on the corner, I loved you. I love you now, still, Pop."

A light rain had suddenly begun to fall, and Born didn't care. He took it as a sign that maybe his father could hear him somehow. Maybe he was shedding tears from heaven. The entire day had been sunny and warm, without a cloud in the sky. And suddenly it had begun to rain, just as he was telling his father about his pain, and about his anger toward him. Born wondered if Leo was trying to tell his son that he was sorry, sending the rain as some sort of apology. Born remained there beside his father's grave, the raindrops feeling like they were washing away his pain. He reached forward, and touched the tombstone. His fingertips brushed across the letters in his father's name. Born kissed his fingers, and touched the tombstone once more. He cried for his father, and for the loss of his own childhood, and for the loss of a woman he loved more than she'd ever know—all of these things Born had lost to a drug he had never even used. He stood up, brushed off his jeans, and put his fitted cap back on his head. Born stuck his hands in the pocket of his jeans, and stared down at his father's grave, with the rain falling harder now. "But you still quit." He said it, and turned and walked back to his car. He felt better now that he had finally said the things to his father that he had been waiting to say.

Born thought then about how Jada had also quit on him. He thought of her as he climbed inside his Denali and checked his eyes, red from crying, in the rearview mirror. Turning the key in the ignition, he drove away and headed home.

29

BETTER TO HAVE LOVED AND LOST . . .

Born took the long way home. He stopped off and picked up fast food and sat right there in his car and ate it. He finally went home at around ten o'clock that night, hoping that Jada had sense enough to be gone. He had seen it all with his own two eyes, and there was nothing more to discuss. He hoped now that she would have the decency to spare them both any additional confrontations by leaving. She had to know the relationship was over. There was no way Born would continue to be in a relationship with a crackhead. If she knew him at all, she had to know that much.

Throughout their relationship, Born had considered Jada more than a lover. She was his *friend*. There had never been secrets between them, and he had given her his heart. Now he felt like such a fool for ever trusting anyone with something so vital to his survival. Their relationship had sustained him. From the beginning there had been a raw honesty between them, and that was what he loved about it. That's what made their relationship so refreshing. It was sincere; their love was real. Or so he had thought. But knowing that Jada had been getting high all along, that she had stolen from him, and had made a fool out of him, that was a deal breaker. All the trust he'd developed for her, all the love—it made him feel stupid. It made him determined never to love again. Born wanted to take his love away from Jada. If only his heart would listen to his mind.

He walked in, and the house was dark and quiet. Jada was sitting on the couch in the dark, waiting for his return. She wasn't high anymore. Even in the dark, he could tell by the way her body slumped discreetly in the corner of the sofa that she was upset. Her body was tense. He saw her, and he stopped walking, stood still, and stared at her. She waited for him to say something, and when he didn't, she cleared her throat. "Born, I need to talk to you." Her voice was barely above a whisper, and he could see tears on her face in the dark. He shook his head, and took off his jacket.

"Get out." Born said it calmly, with no emotion, and waited for her response.

"I'm not leaving here until you talk to me. Born—" Jada began.

Born walked directly toward her, his pace swift and determined. Jada jumped in defense, wondering if he would hit her for the first time in their relationship. He snatched her car keys off the coffee table then he grabbed her and dragged her, kicking and screaming, toward the door. She held on to the sofa, and tried to anchor herself. "Wait a minute! Born! Please!"

Born wasn't trying to hear a word she said. He silently pried her fingers off the sofa, and dragged her body across the room.

Jada sobbed, "I'm sorry, baby! *I'm sorry!*" She repeated the phrase over and over, but her cries fell upon deaf ears. "*Please!* I'm so sorry!" He dragged her to the door, and opened it. "Just let me talk to you, Born. Please! Let me tell you what happened." Jada clung to the door's frame, and tried to resist his force as he pulled her toward the open air. He was silent, but his lack of words spoke volumes to her.

"Marquis, *Please*! Let me tell you what happened!" Jada screamed, and clung to Born, calling him by the name his mama had given him in hopes that he would see how desperate she was. "I love you! I'm *sorry*! My *God,* Born, please! I just did it once!"

Hearing this, Born became enraged, because he knew she was lying. He grabbed her by the throat, silencing her immediately. Jada's voice got caught in her throat, and she looked terrified, as he squeezed her fragile neck. He knew that by now the neighbors were watching, but he didn't give a damn. The only thing that saved her was the thought of facing his mama after beating Jada's ass. "I don't want to hurt you, Jada." His voice cracked as he said it, because he heard the truth in those words. He didn't want to hurt her, even after all the pain she'd caused him. But God knew he would whoop her ass if she stood in his face and lied to him one more time. It made him wonder how many other times she'd lied. His eyes filled with tears, and Jada noticed it.

"Baby, please. I love you—"

His adrenaline coursing through his veins, he picked her up like she was as light as a feather. He held her hands together so that she couldn't hold on to anything else, and he carried her out to her car. He tossed her across the hood of the car with all his might, sending her skidding across the Acura and smack onto the street on the driver's side. Jada lay on the ground, rolling around and crying loudly. Several neighbors came outside to see what was going on, while Jada sobbed uncontrollably in a heap on the ground.

Born turned and went back inside the house, locking the doors and each of the windows. He went upstairs, and lay awake for the rest of the night, listening to the noise Jada made as she tried desperately to get back inside the house. He heard her yelling, banging on the door, and trying to open the windows downstairs, to no avail. He wondered if the neighbors might call the cops. But they didn't. At close to 1:00 A.M., he finally heard her car pull off, and he closed his eyes and cried in the dark. It was over.

Born sat in the darkness, thinking about Jada, and about all the signs he had missed. He remembered the conversation that he'd had with Dorian about Jada. Dorian had turned to Born and looked at him seriously. *"You better watch her, Born. You know we spend a lot of time away from home, and they get bored. They start looking for all kinds of ways to have fun. You know what I'm saying? Just make sure you always know what kind of fun she's having. Make sure she's keeping her nose clean."* But Born hadn't understood what he'd meant. Looking back now, Born understood completely. He had missed the signs. Jada had lost weight during their relationship. Not to the point of looking sickly, but enough for him to notice a change in her body. She would be restless and irritable one minute, and happy-go-lucky the next. Her voice would be hoarse all the time. He had shrugged these things off, made up excuses in his mind for them. She couldn't be using cocaine again, he'd told himself. The truth was, he couldn't bring himself to admit that Jada might do that to them—to him. Born felt like an idiot.

The next morning, Jada arrived bright and early. She had spent the whole night getting high in her car. She had parked at a construction site where new town houses were being built, and got high until she had no more drugs. All of her money was in her Gucci bag on her dresser. She hadn't expected Born to toss her out with nothing. When the sun came up, she was penniless, hungry, and still in trouble with the man she loved. She pulled up in front of the house at close to ten in the morning, and parked awkwardly at the curb. She was prepared for a showdown today. She knew that the last thing Born wanted was for one of the neighbors to call the cops. She was prepared to use this fact to her advantage.

She walked up to the large oak doors, and began banging loudly. *"Open the door, Marquis! Come on!"* Jada kicked and pounded on the door with her fists. She was torn up inside, reduced to tears in the early morning hours.

She heard the lock turn, saw the doorknob twist. As the door slowly creaked open, Jada perked up, opened her mouth, her eyes streaming with tears, prepared to beg Born's forgiveness, and plead with him to hear her out. But she saw a woman's face emerge from behind the door, and Born's mother stood there, looking at the pitiful young thing before her.

Ingrid shook her head as she looked at Jada's uncombed hair, her makeup dripping down her tear-stained face. She felt sorry for the young lady, yet she had to respect how her son felt about the situation. "Hello," she said. "Jada, Marquis ain't home. I came over so you could get your stuff. I want to talk to you, anyway."

She wasn't so much asking Jada as she was telling her what was about to take place. Ingrid stepped aside, and motioned for Jada to come inside. She did, walking slowly into the house that was her home, wishing more than anything that Born was there to talk to her. Jada knew that she looked terrible, and could only imagine what Miss Ingrid must've been thinking as she walked in. She was looking and smelling like yesterday.

Ingrid ushered Jada into the living room, and sat across from her on the couch. Jada looked around at all the things she had purchased for this home—their home—all the trinkets and furniture, the curtains she'd placed throughout to enhance the decor. She wondered how Born could be so heartless as to throw her out of it now. How could he take away everything he gave her without giving her a chance to explain?

Ingrid read the turmoil on Jada's pitiful face. She looked at the young woman she usually saw dressed in the best, looking like a top model. The creature before her looked frail and weak and lost. She shook her head, knowing that drug addiction was no joke.

Jada knew how much Born loved his mother. She knew how close they were, and that he had probably told Ingrid everything. She decided to try to level with Ingrid.

"I want to tell you that I really love your son. I love him so much." She started crying, realizing that she had blown her one chance at love. "I'm so sorry." Catching her breath, she continued. "I'm not an addict anymore. I was using something years ago. Then I did it again, but not like before. I'm not addicted now. I can stop. I just was doing it once in a while when I was bored. I was at home alone a lot and . . . I'm not addicted, though." In her mind, Jada rationalized that she was doing alright as long as she was snorting with Sunny. It was when she'd gone back to crack that things had fallen apart. At least, that's what she told herself. "I wasn't stealing from Marquis. I didn't take from him." She was lying, and couldn't even look at Ingrid. The pain of what she knew was true made her cry so hard that she could hardly breathe.

Ingrid handed her a tissue and told her, "Pull yourself together, now." She shook her head again, knowing that Jada was in denial. "Girl, let me tell you something. Can't nobody help you get over what you dealing with but God." Ingrid cut right to the chase. "I don't claim to be the most religious person," she said. "I ain't gon' sit here and tell you no lies about me being a saint. But I've seen a lot of things. And I've seen how it is to be hooked on them drugs. Seen the shit up close and personal, sweetheart. So don't think I'm just sitting here lecturing you for the hell of it. I know firsthand how it takes over. That crack can eat you alive, if you let it. The choice is yours. It's up to you now. If you want to keep using, you can do that. But you *are* addicted, Jada. And you're killing yourself. Just know that. You're throwing away what a lot of people would love to have. My son loves you. He don't want to say that, because he's hurtin' right now. You know what I'm saying? But he loves you. You hurt Marquis. You always hurt more than just yourself when you use drugs. You hurt everyone who loves you. But you know that. You went to rehab, you know what they tell you." Jada hung her head in shame, but Ingrid pressed on. "You gotta make up your mind that something is more important than that crack. And if you want to clean yourself up, you have to give it all you got. You gotta mean it." Ingrid looked at Jada, and could tell that she wasn't ready to make the necessary change. She could see in her eyes that the young woman was still in denial about how serious her problem was. Ingrid touched Jada's dirty hands, her nails broken from pounding on the door and prying at the windows the night before. "If you want to turn your life around, you can do it. You gotta ask God for His help. That's the only way."

Jada was so sorry that she'd ever slipped. Sorrier that she'd been caught. Ingrid sighed deeply. "Well, unfortunately, I have to be honest with you here. Whether you want to change or not, Marquis is finished with it. He's not budging. I done talked to him, and told him to hear you out—"

"Did you tell him that I'm sorry?" Jada ignored the snot falling from her nose. Ingrid handed her another tissue. Jada took it, wiped her nose, and cried. She spoke in a low, feeble voice. "You can't tell him that I'm sorry. Only I can tell him that. Why can't you get him to talk to me, Miss Ingrid? He listens to you. He respects you so much. Maybe you can get him to hear me out. I just want to tell him that I'm sorry. I'll fix myself up. I'll do it."

Ingrid looked blankly at Jada, feeling sorry for her pain, but knowing that her son was adamant that the relationship was over. She put her sympathetic feelings aside, and said what her son had asked her to say. "I need you to pack up all the stuff you want to take with you, and I'll help you if you need it. But Marquis don't want you here when he gets back. He left town for a few days to get his head together, and he wants me to make sure you're gone before he gets back."

Jada looked at the older woman, feeling like she was turning a deaf ear to her pleas. "I love your son, Miss Ingrid—"

"I believe you, baby. But he wants you to get your stuff up out of here today. I'm just the messenger. Don't make this hard on yourself." Ingrid's tone was flat. She seemed unfeeling, and perhaps a little cruel in her delivery. But inside she felt pity for the young lady. She knew that Jada was a decent person who happened to have one hell of a monkey on her back. Ingrid had watched her own husband fight the same battle, and she knew that when they fell back into using, it was usually with a vengeance. She could sense that Jada was out there pretty far, by her lack of concern for her appearance. The Jada she knew of would never have been caught outside looking like this, regardless of the situation. Ingrid was embarrassed for her. But she believed that Jada genuinely loved her son. Born, however, was still haunted by the pain of having lost his father to cocaine addiction. He had zero tolerance for someone who allowed themselves to be weakened by narcotics. Ingrid had tried to point out to Marquis that Jada and Leo were two very separate and different people. But Born shut down whenever the topic of staying with Jada was mentioned. He was not hearing anything she said.

Jada closed her eyes, as if she wanted to open them and find that this was all a dream. But it was very real. Accepting this, she stood up slowly, and looked around. What should she take with her? Where would she go? How much should she take? She felt a sudden surge of rage that Born hadn't had the balls to come and face her himself. What kind of man sends his mama to do his dirty work? Jada briefly entertained the thought of spazzing and going toe-to-toe with Miss Ingrid. Shit! This was *her* home, this was her life that Born was taking away. But looking at his mother, Jada knew she didn't want to challenge her. Miss Ingrid probably had a little peashooter in her pocket, and would probably not hesitate to bust a cap in her ass, Jada thought. Besides, Born's mother wasn't the one she was mad at. Ingrid wasn't being mean. She was only doing what her son had asked her to do. But still, her presence signaled that this was serious, that it was final. Jada let go of a sob, wrapping her mind around the fact that it was over. He was kicking her out.

She longed for her friend Sunny. Sunny would know what to do. She would tell her where to go. But she still hadn't heard from Sunny much since she'd gone underground with her baby and her family, after Dorian's murder. She longed for her friend, and was saddened by the realization that once again she had nowhere to go, no one to turn to. She felt sick about it. She thought about her sister. Where was Ava now? It had been over a year since she had last spoken to her. The last time she'd spoken to Ava was the day she'd left her house after discovering Jada getting high. Jada didn't have the heart to call her sister and give her the benefit of saying, "I told you so." Her mother. She was her only option. But Jada didn't want to give Edna the satisfaction of seeing her as broken and beaten by life as she was. She went upstairs, and looked in the hall closet and pulled out her luggage. She also pulled some money out of Born's jacket pocket— a few hundred-dollar bills. She went to her spacious walk-in closet and began the process of packing all the things she wanted to bring with her. She zipped her two furs into garment bags, packed her dresses, shoes, jeans, T-shirts, and purses. Soon she had three large Samsonite suitcases filled to capacity, along with her large Coach tote bag, filled with her jewelry, underwear, and a little cash she had stashed for herself. She had $720 and the possessions she lugged downstairs in suitcases. She and Miss Ingrid loaded up Jada's Acura, and she half expected to find out that Born wanted his car back. But he didn't strip her of that as well, and Jada was relieved for that.

When the car was loaded up, Jada looked at Ingrid. She knew that she smelled bad. She knew that she looked and felt even worse. But regardless of her haggard appearance, she had to tell the truth about her feelings for this woman's son. It might be her last chance to get a message to Born. She looked into his mother's eyes and made a final plea. "I am so sorry for messing up," she said. "I fell. But Born can help me stand up on my feet again. He can help me get right again."

Ingrid shook her head. "You gotta help *yourself*, Jada. You gotta get right for yourself."

Jada stared at her, speechless. Then she sighed. "I love Marquis. I never meant to hurt him. He's my everything. I don't have nobody else." She looked at Ingrid, and saw the pity that she tried to hide from her. "I know I have to leave. And I know he doesn't want me to come back. But just tell him that I love him. Tell him to forgive me." Jada resisted the urge to cry, and to hug Miss Ingrid, and she climbed into her car instead. Ingrid stood there for a few seconds, feeling the young woman's pain, and hoping that she found the strength to get clean and stay that way. Jada pulled off slowly, looking back at the house she used to think was etched directly from the canvas of her dreams. Ingrid walked back inside, and closed the door on a love affair between two people who almost had it all.

Jada's life had taken a sudden plunge, and she was destroyed. She had no place to turn, and nowhere else to go. So she went to the one place that still welcomed her. Back to the streets.

Jada slept in her car for the next several days, and even drove to her old friend Shante's place, looking for somewhere to stay until she got back on her feet. Shante allowed Jada to stay with her for a little while, after Jada enticed her with three hundred dollars toward that month's rent. Jada slept on Shante's futon, and during the day she went out, looking for a job, a place to stay—something. Three months went by this way, and all the time Jada drove past the house she had shared with Born, hoping to see him. She never did. She called his cell phone, called his house phone. Every number had been changed to an unlisted one. She drove past his drug spots, but was too embarrassed to go upstairs to see if he was there. She didn't know if Chuck had survived his beating, and she sure didn't want to face him if he knew that she was the real thief who had caused him to be fucked up. Jada got high every day, copping from her old dealer, Lucas, in West Brighton, whenever she got the chance.

She saw Mr. Charlie a couple of times during her trips to score some drugs in his building. But Jada didn't speak to him. She hated him for contributing to her misery. She hated everything that had contributed to the addiction she now realized that she had. Jada would sleep late some mornings, and on other mornings she would lay on the futon and pretend to be asleep, listening to Shante talk shit about Jada to her other friends.

"Yeah, girl. She's gettin' high again. I know! Lil Miss High and Mighty ain't so mighty no more, but she still high." Shante laughed out loud at her own joke. She listened as the person on the other end of the phone said something. "He left her. He put her out, and that's why she's staying with me. Girl, he kicked her to the curb. She said he had his mama come and help her pack her shit up. Now tell me *that* shit ain't gangsta. No more glitz and glamour for her. Now, it's back to where she started. That's why they say, don't forget where you came from. When he had her in all those jewels and furs, she wasn't coming to check on Shante. You know? It don't matter to me, as long as she keeps putting money in my hand. When his money runs out, I don't know where she think she gon' stay. I feel sorry for her."

Jada lay there with tears in her eyes. She knew that Shante didn't really feel sorry for her. But Jada sure felt sorry for herself. She got up and went out to escape—to get high once again. Soon her money was low, and Shante was fed up. So Jada packed her belongings, and went back to sleeping in her car.

After close to a week of living in her Acura, Jada finally admitted to herself that she had to sell some of her things. She went to a pawnshop and sold all the jewelry Born had bought for her piece by piece. Her jewelry netted her six thousand in cash, and Jada cried her eyes out in the pawnshop parking lot. All her jewelry—the diamond bracelets, rings, and earrings, her Rolex watch, and all the Tiffany pieces, every single thing had once held such special meaning for her. And now they were gone. She sold her two beloved fur coats by placing an ad in Staten Island's local newspaper, and got five thousand dollars total for two furs that had cost seven thousand and ten thousand dollars respectively. She felt like dying. Her entire relationship with Born had been a waste. She had nothing to show for it but a car she could hardly afford to gas up, and a broken heart.

She rented a one-bedroom apartment on Lafayette Avenue and used some of the money to set up house. She got some cheap furniture, and she laughed to herself at the irony that this apartment full of low-budget furniture was equal in price to that of the sofa alone in the living room she had shared with Born. This was a big step down, and Jada hated herself for blowing her chance at happiness with a man like him. Whenever she wasn't high, Jada spent her time crying and regretting her actions. She wished more than anything that she could turn back the hands of time. She had no job, but she had a little money. And most of that money was spent on staying high enough not to think about Born.

She missed him terribly. She remembered all the places they'd been together, all the conversations they'd had. Jada missed his voice, his face, his smile. She couldn't believe that he really didn't want her anymore. She thought that Born couldn't possibly get over her, or over their love, that easily. She thought he must be as miserable without her as she was without him. But then she saw him.

She was at the mall in Staten Island, looking for a pair of shoes to match an outfit she had. She was sick of sitting at home, crying and sad about her mistakes. Tonight there was going to be a local "player's ball," and she was going so that she could let off some steam. She hadn't been out since her days with Born, and she needed to unwind. She went and got her hair done and got her nails done, and she felt better than she had in months. She walked into Aldo and was looking at a pair of sexy sandals when she heard his laugh.

Jada looked up, and Born was walking into the store with a light-skinned black woman who looked to be in her early twenties. She was very pretty, and had an enviable bone structure. Her face was flawless, and her outfit was Christian Lacroix. Her hair was cut into a chin-length Chinese bob with bangs, and she was beautiful. Jada's ego told her that the woman looked like a younger and better version of herself. Was Born replacing her with a carbon copy? Jada was green with envy. She stood there, holding the shoe in her shaking hands, and stared at Born. He didn't see Jada at first. He was too engrossed in whatever joke he and his new friend were laughing at. He had his hand on the small of the woman's back, and Jada couldn't help remembering when he had held her just that way. Born, still laughing, turned his head forward as they entered, and that's when their eyes met.

Jada stared at him, and he at her. She put the shoe down and stepped closer to him to say something. But before she could take another step, Born quickly grabbed the girl by the wrist and led her out of the store.

"Wait a minute, Born," the woman protested. "I want to get the shoes I saw yesterday." She pulled her hand away and stood in the store's entranceway.

Born stood outside, and the look on his face was serious. "Not now, Anisa. We'll come back and get them." He took her by the hand, and they walked off into the mall.

Jada stood there, feeling like a fool. She looked around, embarrassed that Born had run from her that way, and hoping that no one had noticed. She put her head down, and walked out of the store in the opposite direction of Born and his friend.

Anisa, Jada thought to herself. *Her name is Anisa.* She thought about the pretty girl with the pretty name who had taken her place in Born's life. She wondered if she had also taken her place in his heart.

Jada sat at the bar alone, wallowing in self-pity. She watched Born, who was all the way across the room with Chance and Smitty, laughing at something. In her mind, they might as well have been laughing at her. She sipped her Hennessy and glared at Anisa, standing by Born's side in the position that Jada had only recently vacated. She felt hatred toward the pretty young woman Born paraded around now as if she were Jada's replacement—her understudy. Jada wasn't even sure if Born knew she was at the club that night, since he had so far spent all evening in the company of his childhood pals and that bitch Anisa. They were tucked cozily at a corner table, surrounded by partygoers.

Jada was trying to summon the courage to approach Born. She thought that surely he wouldn't cause a scene in a crowded nightclub, when all she wanted to do was talk to him. She drained her glass, and was going to slide off the barstool and take the chance of walking over to Born. But before she could set her empty glass back down, a familiar face appeared at her side.

"Perfect timing, I guess," Jamari said. Without asking her, he summoned the bartender and ordered Jada another of whatever she was drinking. Jada didn't argue, figuring this might be even better than approaching Born. If he spotted her talking to another man, he might feel a twinge of the same jealousy she had felt all night long, watching him with Anisa. Maybe, if she was lucky, Born would even come over there.

Jada still didn't realize that the animosity between Born and Jamari ran deep. She knew him only as a man who she had run into all the time when she was in Park Hill stealing from Born. Jamari sat on the empty stool beside her, and ordered a glass of Hennessy straight. Jada smiled to herself, knowing that this was Born's favorite drink as well. She was clueless about Jamari's childhood friendship with Born, and ignorant to the fact that he had once idolized Born. She didn't know that Jamari had crossed Born, and that the two of them hardly spoke to one another.

She sipped her drink when it arrived, and thanked Jamari for it. He smiled, and said, "You're welcome." Jada realized that he was really handsome. In all the times she'd seen him when she was stealing from Born, she had never really looked at Jamari. She had enjoyed his flirtatious conversations, but had never taken the time to see how good-looking he was. Jamari was tall and thin, with light brown skin and encompassing eyes. He had a smile that never seemed to quite reach his eyes. Jada noticed that his lips would spread into a smile. His perfect teeth would be visible. But somehow, the smile never reflected in his eyes. They still seemed sad, maybe even blank and cold. Jada got lost in them as Jamari spoke.

"Now, why are you all alone over here, while that muthafucka's all the way over there?" He shook his head. "Why would a nigga stand over there all night with some skinny, average-looking broad like her, when your fine ass is over here tossing back glasses of yak?"

Jada smiled, happy that Jamari had cracked on the bitch monopolizing Born's attention. She laughed, and shook her head. This was her fourth drink, and she was feeling it. She spoke a little slower than usual, as she said, "Me and Born broke up. I guess he moved on."

Jamari already knew that their relationship was over. Born had made sure he was seen all over Shaolin with all kinds of women, but most often with the pretty young thang he was currently dancing with. Jamari knew that Born was only trying to save face because his ex-wifey was a crackhead. By parading the new dime pieces in his life around town, he was making it known that he was still the man. Anisa and Born danced to Aaliyah's "If Your Girl Only Knew," while they sipped on Moët. There were four bottles on the table with Born and his crew, so Jada assumed they must be balling, as usual. She was so envious, so beside herself with jealousy. Jamari noticed the green-eyed monster taking residence within her. "He's a fool," Jamari said, nodding in Born's direction. "Some dudes don't miss a good thing till it's gone."

Jada shrugged her shoulders, and took another swig. "I think you're right. But it don't really look like he's missing me too much right about now." Jada looked forlorn. "But that's okay, because I came to have a good time by myself."

Jamari listened to what she said, but could tell by the look on her face that she felt very differently. She sounded very unconvincing. He watched her gaze continuously fall on Born and his new girlfriend, while he made small talk with her. He could tell that she was sick with regret. She caught Jamari staring at her, and she turned and met his gaze.

"I think I'm gonna go," she said. She finished her drink, and set her glass back down. "Thanks for the drink." She smiled at Jamari, and patted him softly on his bicep as she stood from the stool.

"Don't leave yet. Don't let that nigga stop you from having a good time."

Jada smiled. "It's not that—"

"Then prove it." Jamari stood up, towering over her. "Dance with me."

There was a reggae mix playing, and couples littered the dance floor. Jamari led Jada to the center of the floor, and started dancing with her. He put his hands around her waist, and pulled her close. She prayed that Born was watching her, and that he came over and interrupted. She was so desperately longing for this to happen that she grinded on Jamari, turning her back to him so that her ass rubbed up against his body. She wanted him to enjoy the dance, so that Born would notice her.

Born did notice her. Anisa went to the bathroom, and Smitty took the opportunity to point Born in Jada's direction on the dance floor. Born stood there, watching the love of his life dance with the man he despised. He wondered if Jada knew who the nigga was, if she knew their history. What was on her mind? He was tempted to go over there and say something, but he knew that if Anisa came back and saw him fighting over Jada, she would have been mad. It was bad enough that Born had already called Anisa by Jada's name on two occasions. He didn't need to further piss her off by arguing over Jada in the middle of a party in New York's smallest borough.

Born stared at the two of them as they danced, feeling like Jamari was playing a dangerous game with him. Born had let his treachery slide the first time, and he hadn't slaughtered Jamari like he should have. This time, he knew that Jamari was only using Jada as a way to get under Born's skin. So he ignored them, and continued to enjoy the evening as if Jada was nowhere in sight. Born was so angry with himself for letting Jamari live, for letting him continue to antagonize him. He thought about something Dorian had said to him years earlier, when Born had first told him about how Jamari had deceived him: *"If you let that nigga get away with it, he's gonna cross you again."* As Born watched his nemesis dance with Jada, he sipped his champagne, and Jamari looked in Born's direction and smiled. Born smiled right back.

Born felt that his reputation was being challenged. Jamari was calling him out. Born took that dance as a sign that war was imminent. He looked at Jamari, thinking of something his father used to tell him. It was sage advice that Born intended to take to heart from this day forward. "Strike first, and strike hard," Leo used to say. Born smiled, hearing his old dad's voice in his head. He intended to follow his advice to the fullest.

30

LEFTOVERS

Born knew that Anisa had gotten him by default. She was just someone he started to date when he was on the rebound. When he met Anisa, she was a breath of fresh air for him. She wasn't from where he was from. That meant that no matter where he brought her within New York City, she was unknown to the niggas on the scene. No one could say that they'd had her or that they knew about her past. She was from Long Island, and they met while he was out there doing business. He went to a barbecue at an acquaintance's house, and she was one of the guests. She was so stunningly attractive that he had hardly been able to concentrate on anyone else. He got her number before he left, called her the next day, and they began a relationship that blossomed into what it was today. But he knew he would never love her the way he had loved Jada.

Anisa was a very demure and soft-spoken young woman. She listened to Born tell her all about Jada, and about the way she had broken his heart. She seemed sympathetic and understanding, giving him reassurance that he had done nothing to deserve what Jada had done to him. Anisa didn't use any drugs, didn't smoke cigarettes, and rarely drank. She was a safe bet, he figured, and her willingness to listen to his tale of woe was a plus for him. Anisa became like his amateur therapist. She listened to him as he told her about how losing Jada to drugs had almost made him want to give up on women. But Anisa was determined to prevent that from happening. She did everything right. She was quiet when he was in an introspective mood, and she was tons of fun when Born needed to let off some steam. He found himself wanting her company more and more, and she became his good friend with benefits.

Born would never love a woman again. He wouldn't allow himself to fall for any woman the way he had for Jada. That was too dangerous. He was afraid to have his heart broken. Even though Anisa was at times the ideal woman, he kept her at a safe distance, and never let her get too close. Anisa stubbornly played her position, hoping that somehow she could break down his resistance.

But after a while Anisa got sick of hearing about the other woman. One day in particular, Anisa had just given him two explosive orgasms, back-to-back. They had been going strong for close to five months, and she was pulling out all the stops to make sure that her position was secure. Thug lovin' was what she'd done to him. Anisa had tied Born's wrists up in a bandana, and sucked him off intensely. He had splashed off in her mouth, and she had devoured it all, untying his hands and smiling, satisfied, when she was done. They lay together afterward, with Anisa's soft hands stroking his dick. He felt himself growing in her delicate hands, and she grinned at him, naughtily. Before he knew what happened, Anisa had him in her mouth again, and he was rock hard.

He beckoned her closer. "Get on that."

Anisa happily complied, climbing on top of him and putting him inside her. He watched her wind her hips, enveloping him inside her warmest place. He held her hips as she grinded, and it wasn't long before she got him to climax a second time—and this time she joined him in that ecstasy.

Afterward, Anisa had laid her head on Born's chest, with her leg wrapped across his. He was on his back with his hands behind his head, and he seemed completely relaxed. They lay together in silence for a while before he looked at her, and said, "Yo, I can't believe the bitch is fuckin' with Jamari." He shook his head in disbelief, as he thought about seeing Jada with Jamari, and hearing more and more that they were being seen together. "The nigga is a bum. All he do is run behind Wizz all day, trying to be somebody for a change. Jamari and Wizz think they doing something, but them niggas ain't making no money. Them niggas ain't seein' no real paper out there. I shut the hill down, and them mutha-fuckas is nibbling on the crumbs that fell from my plate. Jada's just one of my crumbs."

Anisa stared at him, seeming to listen attentively. But in her mind, she was thinking, *No, this nigga is not laying here talking about another woman when he just finished having sex with me.* She wondered if he had been thinking of Jada while they were having sex. She was fed up.

"You're sick without her. It's so obvious." Anisa had said it calmly, and sat up in bed. She seemed like she wasn't mad, but she knew that his love for Jada was still haunting him, and she began searching for her clothes.

"Nah." Born had denied it. "I ain't sick without nobody."

Anisa looked at him, her lips scrunched up in disbelief. "Well, then stop talking about the bitch, then. I'm getting kinda sick of hearing about her. Especially since I'm the one who just made you cum like that."

Born smiled, and told himself that he probably was talking about Jada more than he should. He made a mental note to curb his mention of Jada's name in Anisa's presence from that day forward. Maybe he was slipping.

He didn't talk about Jada much after that, but she still dominated his thoughts. Jada had no clue as to how deeply he had felt for her. Truth was, Born was brokenhearted. His mama told him that you never get over your first love. Instead, he replaced her with Anisa. She was not Jada, but she was also not a crackhead.

Born had held out hope that Jada wasn't really dealing with Jamari like that. But the more he heard the rumors, the more he felt like Jada had been a complete waste of his time. He knew that he had taught her better than that. Born saw clearly from the beginning that Jamari was only trying to provoke him. He wondered how long it would take before the two of them bumped heads at last.

31

CONSEQUENCES

September 1998

Born sat in Slim the barber's chair at the barbershop on Bay Street. He had just sat down, and his cape was secured around his neck. Slim was called that for a very obvious reason. At six-foot-four and 170 pounds, he was a thin young man who ran his own shop, keeping his eyes open and his mouth shut. He cut Born's hair to perfection every time, and for this reason he counted him as one of his regulars. He worked alongside Barnes and Kevin, two other barbers with decent followings of their own. On this day there were three other patrons in the shop besides Born. Two were young men in their twenties, as Born was. He recognized one of them as Breeze, from the Stapleton projects, while an unknown young man in a red Hilfiger shirt sat in Kevin's chair getting his hair cut. The other customer was an older man in his fifties. Slim began the process of cutting Born's hair into the perfect fade. The mood was calm, it being a cool September morning. The radio played in the background, and the topic changed from local gossip to current events. Soon Slim was putting the finishing touches on Born's mustache and goatee. The older man left the shop, and the subject was hip-hop's East Coast–West Coast beef.

"All I'm saying is, the shit done got out of hand. It ain't about music no more. And once it stopped being about music, I lost interest." Slim said as he maneuvered his clippers skillfully across Born's dome. "What do you think, Born?" he asked.

Born pondered the question as he looked at the reflection in the mirror on the wall opposite him. He could see the street through the mirror, and he watched as cars pulled up, and people came and went. As usual, Born was on point. Although, to those who looked at him it may have appeared that he was simply having a conversation in a relaxed atmosphere, Born was in fact watching the arrival of his enemy. Looking in the mirror he could see Jamari and Wizz approaching the shop as they climbed out of Jamari's car.

Born sighed, wondering if it was coincidence, or if it was just his own rotten luck that he kept running into this dude. He answered the question that had been posed to him, as Jamari and Wizz entered the barbershop. He wasn't facing the doorway, and Slim's chair was in the back. But still, Born's presence was obvious. "Sometimes beef starts out because niggas wanna test you," Born explained. "And then niggas do or say something that crosses the line. Once that happens, you got a problem, because a man has to always defend his honor. Unless he's a coward, and he has no honor. But a real man is gonna step up and call a nigga out. And when that happens, you got beef."

Jamari and Wizz listened, still thinking that Born didn't know they were there. "Wassup, everybody?" Jamari said, expecting Born to look up in surprise at the sound of his voice. But Born didn't move, nor did he respond, as the other patrons greeted Jamari and Wizz.

The guy in the red shirt, who was getting his hair cut by Kevin, spoke once again on the topic of the rap war. "Niggas is dying, you know what I'm sayin'? Once bodies start droppin', I think it qualifies as beef."

Jamari nodded in agreement, although he was coming in on the tail end of the conversation. He sat in one of the folding chairs, and said, "Beef ain't always bodies droppin' and bullets flyin'. Some beef simmers slowly." His tone was suggestive, and Born met his gaze in the mirror's reflection. Born knew there was a hidden message in what Jamari had said. Jamari grinned at Born. "Yo, what up, my nigga. I ain't even see you sitting there," Jamari lied. "How's everything, man?"

Born ignored the greeting and the question and stared at Jamari through the mirror. By now, all conversation had ceased, and this exchange was the focus of everyone present. Only the music drifting from the stereo's speakers filled the void of silence.

But Jamari was determined to spark a conversation with his old friend. "Yo, did you ever make back that money you lost with Chuck?" Jamari was grinning, antagonistically. He had heard about how Born had beaten Chuck within an inch of his life when Jada had been the one stealing from him all along. "You know he's working with me and Wizz, now?"

Born didn't flinch. He stared back into Jamari's cold eyes, as Slim removed the cape from Born's neck. "Nah, I didn't know that," he replied. Born wanted to kill Jamari at that very moment, but there were too many witnesses present. "He's working for you and Wizz now. What's that supposed to be, like a step up or somethin'? You and Wizz ain't gettin' no money. It's like I always told my nigga Chuck, if you hang around with nine broke niggas, you're bound to be the tenth one. He'll see what I meant."

Jamari stared at Born like he wanted to say something. But he uttered not a word. Wizz stood up, and glared at Born. "Yo, what the fuck is on your mind, Born? You walk around here like you're Superman, or some shit. You ain't no fuckin' body! You can bleed just like everybody else."

Slim stepped between the men, as Born stood up. "Don't bring this bullshit in my shop, Wizz. Word is bond."

Born turned to leave, grabbing his hoodie on the way out. "Nah, don't worry about it, Slim. I'm leaving." He looked at Jamari and Wizz, and smiled. "Y'all niggas can't handle the truth." He had his ratchet with him, and he felt the steel press against his rib cage. He smiled at them provocatively, hoping that they'd give him a reason to start shooting. "You can give work to Chuck and any other lil nigga out here you choose. But you're never gonna catch up to me. Y'all ain't never gonna get the respect I get, the money I get, or the love I get."

Jamari grinned now. "But it looks like I can get the girls you get,

Born. Jada said to tell you 'hi.'" Jamari licked his lips, feeling so much hatred mixed with jealousy toward his former friend.

Wizz laughed, but on the inside, he was beginning to wonder if Jamari's beef with Born was more about him wanting to *be* Born. To Wizz, Jamari sounded like a deranged fan. In truth, Jamari was thirsty for Born's position, and he had been since they were young kids growing up.

Born considered murdering both of them right there. But he decided to kill 'em softly instead. "Tell her I said hello. I knew you was fiendin' to sample that. I could tell from the first time I brought her around. Congratulations. She got some good pussy, don't she?" The other customers laughed, and Born continued to smile in Jamari's face. The two other young men in the shop getting their haircuts amped up the backhanded remark. His comment illustrated how little concern he had about Jamari being with Jada. Born had already been there and done that, and he'd had her *first*. In his heart, though, Born was still sick without Jada, and he hated her for being with this lame. But he would never give Jamari the satisfaction of knowing that. "Stick to the script, muthafucka. Stop trying so hard to fit into my shoes, and walk in your own for once." Born looked at Jamari with contempt. Then he looked at Wizz. "You should watch how you talk to me," he said. "You might fuck around and piss me off."

Born opened the door, and walked out, laughing. Wizz and Jamari were both enraged, and Wizz began declaring war. "That's it, my nigga. I don't care what you say. I'ma body that muthafucka next time I see him. I'ma run up in that nigga's spots, and all that. Watch. I don't give a fuck what you say." Wizz was talking recklessly, and the other customers exchanged glances.

Jamari was seething. He hated Born, because he was a constant reminder that there was always someone better than him. Jamari remembered how he had started getting respect only when he came around his peers wearing Born's clothes, rocking Born's jewelry. Jamari had respect for Born, but wanted that same success—wanted those same things for himself. He always got the things he wanted, eventually. But by then

Born would be two steps ahead of him, and always did shit bigger and better. Jamari remembered when he started bringing pretty, light-skinned girls around the way, and he was the man for a minute. Having a light-skinned girl with long hair was a badge of honor in the hood back then. But then Born came through with Jada. And she wasn't even all that light-skinned. But she was bad as hell, and she shut all the other bitches in their circle down. Jamari got an Audi, and Born got a Benz. Jamari rented a house, and Born bought one. Jamari hated the feeling he got whenever Born was around—the feeling that he was never the best. Never quite number one, as long as Born was on the scene. Everywhere he went niggas gave him respect. But Born still treated him like a shorty, and he was a grown-ass man. The truth of Jamari's animosity toward Born had yet to surface, and he never revealed to Wizz his true motivation for hating Born as much as he did.

Not realizing that he was speaking aloud, as he peered out the shop windows at the passersby, Jamari said, "Fuck that nigga. I ain't no shorty no more. Things ain't sweet like they used to be."

Pulling his card, the old man in his fifties said, "Yeah, nigga. You talk all that shit now that the muthafucka's gone. Ten minutes ago, you was quiet as a fuckin' church mouse."

The shop was filled with laughter, as everyone fell out at Jamari's expense. Wizz shook his head, as Jamari stormed out. Their laughter filled his ears as he left, and headed for Jada's house.

Jamari arrived at Jada's house, and she could sense right away that he was upset about something. He seemed uptight. He sat down and explained to her that he'd just had an argument with Born at the barbershop. He told Jada that he had defended her, while Born spoke about her like she was a disease.

Jada's heart beat rapidly. "What did he say about me?"

Jamari seemed not to want to tell her. But she pleaded with him until he gave in, and told her his version of the day's events. "He said that you're a dirty crackhead." Jamari watched Jada's expression change, and he continued. "He started talking about how you were wild in bed, and all the sexual things he used to do with you. He was on some real disrespectful shit. He said you were his leftovers, and that he already used you up. He called you a bitch. The nigga was talking about you like you was some ho in the street, with all them niggas in the barbershop laughing at you, and shit. I defended you, though."

Jamari watched Jada wipe the tears that fell from her eyes. He knew that she still had love for Born, and knew that she was holding out hope that he would take her back one day. But Jamari saw Jada as a pawn, and he manipulated her as such. He walked over toward her and wiped her eyes. He kissed her softly on her nose, and held out his hand to her. When she reached for it, there was a vial of crack in his palm. Jada snatched her hand back as if she'd just stuck her hand in some fire. She looked at Jamari, questioningly.

"Go ahead and take it," he said. "I'm not gonna judge you. I know you smoke. My moms smoked also. So I understand. I'm not here to pass judgment. All of us have our bad habits. I got mine, and Born got his, too. He judges you, but I don't. Go ahead and take it. I got you."

Jada stared at Jamari, feeling two things. She was hurt because of Born's cruel words against her. She had thought that Born was her soul mate, and he had spoken about her as if she was a stranger to him. That hurt. She was also wondering what kind of man Jamari was. True, she *was* smoking crack again. But Jada wasn't accustomed to a man who would just give it to her and encourage her to get high. Only Mr. Charlie had done that, and he had turned out to be a snake. Still, the pain of what Born had said about her needed numbing, and Jada took the crack from Jamari. She watched his reaction, but he simply sat there and sparked a blunt filled with weed, and smoked it. Jamari got high off of hydro, while Jada got high off of crack. Jada felt relieved that she did not have to hide, and that she could let her guard down around Jamari. As her mind swirled around in a haze, Jamari reminded her over and over to be herself. He assured her that she could be who she was around him, that he didn't want her to change like Born wanted her to.

Jada had sex with Jamari for the first time that night. He took his time, and seemed to enjoy every moment. Jada was disconnected, and to her it felt empty. There was no emotion in it at all for her, other than sadness that Born had turned on her so viciously. She disappeared inside of herself, as she had done countless times when she was a prostitute. Jada let Jamari explore her body, and she finally accepted that it was over between her and Born. She thought that she just might find happiness with Jamari, if she gave him a real chance.

After that day, every time he came to see her he had crack for her. She appreciated Jamari's openness and his acceptance. She misinterpreted it as love. Jada lost some weight, but maintained her sexy curves. She had few outward signs of her addiction, other than her dwindling bank account balance. Jamari was proud to be seen with her, and the two of them went out all the time. At first she would hope to run into Born, so that he could see how well she was doing without him. But soon she heard that Born had met an unexpected twist of fate.

32

HIGH PRICE TO PAY

Two days passed after Born argued with Jamari and Wizz in the barbershop. He went about his business, as usual. But he longed more than ever to talk to Dorian. He missed his boy, and was consumed with guilt. He still felt like he was the one to blame for Dorian's death, and he wished that he could go back to the fateful moment and change his actions. He never would have taken his eyes off Raquel. Never would have let her get inside the house. Born felt responsible for Sunny not having Dorian to depend on, and for their daughter not having a father. In short, he missed his friend. He wondered where Sunny was, and he wished she was around to tell Jada to leave Jamari alone. Sunny had all but disappeared after Dorian's death, and he hadn't even seen his friend's little baby girl.

Over those two days, Born thought about how life had changed so much for him. Dorian was gone, and so was Sunny and the baby. Jada was a thing of the past, and even his childhood cronies were no longer as close to him as they'd once been. He knew that, despite the civil nature of their relationship, Martin still didn't particularly like the fact that Born had done his own thing, and left the crew behind. In Martin's mind, Born had been selfish, keeping all his connections to himself, while his former crew was left struggling to keep up.

Born felt alone for the first time in his life. It really was lonely at the top. It was nice having Anisa around. But she was someone who didn't know his story. And he didn't have the energy to share it all with her. She didn't know him the way that Jada had. The sex was good, and her conversation stimulated him. For these reasons alone, he kept her around, and she became the new lady in his life. Somehow, he still felt a longing in his heart for the life he once had. He had had it all. A great best friend and mentor, a lovely lady on his arm whom he loved with all his heart, and an enterprise no one could penetrate. And in the blink of an eye it had all gone away. All but his hustle, and that was what he focused on. His days were spent making moves and taking risks, trying to maintain his hold in the streets. He spent his evenings with Anisa, though his mind wandered to what used to be.

He awoke one morning, and left Anisa at home asleep while he went to the store. He planned to drive a few blocks to the convenience store on Victory Boulevard. But as soon as he pulled out of the driveway and onto the street, he was surrounded on all sides by dark vehicles, and cops started jumping out. He knew what was up, and he put his hands up as the cops closed in and opened his car door, removing him from the vehicle. "Don't move, Marquis!" He was amazed that they knew his government name. From that alone, he figured that they had done their homework. Either that, or they'd been tipped off. He didn't resist, didn't say a word as they read him his rights, and showed him the search warrant. They wasted no time searching both the house and his car. He said nothing, and neither did Anisa, as they led her out of the house in pajamas, and put her in the back of a squad car while they searched the house. Born heard them asking her where she was from and how she knew him. But she didn't answer their questions, and they got frustrated, and left her sitting in the back of the squad car half dressed, while they searched the house with police dogs.

Soon the cops emerged with smiles on their faces, and Born knew they had found the small amount of drugs he had stashed in the kitchen canister. His suspicions were confirmed when he heard one officer say to another, "Got him! We got him!" It was only about ten bags of white powder. Not enough to hit him with twenty to life, but still enough to make his heart sink. Born had never been one to keep the bulk of his drugs where he rested his head. The few bags he had in his residence were nothing compared to what they could have caught him with. He wasn't too concerned, but he also didn't want to get his hopes up that things would work in his favor, when he knew it was quite possible that they might not. He watched his neighbors come out and shake their heads at him, as if they'd known all along that he was unfit for their suburban neighborhood.

He looked through the police car window as they drove him to the precinct. He spoke not a word until he arrived and was processed. Born was booked, fingerprinted, and put in a cell. He called his mother and explained the situation. She promised to be in court in the morning to see what the deal was. Born instructed her to get in contact with Grant Keys, the attorney from Dorian's crew. He asked her to explain what had happened and to see if there was anything Grant could do to help. Ingrid told Born not to worry, that she had everything under control. After talking to her Born felt a lot better. The police questioned him for hours that night. They wanted to charge him with conspiracy, but with no co-conspirators that was impossible. For once, Born was glad that he had no partners, no team. The detectives who questioned him didn't seem convinced that he worked alone. They kept asking him about Brooklyn—who were his connections from Brooklyn? Instantly, he thought of Jamari and wondered if he'd stooped low enough to rat him out. How else would they know as much as they did? But thankfully, they didn't know enough. In order to prove conspiracy, they needed people to say that they worked with him. They didn't have that, and they couldn't get him to talk. Born was mute as they barraged him with questions, insults, and accusations.

Finally, at two o'clock in the morning, they returned him to his cell. Born settled in for the night, refusing to worry too much. But all the while he was wondering what was going on. How had they caught up to him out of the blue like this? Had somebody tipped them off? Over and over he replayed his argument with Jamari and Wizz in his head. He wondered if one of them had dropped dime on him, and realized that it was a very likely scenario. He wondered how Anisa was holding up under all the pressure, and wished that there was some way that he could talk to her.

With very little sleep, Born awoke the next morning to face his destiny. Hours passed before he was finally called to the courtroom, with Anisa standing nervously beside him. He looked at her and nodded reassuringly. Then he scanned the courtroom until he found his mother's face. She winked at him, and Born felt more at ease. Beside her sat Grant Keys and Born smiled, happy to see his face. The judge and D.A. went through their formalities while Born's attorney pled his case. Marc Burnett was the finest criminal attorney in the borough, and Born had chosen him to represent both him and Anisa. When all was said and done, despite the prosecutor's attempts to have bail set at ridiculous amounts, the judge asserted that such desperate measures were unnecessary. Born's bail was set at five thousand dollars, and Anisa was released on her own recognizance. Born glanced at his mother on the way out, and smiled triumphantly. Within an hour both he and Anisa were free to go.

When he was released Born eagerly greeted Grant outside the courtroom. Born told Grant that his attorney was urging him to take the five-year deal that was being offered, since the prosecution was willing to drop all charges against Anisa in exchange for Born pleading guilty. With good behavior, he could be home in three years. Grant assured him that he could do better than that. He told Born that he had a relationship with the judge who was presiding over his case.

"How do you think you got such a low bail?" he asked, smiling. "Give me a chance to go back and talk to him in his chambers, and I'll see what I can do about the deal you're being offered." Seeing the look of relief on Born's face, Grant decided not to let him get his hopes up. "Yo, Born, there's a big probability that you're gonna have to do *some* time. Hopefully, it won't be nearly as much as Burnett said they're offering you now. But he's gotta give you some type of penalty because of the nature of the crime."

Born nodded and stuck his hands in his pocket. He looked at Grant. "Somebody ratted me out, didn't they?" he asked.

Grant nodded. "I'm told it was a confidential informant. They called in an anonymous tip from a pay phone at the Staten Island Ferry terminal."

Born shook his head, knowing that if he saw Jamari or Wizz he would kill them for snitching. Fucking cowards! Seeing the fury on Born's face, Grant put his hand on his shoulder reassuringly. "I'll get back to you about your plea offer, but don't get your hopes up too high. I'll do the best I can." Born shook his friend's hand, grateful that Dorian had exposed him to such valuable connections.

On the way home, Anisa was silent. She had greeted Ingrid stiffly, pissed that she had to meet Born's mother under these circumstances. Anisa was angry, and she was near tears after spending the night in jail. She wasn't prepared for shit like this. The lifestyle Born lived was one that she was enjoying, but prison—that was *never* supposed to be a factor, and Anisa was as mad as hell. She hadn't called her family to tell them about her arrest, since doing so would have meant disgrace for her. She had the kind of family that would have shunned Born for leaving her so vulnerable, and she didn't want that. She knew that Born was a smart man, who would always be successful. She had watched him move and could tell that he was an intelligent hustler—certainly more intelligent than his cohorts in the game. She didn't want to blow what was turning out to be a pretty good thing, by complicating things with family drama. Anisa was getting used to living the life that Born led. She was growing accustomed to the fine linen and exquisite surroundings, the jewelry, the cash, and all the luxury he surrounded himself with. The last thing she wanted to do was become a headache for him. She figured that as long as she continued to play her cards right and be as opposite of Jada as she could, eventually Born would give her everything she wanted. She was counting on it. Born talked to his mother, and Anisa listened to their exchange.

"You should have known better than to have that shit in your house, Marquis."

"I know. Not now, Ma. Please." Born shook his head, and looked out of the window.

"Not now? When, then? You need to be more careful. I know that you know better than that. You're slipping. You know you gonna have to do some time for this, right?" Ingrid took her eyes off the road briefly and looked at her son. "Burnett said they wanna offer you a deal. I ain't saying to take it, but you need to be ready for that possibility. How much money did they get when they raided your house?"

Born had thought about this question, and knew that Ingrid would inevitably ask it. He already knew where this was going. "I had like seven thousand in cash, along with all the other stuff they seized."

Ingrid shook her head. "Well, you know they only turned in seven hundred dollars in cash, along with the drugs they found."

Born nodded that he did know that. "I expected that, though. They never turn in all of it."

"I just don't understand how you could be so sloppy." Ingrid couldn't help leveling with her son. "I know you had to expect that these clowns out here would get sick of seeing you on top. You know the streets only love you until you start doing *too* good. Then they hate you. You gotta watch your back. You should have been expecting them to come to your door eventually, and for that reason you never should have had shit in your house."

Born looked at his mother. His eyes pleaded with her to save this conversation for later. He wasn't in the mood for this so soon after being sprung. She grasped the meaning in his stare, and closed her mouth, driving the rest of the way in silence. As they pulled up in front of the house, Ingrid turned to her son. "I cleaned up as best I could, but the place is still pretty messed up." Born had expected that the police had trashed his home during their raid, and he was grateful that his mother had used her spare key to straighten up his home as much as possible. He thanked her, gave her a kiss on her soft cheek, and climbed out of the car.

Ingrid watched Anisa in the backseat, looking terribly upset that she'd been forced to spend the night in jail. She sat there, not budging as she waited for Born to open her door and help her out of the car. The expression on her face was that of someone who was suffering. Ingrid, knowing that her son would take all the weight, and that Anisa wouldn't have to take a fall in the end, didn't like how the young woman was portraying the role of the victim. Anisa's lips were pouty, and she had her darkest sunglasses on her face, like she was at a funeral or something. Ingrid knew that if you want to be a hustler's wife you need to be able to roll with the punches, and take things for better or worse. Anisa didn't seem to have what it took to stand the test of time. Ingrid took note of this, and added this to her list of reasons for not particularly liking her son's new girlfriend.

Born opened the car door, and Anisa stepped out and bid his mother good-bye. They walked into the house, and both went to take much needed showers. By the time Anisa emerged from hers, Born was hanging up the phone after a conversation with Grant. Born was not disappointed. Grant had made his case sound a lot less grim. He explained that due to the quantity of drugs they'd found and Born's previous arrest record, he would have to do some time in jail. But the judge had called in a favor and the prosecution was seeking far less time than the five years Born had previously been facing. Now Born was looking at a one-and-half-year bid, which he eagerly accepted. The charges against Anisa would be dismissed. He thanked Grant for his help, called Burnett and instructed him to accept the plea deal. He could tell that Anisa was relieved to hear that she would be off the hook. Born, on the other hand, spent the next few weeks preparing for his incarceration and passing his torch in the streets for the duration of his absence.

Now Born wished he had a crew behind him—someone he could trust to hold shit down in his absence. As much as he hated to have to do it, he went back to his old hood and got in touch with his boys from Arlington. Martin was still locked up on the attempted murder charge. So Born called on Chance and Smitty. He explained what Burnett had told him, and turned over the buildings in Arlington to them. His only condition was that they hold it down for him and welcome him back when his bid was over. The three of them spent an evening together like they had in the good old days—drinking and reminiscing, and burying all their old hatchets. He was confident when he left that his cronies would wield their power well. He put Omar in charge of Park Hill. It was an operation that was running smoothly. And since Omar was one of Do-

rian's old cronies, he trusted him. Also, he had the power of Dorian's notorious brothers behind him, and Born figured few would challenge that.
He passed the reins to the people he trusted most, and went to embrace
his fate. He pled guilty, and went in for sentencing. Anisa and his mother
were both in the courtroom as he was led away to begin his bid.

During his months at the jungle in New York City known as Rikers
Island, Born managed to steer clear of catching another case. He was
anxious to leave Rikers, where the C.O.s let the inmates run the jail, and
the gangs ran amok. Born had nothing against the gangbangers. But he
saw them all as bullies. And he only respected bullies who had the heart
to bully all alone—not those with a whole gang behind them. Six weeks
after he was locked up at Rikers, he was transferred to Franklin Correc-
tional Facility in upstate New York. When he got to Franklin, Born went
to reception, and they reviewed his case and all the charges against him.
The decision was made to put him into a drug program for six months.
Born assumed this was due to the fact that all the charges against him
were drug-related. He surmised that they probably wanted to show him
the type of damage he was doing by participating in the drug trade.

During his time in the program, Born was forced to take a look at
himself and his role in the game. He thought about his father, who had
never gotten over his love affair with the fast lane. He started to wonder
if it was time for a change. But prison being what it was, he was forced to
revert back to the devil within daily, and to react to his environment. He
had a few words with his fellow inmates from time to time. But for the
most part he managed to keep himself out of trouble. The part that was
the hardest for him was the constant attempts by the correction officers
to demean the prisoners. Many of them walked around like overseers on
a plantation, barking orders and daring the inmates to cross their invis-
ible lines. They looked for any excuse to toss a nigga in the box, and
many of them were assholes. A couple were cool, though, and those were
the ones who came in and did their jobs without becoming obsessed with
power and control. Born didn't like being told when he could use the
telephone, or what colors he could wear. But he managed to humble
himself and roll with the punches of being incarcerated. While in the

drug program, one of the administrators explained that 85 percent of those inmates who earned their GEDs got paroled. To Born that was a blueprint to get out of jail, and he was determined to be in the next 85 percent. He studied for and passed his GED, and kept his mind occupied with books and magazines.

In the beginning of his bid, Anisa had held him down. She came to visit, put money on his books, sent him books and magazines, food, and some clothes. But it wasn't long before those things began to dwindle, and Anisa seemed to disappear into thin air. He called from time to time, and she didn't answer her phone. Born wasn't completely surprised. He had half expected her to forget about him once he got locked up. He had known in his heart that she wasn't cut out to be loyal, and to make frequent visits upstate. But still Born was bothered by her absence at a time when he needed her most. He thought back on how much time and money he had spent with her, and wondered if he'd ever find a woman who reciprocated for once. Born chalked it up as another reason women couldn't be trusted. Doing time was hard, but he saw every day he spent in jail as being one day closer to going home.

When his six months in the program were done, Born was released into the general population, and he came face-to-face with a blast from his past. Martin was also an inmate there, housed in a separate dorm, but still in close proximity to his former best friend. Since Born's departure from the crew, Martin had never stopped harboring the feeling that he had been slighted somehow. He was still a little pissed that Born had never looked back when he started making major moves. Some of their animosity had been resolved at Born's father's funeral. But still there was uneasiness between the two that had been hard to penetrate over the years.

But up north, Born found himself relieved to see Martin's familiar face. And Martin, being the live wire that he was, had established quite a reputation for himself. Born was happy to align himself with his childhood friend. And as the months slowly passed, the two of them bonded again in the prison yard, or the mess hall, and soon they were close once more. It was like old times again.

During the time he spent in jail, Born lost sight of Jada, and had no idea how far she'd fallen after their split. But some news from home did reach him.

Soon, via the ghetto grapevine, Born learned that his stronghold in the streets of Staten Island was no more. Chance and Smitty had allowed some new niggas to take over their neighborhood drug trade. And to make matters worse, Smitty and Chance were now working for the new kids on the block. They were a disgrace in Born's eyes, because all they really had had to do was to maintain what he had already established. He was disgusted. Upon hearing this news, Born tried to stay to himself in order to avoid anybody pissing him off, and causing him to get in trouble. Any little thing was capable of setting him off. So he stayed away from everyone else, and kept his head in a book to escape. Martin was also irate because of the news that his boys—his brother most of all—had let the block go to some unknown. He and Born both wallowed in regret for making decisions that had cost them both their freedom and their empires. Born stayed in his bunk day after day, and only joined the other inmates when it was time to eat dinner. That was when all hell broke loose.

Born had found out that the man who had killed his friend Bobby years prior, during his crew's shootout with A.J., was now housed in the same prison dorm as he was. The guy was in for drug offenses, and Born wanted badly to keep himself out of trouble. So he had steered clear of the bastard, hoping not to catch any unwanted charges while he waited out his sentence. He figured that the guy, whose name was Ray, would get what was coming to him eventually. Born didn't need the attention that an altercation with another inmate would surely bring. He was still sore about what was going on back home, and filled with worry for his mother, and how she was maintaining out there on her own. The last thing he was expecting was for some old beef to come and provoke his inner monster.

But as he walked past Ray's table in the mess hall, Ray tripped Born on purpose, and caused his food to go flying across the room as he stumbled, trying to regain his balance. Ray sat there and laughed right in Born's face, and Born rushed the man with all his might. Ray wasn't far-ing too well in the fight, and tried to pull out a makeshift shank he had hidden in his waistband. Born saw him going for it, though, and every ounce of anger, every ounce of rage, fueled his fight. He had never felt as strong as he suddenly was. His adrenaline pumped through his veins. They fought savagely, locked in a ferocious battle, as the correction officers closed in to break it up. By the time they pulled Born off of the man, Ray was bleeding from his stomach. Born was holding a bloody screwdriver he'd taken from his job as a porter in the administrative building. He had liked that job because it allowed him access to the visiting room, and to tools such as the rusty screwdriver that he'd used to stab Ray four times in the stomach. Born's intention was to kill the man. That way he wouldn't have to deal with him for the rest of his bid. He had known that, with all the bad news he'd received in the past few weeks, whoever he put his hands on would be in trouble. The officers tackled Born to the floor, and wrestled the weapon from his hands. They dragged him off to the box, and shut him in for the night.

He was transferred the next day to a facility in Comstock, New York, where he spent the next eleven months of his sentence in solitary confinement. Ray had survived, though he was reduced to using a colostomy bag for a long time. And Born knew that this was another beef that would follow him for as long as Ray was still alive.

While in solitary confinement, Born was subjected to twenty-three hours of lockdown in a cell the size of a small closet. They only allowed him one shower, one phone call, and one visit each week. He was allowed one hour of recreation in the yard each day, by himself, usually at five or six o'clock in the morning. And when the guards felt like being assholes, they would tell him that he had overslept and missed his hour in the yard. So Born learned not to look forward to it, so that they wouldn't have the power to deny it to him. He would outthink them, he decided. Half the time it was too cold anyway, he'd tell himself. His hours in his cell were spent either reading or jerking off. He read no less than four books a week. When he could use the phone he called his mother most of the time, and Dorian's brothers as well. He liked to check in on D.J. every now and then to see if he was doing okay. Dorian's brothers and the rest of the crew held Born down while he endured his sentence, sending him food packages, cigarettes, money, and clothes, and he was grateful to them for that.

By the time they let him out of the box, Born emerged looking like Saddam Hussein, unshaven and grimy. He felt like an animal. His time in the box had been designed to break him, designed to dismantle his spirit. He wanted out of prison. He listened to his mother when she told him that he better start thinking about what direction his life was headed in. He saw the wisdom in her advice to turn over a new leaf.

He enrolled in violence-management and parenting classes, and continued to read—now, about two books a week. The parenting classes showed him just how dysfunctional his own upbringing had been. He learned that children interpret and understand what's going on in their environment long before parents usually think they do. He learned that children mimic their parents, and that was certainly true for him. He had patterned himself after Leo from the time he was small. They taught him about good parenting, and until then he hadn't really realized how unorthodox it was to be the child of an addict. To witness drug abuse up close from such an early age. All his life he'd worked with the hand he had been dealt, and never took the time to really see it for what it was. He realized for the first time that so much of who he was, so much of how he lived his life, was attributable to his upbringing. It finally dawned on him just how dysfunctional his childhood had been. The odds had been stacked against him from the very beginning. The ease with which he had merged into the fast lane came from watching his father, and from seeing how Leo had handled power. He had studied and watched his father, and became his duplicate. He realized that, all the while he thought that he had the game figured out, and that he knew how to play it, the game was playing him. True, he hadn't become a drug addict, as his father had. But he was in jail, and there was no victory in that. He thought about the fact that he could have wound up dead instead, and he was grateful that things had turned out the way that they had.

Born began to pay close attention to his fellow inmates. He began to listen when they griped about their lack of family, their lack of a sense of direction, and the fact that they had no plans for their future. But there was one man who was incarcerated with Born who would forever change his life.

Earl "Ace" Frasier, an older cat, was incarcerated alongside Born. He watched as Born took part in classes and read books like crazy. Ace was observant, and he watched in silence as he saw a slow change begin to occur in the young hustler they called Born. Born was also observant, and being a seasoned hustler, he could tell simply from Ace's mannerisms that he was or had been an addict. But despite Born's suspicion, he still found Ace to be a likable enough guy. Ace hollered at him one afternoon, as they both left the visiting room.

"I see you been reading a lot, youngster. Going to all kinds of classes and shit. Tryin' to change your life around? Or are you up for parole soon, trying to make a good impression?"

Born didn't know why he felt comfortable answering the older man's questions. Ace was a tall black man in his forties, who—judging from his prison I.D. number—had been locked up since the early eighties. He was well respected in their dorm, and could often be found giving sage old advice to the younger inmates from time to time. Born had never really socialized with Ace much, outside of the occasional card game. But this day, when he looked at Ace, he decided to answer his questions. "I guess it's a little of both," Born said. "I want to turn over a new leaf. You know what I'm saying? But it don't hurt that the board will see all the stuff I've been doing to change my life around."

Ace nodded his understanding.

They went through the demeaning ritual of being cavity searched as they returned to their dorm, and when they arrived, Ace picked up their conversation where they'd left off. "You know you're not really like the rest of these niggas in here," he said.

Born frowned. "What you mean?"

"There's a certain energy that you have that a lot of niggas in here don't have. I've been in here for a long time. And when you walked in, I could see that there was no bullshit with you. A lot of these niggas around here purposely try to walk hard, talk hard, and act tough. But, you don't seem to be trying. Your shit is natural. You walk with confidence, but there's nothing extra about it. You talk hard, but it ain't hard to tell that it ain't just talk. I see a lot of these dudes around here come and sit by you whenever you come back from your classes. It's almost like they anticipate you coming back, so they can sit around and soak up your aura."

Born laughed, and shook his head. "Whatever! The shit ain't that serious."

Ace smiled. "But it is, though. I can tell the fakes and the phonies. You strike me as a real nigga. That's why the fakes gather around you, trying to soak up some realness."

Born smiled, feeling like he was being flattered unnecessarily. "What you in here for, old-timer?"

Ace shrugged his shoulders. "All *kinds* of shit. But mainly homicide. I killed my brother, and then set his house on fire."

Born stared at him in silence, digesting the information

"I was on crack. Strung out, needed money. I went to my brother's house in the middle of the night to get some. I was hoping that, even if he didn't give me the dough, he would let me in so I could steal something, and sell it to get some dough. It was all about getting high for me that night. So my brother came to the door, and I asked him for money. He wouldn't give it to me, wouldn't let me in the house, and I snapped. In my mind I thought that he was turning his back on me when I needed him, that he thought he was better than me. I stabbed him in his chest about seven times. Then I went in the house, stole some shit I could sell real quick, and then set the whole shit on fire. I never realized that my brother's kids were sleeping upstairs, and I left the house to burn down. By the time I was blocks away getting high, the neighbors were trying to get my nephews out of the house as it burned to the ground. The cops figured out it was me, and I was arrested that same night and charged with murder, arson, endangering the welfare of a child, all kinds of shit. Got sentenced to twenty years."

Born shook his head, his suspicions confirmed about Ace's addiction. He was at a loss for words.

Ace continued. "But the time I've served in this prison is nothing compared to the sentence of having to live with that guilt for the rest of my life. I can never get the image out of my head—the look on my brother's face when I stuck that knife in his chest. I can't escape that. So they can lock me up for as long as they want. I'm serving my own sentence in here." Ace pointed to his head, and looked Born in his eyes. "I can never bring him back. And that's the worst punishment. It ain't like I killed him for betraying me, or for stealing from me, or for fucking my wife. I killed him so I could get high. My own flesh and blood. That's the price of being hooked on that fuckin' crack. You sell your soul for that shit."

Born nodded. "Tell me about it," he said. "My dad was hooked on that shit. So was my wifey."

Ace looked at Born intently. "Yet you still sell this shit to someone else's father and someone else's wifey?"

Born shook his head. "You sound like my moms. I guess you got a point, you know what I'm saying? But I always felt like, if I didn't sell the shit to somebody, another hustler would."

"That's true," Ace said. "But if everybody thought like that, what good would that do? If you let yourself think about every fiend after you serve them, you would feel what I'm talking about. You never let yourself feel the guilt of what you're doing. You get cold to it. You never let yourself feel the desperation of the person willing to give you their body for a hit. If you can imagine how strong a drug must be to have you choosing it over your loved ones! You gotta make a decision for yourself that selling that shit ain't what *you* want to do anymore. Fuck everybody else." Ace leaned forward, speaking with sincerity. "I talk to a lot of young niggas in here like this. Most of them don't hear me, though, 'cuz all they want is to get out of here and go right back to getting money. They want to get back to the block, back to the fiends, the cash, the hoes, and all the other shit that comes along with it. They don't really want to change. But I see you around here going to classes, reading books, staying out of trouble. And it looks to me like you might really have what it takes to get the fuck up outta here and never come back. I fucked my life up. Ain't no hope for me. Most of these young niggas in here are hopeless. They don't know nothing else, and they don't want to learn nothing else. Period. They'll get out of here eventually. But they'll be coming back. Or if they don't come back, they'll end up six feet under. But you're a natural leader, Born. I can tell by how these lil niggas follow you without you even asking them to. And I think if you want to walk out of here and leave this shit behind, you just might be the one who can really make that change. Real talk."

Born listened to Ace talk more about his own life, the depths to which he'd fallen at the hands of the crack he had used. He told Born about the pain he lived with daily, of how he'd destroyed his family, along with any hopes of living a life not plagued by demons. Talking to Ace made Born look at his surroundings through new eyes. He realized how right Ace was. Born wasn't like the rest of the guys he was incarcerated with. There was something about Born that set him apart. He was incarcerated with men who didn't know how to read, men who had never been outside of the cities and towns in which they'd been born. He began to see that there was more to life than what he had limited himself to.

Each afternoon, Born would sit and talk to Ace for hours. Born soaked up the old man's wisdom and life experience. Ace reminded Born of Leo in a way. The fatherly advice he gave made Born miss his old dad even more. At Ace's urging, Born became interested in the notion of higher learning, and this is what he used to deter him from more trouble. He stayed out of further drama and became a model prisoner. Before long, the end of his sentence was near. He gave all of his books and tapes to Ace, promising to keep in touch once he got out. By March 1999, he was going home. Born made a vow to himself and to God that he would never look back.

33

DOUBLE CROSSED

Some folks in the hood wondered if Jamari had ratted Born out. The timing was sure convenient. Born's arrest closely followed his argument with Jamari. Jada never questioned it, though. She had no reason to suspect Jamari of that type of treachery. Not yet, anyway.

When she heard that Born was in jail, Jada couldn't understand why she felt sorry for him. Especially after all he'd done to distance himself from her. She was hurt that Born had tossed her out, with his mother's help, rather than helping her fight her demons the way Dorian had helped Sunny. She was hurt by the things that Jamari had told her Born had said about her in the barbershop. Jada was hurt that Born had abandoned her so coldheartedly. He had thrown her out. Then he moved on with another woman, all while Jada was still sick without him. Born had moved on with his life without her. And she felt that it was time she moved on as well. Yet, she still had love for the man, and her heart went out to him. But she was caught up in her own bullshit. Too caught up to really focus on anything else.

She and Jamari dated exclusively for close to three months. Jada was high every day, and she still had not been in contact with Sunny, or with her sister Ava. Her only family, her only friend, was Jamari. He fed her habit, and that was all that mattered to her. For Jada it was more about companionship than love. But it was mostly about the drugs. Jamari was her pusher, and she depended on him for that. When her savings were depleted, he let her move in with him. She was so far gone that she didn't see that as a setback, but rather as a more convenient way to get high. Now she would be living with the drugs, and she could be high as often as she wanted. She was happy to be living under Jamari's roof, and he was happy to have her there.

Jamari had begun to care for Jada, despite the voice in his head telling him not to. At first, he'd wanted to seduce her, clean her up, and then flaunt her in front of Born. He wanted to turn her against him. But Jada wasn't so easily brainwashed. He could tell that she was still in love with Born, and he hated her for that. He hated the thought of Born still holding a place in Jada's heart. Jamari wanted to be the only man in her life, and even in Born's absence he couldn't fill his shoes.

He felt like a loser, but his feelings for Jada persisted. He was eager to have her in his home, and in his bed every night. At last, she was all his. He set about the task of locking her down. He controlled the purse strings, and Jada went along with what made him happy. Jamari saw Jada as a possession. He would have done anything to keep her with him. He showered and spoiled her. He let her get high, as long as she did it with dignity. He tried to fill her every need, so that she wouldn't need another man for anything.

When Jada told Jamari that she was pregnant, he was thrilled. What he didn't say was that he'd been watching Jada closely. Watching her comings and goings in order to determine if she was playing him. He followed her to see if she was cheating on him. He watched her patterns, and knew when her period was due, and documented her menstrual cycle so that he could tell if she was pregnant. So when Jada told him that she was indeed pregnant, Jamari was elated, but he already knew. He was relieved that she told him rather than sneaking off behind his back to have an abortion. He took that as a sign of her affection for him. And that encouraged him a great deal. He was going to be a father, and the woman who was giving him a child was the woman Born loved. Nothing was better than that.

Jamari did whatever it took to make Jada smile. All because his overall goal was to keep her with him. The baby seemed like the perfect solution. But he was disappointed to hear that Jada wasn't sure she wanted to keep it.

Jada asked him one day if he would be mad if she got an abortion. "I'm not sure if I'm ready to be a mother," she said. She saw the dejected expression on Jamari's face, and tried to soften her approach somewhat. "I'm just having second thoughts about this. I mean, especially because I like to get high. How can I have a child? The very meaning of motherhood is being unselfish. It's about loving someone more than you love your own self, and your own happiness. I don't know if I can be that unselfish. I've never in my life been that unselfish." Jada sighed, and felt her eyes well up with tears. She hadn't been high in days, and now all the pain she'd suppressed was bubbling at the surface. "Every day when I wake up, I think about my life. What's my plan for the day? That's what I ask myself. And then I'll think about yesterday. How I got high all day, or how dirty the house looked because I was too high to clean it. I think about the day before that. How I still haven't heard from Ava. How my own mother wants nothing to do with me. And I even think about Born." Jada saw Jamari's jaw tighten at the mention of her former love, and she quickly explained. "I think about how I hurt him, when all he tried to do was love me. Sometimes I hate who I am and what I've become." Jada shook her head, hating the very thought of all the pain she'd caused, all the pain she'd seen in her lifetime. Jada would think about Mr. Charlie, and all the men she'd traded sexual favors with in order to get high. She'd think about her family, particularly Ava, and how she'd caught her snorting coke, and threatened to tell Born.

Born. It was thoughts of him that usually sent Jada searching for her usual escape. "Jamari, I get high just to make it through another day. Where would a child fit into all of that?" Jada waited for his response, angry with herself for the fact that Jamari had ever even hit it raw. She knew she'd gotten pregnant when she was high, because that was pretty much the only time she had sex with him without a condom. She'd been too high to care. She wanted to kick herself now for being so careless.

Jamari looked at Jada sympathetically. He heard her reasons for doubting whether she was ready to be a mother. But in his heart he truly believed that having this baby would be good for Jada. Maybe this would help her leave the drugs alone for good. He thought motherhood might be good for Jada, that it might teach her how to be unselfish for once. But he also knew that this was a surefire way to hold on to her. Having his baby would ensure that she would always be a part of his life in some capacity. Jamari was prepared to beg her to have the baby.

"Don't kill my baby, sweetheart," he said. The words tugged at Jada's heart, as he said them. "Don't you think it's time to do something with your life? This baby will be your reason to take a step back from the drugs and give your body a rest. It might even be enough for you to stop altogether." Jamari knelt in front of her, and took her hand in his. "Jada, please. I'm begging you. I swear it'll be alright. We'll make it work. I promise I'll be with you every step."

Jada listened to him plead his case, but made no decision that night. Jamari's begging went on for seven days. And then she yielded. She awoke beside him one morning, and looked him in the eyes. "I'll have the baby," she said. "I think it's time I turned my life around."

Jamari was ecstatic. He kissed her over and over again, and his smile spread all across his face. Things were better than ever between them, and he was at Jada's beck and call.

As the months went by, and her slim and sexy waistline made way for a bulging tummy, Jamari beamed with pride. Jada had mixed emotions. She had never been in love with Jamari. But she felt like it would be cruel for her to have an abortion after all he'd done for her. And little by little, she began to warm up to the idea of being a mother. She would soon have someone to call her own. Someone that she could love, and who wouldn't desert her like everyone else in her life had.

She stopped smoking crack while she was pregnant. It was hard, because she wanted it so bad on a few occasions. But she stayed clean. She did smoke a little weed during the first trimester. She wasn't proud of that fact. So then she went cold turkey, and really gave it her all. But it wasn't long before she noticed Jamari becoming more controlling. Now that Jada was no longer getting high, she started to notice that he wasn't as likable as she had thought he was. She couldn't tolerate him as much as she used to when she was always high. And, he wouldn't leave her alone, so she was forced to endure him. Jada started feeling trapped.

When she complained, Jamari lightened up. He would pretend to be understanding and supportive. But, it wouldn't be long before he started tightening the reins around Jada's neck. One day, the subject of Jada's relationship with Born came up. Jada shared with him the fact that she had a lot of regrets when it came to their relationship, particularly how it had ended. Jamari went ballistic.

"You're playing yourself," he seethed. "You're pregnant with my baby, and you got the nerve to sit here and express regret over the next man." His face was twisted into a look of disgust.

Jada tried explaining that she had a lot of history with Born. "You said I could talk to you about anything. Well, that's how I feel. I can't control the way I feel, and I'm entitled to my own emotions, whether you like it or not."

Jamari laughed at her. "Regardless of what you're feeling, Born would never take you back now."

Jada sat in silence, thinking about the truth in his words. No matter how much love she still had in her heart for Born, she was pregnant with someone else's baby. All the regret in the world wouldn't change that. She looked at Jamari, who smiled at her sinisterly, and saw for the first time just how cruel he could be.

She was still little then, even though it was almost her fifth month of pregnancy. Jada was hiding her belly behind cute outfits. The pregnancy was progressing normally. The only problem was Jamari's personality. At first she dismissed it as her irritability due to pregnancy hormones. She figured he was getting on her nerves more because she was more on edge than usual. But when she mentioned Born, Jamari got too personal with what he was saying about him.

"That nigga ain't shit!" he yelled. "I used to be friends with the muthafucka back in high school. Both him and his crackheaded daddy wasn't shit." Jamari was really saying some disrespectful shit! It seemed like he had real hatred in his heart for Born, and Jada couldn't understand why. So she asked him about it.

"What's the deal with you and Born? How come you hate him so much? It's almost like you're trying to turn me against him or something."

Jamari frowned, and shook his head. "I ain't trying to turn you against nobody. I know that y'all got history together, or whatever. But I happen to know the nigga longer than you have, and I know he ain't the hero you try to make him out to be."

"What happened to make y'all stop being friends? You said you two used to be close." Jada took the direct approach. She got results, too.

"The nigga thought I stole from him. He took a loss on five grand, and acted like it was fifty grand."

"Did you steal it?" Jada looked directly in his eyes, the way that Born had always taught her. She was searching for the truth.

Jamari shook his head, and diverted his gaze. "I ain't steal nothing from Born. Fair exchange ain't robbery. I did a lot of work for that nigga. I took a lot of chances, and made a lot of moves for him. And I never got compensated for those things. I ain't never complain. The one time he took a loss on my end, he acted like it was the worst thing in the world. The nigga cut me off like we were never close at all. He did it to you, too! So you should know exactly how I feel."

"He did, but I deserved that. I never knew him to do nothing to anyone that didn't deserve it. He's not that type of guy. And I'm starting to wonder if you really did steal from him. Born's a smart man—"

"If he's so fuckin' smart, then he must be right about you. You must be just a fuckin' crackhead who ain't never gonna change."

Jada looked crushed.

"I don't think that's what you are," Jamari clarified. "But that's what *he* said you are. And if he's so smart, then that must be true."

Jada stared at Jamari, her eyes probing. "There's more to the story that you're not telling me. I know there is."

Jamari looked at her, and wanted to tell her all of it. But he knew that the truth would make her cringe. He wasn't sure if she was worthy of knowing. But he reconsidered, realizing that she was about to be the mother of his child. She was entitled to know the truth, for whatever it meant to her. She needed to know why, as his child's mother, she had to forget about Born.

"Sit down," Jamari said. Jada obliged, hoping to gain some insight into why he hated Born so much. She wasn't disappointed.

"I grew up, like, ten minutes away from where Born grew up. We went to different schools until we got to junior high school. That was when we started hanging out, and he would invite me to his hood, and all that. We got to be good friends, but for some reason, my mother didn't like the idea at all. At first she asked me what his last name was, and what his mother and father's names were. She pretended not to know them, but she said that she had heard bad things about Born being a troublemaker, and all that. She kept telling me he was nothing but trouble. She told me she had heard all about Born, that he was a bad influence. I didn't listen to her. I just kept doing what I was doing. My mother had a habit, so I wasn't sure if she was one of Born's customers on the low, or some shit like that, you understand?"

Jada nodded, since Jamari had told her long ago about his mother's addiction. She understood why he would question what his mother had really had against Born.

Jamari took a deep breath, and looked at Jada to see what her reaction would be. "I never knew my father. Whenever the subject came up, my moms would tell me that it didn't matter. The nigga never did shit for me, so what difference did it make what his name was—that's what she'd tell me. So my mother waited until I was twelve years old to tell me that me and Born had the same father."

Jada gasped. "Are you serious?"

Jamari nodded. "His pops and my mother were friends. I guess birds of a feather and all that. Anyway, they were friends with benefits. Leo was hitting it, even though she knew about his wife and his family. She was the other woman, and she got pregnant. And she said that when she told him, he told her he ain't want no more kids. He denied me, and he raised another son the same age as me. Good old Leo Graham. She dropped this bomb on me after me and Born were already really good friends. She told me that Ingrid didn't know about me. Leo never told

Born's mother about me, because as far as he was concerned, my mother was just looking for someone to blame for her situation. She said that my father had denied that I was his child. And she was a loose woman, so she wasn't surprised. But when I met Born, and I saw how he lived, and how his mother was different from my mother, that shit bothered me. He grew up with his father, and the same man denied me as his child. That shit hurt."

"Does Born know about this?" Jada asked.

"Nah. My moms made me swear not to say nothing. Remember, Leo was still alive at the time. I guess she didn't want to start no shit, and I respected her wishes. I kept my mouth shut. But it was strange being at Born's house and getting to know his mother. All the while knowing that her husband was my real father. Then my moms died two years after Leo did, and by then, me and Born weren't on speaking terms no more."

"How do you know that your mother was right about him being your father? No disrespect, but you said yourself that she was kind of loose. Maybe she just *wanted* you to be Leo's son—"

"I thought about that. I mean, all I know is what she told me. She said that he was my father, and that he ain't want nothing to do with me. I didn't ask for no DNA test, or no shit like that, so all I can go on is what she told me. Leo never acted like he knew who I was, or knew who my mother was. I don't think he was really thinking about shit like that at that point in his life. He was just as strung out as my mother was at that time." Jamari smiled bitterly, as he thought back on how he felt seeing how Born was living. "But the nigga had them living like royalty at Born's house. They had VCRs, video games, a floor model TV, nice furniture. I never had any of that shit growing up. I used to borrow clothes from Born all the time, spend the night, and all that. Just to have an up-close and personal look at how the other half lived. I used to lay awake in Born's room while he slept, praying for what he had, and wishing that my moms could be how Ingrid was. There was always food in their refrigerator and in their cabinets. But not at my house."

"So were you jealous because of all that?" Jada asked, already knowing the answer. She was amazed, because she knew that Born felt differently about his childhood. Born was so caught up in not having his father there for him like he needed. But one man's trash is another man's treasure. Jamari had obviously wanted what Born had.

"I never said I was jealous."

"But you keep talking about all the things he had that you didn't have. It sounds like you were jealous."

"I wasn't jealous. I felt like I got a raw deal. Born got two parents, while I had one. All I had was my moms, and she was fucked up."

"I understand what you're saying. But even though he loved his father, Born was disappointed in him, because he was an addict. It's not like Born grew up with the Huxtables, or anything."

"But at least Leo was there for him. The nigga was never there for me. I didn't think that shit was fair. That Born grew up with his father and a good mother, and I didn't."

Jada frowned. "Well, it's not Born's fault that he had a good mother. And it's not his fault that Leo loved him. He never even knew that you could be his brother."

Jamari looked at Jada coldly, upset that she was defending Born. "Whether he knew or not, he still played me. The nigga cut me off 'cause of one fuckin' mistake."

"Yeah. But that was a lot of money, Jamari—"

"I *made* the nigga a lot of money! Whose side are you on? I didn't take *shit* from him that wasn't due to me. All the time I spent putting in work for that nigga, and all the times I had his back when the rest of his crew deserted him . . . the nigga owed me more than that. Five thousand dollars wasn't shit to Born, but that money meant the difference between life and death to me. I was the one who never had shit growing up. Not that nigga! It was my chance to do me, and I wasn't gonna let that nigga stop me from doing what I felt I needed to do. He had all the riches to himself all his life. Even the brothers and sisters that he did know about didn't get as much as he did." Jamari took a deep breath, and tried to clear his head. He was very animated, and he didn't want to give off the impression that he was losing control. "All I'm saying is this. When Born cut me off, he made it easier for me to take what I felt should have been mine all along."

Jada looked at Jamari, and saw him in a whole new light. She wondered if she was one of the things Born had once possessed that Jamari just had to have for himself. She started wondering if she was being used as a pawn, and Jada felt played. She felt stupid, and wondered what Born must think about her being pregnant by a nigga who had double-crossed him. Had she known all of this sooner, she would never have allowed herself to become involved with Jamari. Thinking back on her reluctance to be a mother in the beginning, she quickly felt that she had made the wrong decision. She never would have kept the baby had she known the whole truth. She felt stuck, since she was approaching her sixth month of pregnancy.

Jamari saw the look on her face, and assumed that she was upset. "So now what? You feel like I'm a monster or something?"

Jada stared back at him, neither confirming or denying that fact. "I understand this shit between y'all a lot more now," she said. "I understand why you two hate each other so much." Jada stopped talking, and let the silence linger momentarily. "Why would you wait until now to tell me this, Jamari? You knew how I was dealing with Born, and from the beginning you never let on about any of this. And both of you have this hatred toward each other. Why didn't you tell me?"

"Born never told you," Jamari said. "He never mentioned how he thought I stole from him. So why should I have told you?"

Jada shrugged, unwilling to try to explain it. "I still think you should tell Born about you being his brother—"

"For what? That ain't gonna change shit. We're grown-ass men now. I don't need him to be my brother, and Leo ain't around to be my father. Fuck it. That's the hand that I was dealt." Jamari shrugged his shoulders. "But that nigga Born is gonna get what's coming to him, though. No matter what happens, I know he's gotta get his in the end. The nigga had it too good for too long."

Jada looked at Jamari, and absorbed the words coming out of his mouth. She was disgusted. This nigga—this hating-ass nigga—was the father of the child growing in her womb. From that moment on she hated Jamari, since she felt that he was only out to hurt Born, and was using her to do it. She made up her mind then and there to get him back. Not just for playing her, but for having so much resentment toward Born as well.

Jada knew that Born was a good man. She had let him down, and that was why he'd left her. But Jamari had painted him as some animal, and Jada knew it all stemmed from his own jealousy over Born's lifestyle. She also wanted to pay Jamari back for deceiving her for so long. She started wishing she could undo it all. Just go back and fix her mistakes. But looking at her swollen belly, she knew it was too late.

So instead of aborting her baby and leaving Jamari like she wanted to do, Jada devised a scheme that would have made Sunny proud. She would hit Jamari where it hurt the most, and at the same time give her the resources she needed to leave his sorry ass for good.

Jamari was still hustling with Wizz at that time. Born was gone, and his team had fallen apart. Dorian was gone, with all his artillery and manpower. So Jamari and Wizz were huddled together plotting takeovers like Pinky and the Brain, night after night. Soon they were doing big business, because all the heavy hitters from back in the day were either dead or in jail. The game was changing, and those two knew that they were in the perfect position to shut shit down. They started moving more and more bricks.

Jamari stopped bagging up at home, so Jada didn't see it moving through the house as she used to. He had enough common sense to know that he shouldn't tempt her with it, knowing how she was jonesing for it. But a couple of times Jada was with him when he met his connect, so she had an idea of the type of money that was changing hands. His name was Elliot, and Jada got to know him well. Elliot was Guyanese, and he was handsome. But the nigga was ruthless, too. Jada knew that Jamari was afraid of him, because his whole demeanor changed around Elliot. He would sit straighter and talk more ghetto, and she could tell it wasn't really in him to be all hard like that. He wanted people to think that he was this rugged, thugged-out hustler. But she was finally starting to see that he was a wannabe. Jada had been through these types of meetings with Born, and he had never changed who he was just to be accepted. You took him at face value, or you didn't fuck with him at all. Jamari was nothing like Born.

She had nothing but time on her hands to think. And she thought about how Born had loved her. He had loved her completely. And he had trusted her, even though he didn't trust people easily. She had let him down, and she was sad about that. Then, to find out that Jamari had done him dirty. She wished that she could talk to Born, but she knew that she was probably the last person he wanted to talk to. Jada didn't care about the baby, and stopped taking her vitamins and eating right, hoping to have a miscarriage. She just wanted to get high again.

The difference between Jamari and Born was that Jamari didn't give Jada any money. None at all. If there was no food, he went food shopping with her. If she wanted clothes, he took her shopping. If she had a craving, he took her out to eat. She didn't have any money in her hands from the moment she spent the last dollar in her bank account. Once she ran out of cash, Jamari took care of her, but never gave her her own dough. He knew that would have meant independence to Jada. And that was the last thing he wanted.

After a while, the block got hot, and Jamari's scared ass got nervous. He and Wizz were moving a lot of blow through the borough, and the cops were stepping their game up. Niggas from all the hoods—West Brighton, New Brighton, Stapleton—were getting knocked left and right. Sweeps took place on Jersey Street, Targee Street, Broad Street, and Henderson, and soon half the borough's hustlers were fighting cases or copping pleas. Jamari and Wizz were scared. But they had to make money. The final straw for Jada was when Jamari asked her to make a trip for him. She was visibly pregnant, and the son of a bitch asked her to make a run uptown for him. He wanted Jada to go and get a package from Elliot, and then bring it to Wizz. Naturally, she said no, and told him to kiss her ass. Jamari explained that he was only asking her because the cops wouldn't suspect Jada of anything, with her being pregnant and all. So Jada was mad at first that he asked her to do it. Then she thought about it, and realized that this was her chance.

She waited until he brought it up again, and then she agreed to it. She told him that she knew he was only trying to look out for her and the baby, and that she would have his back the same way he had hers. Jada asked him to tell her what he needed her to do in detail. What she was hoping was that he would give her the money, and she would fake, like she was going uptown, and just break the fuck out. But that's not what his arrangement was. Jamari was getting his shit on consignment. He had set it all up with Elliot, and Jada was just supposed to go and get it, and bring it back. But she had a whole different plan.

When she went to meet with Elliot, Jada was supposed to get two bricks for twenty-three grand apiece. They had to get the money back to Elliot after they moved the drugs. Jamari and Wizz were mimicking Born's operation, and selling cocaine in different forms, from wholesale to retail. Elliot had done lots of business with them. But when Jada went to meet with Elliot, she had to convince him to give her five bricks instead of the two she was supposed to pick up. Jada used her pregnancy as a prop.

She explained to Elliot that Jamari and Wizz really needed five bricks and not the two they had discussed. Jada wasn't sure for a minute if the nigga would go for it. She sat across from Elliot, who stared back at her, suspiciously. She wasn't sure if he was buying her story or not, so she repeated it for clarity.

"I'm telling you, Elliot. He said he needed two before he spoke to Wizz. Wizz told him that they needed more than that. You can call Jamari and ask him."

Elliot did just that. Jada sat there, nervous as hell, even though she knew that she'd taken Jamari's cell phone with her that day. It was downstairs in the glove compartment in her car. He got no answer and left a message demanding an explanation for the surprise increase.

Elliot hung up the phone, and frowned. "Why didn't he mention this shit to me himself? He sends you all the way uptown to do his dirty work? What kind of man is that?" Elliot's voice dripped with his sexy accent.

"Jamari didn't want to ask you, Elliot. He's too scared of you." Elliot looked at Jada as if he hadn't heard her correctly. She smiled. "Don't tell him I said that. And don't act like you never noticed. You know you can tell that he ain't all the way cut out for this game, and you know you see the weakness in him."

Elliot looked at Jada, curiously. "You're telling me that this man is weak. That he has fear in his heart, and that he don't got what it takes. And yet, this is *your* man." Elliot looked her square in the eyes. "Your man whose baby is growing inside you right now."

Jada shifted her gaze, as if she was annoyed that this was a fact. "I got caught up. Hindsight is twenty-twenty, you know what I'm saying? It's too late now. Now I got a baby on the way, and a man who's too scared to step up and ask for what we need to stay afloat. We're fucked up right now, Elliot. Shit is bad. But you got what we need to get back on. Now you know Jamari and Wizz move these bricks. I've been on the scene long enough to see how often they come to see you. We're all making money, and they've never caused you to take a loss yet. Dammit, I'll put my word on it, if that means anything to you. But I need you to give us this shot, Elliot. I need your help. Jamari needs your help. Please do this, and we'll always be in your debt." She rubbed her belly for sympathy, and looked at him innocently.

Jada knew she had tugged at Elliot's heartstrings when he rubbed his goatee as if deep in thought. He looked at Jada, and nodded his head. "I'm gonna give you the shot, *mami*. But you better tell Jamari that I want my money on time, with no excuses. I don't want to hear no bullshit. I mean that. Don't force me to make your child a fatherless bastard. Don't fuck me."

Jada nodded, and smiled. She grabbed Elliot's hand and shook it, and he smiled back at her at last. Truth was, Elliot liked her. She reminded him of his baby sister, who had always possessed a hustler's spirit as well. He summoned his boy, and had the package brought down to them. When it was all there, Elliot had his man bring it out to the car, since Jada was very pregnant, and shouldn't be struggling with a heavy bag. She thanked him, and shook his hand again, knowing that it would be for the last time. As she drove back to Staten Island, she was scared to death that she would be pulled over. She had five bricks of cocaine in her car. She was fully aware of the looming life sentence that awaited her if she was caught. She glanced back at the bag in the backseat containing all five bricks, and headed for Arlington.

34

A CHANGE IN PLANS

Jada called Born's friend Chance, and told him she had an offer he couldn't refuse. He met her in the parking lot behind his Arlington apartment building, and Jada showed him the bricks she had for sale. Jamari was paying twenty-three grand per brick, so five would have cost him $115 thousand. Jada offered to sell Chance all five for a flat seventy-five grand. He went and consulted with his boys, and they bought it, knowing that this was a steal. They never questioned where Jada had gotten the drugs, or why she was so eager to get rid of it for so cheap. It didn't matter. They gave her what she wanted, and Jada took the money and ran.

Jada went by Born's mother's house. She wasn't even sure what made her go over there. She just did. Jada knocked on Ingrid's door, and was thrilled when she opened it. Ingrid was surprised to find Born's ex standing at her door unannounced. Ingrid let her in. She took in Jada's pregnant condition. Jada's belly was big and round, and she seemed happy to see Ingrid.

"Miss Ingrid, I know it seems strange for me to be here," Jada said. She knew that Ingrid must be curious to find out why she had stopped by. So Jada told her the truth.

She told Born's mother that she was with a man who she had thought had her best interests at heart. She told her that Jamari had made her feel like she was a queen, and that it all turned out to be a lie. Jada leveled with her, and told her that she had no one she could trust. No one who she could ask for a favor like the one she needed now.

Jada showed her all the money she had just gotten from Chance. She told Ingrid that she had taken that money for her and her unborn baby. But in her head, Jada knew that she had taken it for another reason. She knew that she would be going to get high that night, and she didn't want to take all that money with her. She knew that she would spend every last dime if she did.

Ingrid listened to Jada's story in silence.

She asked Ingrid to hold some of the money for her until she came back for it. Jada gave her five grand for doing her that favor. Then she put fifty-five thousand dollars of it in a bag, and gave it to Ingrid for safe-keeping. Jada trusted Miss Ingrid, partly because of how she had talked to Jada when Born put her out. She had a motherly quality about her that didn't end with her own child. Ingrid mothered everybody, and that was one of the reasons why she was so loved by all those who knew her. She had always been so nice to Jada. And most of all, Ingrid was her only option. There was no one else whom Jada could trust. She trusted that Ingrid wouldn't spend all the money, because Jada knew she had her own money. Ingrid was a hustler, and so was her son. Jada knew that she was accustomed to seeing that kind of dough. Ingrid promised her that every dime would be there when she came back for it, and then she touched Jada's hand and spoke to her from her heart.

"Baby, you got another life to think about now. It ain't just you no more. You got a baby on the way, and you owe it to that child to do right. It's time for you to get your act together. You're a beautiful girl, and you got too much going for you to throw your life away so young."

Jada told Ingrid that she would think about what she had said. But she knew that she wouldn't think about it much. Jada left with fifteen thousand dollars, and went straight to West Brighton and copped from some niggas on Broadway. She headed back to Brooklyn, and rented herself a room. Then Jada got high for three straight days. She was fully aware of her pregnancy, but she didn't care anymore. The high she experienced was powerful, but when she came down she felt like the lowest piece of shit. She got high again and again to avoid facing reality. Jada stayed in that room from sun up to sundown. She was in outer space somewhere. But then she ran out of crack, and she went to Flatbush Avenue to cop some more. That's when it all came to an end.

Jada had thought that being in Brooklyn would put her out of Jamari's reach. She knew that he wasn't familiar with her part of town, and she thought she had gotten away. But when she went to Flatbush to score more crack, Jada's exchange with the dealer was witnessed by some plainclothes cops. She was under arrest, yet again, and headed back to jail. The *Daily News* ran a story, and that was it. Jamari knew where to find her, but he still had no idea what she had done with the cocaine.

By the time Jada went to court, Jamari was in the courtroom staring at her like she was a piece of shit. Jada knew he was in trouble with Elliot. And to be honest, she hoped that Elliot would kill him.

After her indictment, Jamari came to see her down in the pens. Jada had no idea who he knew or how he got down there to see her, but he came. He walked up to the bars, and Jada was glad that they were there to shield her. She could see the fire in his eyes.

Jamari was so angry that he was trembling. He stared at her for several long and silent moments before he spoke. "My nigga Wizz came to me, and asked me why I was trying to play him. I didn't know what the fuck he was talking about. The nigga said that I got more than what I was supposed to get. He thought I was trying to cut him out of a deal. See, Elliot called Wizz and told him about the shit you pulled. Wizz thought that I was in on it with you, and he came to see me. Me and him were supposed to be partners, and I go and double the take and don't tell him nothin'?! He was pissed off and ready to do me in. But then I told him that you never came back with the shit. I was confused, because I thought you got hurt, or got bagged, or something. I told him that I ain't know what the fuck he was talking about. He thought I was being underhanded, and all the while it was you! That nigga called me a sneak thief, told me that I'm the type to wait till a nigga's guard is down and his back is turned before they take from him. That's the reputation I got now, thanks to you. And on top of everything, now I gotta hide until I find a way to pay Elliot for that shit. How could you do this shit to me, Jada?"

Jada stared at him, coldly. "You did it to Born, didn't you? It was my time to shine," Jada said, mimicking Jamari's own explanation for his betrayal of his former friend.

Jamari looked at her like he hated her. "Where's it at, Jada? Tell me what you did with it."

"Fuck you." Jada folded her arms across her chest.

Jamari stared at her with contempt. "You better tell me what you did with the shit, because my life is on the line here, Jada. I didn't do nothing to you to deserve this."

Jada smirked. "Sure you did. You *used* me to get back at Born, and you didn't tell me the whole story until you had me in a position where I was stuck and couldn't leave. You never cared about me. I was just a part of your plan for revenge. Now Born will probably never speak to me again, and you *know* that was your intention all along! I'm not telling you shit! The cops took the drugs. Just like they took the bail money that you had for Born that time."

Jamari pounded on the bars, causing Jada to step back in fear. "I swear I'll get you back for this. I swear I will. This shit ain't over, Jada. Everything you love, I'm gonna take it from you. Everything. One by one."

"Fuck you." Jada said it calmly, and then went and sat back down on the bench in the cell.

Jamari nodded his head. He stared at her, still nodding, and said, "Okay. I'll see you again soon. Real soon."

He turned and walked away, leaving Jada to await her transport back to prison. She didn't give a damn about Jamari or his troubles. At the moment, her only focus was on getting out of jail.

Strangely, the whole situation with Elliot was resolved in the most unexpected way. Jamari and Wizz knew that their days were numbered. Elliot had put a price on their heads, and the word was out that if someone could find Jamari or Wizz they would be generously compensated. This wasn't just business. It was personal. And both Wizz and Jamari knew that Elliot would surely kill them as soon as he got the chance. Ninety thousand dollars had been taken from him, and somebody was going to pay with their life.

But mysteriously, someone dropped dime on Elliot. Just as Born had been caught off guard with a law enforcement ambush, Elliot, too, was surprised with a DEA raid. The feds swooped down on him in huge numbers, after being tipped off by a confidential informant. But Elliot knew what fate awaited him. With the amount of narcotics he had in his possession, he would likely spend the rest of his life in prison. Elliot shot it out with the cops, alongside several of his boys. And he was killed. The newspapers touted the fact that a narcotics kingpin had been brought down, and Jada was sick to her stomach. She knew in her heart that Jamari's punk ass had ratted Elliot out in order to avoid his wrath. And it didn't take her long to come to the conclusion that he had probably done the same to Born. Jada cried for Elliot, feeling somewhat guilty that she had played a part in how everything had fallen apart. She wished that for all their sakes Elliot had survived and killed Jamari. It would have been perfect.

Jada was sentenced to eighteen months—nine months in prison, and nine months in court-mandated rehab. Her Legal Aid lawyer told her that she should be glad the judge had taken pity on her, because a lot of offenders were getting five years or more for having even small amounts of crack. She'd appeared before a sympathetic judge, whose own daughter was struggling with cocaine addiction. The judge had taken pity on Jada in her pregnant state, when a lot of judges would have sentenced her more harshly because of it. She was lucky. But Jada didn't feel lucky at all. She was distraught.

She looked around the courtroom at her sentencing, wishing she would see a familiar face in the crowd. Her mother, Ava, Sunny—someone who cared about her. But there was no one, and Jada felt desperate to get out. All she wanted was to get out of jail, and get back to her money, so that she could get back to getting high.

While she was in jail they put her in a drug program. It was like being in rehab in jail. She went to talk to counselors, and to meetings and classes about drug abuse and what it does to an unborn baby. That's when she learned what she was really doing to her unborn child every single time she got high. They told Jada that once cocaine enters the baby's blood and tissues, it stays way longer than it does in adults. Jada was getting high for maybe twenty minutes, while her baby would be high for more than an hour. Their undeveloped livers don't filter the drugs that fast, and the drug gets broken down slower. Jada felt terrible for all the problems that her baby could have. She hadn't felt guilty up until then, because she had been hoping that she'd have a miscarriage, so that she could rid herself of any traces of Jamari in her life—including the baby. But she hadn't miscarried. And all throughout her seventh and eighth months of pregnancy, Jada was scared to death. She was worried about what her baby would go through because she had been so selfish.

Prison was not a new experience for Jada, so she knew to watch her back, and not run her mouth. Sometimes bitches would try to test her, and Jada got in her fair share of trouble. Some of the other incarcerated mothers would have given anything to be with their kids. And there Jada was—incarcerated for endangering her child's welfare by abusing crack cocaine while in her last three months of pregnancy. She wasn't a favorite among the other inmates. But for the most part, she managed to stay to herself, and she tried to mind her own business. She had enough to deal with in her own life, and had little time for the usual female "she said" shit.

Jada went into labor in August of 1999, at the end of her eighth month of pregnancy. They didn't rush her to the hospital. They let her pace the jail for a while, until she couldn't take the pain. This would be no easy delivery, where the pain was lessened by drugs. Instead, she felt every contraction, causing her to stop walking every few minutes, until the contractions subsided. Her water broke on the way to the hospital, and she had a police escort with her the whole time. They even shackled one wrist to the bed rail. Jada felt like an animal. But she stopped thinking about that whenever one of the contractions shook her. She was a mess in there, and she felt so much pain. There was one nurse—an Indian woman—who took pity on the poor young thing with no one to help her through the birth of her first child. The nurse held Jada's hand

and talked to her nicely. She told her to breathe, and to relax between the pains. She probably never realized how much she helped Jada that night. But for Jada, the woman was a godsend. For months she'd become accustomed to C.O.s barking orders and inmates yelling obscenities. For once, it was just nice to have a soothing voice in her ear—especially at a time like this.

Sheldon Marquis Ford was born after putting Jada through ten hours of labor. He was so tiny and so fragile that Jada cried openly when she saw him for the first time. He weighed barely five pounds, and he was pale and scrawny. He cried so much, and they poked many needles into him, hooked him up to a machine, and put him in an incubator. As soon as Jada laid eyes on him, she fell in love.

Jada wanted to stay in that hospital for as long as possible so that she could be close to him. She faked aches and pains that she didn't have, so that they wouldn't release her to be returned to jail, and make her leave her baby in that hospital. From the moment she saw him, she stopped thinking of him as Jamari's baby, and she saw him as her child. Her son.

Jada was determined that they wouldn't put him in foster care, and she hated herself for what she'd done to him. But the saddest part for her was knowing that if she wasn't in jail, she would have smoked crack again in order to escape that guilt. That was the point when she finally admitted to herself that she had a problem.

After four days, they told Jada that she was being released in the morning. There was a guard right outside her door. With no place else to turn, Jada called her mother. She had to do something. Jada placed the collect call, and was relieved when Edna accepted the charges. Jada told her the truth of how she'd gotten in trouble. She described how frail and small Sheldon was, and how she had named him after her father—the man in the five-by-seven picture she had stared at every single night before she fell asleep when she was a little girl. Edna listened, and Jada thought it sounded like her mother was crying. Jada begged her to come and get her baby, and help her keep him out of the system. Edna listened, and didn't say anything for a long time before she answered.

Finally, she said, "Jada, this is terrible, and I'm sorry you gotta go through this. But I can't get involved in all this mess. God is in control, so you need to let him have his way. It sounds like your baby has the odds stacked against him already. I'll do what I can to help you. But it sounds like it's up to the authorities now. They got you up there in— where are you again?"

Jada didn't answer her. She held the phone, and she just felt like, *Damn! Can't you ever be there for me, even once?* Jada just hung up the phone, cried her eyes out, and prayed for a miracle.

Jada sat in her bed and summoned up the nerve to call Sunny's mother. She hadn't heard from Sunny in more than a year, and she wasn't even sure if she would want to hear from Jada. She dialed 411, and asked for the number for Marisol Cruz in Brooklyn, New York, and was relieved that her number wasn't unlisted. As the telephone rang, Jada prayed that Marisol would accept the collect call. She wasn't disappointed, and hearing Marisol's thick accent was like music to her ears.

"Thank you for accepting the charges," Jada began.

"Don't worry about it, *mami*. Are you okay? Where are you?"

"I got bagged—"

"For what?" Sunny's mother sounded shocked.

"I was getting high, and I got caught. But the thing is, I was pregnant." Jada's voice was barely audible. She was embarrassed by her own selfish actions.

Marisol listened, and contained the shock she felt. She held her hand silently over her mouth, as she listened to Jada tell her about how she had gotten kicked out of Born's life, gotten pregnant by someone else, gotten high, and gotten arrested. Now Jada needed Marisol's help to get in touch with Sunny, to help her keep her son out of the system. Marisol's heart broke as she listened to the desperation in Jada's voice. She took down Jada's address and prison I.D. number, so that she could try to help.

"Jada, Sunny's been with my sister in Puerto Rico since a month after Mercedes was born."

Jada cried silent tears, as she finally learned the sex of her friend's baby. Sunny had had a baby girl! She could only imagine how beautiful the baby must be.

Marisol continued. "She got a lot of investments and stuff that she cashed in after Dorian died, you know what I'm saying? Insurance and stuff like that." Marisol knew that Jada would read between the lines, and she did. She knew that Sunny had inherited Dorian's drug game fortune, and was laying low for the time being. "I will call her and tell her what happened. But for now, *mami,* you gotta pray for your baby, and ask God to spare his life. He's strong like you're strong, Jada. Don't break down now." Marisol's heavy Spanish accent was a comfort to Jada. She knew that Sunny's mom would do her best to help her, and that was a relief to her after so much bad news.

"Thank you, Marisol. You don't know how much this means to me. Sunny is my last hope. I don't have nowhere else to turn." Jada's voice got caught in her throat as the tears came.

Marisol knew that Jada's spirit was dampened. "Listen, Jada. Let me tell you something. Don't go feeling sorry for yourself, and getting all weighed down by negativity. That's not what you need right now. You are not the first young lady to have a problem like this. Sunny had your same problem once. Right before Dorian died, she was fucked up off that shit. He helped her through it, and she had the baby drug free. But after the baby, she fell back again. Sunny was right back on that shit again. But she went in and got help. Went to a program, you know? You gotta give it a chance. Because Sunny turned it all around, and you gotta see her now, baby girl. She's a whole different person. She still a pain in the ass . . ."

Jada laughed, missing Sunny's one-of-a-kind personality.

"But at least she's clean now. You stay strong," Marisol said. "You're gonna find your way. I will tell Sunny to get in touch with you. You wait to hear from her."

The line went dead, and Jada cried, feeling helpless. She spent the remainder of that night in prayer, asking for forgiveness, and for mercy.

The next day, Jada went back to jail, and she cried all the way back. Her last time touching Sheldon's soft hand through the holes in the incubator, she sang to him. Jada sang "Amazing Grace," and she hoped her son could hear her, even though she sounded bad because she was in tears. Sheldon had to stay in the hospital, because of all of his medical problems. He had stopped breathing twice, and they had managed to bring him back. And now Jada had to leave him there, and hope that he survived. And *if* he survived, she prayed that someone came in time to claim him before the courts sent him away.

Jada stayed in her bunk crying for days afterward. Jada was severely depressed. They put her on suicide watch, and everything. She found out that a custody hearing had been scheduled, and she felt a glimmer of hope. But still she wanted more. Every day without her baby was a day in hell for her.

35

SINCE I LOST MY BABY

September 1999

The visiting room was filled with kids, and Jada's eyes lit up at the sight of so many little ones. Her heart ached for her own child, as she looked around for Sunny's face. She found her friend sitting on one of the orange plastic chairs in the back of the visiting room.

Sunny looked more beautiful than ever. Her brown hair was long and silky, and pressed bone straight, complementing her lovely island-tanned face. When she'd last seen Sunny, her friend had sported a fierce, short haircut that had made her look edgy and sexy. Now her hair was long and beautiful, and she looked absolutely stunning. Jada wished she could have her hair done, since she now wore it in a half-nappy snatch-back ponytail. She was no longer concerned about something as trivial as looks. She hugged Sunny, and realized after so long how much she had truly missed her friend. Sunny began to cry, seeing Jada looking skinny and broken. This wasn't the friend with whom she'd danced the night away all over the city. She remembered the days when they'd gone on thousand-dollar shopping sprees and to parties with the rich and powerful. And now, Sunny had overcome her battles and was watching Jada losing her own. She hugged Jada for a long time, and when she finally pulled away she wiped her tears and looked at her friend.

"Girl, please don't hate me for leaving," Sunny began when they sat down at last. "I'm so sorry. I had to get out of New York after Dorian died. Niggas knew that I was the only one who knew where he kept all his money. Even his brothers and them, they wanted to get their hands on his money. I had to get away, because I was scared. And I was fucked up on that blow, too, Jada. I know my mother told you. When I buried Dorian, I buried a part of me, too. I was a mess. I was depressed, and I wanted to die. I got over that shit, but it wasn't easy. I'm here to help you do it, too. And you're gonna do it. And we're gonna get your baby back."

Jada smiled. "Thank you, Sunny. I need you to get in touch with my lawyer—"

"I already did. I fired him." Sunny crossed her legs, as Jada looked at her with surprise etched on her face. "I hired Nelson Doyle. He's a friend of my family, and he's helping me to try and get visitation with Sheldon."

"Visitation? They put him with a foster family already?" Jada was confused, because the custody hearing wasn't scheduled for two more weeks. When she'd last spoken to her Legal Aid attorney, he had told her that her son was still in the hospital.

Sunny hoped Jada wasn't going to overreact to what she was about to tell her. "Jada, Jamari stepped up and claimed the baby."

"What?" Jada was stunned. "What? How could he do that, Sunny? He can't do that, can he?"

Sunny held Jada's hand. "He went and had a paternity test done; he got a lawyer, and everything. Nelson's handling it, but Jamari's lawyer ain't making it easy. He proved paternity, and they checked him out, and all that. They went all into his background. I heard that the nigga stopped hustling, and everything. He's working at Home Depot, or some shit like that, and cooperating with the social workers. He had Sheldon moved to Staten Island Hospital, and he's got sole custody."

Jada burst into tears. She felt so much hatred surging through her body toward Jamari at that moment. He was rubbing salt in her wounds, and she fell apart. "He don't want me to see my own son?" she asked.

Sunny shook her head. "He's saying some terrible things about you, Jada. He got the doctors on his side, because Sheldon's had a hard time. He stopped breathing four different times, and he's been in the hospital for over a month. They had a closed-door hearing that Nelson said they didn't have to allow you to be present for. He said that since you couldn't challenge for custody as an inmate, you didn't need to be there. Jamari has a whole plan for how he's going to shut you out of Sheldon's life, but we're challenging him every step of the way. We'll be there in court, and we got your mother to come, too. Your mother wants to help you, and she swore she'd do whatever she could. Nelson's gonna put her on the stand and argue that, as the baby's grandmother, she should be allowed to visit with the baby. It might work. But I don't want you to get your hopes up. Jamari's being a real asshole about all this." Sunny looked at Jada, unsure. "Jada, how could you get high when you could feel your child moving around inside of you?" Sunny needed to understand what had sent Jada to such a terrible low. When she'd been pregnant with Mercedes, nothing could have made Sunny use cocaine. Nothing could have made her hurt her unborn child.

Jada nodded, and looked away. "I didn't want to be pregnant anymore. I found out so much about Jamari that made me hate him. And I realized that he only looked out for me in order to make me depend on him. It was all part of some crazy plan. I didn't want to have his baby. I was hoping I would lose it, and then I could be free of him." Jada sighed. "But Sheldon hung on, and I am so sorry that I ever hurt him."

"You should be. 'Cuz he is the most beautiful little boy I've ever seen. He looks just like you. You better thank God every day that Sheldon refused to die. He's a tough little boy."

Jada was grateful to Sunny. Even though her words were blunt and matter-of-fact, they were pure truth. She was glad that Sunny knew what to expect when she faced Jamari in court. Jada told Sunny how grateful she was for all of her help. She didn't know what she'd do without her.

Sunny tilted her head to the side, and looked at her worn-down friend. "How the hell did you get involved with this sucka-ass nigga in the first place? What happened with Born?"

Jada shook her head, and told her how it had all gone wrong. She told Sunny everything she'd been through, from the moment she had lost touch with her friend. She told her how she'd stolen from Born to get high, and how he'd caught her and kicked her out. Jada told Sunny about all the crack she had used, how Jamari had given it to her and hadn't judged her. She told her about the bricks she'd stolen, and the money she'd made, and where she'd stashed it. By the time the visit was over, Jada felt only a glimmer of hope that Sunny might be able to help her to hold on to the child she really hadn't wanted at all. Now she wanted him with all her might.

Two weeks went by before Jada's hearing. When she got to court, she saw Sunny and Edna, and was thrilled to have their positive energy on her side. Her lawyer put her on the stand, and Jada cried her way through her testimony, and promised to get clean. Edna got up there and cried, too. But Jada felt that she was crying for all the wrong reasons.

Edna cried, and told the court about how hard it was to see her child as a crackhead. She told them that she wished she could raise Jada all over again, and make up for all the wrong she'd done. Edna felt that she was being given a second chance with the birth of her grandchild. Jada could tell that Edna's testimony didn't really make her look like the best person in the world. She was scared to death. But her lawyer said that the judge might take pity on her. He might see Edna's desire to fix her past mistakes as a reason to grant Edna visitation rights. That was what they wanted. Jamari's lawyer argued that Sheldon should remain with his father because it was a stable home environment, and he was the child's biological father. Then they began their attack.

Jamari's attorney assassinated Jada's character in the courtroom that day. He talked about how Sheldon only slept for ten minutes at a time, and how he threw up like a faucet. He had seizures, and had to sleep attached to a monitor. That was bad enough. But then he talked about how Jada would have had to get high *repeatedly* throughout her pregnancy in order to do the kind of damage that the baby had sustained. Jamari even stared at Jada from the witness stand, and told her she would never see the baby again, and that he hated her. The judge let him talk freely, and every word cut Jada like a knife.

But he was right. She had put her child's life in jeopardy. And Jamari wanted her to pay the ultimate price. He wanted Jada banned from their son's life, but Sheldon was the only thing she had to live for now. Jamari, himself, had given Jada crack. He denied that on the stand, and told the judge that Jada had been a danger to their son from the very beginning, and she always would be. Jamari's lawyer argued that Sheldon was a neglected child before he was even born, because Jada had put him in imminent danger every time she got high. He said that she had failed as a parent, that she couldn't exercise even a minimum degree of care, since she was incarcerated. Basically, Jamari painted Jada as a danger to their child as long as she was not rehabilitated. He emphasized the fact that she was the sole cause of Sheldon's withdrawal symptoms, and that she was unfit to see him. The judge agreed, and they stripped Jada of all her rights. Her mother had no rights either, since Jamari had his lawyer bring up how terrible Jada's own childhood had been with her mother. His lawyer told the court about Edna's lack of parenting, and implied that had she been a better mother Jada's life might have turned out differently. Edna came across as weak and sorrowful, and the judge didn't feel sorry for them. Jada hated that she had ever shared the pain of her past with the cruel bastard who had fathered her child.

Jada was returned to prison, and she suffered every minute. She wrote Jamari a letter, asking his forgiveness and begging him to at least let her just have a picture of Sheldon, or something. He never even wrote her back. Edna wrote to Jada, though. She wrote to her to ask if she could come and visit her. She sent her Ava's address and phone number. Edna was extending an olive branch to her child. She offered to let Jada call her collect any time she wanted. But Jada just shut down. She didn't write back or call, because she felt like her whole life had been taken away from her. In all, Edna wrote Jada three letters during her incarceration. But Jada answered none of them. She wanted to be left alone. Instead of answering her family's letters, Jada wrote in her journal. She wrote down every emotion, every hurt and pain. In her diary there were dozens of lines of sadness and longing. She filled up several notebooks this way, writing night after night about her pain and anguish. Writing about her guilt. Jada wanted to disappear. She felt like giving up.

But then Sunny saved the day.

February 2000

Sunny sat anxiously, waiting for Jada to make her way over to her at the visiting table. She hugged her, and they sat down, and Jada could tell that her friend was eager. She had something she was itching to share with her. Without a word, Sunny passed Jada the pictures. Jada's heart skipped a beat. Pictures of Sheldon in the park with his father were what Sunny had brought to her. Her eyes filled with tears as she looked at her six-month-old son for the first time. He looked like a replica of Jada, only male and chubby. She smiled and wanted to kiss Sunny. "How did you get these?"

Sunny smiled broadly, thrilled that she could be of help to her friend. "You know I got ways, girl. I got somebody to find out where Jamari takes him to play, takes him to day care, and shit like that. I just want to keep my eye on him, in case the nigga tries to leave town and disappear, or some dumb shit like that. I also want to see if I can catch him in some bullshit that might persuade the judge to see him in a different light. Just keep these pictures in the meantime, so you can see how adorable little Sheldon is."

Jada smiled, and stared at the pictures once more. Her heart overflowed.

"Jada, you *have* to use him as your reason to get clean. When you get out of here, you need to go to a program for nine months. Do that for your survival. I'm telling you from experience. You gotta do this shit for real this time, Jada. No more bullshit, or you may have to say good-bye to your son for good. I don't want to see that happen to you. I'm gonna do everything I can to help you. But you gotta help yourself." Sunny spoke candidly to her friend. As a former drug offender herself, Sunny knew that blunt honesty was the only way to deal with an addict. They had to hear the truth straight, with no chaser.

Jada made up her mind, as she looked down at the photos of her baby boy, that she would have to leave drugs alone for good if she wanted a chance to be in his life. She committed herself to staying clean in order to get her baby back. No matter how hard it was.

As much as she hated Jamari for taking her son away so coldly, Jada had to admire him for how he had managed to care for their son. Sheldon was a beautiful baby, and he looked happy and healthy. After seeing his condition at birth, Jada knew that Sheldon's recovery was a miracle. She could tell that Jamari loved him, and that he was taking good care of him. But she still hated him for depriving her of seeing her baby.

Sunny kept coming to visit Jada, and kept bringing her pictures of Sheldon. Those pictures got her through the hard times. Jada sat on her bed night after night staring at the pictures of her son. Sunny went out of her way to stay on Jamari's trail as much as possible. Since she figured he knew her face from her appearance with Jada in court, Sunny had her mother go to the park and bring Mercedes. She would go and see Jamari there, and let Mercedes play with Sheldon. Jamari didn't recognize Sunny's mother, but little did he know he was helping his son form a friendship with Sunny's daughter. Sunny often laughed at the irony.

Because of Sunny and her mother, and the pictures and stories they gave Jada about her son, Jada went into rehab wanting to get out of there and be clean. Being in jail and having her son stripped away from her had broken her. But going to rehab—for real this time—made Jada see herself so clearly that it changed her life. She was determined to prevail for once in her life, and she was never the same again.

September 2000

Jada stared out the window of the rehabilitation clinic. She knew that lunch was being served, but she wasn't hungry. All she could think about was the fact that her son was growing up without her. He was sitting up without her, and having his first taste of solid food without her. She was envious of Jamari, and of his ability to witness Sheldon's precious moments. She felt sorry for herself, and frankly she was tired of being in institutions. To hell with lunch.

Jada's lawyer was on his job. He filed motion after motion to challenge the judge's ruling. He argued that Jada hadn't used any drugs after her child was born. Granted, that was due in part to her incarceration, but Jada was giving it a real try. He got Jada's counselor, Miss Walsh, to testify about the strides she'd made. Jada had given Miss Walsh a hard time when she first got there. But she told Jada point-blank that she hadn't put her there. She wasn't the reason Jada found herself locked up and in rehab. Jada had done that all by herself. Miss Walsh said that she wasn't there just because she was bored at home. She wasn't there to rub Jada's back, or to pick her up. She was there to help Jada beat this thing, and to make the transition smoother for her, so that she could reclaim her life. Jada wanted that more than anything. Miss Walsh got through to her because of the raw and uncut way in which she dealt with her. She didn't sugarcoat the situation, or pretend that it was going to be easy. Jada needed her type of raw honesty, and it helped her to get the monkey off her back once and for all.

Her attorney argued that the judge couldn't base his decision on whether or not Jada was a *current* danger to Sheldon solely based on Jada's *past* behavior. She hadn't used any drugs since the day she'd been arrested. He argued that she deserved the benefit of the doubt, now that she had been clean for more than a year. It could no longer be considered neglect if Jada had genuinely changed her life, and was now drug free. The judge agreed, and placed a condition on her future with her son. If she completed the program, Jada was entitled to supervised visits. That drove her to finish the program. She had her baby boy to get home to. Jada took her recovery more seriously than ever. And Sunny was there for her every step of the way. At the end of nine months of rehabilitation, Jada left that program clean, and didn't pick up a drug afterward. It was like a switch had gone off in her head once she had seen her baby. For Jada, seeing Sheldon fighting to survive made her want to fight, too. It made her want to beat what was weighing her down, and survive, the same way he had. Having Sheldon saved her life. And even though it would take her a long time to get to the point where she could have supervised visits with him, she was grateful to be in his life at all. At first, a

social worker came along on her visits with Sheldon, watching how she
spoke to him, how she played with him, and observing the way Jada in-
teracted with her son. She was bothered by this, hating the fact that a
stranger had to watch her play with her own child. Eventually, she
earned the right to unsupervised visitation, and a social worker picked
Sheldon up from Jamari and dropped him off with Jada. This was done
so that the two of them could avoid any confrontations that may ad-
versely affect Sheldon's development. Jada preferred it that way. She
didn't ever want to do anything to hurt Sheldon again. He was her whole
reason for living. Jada said a daily prayer of thanks that God had given
her a second chance—not just at motherhood, but at life.

Jada went to see Miss Ingrid about a month after she came home. Ingrid was so happy to see Jada now that she was cleaned up, and had gotten her shit together. She opened the door, and she smiled so big that
you would have thought she was Jada's mother, and not Born's.

"Jada, oh my God. Look at you!" Ingrid was obviously impressed by
Jada's transition. "Girl, you look so good!"

Jada hugged Born's mother, and Ingrid led her into her living room.
"Sit down, and let me get you something to drink." Jada did as she was
told, and Ingrid disappeared into the kitchen. Jada looked around at all
of the pictures of Born gracing the shelves and tables in the living room.
His elementary school picture was the cutest, in Jada's opinion. Born
wore a green polo shirt in the picture, and his two front teeth were missing on the top. He looked so cute, and Jada couldn't help wondering if
their children would have inherited Born's handsome face. She wished
all the time that Sheldon was his child rather than punk-ass Jamari's.

Ingrid reentered the living room, and sat across from Jada. "When did
you come home?" Ingrid asked.

Jada sipped her soda, and said, "Last month. I've been staying in
Brooklyn with my friend Sunny. She helped me out so much, Miss Ingrid. I had a hard time seeing my baby, because my baby's father fought
me for sole custody while I was locked up." Jada sat and told Ingrid
everything. She told her how it had felt to see her baby limp and helpless,

his body frail and bony. She remembered Sheldon as a tiny baby with withdrawal symptoms from the crack. Ingrid listened as Jada told her that watching Sheldon fight for his life had made her want to fight for her own. She briefly explained the long story of her legal battles with Jamari for the right to be a part of her son's life. Ingrid listened sympathetically. "Sunny and her mother snuck, and took pictures of my son, and brought them to me while I was in jail, and in rehab. They helped my attorney prove that I was serious about getting my act together, and I'm so grateful to them for that."

Ingrid nodded. "Your friend Sunny sounds like a real friend. You don't get too many of those in life. You might get *one*. And if you get one, you should consider yourself lucky. If you get more than that, you are truly blessed. You'll come across a lot of different people in your life. Some you'll like more than others. But you gotta learn to differentiate between friends and just plain associates. This girl Sunny sounds like a friend."

Jada nodded. She thought about Shante, who she had once thought was her friend. Now that she had gotten her life together, Jada realized that Shante had only wallowed in Jada's misery and misfortune. But what goes around always comes around, and Shante was still getting high, and looking worse than ever. She had teeth missing and a haggard appearance every time she stepped outside. Everybody looked at her, and saw little more than a crackhead who looked twenty years older than she actually was. Jada was happy that her life hadn't turned out the same way. She had gotten another chance. Ingrid offered Jada a piece of her famous chocolate cake, and that was an offer she couldn't refuse. They ate cake and drank coffee, and chatted like old friends catching up after journeying down a long and winding road. Ingrid explained the importance of friendship to Jada.

"See, this is how I see it. There are so many young women who depend on the men in their lives for everything. They base their self-esteem, sometimes, on the man they love, and on what he thinks. They think that because he says 'I love you,' he's always gonna be around.

That ain't always the case. But your friends . . . your good girlfriends . . . now they'll be there. True friends will help you back up on your feet. You hold on to your girl Sunny. Sounds to me like she got your back."

Jada embraced the wisdom Born's mother imparted to her. It made it easy for her to talk to her about all the things she'd been through. She told Ingrid about her plans to go to school and take up journalism. She told her that writing had been therapeutic for her during her time away, and that she'd love to pursue it professionally. Ingrid was proud of Jada for turning such a negative situation into such a positive one. Ingrid walked to her closet, pulled out a large shoebox, and handed it to Jada. Jada looked inside and found all of her money. She smiled, grateful beyond measure that Ingrid had been true to her word, and had kept Jada's money secure. She wanted to cry, because she knew there weren't too many people who are honest enough to keep fifty-five thousand dollars untouched for close to two years. "Thank you, Miss Ingrid." Jada's eyes were misty. "Thank you so much."

Ingrid smiled back. She sat back in her seat, and folded her arms across her chest. "You did it. You got back up on your feet, and you did it for the right reasons. You did it for yourself, and for your son. I'm real proud of you." Ingrid smiled. Then she let out a sigh, and looked her in the eyes. "Let me tell you something, Jada. And you need to keep this between me and you." Ingrid knew that her son would be upset if he knew what she was about to say, but Ingrid trusted Jada to keep this discussion between them.

Jada nodded. "After what you did for me, Miss Ingrid, you know you can trust me."

Ingrid nodded. "I know my son very well. You know what I'm saying? And I know that he still cares about you. He talks about you sometimes, and he gets this faraway look in his eyes. You didn't hear it from me, but I think my son still has love in his heart for you."

Jada smiled. "Wow. That's like music to my ears."

Ingrid smiled, and sighed. "But Marquis is about to be a father."

Jada's heart broke into a million pieces. She tried to keep her game face on, but Ingrid could see that she was hurt. "With who? Anisa?" Jada asked.

Ingrid nodded. "Yeah." She shook her head in disbelief. "When he was locked up, she forgot all about him. She was there for him at first, but it didn't take Miss Thang long to hit the road. I wasn't surprised, and Marquis said he wasn't either. But I think he was kinda hurt by it, even though he tried to act like he wasn't. Marquis contacted her when he got home to ask her why she had played him like that. Next thing you know, she's pregnant. I can't say she trapped him. I don't know that for sure. But I do know that Marquis will make a good father. I'm sure that Anisa knows she got a good man. And I'm not just saying that because he's my son. Marquis has a big heart, and he's gonna be good to her, and to his child. He won't let her and the baby go without, and for that reason alone Anisa does her best to keep my son happy." Ingrid looked at Jada. "He's about to have a son, and he's real excited about it. But I can tell that Marquis don't care for her like he cared for you."

Jada felt relieved hearing that. Surely the man's own mother wouldn't lie.

"He will probably never love another woman the same way he loved you. But you hurt my baby."

Jada looked at the floor, feeling so small and so guilty. "I know I did. That's something I will regret for the rest of my life."

Ingrid shook her head. "Don't regret it, Jada. Regret ain't nothing but a waste of energy, because you can't fix nothing by regretting it. It's better to have loved and lost than to live with regret." Ingrid patted Jada reassuringly on her hand. "All I want you to know is this: You hurt Marquis, you hurt yourself, and you hurt your son. But now you got yourself together, and I think that your situation with your son will work itself out. You got a second chance with him. Now I don't know if you'll ever have a second chance with Marquis. But just know that, even though he moved on and you moved on, somewhere deep inside my son still cares for you." She smiled. "And for the record, I like you a whole lot more than that chick he's with now."

Jada laughed, and gave Miss Ingrid a high five. She was glad that Ingrid liked her more than Anisa. It didn't change the fact that Born was with the other woman, and that she was about to have his baby. But knowing that she had gotten the stamp of approval from the woman who meant the very most to the man she loved—his mother—made Jada feel like she was the winner after all. Ingrid liked her, despite her struggles and mistakes, and Jada was happy about that. She hoped that someday Born would forgive her as well, and that they could have a chance to at least be friends. She still missed their friendship, and hoped to salvage that, even if there was no chance for salvaging the relationship. "Miss Ingrid, the way I feel for Marquis is everlasting. It don't matter who has his kids, or who lives with him. I know that what we shared is more special than any of that. And I don't think real love expires over time. I don't know if me and Born will ever even be in the same room together again. But when you speak to him, please tell him that I miss him, and that I think about him all the time."

Ingrid smiled, and agreed to do just that. By the time they finished talking and eating, it was almost one thirty in the morning. Ingrid offered to walk Jada out to her car, since it was late, but she insisted that she would be fine. Her car was parked right downstairs, and it was a cold winter night. No one would bother her. As Jada left her house that day, promising to keep in touch regardless of whether she and Born ever spoke again, Ingrid felt like a proud mom seeing her baby girl succeed. Jada had made it through her darkest days, and Ingrid was happy for her. She hoped that Born would get the chance to see how well Jada had fought her demons, and how she had come through the storm, still wearing a smile. And as she watched Jada leave, Ingrid realized that she still believed in second chances. She hoped that Jada and Marquis would have a second chance someday.

36

A VOICE IN THE DARK

Jada left Ingrid's house and headed for Sunny's silver Jaguar, which was parked in the lot behind the building. She pulled the keys out of her pocket and disabled the alarm with the remote. She noticed that a black Suburban was parked beside Sunny's car, and wondered why anyone would park so close to her in a nearly empty parking lot. As she got closer to the truck, she heard a voice behind her that made her stop dead in her tracks.

"You know, I never thought you would really be dumb enough to show your face in Staten Island again." Jada spun around, and stood face-to-face with Jamari in the darkness of the deserted parking lot. Her heart beat rapidly, and she clutched her bag tighter. The money she'd come back to get was in there, and she'd be damned if Jamari would get his hands on it.

"Don't talk to me," she said. Jada hadn't spoken directly to Jamari in over a year. There was a court-appointed professional who coordinated her visits with Sheldon, so that contact between the two parents would be nonexistent. But now she'd had the rotten luck of running into him on her first trip back to Staten Island since her release. "You grimy muthafucka! You stood up there in that courtroom and told them that I was a monster—"

"You *are* a monster. You're a fuckin' crackhead, and you made my son a crack baby. But you really got a lot of nerve coming back to Staten Island after you stole my money. Wizz's money . . ."

"I didn't steal shit from you. Or Wizz. You didn't have to pay for that shit. You were working on consignment, so you didn't take a fuckin' loss!"

"I *did* take a loss, bitch! I had to pay Elliot back bit by bit for that shit before he died." A cold and evil expression flashed across Jamari's face. "I had to rat that nigga out, just like I did to your boy Born." Seeing the surprised expression on Jada's face he smiled sinisterly. "I swear to God, I'm gonna see you dead before I see you in my son's life. Everything you love, I'm gonna take it from you! I swear I'm gonna get you back for everything I ever lost."

"What *you* lost! Listen to you, you selfish bastard. I don't owe you a fuckin' dime. And I don't owe you any explanation. I'm living my life, and I'm going to be a damned good mother to my son. You can't control me anymore. Whatever power you had over me is gone. And now I see why Born hates you so much."

At the mention of Born's name, Jamari seethed. He looked at Jada, venomously. "Is that who you came looking for?" he asked, motioning toward Ingrid's building. "You came looking for Born?" Jamari grinned. "I hope you know that he got somebody else now. She's having his baby, and everything." He smiled at her menacingly, and waited for her reaction.

Jada didn't give him the benefit of seeing her sweat. She was glad that she knew already, so that he hadn't caught her off guard. "I know about that, and I'm happy for him. At least he has the pleasure of having a baby with someone he really cares about. I got stuck having my son with an asshole."

Jamari stepped toward Jada, and she stepped back. He was pissed, and it was visible on his face. "Fuck you!" he said. "You'll be back on that crack in no time. Once a crackhead, always a crackhead."

Jada didn't show it, but those words cut deep. She thought back to what Born had said to her when he found her high in their house that day. *"Once a fiend, always a fiend, huh, Jada?"* Those had been Born's words to her. She still remembered the tone in his voice, the look on his face. It made her heart break all over again, as Jamari said similar words to her now. She ignored his remark, and said, "Well, your mama was a crackhead, Jamari, and look how well you turned out."

Before she knew what happened, he was in her face, and the barrel of his .40-caliber gun was pointed at her temple. Jamari had her back pressed up against the driver's side door of the Jaguar, and Jada was frozen with fear. "You got a lot of mouth for somebody out here all alone in the dark in the dead of winter. I should kill you right here, you stupid bitch!" Jamari was so mad that the vein in his neck was throbbing. "You think I'm gonna let you be around my son when you had him breathing through a machine, and throwing up every fuckin' thing he ate? You had my son addicted to that shit. You dirty bitch! Coming through here in your fuckin' Jag looking for Born. I should kill you just for that shit!" Jada was scared as hell, and he loved the helpless look on her face. "Oh," he said, "what's the matter? You scared?"

Jada nodded, and looked around hoping to see someone she could call out to for help. Jamari saw this, and let out a sinister laugh. "You should be scared. 'Cuz, ain't nobody out here but us. And I want an apology." Jamari cocked his gun, and stared coldly into her eyes.

Jada's whole body trembled, and it made Jamari feel powerful. "Apologize to me, Jada. Tell me you're sorry."

She felt her heart racing in her chest. "I'm sorry." Her voice was barely audible.

"Say it like you mean it," he said, still smiling wickedly.

Jada wanted to cry, but she held herself together somehow. She spoke louder, and said, "I'm sorry, Jamari."

He nodded his head, liking the return of the power he'd once had over her. "Very good. That's more like it. Now, what did you do with the money?" he asked. "You didn't smoke all that money up. Not that fast. Where's it at?"

Jada quickly handed him the bag in her hand. Fuck it! He could have it. Jamari couldn't believe his luck. She had the money with her right then and there! His surprise was obvious, and he lowered his gun, reaching for the bag. But before he could take it away, he heard "click, click!" and he turned to see Sunny standing with a .380 in his face. In the moment of his surprise, Jada ducked out of the line of fire, and grabbed Jamari's gun. Jamari stood still, wondering where this woman had come from. Sunny's smile was as sinister as his had been.

"Hey, muthafucka!" she said. "Hand it over."

Jamari stared at the beautiful woman in front of him, and could tell by the look on her face that she meant business. Her gun had a silencer on the end, and Sunny stood in stiletto boots, jeans, and a black leather jacket, looking at him like she was growing impatient. The driver's side door of the Suburban was open, and for the first time Jada understood why the truck was parked so close. Sunny had been inside the Suburban all along. He handed her the money, while she kept her gun pointed between his eyes.

"Something told me that if my girl Jada came back to Staten Island by herself, you might try some dumb shit. So I took my brother's truck, and followed her here, waiting for you to make your move." Sunny shook her head, looking at Jamari. "You didn't disappoint me. You punk, bitch-ass nigga. You like cornering women alone and putting guns to their heads, Jamari?"

"This ain't got nothing to do with you, ma." Jamari's voice was steady, but the look on his face showed that he was nervous. He thought about trying to take the gun, but knew from the expression on her face that any sudden move would have scratched Sunny's itchy trigger finger. "Jada owes me that money. She took it from me."

"You owed it to *her*. She didn't take it; she was supposed to get that. I heard all about your little twisted games, muthafucka. You thinking Born is your brother; you wanting to be with her so that Born would get mad; you giving her crack, then taking her son. You're a real piece of shit. Now," Sunny looked at Jada. "You wanna off this nigga?"

Jada smiled at Jamari. My, how the tables had turned! She and Sunny had Jamari's life in their well-manicured hands. She looked at him, his eyes pleading with hers to let him go. She thought about her son, and all the hoops she had to jump through just to see him. All because Jamari had assassinated her character in court. She thought about Born, and how Jamari had hidden his history from her, making it likely that Born would never want to see her again. "I want an apology, Jamari." Jada turned his words back on him. Now she wanted what he had demanded of her moments earlier.

He looked at Jada like she had lost her mind. "Fuck you." He frowned, and looked at this woman he had once loved beyond reason. "I ain't apologizing for shit."

Sunny shook her head, ready to blast him, and looked at Jada for a cue. Jada folded her arms across her chest. "You sure about that? 'Cuz, I'm only gonna ask you once more."

Jamari was done talking. He lunged for the gun, ready to kill both of these bitches. But Sunny was faster. Living life as a gangsta bitch had taught her well. As Jamari made his move, Sunny's .380 spit a slug into his brain, sending his eyes flying open in surprise, and sending his body falling to the ground with a thud. Her gun still smoking, Sunny looked at Jada and said, "You got too much fuckin' patience!" The silencer had muffled the sound of the blast, but the dead body at their feet would be hard to explain. "Let's get the fuck out of here."

The two women jumped into their cars and drove off, leaving Jamari to draw his last breath all by himself.

When they finally got back to Brooklyn, Jada was a mess. She was crying and scared, thinking that she was going back to jail, but for murder this time. She figured someone must have seen her and Sunny. Someone must have witnessed the murder they'd just committed. Sunny, on the other hand, was as cool as a cucumber. "Calm the fuck down, Jada! It was like one in the morning. People were probably sleeping, and even if they did see something, they can't prove it was us. You gotta calm down, and let's get our story straight." Jada pulled herself together, and listened as Sunny ran down their makeshift alibi. She was still nervous about what they'd done. But Sunny made her see that at least she was finally rid of the sorry bastard who was her son's father. Maybe now she'd be one step closer to having her son all to herself.

Jamari's murder became another one of Shaolin's unsolved mysteries. The police had come to question Jada, and to ask for her whereabouts on the night Jamari was killed. She had, after all, been locked in an ugly custody battle with him for more than a year. Jada explained that on the night in question, she and Sunny had enjoyed dinner with Sunny's mother and brothers, and that there was no way Jada could have been anywhere near Staten Island. After questioning Marisol, who corroborated Jada's story, the police stopped eyeing Jada as a suspect. Jada was forever grateful to Sunny for saving her life—more than once. But getting custody of Sheldon wasn't such a walk in the park. With his custodial parent dead, the state of New York wanted to place Sheldon in foster care until Jada could petition for custody. But to Jada's surprise, an unexpected ally stepped up to take custody of Sheldon until Jada could wade her way through the mountains of red tape that stood between her and her son.

Jada got a surprise phone call from her sister. The two of them hadn't spoken in years, and it was with mixed emotions that Jada talked with her. It wasn't that Jada wasn't happy to hear from Ava. But she still hadn't forgiven their mother for leaving her to stand alone when she'd needed someone to lean on. And she felt a certain anger toward Ava as well. Ava had left Jada's house after finding out about her drug use, and pretty much never looked back. There had been numerous occasions over the years when Jada had longed for the comfort of her sister, and Ava had been nowhere around. They had written letters to each other during Jada's incarceration. But to Jada that wasn't enough to erase the void Ava had left when she walked out of her sister's life.

Part of her reluctance to talk to her sister stemmed from some feelings that Jada never admitted she had. She felt inferior to her sister. While Jada had done so many things wrong, Ava had done everything right. Sure she had attempted suicide as a teenager, and been a chronic runaway. But Ava had turned her life around, finished high school, gone on to college, and then to law school, and was now a very successful attorney. Ava was a corporate lawyer working at one of Philadelphia's top law firms, and was close to making partner. No kids, no husband. Ava was just living life to the fullest, and traveling whenever the mood struck her. Ava had never been addicted to anything, never been to jail. Next to her sister, Jada felt like a complete failure. Hearing her voice on the phone did little to soothe that.

The conversation was cordial. They caught up on what was going on in each other's lives. Jada told her sister about Jamari's sudden death, and the fact that the police had yet to find any suspects. She told her about the battle she was now waging in order win custody of her son, and how she'd been drug free for nearly two years. And most important, she had managed to do it despite the abandonment she felt from Ava and their mother. Staying clean was an accomplishment that Jada was proud of, and she felt stronger because she had accomplished them without her family's support.

Ava had an ulterior motive for this phone call. She wanted her sister to finally forgive their mother for the pain she had caused her. But when the conversation turned to Edna, Jada shut down.

"I don't really want to talk about her," Jada said. "I still don't see how you could act like she never did anything wrong. It's like you erased all the shit from your memory what she did to us. The things she let J.D. get away with doing to us . . ."

"There's some things that you don't know about Mommy," Ava began. Edna had sworn Ava to secrecy about her recent cancer diagnosis. She didn't want Jada to forgive her only because she was sick and dying of an incurable disease. She wanted her daughter's forgiveness from the heart, and for that reason Ava skirted the real issue at hand. "Mommy wasn't the best mother on the planet," Ava said. "We both know that. It took a long time for me to get over what she did when J.D. was violating me. She didn't help me, and to be honest, she abandoned me. I hated her. I hated her so much. But while I was in the group home, they counseled me. I spoke to people about what had gone on, and I got help for what I went through. Meanwhile, you were out there on your own. And I never realized how unfair it was that I got help, and you just got swept up in the streets. I had a feeling you were using drugs, when we were in high school, because you started losing weight and acting all crazy sometimes. And I've always felt bad because I didn't do anything or say anything to try and stop you in the beginning. Mommy knew, too, but she didn't know what to do about it." Ava sighed. "She understands your anger toward her, Jada. She really does. But she never stopped loving you. Every time I talk to her, she mentions your name. She wants to see Sheldon, and she wants to know if you've even told him about his grandmother. She needs to see him. And to see you . . ."

Jada shook her head, as she held the phone. "Well, I'm not really willing to see her anymore. When I was locked up, and I gave birth to Sheldon, I called her. I begged her to come and take custody of him so that he wouldn't be taken away from me. You know what she said to me? She said God was in control, and she didn't want to get involved. She told me to pray about it. I'm laying in the hospital, the night before they returned me to prison, begging my own mother for help. And she told me to turn to God. Like there was nothing *she* could do for me. I'll never forget that, Ava. You know what happened? Jamari took my baby, and kept him from me for as long as he could. If it wasn't for Sunny . . ." Jada caught herself about to divulge too much information. "All I'm saying is, where was my family? Where was my mother? She came to court, supposedly to help me. And she got up on the witness stand and told the judge that she regretted raising a fuckup like me, and she hoped she could get a second chance, if he allowed her to raise my son. What the hell was that? How could she have possibly thought that would help me?"

"Jada, Mommy is really into the Bible now. She probably said that in the courtroom that day because that was the truth, in her opinion. She wasn't going to lie under oath . . ."

"Well, then what the fuck did she come there for, Ava? What the fuck did I need her for, if she wasn't going to say something helpful? When has she ever come through for me? When? You tell me that."

Ava was at a loss for words, and silence filled the phone. She had known that Jada would have a hard time letting go of the past. But Edna was dying now, and Ava was determined to bridge the gap between mother and daughter. She was tempted to just come out and tell Jada the truth. But her mother had sworn her to secrecy. She wanted to tell Jada herself. If Jada would only talk to her. Ava could see that this would be no easy task.

She talked to her sister for a while longer, and they made plans to get together sometime in the near future. Ava was in and out of New York often, and she told her sister that she would love to see her, and start the process of mending their relationship. Jada agreed, although she knew that she really wasn't ready for that. From that point on, she avoided her sister's phone calls, and went about her life as usual. Fuck her family, Jada felt. All she had was Sheldon, and all he had was her. They were the only family that either of them needed. Sunny had been the only one—family or otherwise—to help Jada rid her life of all its demons. So in Jada's opinion, Sunny and Sheldon mattered more than any sister or mother she'd ever had. She lived her life as such. It was all about Sheldon.

The next few weeks consisted of a series of hearings concerning Sheldon's custody. Jada appeared at each one with her attorney, trying to establish that she was fit to have sole custody of her son. At the final hearing, the judge listened to Jada's attorney explain how she had turned her life around. He gave the judge recommendations from her rehab counselors, and Sunny and her mother Marisol both testified on Jada's behalf. But the judge was reluctant. Jada still had no job, and she had no prospects for getting one with a rap sheet as long as hers. She had her own place—an apartment in Brooklyn—but the court wasn't satisfied that her son would be safe in her care without the supervision of another responsible adult. The charges Jamari had leveled against her were serious. The amount of crack she'd used during her last two months of pregnancy was hard to ignore. As Jada stood in the courtroom, listening to the judge speak, her heart sank. She knew that he was about to deny her custody. But then a voice spoke out in the courtroom, and made Jada's heart stand still. It was her mother.

"I'm willing to take my daughter and her son into *my* home, your honor." Edna stood in the back of the courtroom, and everyone turned toward her.

Jada couldn't believe her eyes. She stared at her mother as if she was crazy. There was no way Jada was going to move back in with Edna. "Your honor . . ." Jada began to protest. Her lawyer cut her off, placing his hand on her forearm. He whispered to her, "Be quiet. This may be your only chance."

The judge motioned for Edna to step forward, and he asked her who she was.

"My name is Edna Ford. I'm Jada's mother. I would be happy to have my daughter and her son come and live with me in Staten Island. I don't work, so I can provide child care for my grandson while my daughter gets herself into school, or gets a job. I'm a Christian woman, and there will be no drugs of any kind in my home. You have my word that I will make sure that Sheldon has the best stable environment possible."

Jada stood there dumbfounded, wondering how Edna had known that she would be appearing in court that day. She wondered what would make her mother think that she would want to live with her. Jada still had not forgiven her. She looked at Edna speechlessly, and the judge spoke up at last.

Looking at Jada, he asked, "Would you be willing to relocate and live with your mother, if you were given custody of your son?"

Jada shook her head. "Your honor, with all due respect, I don't think I need to be supervised . . ."

"May I please have a few minutes to confer with my client?" Jada's lawyer interrupted. She shot him an evil look, which he ignored, and the judge granted them a five-minute recess to discuss the new developments. Her attorney grabbed Jada by the arm, and motioned for Edna to follow them. He led Jada outside of the courtroom, and pulled her into a secluded corner. Edna was right behind them.

Nelson Doyle was no stranger to family court cases before this judge. He knew that Jada would not get custody of her son unless she pulled a rabbit out of a hat. She needed magic, or some kind of miracle, in order to walk out of that courtroom victorious. And when Edna spoke up it seemed to Doyle that their miracle had just arrived.

"Jada," he said, "you should listen to your mother—"

"Nah," Jada interjected, shaking her head. "I don't even wanna talk to her. She's never been there for me."

Edna heard her daughter speak about her as if she weren't there. "I'm here now, Jada. It's not too late for you to talk to me. But one day it might be."

Jada frowned, and looked at her mother. "It is too late. Where have you been all this time? All this time I was out here by myself, fighting for my son, fighting for my own life. And where were you? Now you wanna come in here and . . ."

"And help you get your son back." Edna finished Jada's sentence, and stood there staring at her. "I want to come back, and try to salvage what's left of our family. You deserve the chance to be a mother to your son. I want to help you, Jada. And maybe we can start to fix what's broken with our own relationship."

"I don't *want* to fix our relationship. What's the point?"

Doyle spoke up. "I think the point is that reuniting with your mother could be the one thing that persuades the judge to give you custody."

"How? What is that gonna do for me?"

"It would show him that you're so determined to be a good mother to your child that you're willing to relocate and reunite with your mother. It'll show him that you and your mother are committed to your recovery. That you're willing to make whatever adjustments are necessary to give Sheldon a stable upbringing. If you do this, Judge Blackburne will have reason to believe that sending Sheldon home with you will be a good decision." Doyle saw the pain on Jada's face, and tried to soothe her somewhat. "Jada, I know that you're a good mother. I know that Sheldon will thrive under your care, that you will make sure that you stay clean for him. But that judge doesn't know that. When he looks at you, he sees a drug addict who is still on parole. He sees a mother who got high while she was pregnant, and had an underweight, crack-addicted baby. He's not going to trust that you've recovered fully. Not to the degree of giving you sole custody so soon after your release from rehab, and Jamari's murder. That judge wants to give Sheldon some stability for a change. And he's going to believe that living with your mother will give you that stability." Nelson looked at Edna, hoping she would have something to add to his pitch.

Edna cleared her throat. "Jada, I know that you don't want to come and stay with me. But this is for Sheldon. He needs you. And the only way that judge is going to give him what he needs is if I help you." Edna reached for Jada's hand, which was given to her reluctantly. "There's been a lot of mistakes between us, Jada. You've made them, and I've made them. But we have to put all of that aside in order to do what we can for Sheldon. I wasn't always there for you. You're right about that. But I'm here now, and I'm willing to do whatever it takes to make this work."

Jada felt so awkward. She had been so angry with her mother for so long; so disappointed in the choices her mother had made. Yet she understood the enormity of the situation at hand. Sheldon was inches from her grasp. She'd already missed his first birthday. She was being given a shot at being there for his second—without Jamari or any court-appointed professional to interfere. She wanted to cry. She was frustrated, and felt like she was being forced to forgive before she was ready to do so.

Edna knew what was bothering her child. "Jada," Edna said, softly. She handed her a tissue, and waited as Jada wiped her tears and blew her nose. "I'm not asking you to forgive me right away. All I want is for you to come and stay with me. You and Sheldon. And let's see if we can try to get along. Not for us. But for him, Jada."

Jada dabbed at her face with her tissue, and looked up at the sky for guidance, and sighed. She looked at Doyle, and nodded. "Okay. If it helps me get my son, I'll do whatever I have to."

Doyle breathed a sigh of relief, and led the two women back into the courtroom. The judge reconvened the case, and addressed Jada directly.

"Miss Ford, before the recess your mother indicated that should the court grant you custody, she is willing to allow the two of you to live with her until such time as you've exhibited a determination to remain clean and sober. Are you in agreement with that?"

Jada wondered if she understood exactly what the judge had just asked her. But she thought he was asking if she was willing to go and live with her mother if they gave Sheldon back to her. "Yes." She felt Doyle's reassuring hand on her back, and she exhaled.

The judge addressed Edna. "If I release your grandson to the two of you today, will you accept responsibility as his legal guardian, while the court conducts periodic visits to determine your daughter's suitability as a parent?"

"I will, your honor." Edna nodded her head affirmatively.

"Your honor, Miss Ford and her mother will comply with any regulations the court sets forth should they be awarded custody of Sheldon. There's nothing like a mother's love. And in this instance, Sheldon would be benefiting from the love of not one, but two mothers—"

"Spare me the melodrama, Mr. Doyle." The judge looked annoyed. "I don't need to hear that. I've made my decision. Sheldon Ford is released into the custody of his mother and grandmother for the period of six months. During that time, the court will appoint a social worker to go out to the custodial home for unscheduled visits with the child and his guardians. Is that understood?"

Jada wanted to cry for joy. "Yes. Thank you!"

"He will be monitored closely for signs of abuse. The home will be inspected for safety, and for any signs of neglect or unsanitary conditions. You will be required . . ."

Jada had stopped listening. All she knew was that her son was going home with her. She was getting Sheldon back. She was turning over a new leaf in her life, and she wanted to laugh and cry at the same time. She waited until the judge banged his gavel, and she hugged her lawyer tightly. Nelson Doyle hugged her right back, and then shook Edna's hand firmly. "Good luck to you two. Congratulations!"

Doyle left in order to complete the necessary paperwork to facilitate Sheldon's release. And Jada was left standing with her mother, shrouded in an awkward silence. Finally, Jada made eye contact with Edna, and saw a strength in her eyes that she had never seen before. "Thank you," Jada said. "I appreciate you doing this for me."

"You don't have to thank me, Jada. I owe you for all the times I let you down. I can probably never make up for what I did in the past. But I want to try. If you'll just let me."

Edna wanted to hug Jada, but decided against it. She wasn't sure if Jada was ready for that. Instead, she reached out her hand, and let Jada make the decision of whether or not to take it. Jada stood still, and hesitated briefly. She looked at her mother long and hard, seeing how beautiful Edna still was. Edna had lost a lot of weight, and her hair that had once been long and flowing was now cut short in a choppy style. But she was still such a pretty woman. Throughout her childhood, Jada had thought her mother was as lovely as she was shy and reserved. She smiled inwardly, seeing that Edna's beauty hadn't diminished over time. Jada was so happy to get her son, and so grateful to Edna for coming to her rescue at last. She took her mother's outstretched hand, and managed a weak smile. Together they went to bring Sheldon back home, where he belonged.

Jada moved out of her Brooklyn apartment and into Edna's home in Staten Island. The first few weeks were tense and awkward in the home. The two women rarely spoke to one another, unless it regarded Sheldon's well-being. Jada wasn't ready to make nice with her mother, and Edna didn't want to push too hard too soon. But one night Sheldon awoke after having a nightmare. And both women rushed to his bedside simultaneously. Jada scooped him out of bed, and cradled him lovingly in her arms. She rocked him back to sleep, as Edna stood in the doorway watching. As Sheldon fell into a deep sleep in the comfort of his mother's arms, Edna smiled.

"You know it's still amazing to see you now as a mother. I remember—it seems like just yesterday—that you were in my arms just that way."

Jada smiled, wishing that she, too, could remember. "I bet you wish you could snap your fingers, and start over. I guess I should cherish him being this little, huh? Someday he may be as much of a headache for me as I was for you." They both spoke softly, so as not to wake Sheldon.

Edna stepped into the room, and leaned against the dresser. She was so glad that Jada finally seemed ready to talk. "Your son is a lot like you were. He looks just like you, that's obvious. But Sheldon is also very strong-willed. He's very bright for his age, just like you were. And he smiles, and it melts the coldest heart."

Jada looked at her mother. She was happy to hear Edna say such nice things about her. But she was still getting used to their new relationship. She wanted to know what had prompted it. "Why did you come to court and do that for me?" she asked, getting right to the point. "How did you even know that I had a hearing that day?"

Edna pulled her bathrobe tighter around her small frame, and leveled with her daughter. "Your attorney called me. Your friend Sunny told him that he should see if I was willing to step up and help you win custody. They told me that they were threatening to put Sheldon in foster care because Jamari was dead. Sunny said that you were too stubborn to ask for it on your own, but she thought you needed my help. I told him that I would do anything to help you."

Jada laid Sheldon gently back in his bed, and tucked him in. She continued to sit on the edge of his bed, and she looked at Edna. "So Sunny orchestrated the whole thing, huh?" Somehow Jada wasn't surprised.

Edna nodded. "I'm glad she did. I was waiting for a chance to talk to you about everything that was happening. Everything that happened before." She searched for her daughter's eyes in the darkness of the bedroom. "Jada, I knew for a long time that you were using drugs. I knew when you were living with me, and you would come home high. You thought I didn't know, but I did. The same way I couldn't stand up to J.D., I couldn't stand up to you."

Jada hung on her every word. Edna folded her arms across her chest, and kept talking. "So I ignored it. I started going to church, and praying for you. I remember I used to beg you to go with me, and you refused. So I went by myself, and prayed and prayed for you. They kept saying that prayer changes things. And I wanted my prayers to change your problems. Every week I went to church, every night I pulled out my Bible and prayed for you. And then I caught you with Charlie."

Jada looked at the floor in silence, feeling ashamed. She hated that she had done that to her mother. She hated that she had fallen that far down to do something so terrible.

"Jada, I was so hurt when I found you doing that with him. But I wasn't just hurt because I liked Charlie. I made you get out because I couldn't handle it. I saw for the first time, just how strung out you really were, and I felt like you and Charlie had betrayed me. It was obvious that he knew you were using. Why else would a beautiful young girl like yourself want his old behind? I felt like an idiot. I was embarrassed. I was an emotional mess after that. I lost contact with everyone—you, your sister—everybody. Ava didn't hear from me for years, and I know you and her didn't speak either. I got a letter from you while you were in rehab for the first time. I read that letter so many times that the pages started to fall apart from all the folding and unfolding. But I couldn't find the words to write you back. What could I say to you? I was so angry with you, so disappointed. I just went into seclusion and all I did was go to church. I prayed for you all the time. I prayed for Ava, too. Ava wrote me a letter after Ms. Lopez, her counselor, convinced her to do it. And I wrote her back. One letter at a time, we put the relationship back together, and it wasn't easy." Edna took a deep breath, as if she was admitting something out loud to herself for the first time. "I don't want you to think that I love her more because I wrote back to her and not to you. It wasn't that. It was that her problems were small compared to yours. Our problems were easier to fix." Edna sighed. "I was never strong enough, Jada. I would always hide when the going got tough. And I hid when you got caught up. I ran to God, and threw my problems on the altar. People would come up to me and tell me that you and Shante were smoking crack. All I could do was keep praying. Looking back now, I think the Lord was telling me to go and find you and bring you home. But I couldn't do that. I didn't want to do that. And then, I saw you for myself."

Jada held her breath as she listened to her mother, and remembered the encounter vividly.

"You were in the corner store in West Brighton, and you looked a mess. I wanted to cry out to you, and hug you, and bring you home. And

I wanted to hit you all at the same time. But I didn't know how you would react to me, or if you wanted to talk to me. As grown as I was, I was scared of what you might say to me. So I walked away from you. That was the most heartache I have ever felt in my life."

Jada let the tears fall from her eyes, as she recalled the day her mother had walked past her in the store. Jada had been so desperate to get high, had no money, and was really at one of her lowest points. She remembered crying on her way home, devastated that her mother had walked past her. Now she understood that it had hurt Edna just as much.

Edna watched her daughter cry in the dark, and she knew that Jada remembered the day. "I wanted to reach out to you, but I was afraid. And the Bible says that God has not given us a spirit of fear. But he has given us a spirit of love, power, and a sound mind. So that voice in my head telling me not to reach out to you, telling me not to bring you home again—that was nothing but the devil. I didn't see it that way then. I thought that you were too far gone for me to help you. But then Ava told me about you and Born. How you got yourself together, fell in love, and you were living happily ever after."

Jada smiled at this, her face still slightly damp from crying. She knew that hers had been anything but a fairy tale. "Yeah, right."

Edna smiled, too. "Well, she was happy for you. And that was when Ava began trying to get you to come and talk to me. But you weren't ready, and I understood that. I was happy that you had cleaned yourself up. I thought that my praying had finally done the trick. Then Ava found you using one day at your house, and she left and came to stay with me. When she came to my house in tears, and I found out that you were back on drugs, I was devastated. I kept praying for you, Jada." Edna let a tear fall from her own pretty eyes. Her heart was breaking for her daughter's pain. "And the Lord really does work in mysterious ways. I picked up the paper one day, and saw that you had been arrested. I saw that as a blessing in disguise. At least you were going to get help. I wrote to you while you were away, and you never wrote me back."

Jada shrugged. "I didn't write you back because by then I felt like I didn't need you anymore." Jada knew that she was speaking bluntly, but she had little concern for whether Edna was disturbed by what she was about to say. "I don't think you really understand how terrible it was for me being out there all alone."

Edna was ready to listen, and really wanted to hear what her daughter had been through. "Come in the kitchen, and let's have some tea or something. We shouldn't talk in here and wake Sheldon back up."

Jada agreed, and followed her mother into the kitchen. She sat at the table while Edna got some water boiling for her tea. Edna turned around, and faced her daughter. She knew that this would be the night that it all came pouring out. Sitting before her was her child, who was no longer a little girl. Jada was a woman, with a child of her own. And both women had a lot to reveal. There was a lot to discuss.

"Jada, I want to tell you some things that you may not know. But first I want you to tell me everything that I don't already know. We both have a lot of catching up to do. For the past few weeks, we've been living under the same roof, barely speaking. I want to rebuild our relationship. But before we can do that, we have to clear the air. Tell me everything that you went through. From start to finish. I want to know when you started using cocaine, and everything that happened to you after you left." Edna sat down, across from her daughter, and waited for her to begin.

Jada took a deep breath, and began her story. She told her everything, from the time she and Shante started smoking crack to the day Jada got arrested while pregnant with Sheldon. She pulled no punches, and held no details back. She revealed to her mother how she'd resorted to selling her body for crack. She told her all about Mr. Charlie, and how he'd taken advantage of her vulnerable state of mind in the midst of her addiction. She told Edna about meeting and falling in love with Born, and how she'd lost him because she couldn't end her new relationship with drugs. Jada told her mother about the day she'd come looking for her mother, and that she'd known that Edna had been home that day, yet had refused to answer the door. She told her about the bricks she'd stolen from Jamari, and how she'd stashed the money at Ingrid's house. The only detail she left out was her and Sunny's roles in Jamari's murder. That would be one secret Jada would never reveal. She watched as her mother cried tears of regret as she listened to her daughter's heartbreaking story. Finally, when Jada was done, Edna wiped her eyes, and looked at her child.

"Jada, I know that saying sorry doesn't fix anything. Sorry is only a word. I can't change the fact that I left you all alone for so long. And I was home that day you came by to see me. I saw you through the peephole, and I couldn't bring myself to open the door. I thought I was giving you tough love. I thought that we had years ahead of us, and that forgiveness could come later on. But I see now that I was wrong." Edna sighed deeply, and shook her head. "I never should have turned my back on you. I gave up. I quit. And I should have had the strength to fight for you. But I didn't." She reached across the table, and took Jada's hand in hers. "When you were in the hospital, and you called me to come and get Sheldon, I wish I had come to get him. I really do. But I think now that maybe you had to come that close to losing him before you realized how glad you were to have him." Edna sounded like she was speaking from experience. "I have something to tell you, too," she said. "I found out a couple of years ago that I have breast cancer."

"*What?!*" Jada's face registered pure shock. "Why didn't you tell me?"

Edna shrugged her shoulders. "Well, for one you weren't talking to me, Jada."

"But I would have listened if you told me you were sick! Why didn't you make me listen . . ."

"I didn't want your forgiveness just because I'm sick. I wanted us to fix our relationship because we both wanted to. I didn't want your sympathy. To be honest, I don't think I deserve it. After all the pain you've been through, all by yourself . . . I have no right to expect you to feel sorry for me."

Jada began to cry. "So you still have it? Can't they treat it?"

Edna nodded. "I've been through chemotherapy. I've had a couple of operations to try and remove it. But it's spread, and now I have to get a double mastectomy."

Jada gasped, and the tears flooded down her cheeks. She understood finally why her mother looked so much thinner, why her once long hair was now cut so short. She imagined the pain Edna must have gone through while Jada was busy getting high. Jada imagined her mother's anguish, knowing that she had to have her breasts removed in order to try and conquer the disease that was ravishing her body. "Mommy, I'm so sorry." The words got caught in Jada's throat. Edna got up and walked over to embrace her daughter. They sat and cried together in the kitchen for all the years wasted with anger and bitterness. And when the tears subsided, they looked at one another with so much regret.

Finally, Edna spoke up. "I want to tell you what I've learned. Listen to me carefully." She held Jada's hands once again. "God is the only reason I'm still standing. He is the only one you need to get you through. Trust Him. I know I've made mistakes, and so have you. But the Bible says that all have sinned and fall short of the glory of God. Even as messed up as we are, He still loves us. You have a second chance with your son. And I have a second chance with my daughter. But the only way that we can even begin to fix what's been wrong for so long is if we lean on Him for strength. I'm not asking you to make a change overnight. But I will tell you this. You are not strong enough to beat this addiction by yourself. I know that you haven't used drugs in a while. But every day there will be hardship and pain, and you will be tempted to go back to the one way you know to numb that pain. The only one who can give you the strength to fight it and stay clean is God. That's your only hope. You have to pray, and trust that He will clean you up, and help you stand. I'm a witness, Jada. When I went to the Lord, I was a weak and broken woman who couldn't find the courage or the strength to fight the demons in my life. But He changed that. He is my strength. And He will be yours, too. All you have to do is let Him."

Jada nodded her head, listening to her mother's advice. She knew that if God could change Edna from the pushover she had once been into the survivor that sat before her now, that He could do the same for her. She hugged her mother, and they began from that evening on to mend their torn relationship. Jada accompanied her mother to church on Sundays, and every night they sat up after Sheldon went to sleep and talked about

any- and everything. Every day they added a piece to the puzzle until finally it looked like their relationship might reach completion. It was a
dream come true for both women, as they began to become friends as
well as mother and daughter. Edna had surgery to remove both breasts,
in hopes that the cancer would be completely removed. Jada helped her
mother through her recovery, and they shared many laughs and good
times in the months that followed. Ava came to spend the weekend once
a month, and the three women all enjoyed themselves spoiling Jada's son.
They played cards. They played Bingo for loose change, and baked cakes
together, just like the good old days, when they were little girls in Brooklyn. Jada helped her mother cook, and learned all her best recipes. And
Ava would brush, cut, and style Edna's hair. They had beautiful times.
Sheldon was thriving, and Edna's cancer seemed to be in remission. It
seemed as if they might get the fresh start they all needed as a family.

In June of the year 2000, the court deemed Jada a fit parent for Sheldon. She no longer had to submit to visits from Administration for Children's Services, and she was officially Sheldon's sole custodial parent.
Jada knew that she had gotten a second chance, and she thanked God for
it every day. Sheldon was almost two years old, and he was such a smart
and beautiful child. Jada loved him beyond measure. She used the money
she'd gotten from sheisting Jamari, and bought herself a house in Staten
Island, so that she could be close to her mother. She put the rest of her
money in the bank. Jada studied for and passed her GED and was proud
of herself. Through one of the members of Edna's church congregation,
Jada got a job working as an entry-level clerk in the accounting depart-
ment at a consulting firm. She was working full time, Monday through
Friday, and it wasn't long before she pursued her dream of going back to
school. She majored in journalism, and focused hard on completing her
education. She attended school three nights a week and on Saturdays.
She was determined to turn her life around, for good this time, and to
make her family proud. Edna watched Sheldon while Jada went to work,
and to school. He loved his grandmother to death, and she loved him
even more. They sang songs together, and played and danced together,

and Edna got the chance to be silly with her grandson, and to forget temporarily about all the pain, both emotional and physical, she'd endured in her lifetime.

Jada graduated from college in May 2005. Edna, Ava, Sheldon, Sunny, Mercedes, and Sunny's mother, Marisol, all came to cheer her on. As she walked across the stage and accepted her degree, they all cheered loudly for her. They didn't care how ghetto they sounded to the other people present. Only they knew the depths to which Jada had fallen, and they were proud of her meteoric rise to the top, where she belonged. Tough as she was, Sunny cried tears of joy for her friend. She was proud of Jada, and proud of herself for all that they had managed to accomplish despite their pasts.

Over the next two years, Jada became an assistant editor at a premier black women's magazine. She and Sheldon were closer than ever, spending their weekends taking road trips with Sunny and Mercedes, or just cuddled up on the sofa watching DVDs. They went to Edna's house every Sunday for her delicious home-cooked meals. Those Sundays were so special, and Jada found herself anticipating them each week. And then Edna had a relapse. Her cancer had resurfaced, despite the double mastectomy, and she was hospitalized. The doctor told Jada and Ava that Edna's prognosis was grim. Cloaked in sadness and regret, the sisters held vigil at their mother's bedside, trying to liven Edna's cold hospital room with laughter and memories. They would lie with Edna in her hospital bed, and reminisce on the good days, never mentioning the bad days. Despite the pain and the weakness Edna was enduring, those last days with her daughters made her smile. After being hospitalized for three weeks, Edna died, with Jada and Ava at her bedside.

Jada was distraught. Now that she had the relationship with her mother that she had longed for all her life, she was gone. Jada cried not only for the loss of her mother, but for the years they'd lost being mad at each other, and unwilling to forgive. She found solace only in the fact that she'd forgiven her mother before she died. She was happy that Edna had gotten to know Sheldon, and that he had been given the gift of having a grandmother who loved him. Despite all the pain she felt her mother had caused her, Jada missed her terribly. With Ava working on some big legal case in D.C., the responsibility of making Edna's funeral arrangements fell on Jada's shoulders. She set about the task of burying her mother, and of burying the pain of her past along with her.

AFTER THE RAIN

37
FORGIVENESS

January 9, 2007

Jada held her head in her hands, as if doing so would prevent her from remembering all the pain of her past. It was all more than she could stand at that moment. The last thing she needed was to be remembering these things, feeling this pain again. Getting the flowers that Born had sent to her, reading his note . . . it was enough to send her back along all the corridors of her recollection to places she hadn't visited in years. Jada was overwhelmed with so many emotions. Instinctively, she picked up the phone and called Sunny. Sunny had been her friend for so long. She knew Jada better than anybody. As dependable as ever, Sunny answered on the third ring.

"City morgue. You kill 'em, we chill 'em," Sunny answered, jokingly.

"That's not very funny, since I'm in the process of burying my mother, Sunny." Jada's voice was trembling as she shook her head at her friend's twisted sense of humor.

"Sorry. I didn't even think about that. I was only joking, girl. How you holding up?" Sunny asked.

"Not too good."

"What's the matter?"

Jada sighed, rubbing her head to try and stop the headache creeping up on her. "I got a package from Born today."

Sunny didn't respond right away. Instead, she let Jada's words linger for a few moments. "Wow. What was it?"

"Some flowers. He sent a note with them, and it didn't say much. But now I can't stop thinking about him, and about us. I thought I had dealt with all this shit, but—" Jada's voice trailed off, as she fought to compose herself.

Sunny listened intently, and heard the pain in her best friend's voice. "You want me to come over?" she asked.

Jada closed her eyes, and gripped the receiver tighter. "Yeah, could you? I need to get some of this shit off my chest."

Sunny knew that was exactly what Jada needed. "I'm on my way."

Born walked into his mother's apartment and smiled at his favorite girl. She stood in her kitchen, shredding cheese for her famous macaroni. "Wassup, old lady?" he asked playfully, kissing his mother on her round, brown face.

Smiling back at her only child, Ingrid said calmly, "I got your 'old lady.'" She swatted Born's hand away as he reached for a piece of cheese. "Don't come in here trying to eat up this cheese. Go on and look in the fridge and find something." As Born walked to the refrigerator, and looked around inside for something to nibble on, his mother watched him sideways. She loved to see her only child whenever he walked through her door. He was like a ray of sunshine in her life, and she loved him tremendously. She thought of how proud her husband would have been if he had lived to see his baby boy. No longer a baby, Marquis Graham was a tall young man, solid and well toned. He was always dressed to impress, even if he wasn't trying to, and his smile could be either mocking or sincere. His brown skin was reminiscent of his father's caramel complexion, and Ingrid knew that her husband would have been proud.

Born pulled up a chair at the kitchen table, and poured himself a bowl of Froot Loops. He ate his cereal as his mother filled him in on gossip he cared nothing about. He wasn't thinking about the goings on in the hood at that moment. His mind was on Jada. Born knew that she must be heartbroken about her mother's death. When he'd been with Jada, she was never close to her mother. But Born knew that she was hurt by Edna's absence in her life, and he had no idea whether or not they had reconciled prior to her death. When he'd seen Edna Ford's obituary in the paper, he couldn't resist the urge to send his condolences. Thinking about her, even after all this time, made him feel all the love he had tried to suppress for so long. *Jada.* Her name made his heart pause. Jada had taught Born about love, and about disappointment. She still had a place in his heart.

When Born was in prison, during his conversations with Ace, he realized that he had blamed her for more than just her own addiction. Born had told Ace the whole story of their relationship. Ace had listened, and he asked Born if he was so mad at Jada because of her own mistakes, or because she had repeated his father's mistakes? That made Born wonder if he should have handled things differently. Should he have gotten her into rehab and loved her out of her addiction? Or was walking away from her the right thing to do? He wasn't sure. But he knew that he had never been able to forget her. Almost ten years had passed, and Born still thought about her all the time. A song would come on the radio, and he'd remember dancing with her or singing to her. A movie would come on television, and he'd remember her persuading him to watch it with her. Someone would say a phrase that Jada used to say all the time. It seemed that there were reminders of their love everywhere he looked. There had been a time when it hurt to think about her. He had once believed that Jada had quit on him. But he wondered sometimes if it was the other way around.

"I sent Jada some flowers today." Born said it so matter-of-factly that Ingrid wondered if she'd heard him correctly. She turned and faced him, placing the cheese on the counter.

"You sent flowers to who?"

Born smiled slightly. "Jada, Ma. Her mother died. I saw the obituary in the newspaper. I don't know why, but I just felt like I had to send her something to let her know that I know how she feels."

Ingrid looked at her son. She heard what he wasn't saying. He made it sound like his concern for Jada was only about the death of her mother and how she must be affected by it. True, Marquis would understand what Jada must be feeling, since he himself had lost a parent. But Ingrid knew that there was more to it than that. She knew her son better than he thought. "How did you find out where she lives?" she asked, continuing the preparation of her macaroni and cheese.

Born sat back in his chair, and cleared his throat. "I called her sister. Ava gave me her address."

Ingrid stopped making the macaroni again. She turned and looked at her son, and wondered if she should ask her next question. "Her sister? Why are you keeping in touch with Jada's sister?"

Born shrugged his shoulders. Then, realizing what his mother suspected, he shook his head. "I know what you're thinking. It's not even like that, Ma. I never did nothing with Ava. That's my word. I wouldn't do that."

Ingrid scrunched up her lips in disbelief. "Since when wouldn't you do that? You forget that I know you, Marquis. I know that when you're hurt, there's really nothing you *won't* do to get back at the person who hurt you. I remember that child who cheated on you back when you were younger. What was her name? Well, whatever her name was, you sure did start screwing her best friend when you found out what she was doing while you were away. Don't think I forgot."

Born smiled, and shook his head. Damn, his mother had a good memory! Like an elephant. "Well, I didn't do that this time," he said. "I saw Ava when I was over in West Brighton handling some business, like a year ago. She was out there to see her mother, and I was standing in front of the store talking to my boy. She came over to me, and said 'hi.' I hadn't seen her since the time she stayed at my house for spring break. She told me that the real reason she had left so fast, when she came to stay with me and Jada, was because she had found out that her sister was using cocaine again." Born recalled his conversation with Ava that day in West Brighton. She told him about discovering her sister snorting a line in her bedroom, and explained the argument that followed. Ava had also been honest enough to tell Born that she was feeling him back then, and that that had been part of her reason for leaving. She had wanted him, and when Jada accused her of being jealous, Ava had to admit to herself that there was some truth in that. Ava had explained that she was in a committed relationship now, and happy. "But I had a crush on you something serious back in the day! I always knew that Jada was a lucky girl," she had said.

Born was flattered. After all, as pretty as Jada was, Ava was breathtaking. But Born's attraction to Ava had been purely physical. What he had felt for Jada went beyond all of that, and he was kind of glad that Ava had left when she did. If she hadn't, there was no telling what mistakes his libido would have caused him to make. As he stood and talked to Ava that day, Born had listened to her explain how Jada had gotten her life together. She told him that Jada had graduated college, and was doing big things. Born was happy to hear that Jada had pulled herself together.

As Ava spoke to Born that day, and saw that he still looked good, and that not much had changed, she couldn't help feeling like her sister had fucked up a good thing. She remembered the way he'd looked at her that day, when he'd found her naked in the bathroom, and she wondered if he replayed that day in his mind as often as she did. Born was sexy, and even though Ava was involved with someone she loved, she couldn't deny the fact that the mere sight of her sister's ex made her panties wet. But then guilt set in. This was *Jada's* man—well, at least he used to be. To get with Born would cross a line that Ava would never be able to come back from. She and Jada were still not as close as they had once been. But Ava wasn't grimy enough to play her sister and fuck her former man. She had cleared her throat and put her hormones in check. And then she gave Born Jada's phone number, so that he could call her if the mood struck him. She also gave him her business card, and smiled when his eyes widened upon discovering that Ava had become an attorney. He was impressed.

But Ava had unselfishly steered the conversation back to the subject of Jada. "I know she still loves you, Born," Ava had said. "Don't tell her that you got this from me, but you should call her someday. I'm sure she'd be happy to hear from you." And as hard as it was for her to do, Ava walked away from Born, and hoped that he would call her sister.

Ingrid nodded. "So you think Jada will be happy to hear from you?" she asked. "Y'all haven't spoken to each other since . . ." Ingrid stopped cooking for a moment and thought about it. "How long has it been since you last saw Jada, Marquis?"

Born finished chewing his cereal. "Almost ten years. We broke up in ninety-eight. I think she got locked up the following year, and by then so had I." Born chuckled at the irony in that. Both he and Jada had gone to jail, and it had changed their lives for the better. Ava had told him that her sister was clean, and that she had regained custody of her son after Jamari was killed. Born still hated the thought of Jada having Jamari's baby. Even though Jamari had been slain in a late-night drug deal gone bad (at least, that's what the police had called it), Born still hated Jamari, and he hated the thought of Jada ever letting him get close to her.

"Do you still love her?" Ingrid asked, without turning to face him. She didn't need to see her son's face in order to know if his answer was sincere or not. She could tell simply by the tone of his voice.

Born hesitated. He thought about it. And then he leveled with himself. "Yeah." He shoveled the last of his cereal into his mouth, and sat back in his chair. "But I'm having a hard time forgiving her. She hurt me." Born shrugged his shoulders. "And I still can't help it that I love her. I don't want her to feel no more pain."

Ingrid smiled with her back still turned. At least Born was admitting it now. "So what if she calls you?" Ingrid asked. "You know. To say thank you for the flowers. Will you meet with her?"

Born shrugged his shoulders, as if it didn't matter. But deep inside he was praying that Jada would call. "Yeah. I would meet her for drinks, or whatever, you know what I'm saying?" He tried to sound nonchalant. "If she calls."

Ingrid nodded outwardly, and inwardly said a silent prayer that Jada would pick up the phone and call Marquis. This was her big chance!

Sunny sat in the backseat of the red Aston Martin, her Dior shades perched perfectly on her nose. She looked across the water as they crossed the Verrazano Bridge. She loved autumn in New York City. The trees were all shades of red, brown, green, orange, and yellow blended together into a beautiful mosaic. She inhaled the cool air from the partially opened window and was so grateful to God for a chance to see such a beautiful day. Thinking back over her life, there had been many times she didn't know if she'd make it to see and appreciate a day this blissful.

Sunny's driver that day was Raul, a middle-aged black man. He was a good driver; kept the radio tuned to one's liking, and talked very little. Sunny liked that about him. She couldn't stand drivers who wanted to discuss current events or politics, sports or whatever else. Those types were never employed by her for very long. Sunny preferred a silent driver, like Raul. She had a lot on her mind.

She thought about Jada and about how sad she had sounded on the phone. They had both had more than their share of heartache in their lives. Both had been through hell. But Sunny always felt she was made of stronger stuff than Jada. Sunny was a bad bitch, and she knew it. But Jada was not as tough, despite her efforts to make the world believe otherwise. In Sunny's opinion, Jada was fronting. She could make believe real well, pretend that she wasn't incomplete in some places. But Sunny knew the truth. She knew that inside of Jada dwelled pain and distrust, and plenty of untold stories.

As they approached the toll plaza, headed for Staten Island, Raul held the EZ Pass up on the windshield. Sunny looked beside her, checking on her most precious cargo. Her nine-year-old daughter, Mercedes, sat calmly beside her in the backseat. Dressed in calf-length brown suede boots, a brown turtleneck, a denim jumper, and a matching jacket, Mercedes looked like a living ad for any children's clothing line. She looked as sweet as pie, with her light brown complexion and soft light brown curly hair. She was adorable. Seeing that Mercedes was secure, Sunny relaxed and directed Raul to Jada's place. The radio was tuned to KISS-FM, and Sunny couldn't help singing along to the oldie but goodie as it played: "I'm wishing on a star, to follow where you are . . ."

Raul smiled as Sunny continued singing off-key all the way to Jada's house. Raul couldn't help laughing at her. She was a gorgeous girl with a filthy mouth and an effortless charm about her. Sunny could make you cry from her verbal tirades, or melt you with her silky, sexy words, depending on her mood. She was, indeed, a handful.

But when it came to little Mercedes, Sunny was a pussycat. She loved her daughter, almost to the point of adoration. It seemed that, despite the hard life she had obviously lived, when Sunny gave birth to Mercedes, her life had reached its fulfillment. It was intriguing to all who knew Sunny as the hard rock from around the way to witness her melt like butter in the palm of Mercedes's hand.

By the time they pulled up in front of 104 Christopher Lane, Raul was happy that the trip had come to an end. Sunny may have been beautiful, but her singing voice was anything but. Sunny looked around at Jada's neighborhood and couldn't help feeling proud of her friend. The two of them had seen all types of shit—from back alleys to penthouse suites. And now Jada was living in suburbia—a cozy, quiet, tree-lined street in Staten Island, while Sunny resided in a deluxe Manhattan high-rise apartment building, complete with a doorman. She and Jada had once lived self-destructive lives. And now they both lived tucked among doctors, lawyers, and accountants. It was truly remarkable. But damn, what a high price they'd paid to get there.

Sunny was modeling now. She was no Tyra Banks or Naomi Campbell. Not yet, anyway. She did mostly print work and magazine ads, a couple of runway shows here and there during Fashion Week, but it was work nonetheless. Finally she was living her dream. The only thing working against her was her age. Sunny was in her early thirties, and in the modeling world that was considered very old. Most of the girls who got the big ad campaigns were in their teens and twenties. The competition was fierce, but Sunny was holding her own. Having invested much of what Dorian left her hadn't hurt either. Sunny was a rich socialite, spoiling herself and her daughter with the fruits of Dorian's labor, and with her own. She wanted for nothing, and she had enough money to live lavishly.

She dated smartly. A Knicks player for close to two years, and most recently a Golden Globe–nominated actor, whom she'd accompanied to the event. She was doing her thing and helping Jada pen a novel about the nightlife they'd enjoyed in their pasts. The two of them were learning how to balance motherhood and the single life. And more important, both of them were no longer addicts.

Sunny handed Raul a crisp fifty-dollar bill as he helped her from the car. He promised to return for her as soon as she called, and she smiled graciously. She helped Mercedes step from the car, and the two walked hand-in-hand up Jada's driveway.

Sunny rang the doorbell, and ran her fingers through her natural brown hair, which was long and luxurious. Her makeup was flawless, as usual, and Mercedes looked up at her mother adoringly. Sunny tapped her foot as she waited for Jada to open the door. When the door at last swung open, Sunny could see that her friend had been crying. Her nose was red, and her eyes were puffy.

Sunny hugged Jada, and rubbed her back. "Here you go with this crying shit again," she said.

This remark made Jada laugh, and Sunny smiled as she walked inside. Jada hugged Mercedes warmly, admiring her cute little outfit. "Baby girl, you get more beautiful each time I see you."

"Damn!" Sunny looked around at all the flowers that had been delivered, and shook her head. "People go too far with their condolences sometimes. It smells like a damn funeral parlor up in here!"

Just as she strolled into the living room, Jada's eight-year-old son, Sheldon, rushed over and threw his arms around Sunny's waist. "Wassup, Aunt Sunny!" He said it enthusiastically, genuinely happy to see her. Sheldon was always happy to see Sunny, the two of them sharing a unique bond. Over the years Sunny had spoiled him beyond reason. Sunny knew that she would never have another child. Mercedes would be her first and last. And aside from D.J.—Dorian's son with Raquel—she knew that Sheldon was as close as she would ever come to having a son. She gave him everything he wanted. Every chance she got, Sunny sent Sheldon presents, and she took him on expensive vacations. Jada smiled, grateful once more that her friend was such a positive force in Sheldon's young life. At a time when Jada was cloaked in darkness, it had been Sunny who had held up a flashlight for Jada to find her way. For this, and for many other reasons, Jada was eternally grateful to Sunny.

"Wassup, Sheldon?" Sunny pinched his cheeks as she always did, and Sheldon blushed. "Your face looks older, you're getting all tall. Pretty soon you won't have no time for Aunt Sunny."

"Nah, I'ma always have time for you, Aunt Sunny." Sheldon looked away shyly, and Jada laughed.

"Stop making my baby get all sensitive." Jada smiled as she said it. Sunny ignored her completely.

"Mommy's just hatin' 'cuz can't nobody make her big behind blush no more!" Sunny joked. Sheldon laughed, as Sunny tickled him.

Jada also laughed at this remark, because at five-foot-three and a solid size six, Jada was anything but big.

Sheldon hugged Sunny once more, and then smiled at Mercedes, who waited patiently on the sidelines. Mercedes loved Sheldon, and each time they played together she would entertain her mother with tale after tale of their adventures. They were so close in age that they played together for hours at a time. Grabbing her by the hand, he ran back to his room so that they could play with his Xbox. Sunny plopped down on the sofa, and Jada sat down as well. The card she'd received from Born sat looming on the coffee table.

Sunny scooped it up, and read it. When she was done, she sat back and looked at Jada. "So?" she said. "How did you feel when you got this?"

Jada shook her head, at a loss for words. "I felt like somebody sucked all the air out of my lungs. I haven't heard from him since . . . it's been years. It's crazy that he would contact me after all this time. How the hell did he know where I live?"

Sunny pursed her lips, and sucked her teeth. "Girl, please! He's the man out here. He knows everything that goes on in Staten Island. You can believe that. He's probably known where you've been since the day he last saw you." Jada closed her eyes at the thought of that, and Sunny crossed her legs. "So how do you feel about him after all these years, Jada?"

Jada chuckled somewhat, and looked helplessly at the ceiling. "I still love that man as much as I did almost ten years ago."

Sunny frowned. "How? Explain that to me. How can you still love a man who did that to you?"

Jada fell silent, and looked Sunny in her eyes. "He was the love of my life," she said.

Sunny looked at her friend like she was crazy. "He was the love of your what?" She was dumbfounded. Sunny pulled a cigarette out of her purse. She'd been swearing she was going to quit, but it was shit like this conversation that sent her reaching for a square. She lit it, and exhaled the smoke. "Don't get me wrong, Jada. I always liked Born. Him and Dorian were tight like brothers. And when y'all were together, I thought he really loved you. But I lost some respect for him after what he did to you. Girl, the nigga threw you out on the street with a muthafuckin' monkey on your back. And he was the love of your life?" Sunny's expression was incredulous.

Jada sat back, and folded her arms across her chest. "I hate him for throwing me away like garbage. But I can't help loving him still. I can't explain it. It probably sounds dumb, or whatever. But I think I'll always love him." Jada looked away from Sunny, her eyes staring at nothing in particular. "I guess it has a lot to do with his relationship with his father. But that's a long story."

Sunny stood up and walked over to Jada's small bar. She poured herself a drink, and returned to her seat on the couch. "Well then, start talking, girl. 'Cuz I got all night." Sunny stretched her legs across the sofa's cushions and got cozy.

38

SECOND CHANCES

Born walked into Anisa's house, using his own key, and dropped his jacket on the leather recliner. Seeing his son, Ethan, stuck in his usual spot on the floor in front of the TV playing Def Jam Fight For New York, Born smiled, happy to see his boy.

"Wassup, Dad?" little Ethan greeted his father.

"What up, boy?" Born lovingly rubbed his son's head and glanced at the TV screen in time to see Method Man knock Snoop Dogg into the path of an oncoming subway train. Born glanced at all the games Ethan had—Xbox, PlayStation, Game Cube, even the new PSP. He had the hottest games for each and every system. Born knew that it was overkill, that all of this was too much for one seven-year-old to have. But Born was determined that Ethan would have his every heart's desire provided to him by his father. For that reason, he went out of his way to fill Ethan's closet with every designer children's outfit by the likes of Phat Farm, Sean John, Rocawear, Akademiks, etc. Ethan had eleven pairs of sneakers—Jordans galore, Timberlands, Uptowns, and all that. Every two weeks he got a new pair of sneakers. The boy had a leather jacket, a Sean John snorkel, a suede Phat Farm coat, and a gold chain. Born even brought a hot hero from the local pizzeria to Ethan's school each day so that his son wouldn't be subjected to the school's lunch. Anisa refused to make his son lunch every night, so Born bought it for him, since Ethan hated the cafeteria food. It was that serious. He had everything a kid his age could ever possibly want, and his father was proud of that. Born enjoyed seeing Ethan enjoy the finest things.

To him, that was one of the marks of being a good father, ensuring that your child's wants and needs were fulfilled. Born wanted to do whatever was necessary to ensure that Ethan knew his father had his back no matter what.

Ingrid often told her son that what he did for Ethan was excessive. He was spoiling the child, giving him more clothes than necessary, more toys than any child could ever play with. But to Born, it was all part of doing whatever it took to feel like he was doing a better job at fatherhood than Leo had. Born's disappointing relationship with his father shaped the type of father he was to his own son. In his lifetime, Born had seen his share of death and destruction, sorrow and sadness. But on the day that Anisa gave birth to Ethan, he had finally witnessed the miracle of life. He had seen life and hope, and his outlook had changed drastically. For the first time in his life, he had a reason to live. Ethan was his everything.

His relationship with Anisa had changed long ago. They'd gone their separate ways not long after Ethan was born. When Born had first come home from jail, he had called Anisa, wanting an explanation for why she'd left him all alone while he was away. Anisa had apologized for her disappearing act, and begged Born to come and see her. He did, and he spent some time with her, and caught up on some much needed sex with her. But to him, that's all it was. Sex. Then, to Born's surprise, Anisa had discovered that she was pregnant. When she'd first told him about her pregnancy, Born had mixed emotions. His intention had never been to get involved seriously with Anisa. She was just a plaything for the time being, and he wondered if he could trust her. What if she was lying about him being the father of her child, in order to trap him? To be certain, he insisted on having a paternity test when Anisa gave birth. Sure enough, Ethan was his son, and Born assumed the role of fatherhood like a pro. He changed Pampers and went to doctor appointments. He was such a good father to Ethan that Ingrid couldn't help beaming with pride whenever she saw them together. From day one, he was hands-on.

He wished Anisa hadn't been the one who wound up being his baby's mama. But he was happy to have his son, and knew that Ethan would be the reason that he changed his life for the better.

Born had given Anisa a chance to redeem herself after Ethan was born. And he tried forgiving her for the sake of their new family. But something inside of him wouldn't let him get past the way she'd abandoned him while he was locked up. Something wouldn't allow him to let go of the fact that she had proven herself to be untrustworthy. Anisa tried to look and act the part of Born's ideal woman. Still, no matter how she tried, in Born's eyes she was just the young lady who'd been lucky enough to have his firstborn. He still hit it every now and then. But Born knew that there was no real future between them. Still, in his determination to ensure Ethan's well-being, Born set her up in a nice one-family home on Bement Avenue. He spent the night with her every once in a while. But he had his own home—a duplex condo off of Richmond Avenue—where he spent the majority of his time. He gave Anisa money for whatever she needed, and spent tons of money on their son. This was his way of ensuring that Anisa didn't cause him any baby mama drama, and also that she wouldn't move too far away from him and take his son away. Anisa didn't date much. Not publicly, anyway. She had one or two "maintenance men," whom she called for physical emergencies, whenever Born got tired of servicing her. But she dated none of them seriously. Anisa held out hope that she could sucker Born into having another baby with her. That, she figured, might restore her to the number-one slot in his life. Especially now that he was getting involved in the entertainment industry.

Born had come home from prison, and gone back to getting money with Dorian's crew. But it didn't feel right to him anymore. Born was growing tired of the game. Having had so much time to think while he was away, he'd come to some conclusions. Drugs had destroyed the lives of those around him, and they had come damn close to destroying his. Leo was gone, and so was Jada, in a sense. He thought about Ace, just coming down from a twenty-year bid, and about his half siblings, who were still strung out in this day and age. And he thought about all the years he'd spent in jail, years he had lost forever. He wanted to be there for his son, and the risk of going back to jail or being killed in the streets was a risk no longer worth taking. Born began looking for an exit from the game.

While still doing business with Dorian's crew, Born opened a sneaker store in Park Hill, on Targee Street. He did good business with that, and used it as a front for the few shady dealings he still had left to handle. He enjoyed the day-to-day operations of running his store, but the money wasn't nearly enough to entice him to leave the game alone completely. Eventually, he also took over Slim's barbershop, and that business was successful as well. Still, Born was reluctant to do anything other than the one thing he'd done all his life—hustle. The legitimate businesses were merely excess income. It just allowed him to keep putting money away for Ethan's future, as well as for Dorian's son.

D.J. was being raised by his uncles. And part of what bothered Born was the fact that he knew that Dorian would have been displeased with how his son was being brought up. Born knew what Dorian had wanted for D.J.'s future, because it was very similar to what he wanted for his own son. An education, without having to worry about paying for it. A chance to go to college, or to play professional sports, or to get into the entertainment industry. The sky was the limit for their sons, because of the work their fathers had put in, and the connections they'd made along the way.

But D.J. was being groomed to be a heartless, fearless hustler. Born knew that Dorian would not have wanted that life for his son. Not so soon, anyway. D.J. was fifteen years old, and rarely went to school. He was constantly on the road with his uncles, learning the game and soaking up all the wrong shit. Born felt a sense of responsibility toward the youngster. After all, he himself had once been groomed as Dorian's successor. He began to put in more time with Dorian's son.

D.J. wanted to be a rapper. And he was good enough to be a multi-platinum success, if only he were given the chance to do something other than learning the game. Whenever Born went to spend time with D.J. — as he constantly did, often for days at a time—he took him to a recording studio to help him learn the industry, meet artists, and cut demos. Born used his connection with Zion, his childhood friend who was well connected in the music industry, which allowed him access to all the best studios in New York City. They spent hours at the Hit Factory, where hundreds of artists over the years had created timeless classics. Born drilled it into D.J.'s head that someday he might be among those who had created number-one hits in that very same studio. D.J. was excited whenever Born came to pick him up, because he knew that Born took a genuine interest in what interested D.J. Music. And getting into the industry seemed like an attainable goal, not something that was beyond his reach.

Born also talked to D.J. about his father all the time. Not in the way that D.J.'s uncles spoke about Dorian. They made him sound like a Nino Brown type of guy, who had made a fortune by taking no prisoners in a game so ruthless that it would chew you up and spit you out if you weren't careful. They made Dorian sound like he was 100 percent hustler, and nothing else. But that wasn't how D.J. remembered his father. He remembered Dorian being a very handsome man, who drew all the attention whenever he walked into a room. He remembered Dorian as the ideal father, who taught his son to play ball and shared a love for music with him. He remembered Dorian as a good man, just as Born remembered him. A loyal and trustworthy friend with a heart of gold. Not one made of stone, the way D.J.'s uncles portrayed him. As young as D.J. was, he knew that Born had been a true friend to his father. He could tell by the way Born took responsibility for him, as if he were his own son. Born talked to D.J. about girls, about life, in a way that a father would. He didn't sugarcoat his past. Instead, he described in explicit detail the way he had come to know Dorian, and the ways in which they'd taken the game and played it to the end. Born let D.J. know all the pitfalls that came along with being a hustler. He explained why he wanted to get out of the game, told him all about his past. And, by leveling with Dorian's son as if he were a *young* man as opposed to a *grown* man, Born gained D.J.'s respect and admiration. D.J. could clearly understand why the man who had become his mentor and father figure had also been his father's best friend.

Seeing how D.J. related to him made Born extremely proud. He loved him as if he were his own son, and he knew that Dorian would be proud of how Born was helping to shape and mold him into a strong and determined young man.

His time in the studio began to pay off. D.J. auditioned for a chance to battle on *Cipher Sundays,* a rap freestyle competition, in which contestants battled for the chance at a recording contract. He was thrilled when they called him for the show, and Born worked with him to get ready for his big shot. He really believed that D.J. had what it took to go the distance. Already, he'd been in freestyle ciphers in Brooklyn, and uptown, and D.J. had held his own, and made Born proud. Born had ensured that D.J. had been exposed to all the areas of the industry that he himself had access to. He figured Dorian's son was ready for the world.

When D.J. won the first round of the competition, everyone began to pay attention. Dorian's brothers, who up to that point had only seen rapping as a pastime D.J. enjoyed when he wasn't soaking up the game, began to take notice. They were still a little skeptical that he had what it took to compete on such a high level. Many youngsters dreamed of being famous rappers, yet few actually achieved that goal. But after watching him on TV, and seeing him demolish the competition, everyone in their family began to take notice of his talent. For five consecutive weeks, D.J. conquered opponent after opponent, and the title of *Cipher Sundays* Champion was within reach.

Dorian's two brothers—William and Lamont—invited Born over for a meeting at Lamont's house. They explained that they wanted to talk to him about D.J. and his career. When he got there, D.J. had smiled at him as if he knew something that Born didn't know. He did. Dorian's brothers sat Born down, and explained that they'd thought D.J. was best suited to follow in Dorian's footsteps in the streets. But after seeing D.J. pummel the competition for more than a month on *Cipher Sundays,* they were convinced that he had a different destiny. Finally, they believed that

D.J. had what it took to be a rapper. And, they explained, the reason they had called Born over to discuss this was because they wanted him to be D.J.'s business manager. D.J. already had a terrific chemistry with Born, and it didn't hurt that Zion—a man with considerable industry connections—had suggested, and almost insisted, that Born be the man chosen to manage D.J. Both Born and D.J. were thrilled at their new business relationship, and Born began to see that this might be his big chance to get out of the game once and for all.

D.J. went on to win the last two rounds of *Cipher Sundays,* and everyone was ecstatic. It was on! D.J. was the champ, and almost every major record label was interested in signing him. He was a teenage ingenue, with the charisma and personality of a seasoned hustler. His interviews were flawless, and D.J. effortlessly displayed a mixture of humility and pride that made fans embrace him by the thousands. Born spent his days negotiating contracts, and getting D.J. in the studio. Born gave him feedback on his songs, suggesting lyrics from time to time. But for the most part, D.J. wrote his own rhymes, and Born offered constructive criticism, helping D.J. shape an image for his growing legion of fans. Zion assisted him in choosing producers, and in obtaining media coverage for D.J., and soon they inked a great deal with one of the biggest labels in the industry. D.J. was featured in major urban magazines, as well as on MTV and BET. He was on his way. Everyone could tell that this was only the beginning for the young powerhouse.

And ever since she'd heard the news, Anisa had been more anxious than ever to sink her claws back into Born. She knew that, as he began touring with D.J., he would inevitably meet beautiful and successful women. She wanted to try and get back "in" before that happened. Born saw her clearly, though, and he paid her no mind.

Born left Ethan in front of the television and walked into the kitchen. He found Anisa sitting at the table with her two good friends, Kiara and Precious. Born groaned inwardly, not exactly thrilled to see these two bitches sitting in the kitchen.

"Hey, baby." Anisa smiled at Born as he entered. Her hair was freshly done, highlighting perfect cheekbones and a glorious smile. She was a pretty girl; still, Born knew that an ugly side existed within her. Anisa was all about the Benjamins, and Born knew that, since she was being nice today, she must want some money.

"Hey," Born greeted Anisa, and said, "Wassup, y'all?" to the other two.

"Whattup, big baller, shot caller?" Precious's ghetto ass responded. "You came just in time. We was just talking about Anisa's birthday, which you should know by now is coming up. And we think you should get us a limo and let us take Anisa to Atlantic City to celebrate."

Born walked over to the refrigerator, completely ignoring Precious's audacious comment. Kiara chimed in. "You only turn thirty once, Born. Don't you want Anisa's birthday to be memorable?"

What Born wanted was to tell these gold-digging hos to get the hell up out of his house. After all, it was *his* house. Anisa just lived there. But instead of saying that, he poured himself something to drink and continued pretending he hadn't heard a word. Finally, Anisa spoke up.

"Born, you don't have to be so rude. You could just say yes or no. It's that simple." She folded her arms across her chest, sat back in her chair, and rolled her eyes at his back. Precious grimaced at Born from behind, and Kiara giggled quietly.

Born sipped his iced tea, and turned around to face the women in his kitchen. "Y'all bitches is crazy if you think I'm coming out of pocket to send y'all *anywhere*."

"Born!" Anisa cried, defending her friends.

He continued talking. "Y'all better roll some quarters, or sell some ass, or do something so you can go to Atlantic City. 'Cuz I ain't paying for a muthafuckin' thing. Don't come at me with dumb shit."

"Born!" Anisa looked steamed.

"What? You knew that shit was dumb when they started talking." Born frowned, turned, and walked out of the kitchen.

Anisa avoided looking at her friends, until finally Precious said, "I told you his cheap ass wouldn't pay for it."

Born went back into the living room, picked up the extra joystick, and played a game with his son. He could hear Anisa's voice mixed with those of her friends as they continued talking and cackling in the kitchen.

Within an hour or so, the two guests left, and Anisa came to see what Born was up to. He knew she had an attitude about how rude he had been to her friends, but Born didn't really give a damn.

"Why you had to be so mean, Born? You know how Precious is. You know how she acts. She didn't mean no harm."

Born shrugged. "I don't care what she meant by it. Ain't no free rides over here. Whoever don't like that, they can kiss my—"

"Okay, okay. I get the point. But, it *is* my birthday weekend, and I *would* like to go to Atlantic City with my friends. So can I have some money to pay for the hotel room—"

"Hotel room? How long are you planning to stay there? It's, like, two hours away, so what the hell do you need a hotel room for?"

"Just for the weekend, Born. And this is all I want you to give me for my birthday." Anisa batted her pretty, long eyelashes at him. "Pleeeease. It's close by, so you'll be able to get in touch with me if Ethan needs me, or something."

Born knew that Anisa really didn't concern herself with Ethan as much as she should. Born played the role of Mr. Mom, while Anisa was busy being a diva. She was a good mother, but not what one would call a supermom. Born decided to give in so that he could have some valuable alone time with his son. He figured it would be better to have Anisa out of his face for a little while. Fuck it. "Go ahead and make the reservations, and I'll pay for your room," he said. "But you three can get down there the best way you can."

Anisa smiled, pleased with the outcome. She didn't need a limousine, as Precious had suggested. She could always drive her Range Rover instead. She hugged Born, and then ran off to call her girls to give them the good news. Born finished his game with Ethan and made sure that he ate dinner and took a bath. Then he tucked Ethan into bed, kissed him good night, and prepared to head home.

But when he peeked his head inside Anisa's bedroom to say good-bye, she pulled him inside and kissed him deeply. She pulled him closer to her, until the heat of their bodies was too much for either of them to ignore. They had sex on top of the covers of her queen-size bed, and then

Anisa fell asleep almost immediately. Born laid in bed beside Anisa, watching her sleep. He thought about slipping out while she snored softly. But instead, he lay there fitfully tossing to and fro, not realizing that Anisa's peaceful slumber was a hoax. She knew, as she feigned sleep, that something had Born lying awake later than usual. Something had him troubled.

Born thought about Jada. He thought about her voice, the way she sounded so sexy, especially in the morning when she first woke up. He remembered how they used to talk until the wee hours of the morning about any- and everything. Jada had stimulated his mind like no other woman since. She had made him think about things that he probably never would have thought about otherwise. And he missed that.

Sunny was exhausted. After drinking a whole bottle of Hennessy, talking to Jada for hours about their past, and ordering pizza for Sheldon and Mercedes, she had finally ended her conversation with Jada and gone to sleep beside her daughter. It wouldn't be the first time Sunny had gotten lit and camped out at her friend's place. The two of them were so close that they made themselves at home whenever they visited one another. Jada looked in on Sunny and Mercedes sleeping comfortably in the guest bedroom. Sunny was sprawled out in the queen-size bed, with Mercedes nestled peacefully beside her.

She shut the door and then looked in on Sheldon, who was knocked out in his own bedroom. Jada looked at the assorted sports paraphernalia scattered throughout the spacious room and smiled, thankful for the second chance she'd been given to be a mother to her child.

She took a long, hot shower, and washed and conditioned her hair. Then she moisturized her skin with lotion and pulled on an oversized T-shirt that she liked to sleep in. She wrapped her hair up in a silky scarf and walked into her bedroom. Her feet sank into the plushness of her thick carpet. She loved the feeling of climbing onto her pillow-top mattress and lying back across her sky blue comforter. What a day it had been. Her conversation with Sunny had conjured up lots of things she'd long ago forgotten. She stared at the ceiling, thinking about all the memories her conversation with Sunny had brought back. Jada toyed with the card in her hand and read Born's script for the thousandth time:

Believe it or not, I still think about you all the time. And I'm sorry for your loss.

She smiled. He still thought about her. He was sorry for her loss. She wondered why those words meant as much to her as they did. She thought about their story, about all the things that she and Sunny had discussed that evening—both good and bad. Jada remembered the love she had shared with Born, and the pain of losing him, as if it were all recent. But at that moment, what consumed her was an overwhelming need to talk to him.

Jada fluffed up one of the seven pillows on her bed, and laid her head on it. She closed her eyes, and could see Born's face so clearly. She could see his lips vividly, lips she used to love to kiss, lips that had taken her to ecstasy countless times. Jada opened her eyes, hating herself for ever going back to where she swore she'd never go, back to the drugs and the crazy lifestyle, and leaving Born and all his love for her behind.

She picked up the phone and dialed the cell phone number quickly, before she could think better of it. She listened as the phone rang several times, and she tried to control herself, tried to calm down. After five rings, Jada got ready to hang up. But as she pulled the phone away from her face, she heard his voice.

"Hello?" Born sounded like he was asleep. She put the phone back to her ear and waited. "Hello?" he repeated, his voice husky, and so damn sexy after all these years.

Jada sat there in the silence of her bedroom, and realized that she had no idea what to say. She hung up without uttering a word, and she buried her face in the pillows. Damn! He still had a voice that melted her like butter. Jada's heart beat rapidly in her chest, and she hugged her pillow close to her. The man still had the power to make her weak.

Born woke up to the ringing of his cell phone. The caller ID read "Unknown Number," and he wondered who would be calling him this late from a private number. He couldn't sleep as it was, although he had been lying in the dark for about two hours. He got out of bed, and walked into his son's room. He saw Ethan sleeping peacefully, and he was content with that. Born walked downstairs and sat on the couch in the dark. His eyes were completely adjusted to the moonlight glowing in the windows. He sat down, and once again, she was on his mind. Jada. He wondered if it was she who had called.

Born fell asleep on the sofa downstairs, sitting alone in the dark, thinking about the past. He dreamed that they were all together again: him, Jada, Dorian, and Sunny, all together in a car, driving to an unknown destination. In his dream, Dorian looked over at Born riding shotgun. The ladies were chattering as usual in the backseat. Dorian smiled at Born, and said, "I been in this game a long time, my nigga. You feel me? I've seen a lot of things, and met a lot of people, made a lot of connections. But you are the best friend I've ever had. You got what it takes to do everything I did, and then some. So remember this. You only get one shot, Born. You hear me? Just one shot." He held up his index finger to illustrate his point.

In his dream, Born didn't ask what Dorian meant, because in his heart, Born already knew. He meant that you only get one shot at life. And you damn sure better not waste it.

39

BURYING THE PAST

Jada woke up the next morning with the difficult task of her mother's wake looming ahead of her. The viewing of Edna Ford's body was to be held that evening at seven o'clock, and Sunny had agreed to watch Sheldon while Jada handled her daughterly obligations. Jada wanted to spare Sheldon at least one day of sadness and grief. He would attend his grandmother's funeral, but he didn't need to be present at her wake. The wake was still hours away. Jada sat at the breakfast table, amazed that Sunny had prepared French toast, eggs, and sausage all by herself.

"Girl, I didn't know you had it in ya!" Jada munched on the soft, sweet bread drenched in syrup. "You have never been domestic. When did you learn to cook?"

Mercedes and Sheldon smacked their lips as they devoured Sunny's breakfast. Sunny laughed, pleased that everyone was enjoying her cuisine. "I learned how to cook after Mercedes was born. Even though I have Jenny G., I still like to cook for her myself every now and then." Jennifer Gonzalez was Sunny's housekeeper. She came by every day, except Sundays, to clean up Sunny's spacious high-rise apartment, and to prepare meals for her and Mercedes. Sunny paid Jenny G. a very competitive wage, and in turn she got whatever she needed from the Dominican woman. She cooked, cleaned, ironed, ran errands, answered phones. Whatever Sunny wanted, Sunny got it, and Jenny G. was more than happy to do it. After all, she was an illegal immigrant who spoke little English. Sunny spoke Spanish, thanks to her mother, and was happy to have her daughter exposed to a second language as well. In spite of her lack of credentials, Jenny G. was getting paid in full, and she knew well enough to shut the fuck up and jump whenever Sunny told her to. Jada had never guessed that Sunny knew how to cook. For Sunny, it wasn't that she didn't know *how* to do it. She just very seldom *wanted* to do it. "There's a lot that you don't know about me," Sunny said, winking at Jada.

Jada laughed. "Yeah right. I know everything there is to know about you, Sunny. I could write a book on your behind!"

Sunny smiled big at the thought of that. She nodded. "And it would be a bestseller!"

The women slapped each other five, and enjoyed their food. When the kids were done eating, they went to watch TV, and Sunny looked at her friend from across the table. Jada looked bewildered. "What?" she asked.

Sunny folded her arms across her chest, and sat back in her seat. "Last night, when we went to bed, I did a lot of thinking before I fell asleep. You should call Born. He's obviously thinking about you." She shoveled some food in her mouth, and looked at Jada expectantly.

Jada shrugged. "That's easier said than done," she said. "I mean, I would definitely like to talk to him. But what would I say? Where the hell do I even begin?" She shook her head. "I'll think about it."

She finished her breakfast and then went to get dressed. Jada put on a black Donna Karan pantsuit and went on her way to her mother's wake. She paused at the door, and looked at her watch. "Ava's supposed to meet me at the church before the wake begins. We'll finish talking when I get back," she said to Sunny as she kissed Sheldon good-bye. Jada headed down the driveway and got inside her SUV. Sunny shut the door and returned to the living room, while the children played in Sheldon's room.

Sunny sat on the sofa and looked at the photo albums stacked on Jada's coffee table. She picked one up, flipped through it, and saw a picture of Jada and her sister as children. They looked like two peas in a pod. She saw some other pictures that she assumed were pictures of family members whom Sunny didn't recognize. And then she saw it.

A picture of Born at the birthday party they'd thrown for him aboard the cruise ship was on a page all by itself. Born was smiling, his dimples prominent. She looked at the man standing beside Born with his arm flung over his young apprentice's shoulder. *Dorian.* He looked so happy, with his sexy smile gracing his brown face. The stars over New York Harbor twinkled in the background, and Dorian's eyes seemed to sparkle just as brightly.

Sunny sighed, and thought about how things had changed after her confrontation with Dorian that night. Born's party had taken place on the same night she had confronted Dorian about his infidelity, and he had confronted Sunny about her addiction. With Dorian's help, Sunny had cleaned herself up. Dorian had helped her every step of the way. She thought about how much she loved that man. How much she truly missed him. Sunny shed some long overdue tears, and she reminisced on the love they'd had. Damn, she missed him. Not a day went by that he didn't cross her mind. Sunny sat there alone, and cried for the love she'd been stripped of way too soon.

Meanwhile, Jada entered the church on Richmond Terrace, and smelled a sanctuary full of flowers that had been sent over to commemorate Edna Ford. Edna had been heavily involved in the church, and was a born-again Christian. Over the years, she had become a fixture at Sunday service, and at Wednesday night Bible study. And during the time that Jada had lived with Edna, she'd accompanied her mother to church every Sunday. The whole congregation had embraced Jada. And she had learned that you don't have to pray using big words, or a scripted monologue. You could speak to God from your heart, and he would still hear you, and still listen. Jada had prayed at the altar countless times, holding her mother's hand. She'd prayed for strength to stay clean and sober, and she hadn't touched any drugs in eight years. She had prayed for a job so that she could support her son, and one of the members of the congregation had helped her get the job she now held at the magazine. She had prayed for forgiveness for all the things she'd done wrong in the past, and that she continued to do wrong. And she hoped that God had heard, and had answered that prayer as well. These days Jada no longer went to church every Sunday. Instead, her appearance at Sunday service was more like an event that took place quarterly. But she still prayed every day, and she was grateful that her mother had brought Jesus into her life. She sure did need Him now.

She saw the undertaker from Sanderson Funeral Home standing at the altar near Edna's casket, preparing the body for the viewing at that evening's wake. Jada's heart caught in her throat, as she realized *fully,* for the first time, that this was it. This was final—death. Her mother was gone forever, and she'd never get the chance to play cards with her or cook with her, or even to pray with her, again.

But that was her reason for being an hour early. The wake began at eleven o'clock and it was only ten. Jada needed some time alone with her mother. She allowed the undertaker a few minutes to complete his duties, and then she gingerly stepped closer to the coffin. Her mother lay there, her body thin and frail, and her hands folded across her belly. Jada looked at her mother's face, and she smiled. Her face was still as lovely as it had been when Jada was a little girl, staring at her mother in awe.

Her gaze fell again to the hands that told the true story. Her mother's hands, with wrinkles and veins looking as twisted as the journey Edna had taken through life. Edna's hands were folded across her stomach— over her womb. Jada thought of the irony of Edna's hands being clasped over her womb—the same womb that had held her and Ava. But in Jada's memory, the womb was the only time Edna had offered protection to her young daughters. Once they had emerged into the hard, cold world, Edna had let them fend for themselves. But when she had needed her most, Edna had finally stepped up and given Jada the love and attention she had needed to clean up her act. Edna had saved not only her relationship with Jada, but also Jada's relationship with her son.

"Wow," she said, wiping the tear that had rolled down her right cheek. "I think you look lovely in that dress." Jada had chosen the cream-colored silk dress for her mother, thinking she would look pure and free. Looking down on her mother now, Jada thought she looked angelic.

"I don't even remember the last time I actually told you that I love you," she said, gently touching her mother's body. "But I do. I love you."

"She knows you do, Jada."

The voice came from behind her, and Jada spun around to face it. She smiled through her tears, as she saw her sister standing there. Ava looked amazing as usual. Her long hair still hung past her shoulders. She wore a tailored black suit, and her figure was flawless. Ava took off her Gucci shades and closed the distance between them, walking toward Jada. Jada wanted to jump for joy as she embraced her sister, still crying. When she hugged Ava, it felt the same way it had the night that they had cried together before Ava's suicide attempt. Once again, they were scared little girls from Brooklyn left to find their way together. Once again, they were yearning for their mother's protection, which would never be theirs again.

Their hug was so intense that they clung to each other, both of them needing their sister for strength. Ava finally pulled back and looked at Jada.

Jada smiled, but it quickly faded. "I don't know how I feel about this." Jada was being entirely honest. "I don't know if I feel more happy that she's not suffering through treatment anymore, or sad that she's gone." Jada wiped her eyes. Sadness and pain weighed heavily on Jada's heart. She looked silently at her mother's dead body and held tightly to her sister's hand.

Ava looked at her sister and said nothing for a few silent moments. Then she led her to the very first pew in the church nearest their mother's casket. She sat down, and Jada sat beside her, and they looked at each other.

Ava crossed her legs, and propped her elbow on the back of the cushioned bench. "Mommy loved you more than anyone else in this world," she said.

Jada shook her head in disbelief. She knew that Edna had cared for her, but surely Ava must have been her favorite. Ava had done everything right. She had never gotten addicted to any drugs, never been arrested. Ava was the "famous" attorney who Edna always bragged about when she was working on high-profile cases. Ava was well traveled, and wasn't weighed down by a relationship or kids. She was free, and living her life perfectly. Jada was just the black sheep of the family who had turned her life around in time and had managed to become a success after being a failure for so long. "I don't think that's true," Jada said.

Ava grinned. "I'm telling you, Jada. During the years that you weren't speaking to Mommy, me and her did a lot of talking. I would come back to New York to check on her, and to see if she was lonely, or if she needed anything. And every time I came to see her, she talked about you. She admired you so much, even when you were strung out. I have her personality. I'm reserved, and I play it safe, and all that. But Mommy said that you were more like Daddy. She said that he was never the type to back down from a fight. That he was fearless and bold and sometimes loud."

Both sisters laughed, knowing that Jada had been a hell-raiser in her youth. Ava continued. "But Mommy admired that about you. She said that you got all the strength that she never had. And she said that you were stubborn, and that was why you had such a hard time forgiving her. But when you went to live with her, she was the happiest I had ever seen her, Jada. She had you back, and she was so glad. She knew that you forgave her. Even if you never said it. Because actions always speak louder than words. She knew that she had your forgiveness. And you should know that you had hers, too." Ava looked at her sister, still beautiful after all the storms she'd weathered. "I used to be so jealous of you, Jada."

Jada frowned, and looked at her sister in surprise. "Jealous of what? You lived your life way better than I did."

Ava smiled. "Exactly. I felt like I had done it all the right way. And yet you still managed to get all the attention, all the time. You got the great guy. Born was so sweet, and so handsome. You had the cool girlfriend, and the fabulous wardrobe. The day I walked in on you getting high, you said that I was jealous, and wanted what you had. In a way that was true. And even Mommy longed for you. I always knew she loved me, and that she was glad that I forgave her. But she missed you. She was incomplete without you. She wanted your forgiveness so badly. And when she got it, she started living again. I was hating a little sumthin'."

Jada smiled, amazed, because she'd never suspected that this was the case. "Well, you never showed it. I wouldn't have guessed that. For so long I was jealous of you, too. But I think she loved both of us equally. She was probably just happy that I managed to clean up my life's mess."

The pastor entered the sanctuary, and cleared his throat. He saw the siblings in the midst of what had obviously been an emotional discussion, and he was sorry he had to interrupt.

"Ladies, it's eleven A.M. now, and I see some cars pulling up. I just wanted to let you know, so that you can prepare yourselves for that." Reverend Wilkins was a distinguished older man in his fifties. His salt-and-pepper hair was always styled to perfection, like Steve Harvey's, and his suit was well fitted. He was a good man, with a virtuous wife and a devoted following. He smiled warmly at Edna's daughters, and felt like he knew them well. Edna had spoken of them during her testimonies over the years. She'd shared with them the pain of having a daughter addicted to crack, and then the pride of having a daughter turn a horror story into a success story. He had prayed with Edna for Jada's recovery, prayed that God would loose the young lady from her shackles. And he hoped that Edna could see now that prayer really changes things.

The sisters thanked the pastor for his help, both of them shocked that an hour had passed so quickly. Jada turned to her sister, and felt the sorrow they both were cloaked in. She said, "I know I should have told her this more often when she was alive, but I loved her. I love you, too, Ava. I mean that."

Ava smiled, big and beautiful. "I love you, too, Jada." They hugged, and fixed their clothes in preparation for the process of greeting the well-wishers.

"Where are you staying while you're in town?" Jada asked.

Ava shrugged. Jada nodded. "You're staying with me."

Ava smiled, took her sister's hand, and they greeted the mourners who came to bid farewell to Edna Ford. It was the end of one chapter, and the beginning of one brand-new for them, as their sisterly bond was renewed.

When Jada arrived back at her house, with Ava in tow, Sunny was sitting on the couch with the kids, cracking up at an episode of *South Park*. Jada shook her head as she entered, and said, "You know damn well these kids don't need to be watching this, right?"

Sunny turned around, and saw the two sisters. It was Sunny's first time seeing Ava since 1996. She stood up, and hugged Jada's sister, truly happy to see her after all the time that had passed. She stood back and looked at her, noting that her suit was Prada and her shoes Manolo Blahniks. Yes, Miss Ava had done alright for herself.

Ava smiled at Sunny, thrilled to see the woman she had always secretly looked up to. Ava liked Sunny's outgoing nature and her bubbly personality. Sunny had a vivacious spirit that neither tragic loss nor addiction had been able to break. She was thirty-six years old, and she still looked twenty-one. She was a diva without trying to be.

"You look *fabulous*," Ava told Sunny, looking at her outfit. Sunny was dressed in painted-on DKNY jeans, cuffed at the calf, with a pair of Prada boots and a Prada blouse. Her diamonds gleamed in the light, from her ears, neck, wrists, and fingers. She looked brand-new.

Jada looked at Sunny, and frowned. "How did you change clothes?" she asked.

Sunny waved her hand, as if bothered by the question. "I called my driver, Raul, and he came to get me and the kids. We went to my place, and I packed some stuff for me and Mercedes. We're gonna stay here until after the funeral. You know, just in case you fall out or some shit."

Sunny said it so bluntly that Ava and Jada both cracked up laughing at her crass remarks. Sunny knew that she really wanted Jada's company as much as Jada would probably need hers. Talking about Dorian after so many years had tugged at her tough heartstrings, and made her remember the love of her life in such detail that it almost scared her. She could still hear Dorian's voice in her ears, still feel his breath on her neck as he woke up nestled beside her every morning.

Jada shook her head, and smiled, not at all surprised that Sunny would invite herself to stay at her place. Sunny had cunningly made it sound as if she was doing Jada a favor, but she knew that her friend needed her, too. Sunny wanted everyone to think she was made of steel, but she was fragile at her core, and Jada knew it.

"Well, Ava's staying here, too, so it'll be like old times." Jada smiled.

Ava smiled, too, anxious to catch up with her sister. But first she hugged and kissed her nephew until he begged for mercy. Ava kissed him all over his handsome face, and hugged him tightly. She wanted children desperately, and envied Jada for having such an adorable son.

Soon the kids went off to play and to watch their shows on Nickelodeon and Disney. Jada and her sister changed into sweats and T-shirts and joined Sunny in the living room. They sat around with a bottle of Sunny's finest white wine. It was a vintage bottle of Moscato from some valley in the south of Chile. And it was delicious. Sunny, true to form, kicked off the night's discussion.

"Here's a toast," she said, raising her glass with her wrist perfectly poised, diamonds glistening. "To the women who weathered the storm. The men may not have made it to shore. Or if they did, they still have a lot to learn." She looked at Jada. "But we're still standing, and we're still here to tell the story. To us!"

Ava nodded, and Jada smiled, as they clinked glasses like they had done once many years before. So much had changed, so many lessons had been learned. So many doors had been open and shut since the last time the three of them had sat together as they did now.

Ava looked at her sister. Jada was still lovely, despite her trials and tribulations and the rough roads she'd traveled. She had so many questions for her sister about what her life had been like. She had so many things to tell her sister about her own life, now that they were older and relating on a new level. But first, Ava addressed Sunny. "Sunny, I'm so sorry about Dorian. I know you two loved each other, and I know you miss him."

Sunny looked at the floor. "Yeah. I thought about him a lot today, while y'all were at the wake. I think of him every day. Every time Mercedes smiles, and her eyes light up the way his did, I see him. I see his face in hers. I hear his laugh when she laughs. But I had forgotten what it was like to see him every day. To sleep beside him, and to walk into a room with him. I didn't let myself think about that too often." Sunny's voice cracked, and she cleared her throat. "But today, I started thinking, and looking at old pictures, and I just miss him so much."

The women sat silently for several poignant moments. Ava took a deep breath, feeling the gravity of Sunny and her daughter's loss. They began to discuss the old days, particularly how everything had gone so wrong after Dorian's death. Jada laughed at some memories, and was moved to tears by others. And as they sat in her living room reliving the past, it was like a spring rain had washed over them, and they were cleansing old wounds. It was time for letting go.

40

TROUBLE SLEEPING

As Jada filled her sister in on all the details of her past, Sunny slipped up-stairs and changed into her pajamas. Knowing that the sisters needed time to talk, she made sure that the children ate dinner, and then she re-joined the sisters in the living room.

Sunny came back, and listened as Jada was filling her sister in on the delivery she'd gotten from Born. Sunny had on a Victoria's Secret silk gown and matching robe, and Jada laughed at her friend, the diva. "Why are you dressed head to toe in silk, like there are men here to impress?"

Sunny smiled flirtatiously, and sang, "I'm feeling sexxxxyyyyyyyy," like Beyonce sang in "Naughty Girl."

Ava laughed, and shook her head. Sunny would never change. "Well, girl, there's nothing wrong with feeling sexy sometimes. Shit, I feel like that all the time."

Sunny slapped Ava a high five, and then sat down on the sofa beside Jada. She looked at Jada, and asked, "So, what did I miss?"

Jada shrugged. "Not too much. I was just about to tell Ava how I got the flowers from Born, and started reminiscing." She looked at Sunny, who was yawning and stretching, and obviously tired. Jada herself was exhausted. "I'm sure you're riveted by my life story, but I need to get some sleep. So do you, Ava. We have to bury our mother in the morn-ing." Jada closed her eyes, partly from fatigue, and in part to picture Edna Ford's face one more time. It would be a bittersweet good-bye. Jada was missing her mother, and the good times they'd managed to have after all their turmoil. But part of Jada was anxious for the closure her mother's death had brought her. It was time to let go of old pain, and old regret. Time to move forward and embrace what was yet to come.

Ava agreed, and stifled a yawn of her own. They found Sheldon and Mercedes already sleeping in his bed, and decided to leave them. Sunny insisted on sleeping on the couch, and Ava took the guest bedroom. Jada went to the sanctuary of her own room, and stretched out across the bed.

She lay back in the dark, thoughts swimming around in her head. She couldn't fall asleep, and she got sick of tossing and turning. She looked at the clock, which read 3:54 A.M. She wanted to call Born. But she questioned what she would say to him. She had so much to say, and wasn't sure where to begin. She wondered how she would start the conversation. But more than anything, she just needed to talk to him. She had to get some closure for once. Without second-guessing herself she reached for the phone. He answered on the fourth ring.

"Hello?" He sounded sleepy, just as before.

"Born?" she said. "It's Jada." Her heart was pounding at the sound of his voice.

She heard a loud thud, and then some commotion, before he came back on the line. "I'm sorry," he said. "I dropped the phone."

Jada laughed, silently. She knew that hearing from her must have been the last thing he expected. Especially at four o'clock in the morning. "I'm sorry I called so late," she said. "I should have waited until the morning—"

"Nah, Jada," Born said, getting out of bed and whispering, so as not to wake Anisa. He was glad that his fumbling the phone hadn't woken her up. He was in a state of shock, hearing Jada's familiar voice over the phone after so many years. He walked downstairs quietly and slipped into the kitchen to avoid being heard. "I'm glad you called me." His face bore a smile so wide that his whole face lit up. "It's good to hear your voice."

Jada, too, was smiling. She hadn't heard him speak her name in far too long. "Thank you for the flowers," she said. "I was real surprised when I read the card. I didn't expect to hear from you again."

Born had almost forgotten the sad occurrence that had prompted him to contact Jada in the first place. He apologetically said, "I'm sorry, Jada. I'm sorry to hear about your moms dying." Born knew how strained Jada's relationship with her mother had been. There were many times over the years that he had sat and listened to her tell him story after story about her childhood, and about how her mother had let her down. Still, even with all their faults, Born knew that when one loses a parent, there's a terrible emotional barrage that accompanies that loss.

"Thanks," she said. "I'm dealing with it." Jada switched the phone to her other ear. Jada's voice was tinged with regret. "I wish I could have told her that I forgave her." She sighed, thinking of her mother's delicate face, her soft voice, and her calm demeanor. Jada had never wanted to be as soft, as weak as her mother. But after a day spent thinking back on her addiction, she realized that she had been just as weak, just as pathetic.

Born cleared his throat. "I know how that is. I had a lot of shit that I never got to say to my father before he died."

Silence filled the conversation, as the two of them searched for what to say. So many days, months, and years had passed since their last conversation. So many things had taken place, and the two of them were so very different from the people they'd been when they were younger. But they were also still very much the same.

Jada searched for something to say, but it was Born who filled the silence. "I think about you all the time," he said. He was being honest. "I really do. I know that the last time we saw each other, it wasn't nothing nice. But I just want you to know that I still think about you. I think about you a lot."

Jada wanted to cry and smile at the same time. His words were such a comfort to her, and yet it hurt her so badly to know that he still cared for her after all she'd done. "Born, I'm sorry that I ever hurt you. I don't know what to say to explain why I did what I did." Jada paused, knowing that there *was* no excuse for what she'd done. Born had loved her enough to make up for all the love she'd never had. And that hadn't been enough to keep her from going back to drugs. She knew that she had let him down just as much as she'd let herself down. "All I can tell you is that I never meant to hurt you. I always loved you, and I'm so sorry for everything."

Born held the phone, with his eyes closed. Hearing her say those words, he felt her sincerity. He knew in his heart that she hadn't meant to cause him any pain. "I wanna see you," Born said before he realized it. "I need to see your face."

Jada held her breath, completely mesmerized by what he'd just said. She was still amazed at the fact that she was talking to her soul mate after so many years, and so many tears. "I want to see you, too. We've got so much catching up to do."

"Good, so let's meet somewhere tomorrow," Born suggested, wasting no time.

"I can't tomorrow. I'm burying my mother tomorrow. Ava's staying with me, and Sunny's here with her daughter. I got a house full of guests coming, and I can't slip away, even after the funeral."

"I understand."

"But what about the next day? Friday. Can't we see each other then?"

Born thought about Anisa's birthday plans. She was going away on Friday with Precious and Kiara to Atlantic City. He smiled at the perfect timing, and agreed. "Yeah. That's perfect. We can get together on Friday." He was glad that he'd allowed himself to be suckered into footing the entire bill after all. He would be rid of Anisa for the weekend, and free to catch up with Jada, the one who still held the key to his heart. The situation was a win/win.

"Good. I can't wait to see you." She paused, summoning the courage to say what was on the tip of her tongue. She could feel her heart racing in her chest. "I miss you." Jada's voice sounded soft and unsure.

Born pictured her face, and wondered why he started smiling. "I miss you, too."

They hung up after agreeing to meet at a new soul food restaurant on Forest Avenue that Friday. They both fell asleep with thoughts of each other running rampant in their minds.

The next day Jada and Ava set about the task of burying their mother. She didn't mention to Sunny or to Ava that she had spoken to Born the previous night. She kept replaying their conversation in her head, as they headed to the church. Throughout the ceremony, Jada cried and Ava consoled her, and then they'd switch roles. Sunny sat with Sheldon and Mercedes, trying to keep them entertained in the somber setting. She played a game of hangman with them silently in the last pew of the church, while some of the older women in the congregation looked at her disapprovingly. One of the ushers whispered loudly enough for Sunny to hear that it was wrong to play games in God's house. Sunny resisted the urge to give the Christian women the finger, and simply ignored them, while she continued playing with the kids. The service was beautiful, and when it was concluded, they all piled into the limousine for the journey to Edna's burial site. Ava had her Gucci shades on to hide her eyes, bloodshot from crying all day. She turned to Jada and held her hand. "I want you to know that it wasn't easy for me to forgive her either, Jada."

Jada squeezed her sister's hand. She had often wondered how Ava had been able to forgive Edna after all their mother's emotional neglect had driven Ava to run away and to attempt suicide.

"I couldn't forgive her at first, because I knew that she suspected J.D. was pushing up on me long before I told her that he was. Later on, after me and her started speaking again, she admitted that she was suspicious and that she was in denial. She said she wanted to keep us and keep J.D., and so she made herself see what she wanted to see rather than what was really going on. The picture-perfect family she wanted outsiders to see was really a twisted mess. She tried to hide it. That was her way of dealing with things at that time. Mommy never found the courage to fight until she found Jesus." Ava wiped her eyes. "It took me a long time to forgive her for being so weak. So don't think you're the only one who wasted valuable time being angry. I did, too."

Sunny handed Ava a tissue, and Jada rubbed her back to comfort her.

At the cemetery, the entire congregation seemed to be present, as they all circled Edna's final resting place. Jada held Sunny's hand, and Ava's, and they prayed with the minister, who said a final prayer for the soul of Edna Ford. As soil was thrown upon Edna's casket, the minister said that from dust they had all come, and to dust they would all return. Jada glanced around as Edna's fellow parishioners gathered around her grave. She smiled, seeing that her mother had made such an impression on so many of the members of her church. It seemed like the entire congregation had come out for Edna's funeral. Jada was happy that her mother had managed to find solace in her faith. She held Ava's hand, as Ava cried softly with her head on her sister's shoulder. As they headed back to the limousine for the ride to Jada's house, Sunny put her arm around her best friend's shoulder. "Your mother must have been so proud to see who you are now, Jada. You came a long way, and I'm proud of you."

Jada smiled, and held Sunny around her waist as they walked back to the car. She nodded her head, too choked up to respond verbally. Because after all she had been through, Jada was proud of *herself*. They piled into the limo, and headed to Jada's house to welcome the steady stream of well-wishers that they knew would surely come. Some of Edna's friends would be there to show support, and to genuinely express their condolences.

Others would only be coming to see what was what. They had heard about Edna's two daughters—one who was a recovering crackhead, and the other, a successful attorney from Philly. They wanted to see what they looked like, and how Jada's house looked. For that reason, Jada began to straighten up the house, so that the nosy broads coming to snoop would have nothing but good things to run back and tell the rest.

Soon the guests began to arrive, and they all had stories about Edna. One after another, they regaled Jada and Ava with story after story about Edna's acts of kindness. How she'd volunteered at soup kitchens, and visited the sick as a member of the missionary board. The solo that Edna sang off-key whenever she got the chance. They all spoke of Edna's faith and devotion to the church. Jada and Ava were soon overwhelmed with hearing all the wonderful stories about their mother. Jada listened, happy that so many people had come to love her mother. She continued playing the perfect hostess, as guests milled about her house. But her mind soon drifted elsewhere.

All she could think about was Born's voice in her ear. He missed her.

He didn't hate her. He thought about her all the time. Jada went through the motions of entertaining her guests, and she counted down the hours until she could see the man she still loved once again. The hours ticked by so slowly, and she could hardly wait to see his face once again.

Born sat at the corner table in the back of the soul food restaurant, wondering why he felt strange sensations in his stomach. Could it be that Jada still made him feel this fire after all these years? Born was anxious to see her, but nervous at the same time. So much time had passed since the last time he'd been face-to-face with her. He sipped his drink, glancing periodically at the entrance, waiting for the moment that she would walk through the door. She didn't make him wait very long.

Jada entered the restaurant, greeted all the regulars, and scanned the room for the love of her life. She felt a knot in her stomach from anticipation. It had been so long since she had last seen Born that she wondered how he had changed, what was different. She wondered if he would think she looked the same, or if she had aged. Would the few pounds she'd gained over the years be instantly recognized? These things she wondered about as her eyes subtly perused the scene.

Jada glanced down at her clothes, unsure. But she decided that the 7 For All Mankind jeans, salmon-colored top, and matching stiletto boots she wore were fine. She couldn't believe her hands were actually trembling from jitters. Born took it all in, noticing how sexy she still was. Her body was still exquisite; she looked even better than she had the last time he had seen her. He sat dumbfounded, in awe of her, and remembered the very first time he had laid eyes on her. Strutting down the street, with all that body and so many secrets. All the years of loving her came flooding back. Jada turned, and their eyes met across the room. She spotted Born at the table in the back, where she knew he had strategically placed himself to avoid being seen. Born had always been the type to lay in the cut, and avoid detection. She headed toward him smiling, her heart racing all the way. He still looked so good. His smile was so familiar, the way the corners of his eyes creased when he did so. His dimples, which

Jada loved so much. Jada felt his eyes penetrating her, and she grabbed her snakeskin clutch tighter in the palm of her hands, and scanned his face as she walked toward him. She felt like time was standing still as she approached his table. Each one step felt like two.

Born stood to his feet, and Jada realized that she had forgotten just how powerful his presence was. He towered over her, fifteen pounds heavier than the last time they'd seen each other, but still so handsome, still so incredibly sexy. He wore a button-up Rocawear shirt, matching jeans, and a pair of Uptowns. His icy chain, dripping in brilliant diamonds, hung low on his chest. She took all of him in, and he could see by the look on her face and the sparkle in her eyes that she liked what she saw. Her smile made his heart race. He pulled her close to him in a firm embrace that was so long and so meaningful that some of the other patrons turned and smiled at them, seeing that there was obviously love between these two. The years had passed, so much had changed, and yet his arms—these arms—felt so familiar. Jada lost herself in them briefly. For several moments, he held her. Then he pulled back ever so slightly and gazed into her eyes, seeing the tears that she was trying so hard to hold back.

"You're still gorgeous. You know that?" he asked.

She smiled, shyly, getting butterflies after all this time. "Thank you." Jada smiled, still holding on to him for dear life. She felt that if he let go she might not be able to stand on her shaky legs. "And you're still the flyest nigga on Staten Island."

Born smiled, and hugged her once more. Then he released her body's familiar softness, and pulled Jada's chair out for her. She sat down, and he sat across from her. Jada felt like she was sitting in the middle of a crowded room, and all she could see was Born. She knew that he saw her clearly. She felt transparent, and naked, like she had felt the first time they made love. This was the one person who knew her inside and out. And she knew him just as well.

Born sat there looking at her for several moments. No words were necessary, as they took in one another's presence. He had seen her in his dreams countless times, pictured her face perfectly in his imagination. But seeing her now—in the flesh—brought him a joy that was unexplainable.

Jada broke the silence that lingered, saying simply, "Wow." She looked at him staring back at her. "I can't believe it took us this long to see each other again."

He shook his head. "Me, either. Yo, I thought about what it would be like to see you today, and I never thought it would feel like this."

Jada frowned, slightly. "Feel like what? How do you feel?"

He shrugged. "I can't explain it. I feel so fuckin' . . . happy," he said, grinning from ear to ear. "Man, if you only knew how fast my heart started beating when you walked in here!"

He looked at her pretty doelike eyes. He collected himself, and said, "I'm really sorry to hear about your mother."

She thanked him, and Born looked at Jada. He saw her through new eyes as she sat there, so vulnerable still. He remembered when he'd hated that vulnerability, recalled that he'd seen that as a weakness. The same type of weakness his father had shown. They were one and the same in his mind all those years ago. But now he realized *how much* he had held Jada accountable for how Leo had let him down, and he was sorry for that. It wasn't weakness he seen in Jada. It was tenderness, underneath all that tough talk. It was gentleness and vulnerability beneath the surface of her rough layers. What she had needed wasn't tough love, but a love that would have helped her overcome any obstacle. Looking at Jada, he felt like he had let her down as much as she'd him. He could only imagine what depths she'd fallen to before climbing her way out and rising to the top of the heap. He was proud of her for being strong enough to pull herself up. For being stronger than his father had been.

Jada, on the other hand, stared at Born, realizing just where she'd gone wrong. This man before her was just a man. Nothing more. She had expected him to save her. To change her life and right all the wrongs she'd suffered. And for a while Born had done just that. But it wasn't up to him to save her life. She'd had to do it for herself. Just like Miss Ingrid had told her. Jada understood how true that was now. She had had to fight her own demons, just as her mother had learned. Like Edna, Jada had wanted to relinquish control completely. She'd wanted Born to rush in and save her. Writing had become more than a job for Jada. It was so therapeutic, and Jada had learned a lot about herself through her writing. She had realized that she had been longing for a father all her life. When she was angry with Edna as a teenager growing up, part of that anger stemmed from the absence of her father. Jada had never really grieved his loss. Instead, she'd mothered Edna back to life, and then gone in search of someone to take her father's place. Someone to fill the void of a daddy's love, which every girl needs so desperately. Born had become that father figure to her, and she had depended on him for everything. She had expected Born to rescue her from addiction. But instead he had left her to fend for herself, and for a long time Jada had been angry with him for that. Now she understood that Born was not to blame. She knew that it had been her fault that she'd sunk deeper into addiction and further away from herself. When Born left her, she still had herself. It took her far too long to realize that she was all she needed. Still, Born had left her *alone*, when he said he'd never do that. And as much as she loved this man—as much as she adored him and the memories they'd shared together—she somehow couldn't forget how easily he'd abandoned her.

"Born, I want to talk about what happened between me and you."

He nodded, glad that there was no need for awkward small talk. Jada had dived right in. "Listen." He paused, and took a deep breath. "There's some things I want to say to you about that." He drained his glass, and felt his chest burn from the alcohol. Then he looked at her intently. "I was never good at trusting people. I don't usually allow people to get that close to me. But I thought we were friends. I thought we had honesty and love between us." Born couldn't hide the pain in his eyes. "You lied to me. You stole from me, Jada. I never cheated on you. That was the first time in my life that I was faithful to any woman." He looked at her, curiously. "Did you cheat on me?"

Jada shook her head. "No," she said, truthfully. "I swear I never did." And she was relieved to know that he hadn't cheated on her either.

Born continued. "I was good to you, and I had so much love for you.

I tried to show you that. I accepted you and your past . . . all I ever asked was that you keep it real with me. I trusted you." He paused, and looked at her. "You broke my heart, baby girl. And I wanna know why you did that to me."

Jada felt so sick as she looked at him. She knew that she couldn't even begin to tell him how much she loved him. How many times over the years she had longed for him, and wished that he would come back and get her. Now that he was sitting right across from her, she had no idea where to start. So she was honest, and told him exactly what she was feeling.

"Born, you were the first man to ever love me for me. You knew what I was, and what I had been through. You knew all the mistakes I made, and all the shit I had done. And you still loved me, anyway. You never held my past against me. You made me feel accepted, and beautiful, safe and loved. And I blew it. I messed that up." Jada sighed deeply. "I fucked up. But I never stopped loving you, Born. Not for one second. You've always been my soul mate. I was just too stupid to see that your love should have been enough to keep me from going back to the drugs. But loving you was something I never stopped doing."

He was the person who had mattered most in her life. She knew that, even after all this time, she owed him an honest explanation. "I never wanted to lie to you. I loved the honesty in our relationship, too. In the beginning it was just me and you. And I was alright then. I was good, and I loved you so much. Then, when you and Dorian started working extra hard, and me and Sunny started spending more time together . . . I got strung out, Born. I wouldn't admit it to myself, but I was twisted." Jada took a deep breath, and she explained how she'd taken her first trip across the white lines with Sunny in the men's room at his friend's party. "I came face-to-face with cocaine with no one around who would judge me, and I couldn't walk away from it. I remember standing there staring at it, and knowing that I wanted it. I pushed the thought of you out of my mind. Told myself that I would only do it that one time. Just to make the party more enjoyable. And that night I felt so guilty. I hadn't lied to you or stolen from you yet. But I knew I'd let you down. After that, I would get high in order to escape the guilt of what I was doing behind your back. I know it sounds crazy, but it's the truth. I owe you the truth." Jada was raw and honest as she described the times she and Sunny had gotten high together, and how she'd resorted to stealing from Born once Sunny disappeared. She looked at Born lovingly. "I'm so sorry that I hurt you. It was the last thing I ever wanted. I wanted to be the woman you wanted me to be. I wanted to be the Jada that you fell in love with. But part of me enjoyed being the Jada that got high behind your back, and was the life of the party."

"So, Sunny got you caught up in all that? I didn't know she got high, or I never would have wanted you to be friends with her."

Jada shook her head. "I can't blame Sunny. I knew I shouldn't have done it. But I was having fun when I was high. When I was high, I was happy. I had money, I had love, I had friends, and life was a party. But when I wasn't high, I was ashamed, because I was a cokehead, and I had betrayed you. I was living a double life. But in the midst of all of that, I didn't ever want to cause you any pain. I loved you. I never wanted to hurt you, Born. I only wanted to be one thing to you, and another thing the rest of the time. I was selfish."

Born watched her talk, and listened to what she said. He saw so much growth in her. The fact that she was taking responsibility for her actions was impressive to him. She had been in denial for so long, it was a relief to hear her admit that she'd been wrong. He remembered the lies she used to tell, and was relieved to hear some honesty from her at last.

He thought back to the days when they had walked with their fingers laced at the mall. The days when they had put on their flyest shit, and gone to rap concerts or parties. He missed this woman, his baby girl. And now that she was here, he could barely keep his hands to himself. He reached for her across the table, and she gave him her hand, willingly.

The waitress walked over, prepared to take their orders. Born ordered roasted chicken and mashed potatoes. Jada ordered the same. He smiled, remembering that she had always followed his lead. Except for the one time it mattered.

The waitress took their drink orders, and set out to retrieve them. Born continued stroking Jada's hand, and she looked into his eyes.

"Well, I have some questions, too," she said. Born leaned back, and prepared himself for the inquisition. Jada needed answers of her own. "How could you leave me alone like that? And why couldn't you face me, instead of sending your mother to kick me out of our house?"

Born nodded his head, feeling that these were valid questions. "I reacted like that because I was hurt. I had a whole lotta faith in you, and I was so mad that you lied to me. You made a fool out of me. I just wanted you to go away from me." He looked at her sincerely. "I could have really hurt you. I wanted you to feel the pain you made me feel. And the only way I knew how to do that was to physically hurt you. Deep down I really didn't want to do that. So, I just cut you off. I let my moms speak for me. Looking back on that, I can see that wasn't really a good look. But I didn't know how I would react to you if I saw you face-to-face." He recalled gripping Jada's throat as he tossed her out of his life. He had known that he was angry, and powerful enough to snap her neck with his bare hands. All the love he'd had for her had been replaced by rage, and he was dangerously close to hurting her. "I think it would have ended a lot worse if I would have been there that day instead of my mother." Born shook his head. "You made me give up on love. I'll never give another woman my heart. It hurts too bad when you trust somebody, and it turns out that they lied to you. My heart is off-limits."

He ordered another drink, and decided to ask another question. "What happened to you after we broke up. How did you start fuckin' with Jamari?"

Jada took a deep breath. She felt herself well up with emotion at the thought of the rocky road of her past. "When you left, Marquis—" Her voice trailed off.

Born wanted to prevent her from having to feel all that pain again. "I know it wasn't easy."

"Nah." Jada sat back, shaking her head. "You have no idea. You cannot imagine what it was like for me. I had a hard time. You know what I'm saying?" She looked at Born directly. "It wasn't easy for me to live without you. And I had a real hard time at first."

Born noticed that she looked at him unflinchingly. Her gaze was steady. He remembered that she used to have a hard time maintaining eye contact with him. And he noticed that she had no problem looking him in his eyes now. She was direct, and the tone of her voice was firm. It seemed like she had waited a long time to get this off her chest, and he sensed that she needed to say this to him. Jada took a sip of her drink. Born listened as she told him her story.

"When you threw me away—when you let me go—I felt like nobody else was in my corner, like nobody else had my back. And it was all about me from that point on. I felt like all I had was me. I went through my phase of feeling sorry for myself, being depressed and all that." Jada paused to sip her drink, remembering how she had kept her outer appearance flashy and classy, while on the inside she felt dirty and unwanted. "And, then I saw you and Anisa in the mall. You grabbed her, and walked away from me. Then I saw you at a party that night. You avoided me the whole night. I was crushed. So, I dealt with Jamari, knowing that for me it was all about his paper, never about any love on my part. I was playing him. I thought that I was in control. But he was playing me, too, because I was always high." Her eyelashes fluttered daintily, as she blinked away the memory. "And he knew what I was doing. He would give me the shit, buy it for me. He had me right where he wanted me, and he knew it."

Born frowned, disturbed by what he was hearing. "You're telling me that he *gave* you crack, and he knew you were smoking?" His facial expression was one of pure amazement.

Jada nodded. "He did. The first time he gave me drugs was when he told me how you put me down when you and him argued in the barbershop."

"I didn't put you down. If anything, I gave you a compliment." Born chuckled at the memory. "The nigga was in there talking shit about how he was with you now, and I wasn't. So I just said, 'Yeah, she got some good pussy, don't she?' I didn't put you down."

Jada set her glass back down. "That's not all you said."

Born looked her in her eyes. "Yes, it is." He shook his head, already assuming that Jamari had told her something far worse. "What did he tell you I said?"

Jada shook her head, feeling played once again. "He said you told them about how I sucked your dick—"

"*What?*" Born's face was twisted in disbelief. "That nigga was lying. I ain't never said no bullshit like that about you."

Jada shook her head. "Well, he said that you were saying some pretty foul shit. And then he gave me crack, and told me that I could smoke if I wanted to. That he wouldn't judge me, like you did."

Born laughed, uneasily. "Well, he didn't love you then. If he cared about you like I did, he wouldn't have ever let you do that in front of him."

Jada nodded. "Eventually, I saw that. I realized that he was just too willing to accept my addiction, and it seemed like to him it was no problem. The only time me and him had a problem was when your name came up. At first I thought that he didn't like you just because you were my ex. But then he told me about you. He told me how he betrayed you, and how you cut him off. He said some really fucked up things about you. And I never saw him the same way after that." She paused, wondering if she should reveal what else Jamari had said.

Born sensed her hesitation. "What?" he asked. "What else did he say?"

Jada sat back, and looked at Born. "He said you were his half brother."

Born nearly spit out his drink. "Whose half brother?"

"He said that you were his half brother," Jada confirmed. "He told me that Leo was messing around with his mother behind Miss Ingrid's back. They both used crack, so Jamari said they were getting high together, and doing their thing on the low. Anyway, his moms told him that your father was also his father. But apparently Leo denied him, and raised you instead. Jamari had resented you ever since his mother told him that. He was jealous that you had your father there all your life and he never had that."

Born sat staring at Jada for a long time. "That nigga really was crazy!" Born shook his head, and laughed uneasily. "He *wished* we had the same father."

Jada shrugged her shoulders. "Well, he really believed that, and he was so jealous that Leo was there for you and not for him."

Born got lost in thought for several moments, trying to think of whether this scenario was at all possible, or likely. But he quickly brushed it off, thinking to himself that Jamari was just delusional.

Jada continued. "When he told me that, I started to see things clearly. I realized that he didn't care about me. It was all about getting back at you. I could tell that he was just using me to make you mad, and I felt like such an idiot. But by then, I was already pregnant." She paused, and sipped her drink. "I was so mad at that nigga for playing me, and mad at myself for not seeing it from the beginning. So I figured out a way to get revenge—for me, and for you. I stole his package, and I sold it and kept the money." Jada looked at Born to see if he looked confused. He didn't. Born knew all about the heist that she had pulled off. His friend Chance had told Born about it when he came home from prison. Plus, his own mother had held the money for Jada until she came back to claim it. Jada wasn't the least bit surprised that he knew either. Born was always a step ahead of everybody else. He knew about every card game, every dice game, every number runner, every loan shark, and all the angles to get money in the streets. So it didn't surprise Jada at all that he didn't flinch as she continued her story.

"He was heated. Elliot—his connect—wanted to kill him and Wizz, and I was on the run. I didn't know if Elliot might want to kill me, too. I took the money, and got the hell out of dodge. I went back to Brooklyn, and I was getting high again. Then I got arrested, trying to buy crack." She shook her head, still disturbed by the fact that she had fallen so far down that she had been getting high while she was pregnant with her beloved only child. "I went to jail, and that's where I had Sheldon. Jamari waited until after I gave birth, and then he snatched him from me. He took custody, and painted me as a horrible person. I guess I was, but

I needed *help*. I didn't need to have my lifeline taken away from me."
Jada felt that Born had also taken her lifeline away once. But Jamari was
the one who had tried desperately to break her spirit. "He took my son
when Sheldon was all I had to live for. He kept him from me for the
whole time that I was locked up. The nigga dragged my name through
the mud, and all that. He made me regret the fact that I got pregnant."
She saw the expression on Born's face change, and she clarified her statement. "I don't regret it now. But back then I did. I was so mad, because
if I had known the whole story, I never would have gotten in so deep
with him."

Born understood what she meant, and he hated Jamari even more for
putting Jada through so much hell. He felt better hearing that Jada had
had no clue about Jamari's beef with Born before she got involved with
him. He just wished that she hadn't gotten involved with him at all. "So
how did you get your son back?" Born looked incredibly moved by her
story. He loved and adored his son like no one else. To be deprived of
being a part of Ethan's life would have killed Born. He empathized with
her situation, wondering how a nigga like Jamari could be so cruel. Then
he realized that he, too, had once been just as cruel to Jada.

"It wasn't easy," she said. "I had to fight to get him back. Jamari told
them that I was using crack during my pregnancy, but he didn't tell him
that he was the one giving it to me! When I mentioned that in court, he
called me a liar. He was the worst." Jada paused. "It wasn't that I didn't
realize that I had done wrong. Using crack while I was pregnant was like
putting a loaded gun to my baby's head, and I realized that. I knew that
I was wrong for that. But I was sick, and Jamari took no responsibility for
his role in my addiction. He had never once tried to help me. All he
wanted was to control me. Sunny kept me from losing my mind, because
she told me that if I crumbled, if I gave up, then Jamari had won. I
didn't want him to win, but he was making it so hard for me to fight. But
I got back on my feet one step at a time. I stayed clean, got an apartment,
and I started with supervised visitation. The social worker sat and
watched how I talked to my son, how I played with him, what my home
looked like, how much food was in the fridge, and all that. Then I got

unsupervised visits. A social worker would go and pick Sheldon up from Jamari and bring him to my house. I was so glad that they assigned us a go-between. I couldn't stand the sight of Jamari, and I didn't want to have to see him every time I wanted to see my son. And then somebody killed the muthafucka." Her voice was flat as she said this, and both she and Born knew that that had been one of the best days of her life. "I guess he got what his hand called for." She sipped her drink again.

Born watched her closely. He was looking for a sign that Jada was leaving out part of the story. "You went to see my moms the day that Jamari got killed." Born watched the surprise on Jada's face emerge, and then quickly disappear. Jada hadn't thought Ingrid had told Born about that visit. Ingrid had surely not missed the coincidence in the fact that Jamari was killed within minutes of Jada's departure from her apartment.

"Yeah. I did." Jada said it, but didn't elaborate.

Born smirked. "Did you do it?"

Jada looked away, and wanted to tell Born the truth. But that would mean incriminating her friend. And even though she trusted Born not to tell another soul, Jada couldn't risk getting Sunny implicated in Jamari's murder. There was no statute of limitations on homicide. "Nah," she said. "I didn't kill him. But I was glad that somebody did."

Born nodded, and took another swig of his drink. "So you and Sunny gonna take that shit to your graves, huh?" He asked the question, and smiled. Then he sat back in his seat.

Jada looked at him, not blinking for several moments. She didn't know how Born had figured out the truth. But she sure wasn't going to elaborate. "Me and Sunny will take a lot of things to our graves. Death before dishonor, you know what I'm saying?"

Born nodded again. He had taught her well. What Jada didn't know was that Ingrid had watched the entire episode play out from her apartment window. She had seen Jada and Jamari arguing and she was preparing to go out there and help. Then she had seen a very attractive and well-dressed woman come to Jada's aid. Ingrid saw the exchange between the three of them, and saw Jamari get shot and the two women make their escape. It didn't take Born very long to surmise that Sunny had been the woman Ingrid had seen. He smiled, knowing all that Jada wasn't saying.

Jada directed the conversation to safer territory. "If it wasn't for Sunny and her mother, Marisol, I don't know if I would have made it through all that. Sunny helped me out a whole lot. She took pictures of Sheldon, and brought them to me. She was my only hope for a long time. For that, I will always be grateful to Sunny. For real." She sighed. "I got my GED, and I petitioned for sole custody of my son. But they gave me a hard time about it. I had to live with my mother in order for me to have Sheldon with me. They wanted to be sure that he was living in a stable environment, and I had been unstable for so long. So I lived with her until they said that I could raise him on my own."

Born nodded. "So that must have been awkward at first. You and her living under the same roof after all those years of not even speaking to each other. What was that like?"

Jada shook her head. "At first, it was real tense. I wouldn't talk to her. I thought she was wrong for shutting me out. But I realized that she was angry with me, too, and she had every right to be. So once we finally started talking, we both got to say some things that needed to be said. We got to reconnect as a family. And I'm grateful that we got the chance to do that before she died. I'm glad she got a chance to see that I turned my life around."

Born looked at her, truly proud of what she'd done for herself. "So, do you ever get tempted to use drugs now?"

Jada looked at him, knowing that he wondered if she was clean for good this time. "No. I don't get tempted at all. When I think of all the things I did to get high, and to stay high . . . I would never put myself or my child through that again. Sheldon is all the reason I need not to ever go back to that life again. I love him too much for that. When I look at him, I don't see his father. I see my baby, *my* son. I was so far gone that I put his life in jeopardy. I owe him my very best for the rest of his life. I don't want to let him down like I did in the beginning. He's my everything." She felt herself getting a little misty-eyed, and she looked away briefly before continuing. "I never want to be without him again." Jada told Born about her mother helping out with Sheldon while she got her life together. "I went to college, and graduated with a degree in journalism. Me and Sunny are collaborating on a book now. I think it'll be a bestseller."

Born smiled. "I bet it will."

Jada smiled, too. "I'm living a very different life than the one I once lived. I'm not gonna fuck it up again."

Born listened quietly, soaking all of it up. His mind was like a sponge, absorbing each detail. He had known that Jamari had taken custody of Jada's son. But he had not known the lengths to which Jamari had gone to ensure that Jada was humiliated every step of the way. Knowing her story—knowing that Jada had been subjected to humiliation at the hands of men for most of her life—he felt sick to his stomach with pity. He was mad at himself for all the pain he had caused Jada. He was also somewhat mad at *her* for falling prey to a nigga as corny as Jamari. He hated Jamari for taking her child away from her, because Born knew that Jada—like him—needed her child to survive. Born felt that Jamari had taken advantage of Jada's weakness, and had used it to feel powerful for the first time in his life. His rage was evident on his face, and Jada spoke on it.

"Cat got your tongue?" She sat back, drained her glass, and looked at Born dead-on. She smiled at him, looking relaxed from the effects of the rum.

Born recalled saying that same thing to her so many times over the course of their relationship. He used to always use the phrase when an awkward silence fell between them, because he knew that Jada would be far off in her mind, deep in thought. Hearing her say that now—"Cat got your tongue?"—it made him smile inside.

Jada read him perfectly. "I remember," she said. "I remember everything." She stared at him, wondering about Anisa. "Earlier you said your heart is off-limits because of how I hurt you. So how is it that you have a son with the woman who took my place?"

Born grinned a little, flattered that she was still jealous after all this time. "Nobody ever took your place. That's first of all. And Anisa never even came close. She just got pregnant." He loved Ethan with all his heart, and took the role of fatherhood very seriously. Born had always felt like his own father had disappeared when he needed him the most. He was determined not to disappear from Ethan's life, despite the fact that his relationship with Anisa was basically over. "Anisa takes pretty good care of him. But, even though she may not have been the woman I *wanted* to have my child . . ." Born looked at her suggestively. "I'm glad she had him for me, because he made me want to turn my life around."

"How is he? Is he bad, or is he a good kid?" she asked, wishing all the while that he was her child.

Born noticed the sadness in her eyes as she asked the question. "He's good. Ethan really has a lot of my ways, a lot of my habits. He's something else." Born smiled, thinking of his boy. "How is Sheldon doing? He's healthy and all that?"

"He's great." Jada, too, smiled. "He's so beautiful, and so smart. He has such a crush on Sunny that it's ridiculous." She laughed.

Born laughed, as well. He could see how a little boy would have a crush on Sunny. She always dressed sexy, and D.J. had told Born about his "funny feelings" whenever Sunny came around. Sunny had remained a part of D.J.'s life after Dorian's death. When he and D.J. got together, he often told Born about his visits with Sunny and his little half sister, Mercedes. But Born hadn't had the pleasure of crossing paths with Sunny in years. "Good ole Sunny! How is she? She still the same live wire she always was?"

Jada nodded, as their second round of drinks arrived, a rum and Coke for her, Hennessy straight for him. "She'll never change too much. Having Mercedes calmed her down, but Sunny still has the same loud mouth she always had. But I love her to death. She helped me out a lot with Sheldon when I was in trouble."

Born smiled. He cleared his throat, and tried to sort through all the things they'd discussed. "What do you tell your son about his father? Does he ask you about him?"

Jada nodded. "Yeah, he does, sometimes. Like any kid, he wants to know what his father looked like, and why he's not around anymore. Of course he was too young to remember Jamari, because he died when Sheldon was a toddler. I just try not to talk shit about him around my son. That's not easy to do, because I still have hate in my heart for him. I just tell Sheldon that his father loved him very much. But he wasn't living his life right, and he died young. That's all I can tell him right now. Someday, when he's older, I plan to tell Sheldon the whole story. I know it won't be easy. But I'd rather him hear it from me than from anybody else." Jada often worried about the day that she would have to explain her past to Sheldon. She and Sunny went about raising their children, and Sheldon and Mercedes didn't know about the past that both their mothers kept secret. Sunny often joked that one day she'd tell her daughter the story of her life, and poor little Mercedes would never be the same. Jada, however, dreaded the inevitable day when she would have to reveal to her son that she'd once been a crackhead. But she took comfort in one simple fact: She wasn't a crackhead anymore. And she never would be again.

"You know, I named him after the only two men I've ever loved in my life. My father, and you."

Born put his drink down, and looked at her. "Are you serious?" Born looked at her as if he wasn't sure if he should take her seriously. He was flattered, though, and he smiled, once more revealing those beautiful dimples Jada loved so much.

Jada nodded. "Yup. His name is Sheldon Marquis."

"Wow," was all Born could think to say in response. But he couldn't stop smiling. He knew that must have made Jamari sick!

Finally, their food came. Born, as usual, bowed his head, and prayed. Jada prayed, too. "That's the first time I've ever seen you pray, Jada. You born again now, or something?" He asked this as he poured salt on his mashed potatoes.

She looked at him, and spread butter on her potatoes. "I pray every day. I used to go to church with my mother back when I lived with her. She was really into church, and all that, and I guess some of it rubbed off. I know that I wouldn't have been able to get clean and stay clean if it wasn't for God. He's important in my life, but I wouldn't say that I'm born again. I don't wanna lie like that. I don't want to pretend to be so devout, and then do dirt when the prayer is finished . . . like some people." Jada winked at him, suggestively, and shoved a forkful of chicken in her mouth.

Born laughed, loudly. "Wow!" he said. "I forgot that you got all that mouth. You really do know how to put a nigga in his place."

She smiled. "I was only speaking hypothetically," she lied. "I wasn't talking about you in particular."

True to form, Born filled his mouth to twice its capacity, and proceeded to chew with his mouth half open. Jada frowned in disgust, and he seemed pleased by this, smiling as he chewed.

"I missed your old stankin' ass," he said.

Jada laughed. "I missed your old stankin' ass, too."

Born drank some water. "So, tell me this. I know you told me you got your degree, you're writing a book, you bought a house, and all that. So you got a man?"

Jada nodded. "Yup. His name is Sheldon. My son is my man, and I'm totally committed to him."

Born smiled. "I hear that."

Jada laughed. They shared their meal, and some small talk about the other aspects of their lives from the time they'd been apart. And they began to reconstruct the friendship they had once had, before disappointment got in the way. Born told Jada about how he'd been arrested and incarcerated. He told her about the time he'd spent in solitary confinement, rethinking the direction of his life. He explained that he had gotten out of prison, and opened a sneaker store, then bought a barbershop. How he'd continued doing business with Dorian's crew until it became apparent that D.J. had a gift that couldn't be ignored. He told Jada about his new role as D.J.'s manager, and about how that had been enough to finally get him out of the drug game.

Jada smiled. "You're the perfect manager for him."

Born smiled, too. "Yeah, I got love for the kid. I won't let nobody take advantage of him, or exploit him. I feel like I owe it to Dorian." He looked at Jada, knowing that she had witnessed him mourning the loss of his boy. Jada knew his history. She had held him when he got weak enough to cry over the loss of his friend, and she didn't need any further explanation. Born was glad to be sitting there with Jada, enjoying a meal and making amends. He was amazed at how mainstream their lives had turned out, with him working in the entertainment industry and Jada having a career of her own. It seemed that they had both learned from their mistakes, and made the best out of bad situations.

By the time they finished eating, they had fallen back into their old ways—somewhat. Their conversation had turned to the good old days. They reminisced on the times they had shared when they had been happy, and such a good team. They laughed at old jokes and recalled things that had been special to both of them. Jada realized how much she had missed him, and their love. She enjoyed watching the way he moved, the way he talked, his voice, and his laughter. And as they ordered another round of drinks, Born found himself wishing that things had turned out differently between them. No one had ever made him feel the way Jada had. He had never loved a woman as completely as he had loved her. Seeing her now reminded him why he had loved her so much.

Jada stared at him, wishing they had never parted. She had one more bone to pick with him, though. "When you threw me out, it seemed like you had Anisa waiting in the wings to take my spot. Are you sure you never cheated on me with her?"

Born frowned. "I never cheated on you, Jada. I was faithful to you always." He saw the skeptical look on her face, and got defensive. "Is that what you thought? That I cheated on you?" He shook his head. "I never played you. Never."

"Well, shit! You started seeing her damn near the day after me and you broke up." The contempt was so evident in Jada's voice as she spoke. In her mind, she thought, *You didn't even wait!*

Born sensed her disdain, and he looked at her dead-on. "I know you're mad at me for that."

Jada started to deny it, but it would have been pointless. "You gave it *all* to her, Born. Everything that used to be mine. She got your attention, your lifestyle, your friends, your son." Jada fumed inside. "I hated her. I hated you. You would see me, and you just walked on by like I was a stranger. Like I was never your girl, and we were never in love. You kicked me out of that house, and out of your life. All our mutual friends became your friends and her friends. I was on the outside looking in. And I thought you were being so cruel. It took me a long time to stop feeling like that. I had to understand that you just moved on."

Born heard the pain in her voice. "I was hurt, Jada. You made a fool out of me. Niggas in the street were coming to me, and telling me that they saw you high, that they saw you embarrassing yourself. I felt betrayed. And I guess Anisa helped me forget about the hurt I was feeling." Born stared at her intently. "I never loved her the way I love you," he said. "Anisa looks good, she gets attention. But she's not you. She doesn't move me anymore. It's been a long time since I can honestly say I felt any type of love for her."

"Do you still feel love for me?" Jada surprised herself that she'd asked the question.

Born was also surprised. He thought about the years without her in his life. He realized how much he missed her input, her smile, her voice. He wondered if she had any idea how difficult it had been for him to walk away from her all those years ago; wondered if she knew how hard it had been for him not to call her or go after her. He had watched her blossom from a young lady to a woman over so many years. And leaving her behind had been no easy task. Looking at her now, all grown up and standing on her own two feet, he was so proud of her. Jada had been his ride or die chick. And sitting with her in the back of that soul food joint, he realized that she still held his heart after all these years. Their love had been a fairy tale, only their story's ending had had a sordid twist. "Yeah. I still love you a whole lot."

Jada smiled, glad to know that Born still had a genuine love for her; glad to know that her feelings hadn't been hers alone. "I still love you, too." She blushed slightly, feeling vulnerable. "Do you forgive me, Born?"

He nodded. "Yeah. I forgive you," he said. "Do you forgive me?"

Jada smiled. "Yes. I do."

Born reached for her hand, and kissed it. Both of their hearts were comforted being in one another's presence after so long. They finished their drinks, and Born paid the check. Yet the two of them sat there, not moving, neither of them wanting to end the evening. Finally, Jada reached for her purse, and slid her chair back. "Thanks for a lovely meal," she said, half jokingly. Things had never been that formal between them. She smiled. "I have to admit that I don't want to go right now—"

"So don't." Born smiled back at her. He wanted nothing more than to kiss her, but he held back. He couldn't believe that he was with Jada after all these years. Yet, despite the affection he felt toward her, there was still a wedge between them of pain and disappointment.

She was thinking the same thing. So many years ago, this man had made the kind of love to her that makes you want to kick up your leg like one of the Rockettes. She remembered how she literally had felt every nerve in her body respond to Born's touch. He had loved her perfectly, once upon a time. Jada shook her head, trying to break free of the memory. "I have to," she said. "If I don't leave now, I probably never will." Jada stood up, and Born followed suit.

Jada stepped around her chair, and walked closer to Born. She wrapped her arms around his neck, and pulled him into a firm embrace. He hugged her back, and held on tightly. "You can call me, and I plan to call you, too. I'm glad we're on good terms now, Marquis." He smiled at her calling him by his government name. "I missed you," she said.

Born got a little choked up, but kept his game face on. "Yo, I missed you, too. A whole lot." He hugged her tightly, grabbed her by the hand, and led her out of the restaurant. They said good-bye to the friendly restaurant staff, and walked out hand in hand. Jada showed Born where she'd parked her car, and he walked her toward her silver Buick Rendezvous. He complimented her on her taste in SUVs, and then they stood awkwardly beside her truck.

"Jada, I want you to know that I wish I would have reacted differently when I walked away from you. I wish I had been strong enough to help you through it. I didn't know how to handle that. But now I know that if I really loved you, I should have tried to help you. I didn't have it in me to help you, so I shut you down. I'm sorry, baby girl." He moved closer to her face, and caressed her cheek with his hand. "I'm so sorry."

Jada tried to control her runaway heartbeat. She felt flutters in her gut, as she felt his warm breath on her face. Then he kissed her gently, and she let go, kissing him back fully. His tongue tasted sweet in her mouth, and she kissed him with an intensity that surprised both of them. Their kiss lasted several moments, and not once did they stop to think about their public display of affection.

Born didn't care who saw them. In his arms he held the love of his life. Whoever didn't like it would just have to kiss his ass. When he pulled himself away from her, he kissed her once more gently on her lips. Then he looked at her, his expression full of regret, and full of love, even after all this time.

Jada's eyes were tear filled, and she looked away in order to blink back the waterfalls. She laughed uneasily, and said, "I need to go." She took her keys out of her purse, and looked at Born. "I'll call you," she said. Born watched her climb inside her truck, and she rolled down the window to talk to him.

"Think about this," he said. "This don't have to be the end of our story. It might be the start of a whole new chapter. We said we'd always be friends, right?"

Jada nodded.

Born smiled at her. "Well, if you ever need a friend, holla at your boy." She smiled, as Born walked away backward. He winked at her. Then he put his hands in the pockets of his jeans, turned around, and walked away. Jada sat watching his familiar stride as he walked. She put her key in the ignition, and started to drive away. But she couldn't help feeling like her heart was breaking all over again. She called out his name, and Born stopped walking and turned back to her.

"Why don't you come by my house? I think Sunny would be really happy to see you."

He nodded, grinning that same irresistible grin he always had. "I'll follow you," he called out. Jada smiled, and waited for him to pull his car up behind her, so that they could drive to her place. She wanted to jump for joy, but she contained her enthusiasm as they headed for her house.

41

UNFINISHED BUSINESS

Born followed Jada inside her house, and they were immediately greeted by two kids. Sheldon and Mercedes ran to Jada, and hugged her. Born looked at the two happy children and smiled. Sheldon looked so much like Jada that it was obvious to him that this was her son. She introduced them, anyway.

"Sheldon, this is my friend Born." Sheldon shook Born's hand, and Born smiled at him.

"Wassup, little man?"

"Wassup?" Sheldon responded.

Born noted how handsome Jada's son was. He turned his attention to the pretty little girl standing next to Sheldon, and Born had to fight the urge to cry.

Jada pointed to Mercedes. "This is—"

"I know who she is," Born said softly. "She looks just like her father." He looked at Mercedes, and saw Dorian's features all in the beautiful girl's face. She had Sunny's long brown hair, and her light complexion. But everything else was Dorian. Born felt the guilt he still couldn't shake after all these years pounding in his heart. "Hi, Mercedes."

Mercedes smiled at the tall man who was smiling at her. "Hello. Are you Aunt Jada's boyfriend?"

Born laughed, and Jada wanted to die from embarrassment. "I used to be Aunt Jada's boyfriend," Born explained. "But now I'm just her friend." He smiled. "And I can see you got your mother's outgoing personality!"

"Ya damn right, she did!" Sunny stood behind Born with her hands on her hips. He turned around, and saw her standing behind him with a smile plastered across her lovely face. She opened her arms to him, and said, "Wassup, baby?"

Born hugged Sunny for a long, long time. Seeing her and Mercedes made Born feel so good and so bad at the same time. He felt happy to see Sunny, who still looked like the star she had always been. He was also happy to see her daughter for the first time. But seeing the two of them also brought back the feeling that he had let his friend down, and cost him his life. And that made him want to cry.

Sunny smiled at Born. "Now you're the last person I expected Jada to bring home." She looked at Jada, curiously. "Where the hell did you find him?"

Jada smiled back. "I called him. We met for lunch, and I invited him back here."

Sunny nodded, and was glad that Jada had taken her advice and called him. She looked at Born, still smiling. "Well, I'm sure your ears have been ringing 'cause we've been talking about you for days!"

Jada frowned at Sunny, not wanting Born to know that he had been the topic of so much of their conversation over the past couple of days. Born frowned, too. "What were y'all talking about?"

Just in the nick of time, Ava emerged from the kitchen and saw Born standing in the foyer. "Oh, my God!" she exclaimed. "Hey, Born. What's up?"

Born smiled back at Ava, as she came over and hugged him. She still looked good, and Born recalled the day he'd seen her naked. He was glad now that he hadn't violated Jada's trust by sleeping with her younger sister; otherwise this reunion would have been very uncomfortable. She smiled at him. "When did you get here?"

"Just now," he said. Jada ushered Sheldon and Mercedes back to their room so that the grown folks—particularly Sunny—could talk freely. She came back, and ushered everyone into the living room, and then gave Born a tour of her home. He was amazed at how well Jada had done for herself. He was proud of her for spending the money she had taken from Jamari to put a down payment on this house. It seemed that Jada had turned a major corner in her life, and Born was happy for her. He commended her for having the courage to turn her life around, and they prepared to head back downstairs.

Born stopped Jada at the top of the stairs. "I wanna say something to you before we go back down there."

Jada looked at him, wondering what was on his mind.

"I'm so proud of you," he said. "You did all this by yourself. You stayed focused, and you did what you had to do. And look at you now. I know I ain't no one special, or whatever. But I just wanted to say that I'm proud of you, and I really admire you for being strong enough to do all of this on your own."

Jada smiled, truly thrilled that he had noticed how extraordinary her accomplishments were. It had been no easy task for her to stay off drugs, to fight for her son, to go back to college, and to buy a home for her family. She knew that it was her own strength, and God's grace, that had gotten her through it all. But she also knew that there was one other contributing factor. "I had a good teacher," she said. "You taught me how to be a survivor, and how to fight my way to the top. I owe you so much for all the things you taught me."

Born shook his head. "You don't owe me nothing. In fact, I'm the one who owes you. I know I can't make up for walking away and leaving you by yourself. But if there's ever something I can do to help you in any way, Jada, I'm here."

Jada looked around for Sheldon or Mercedes. Satisfied that the coast was clear, she leaned in and kissed Born softly. His lips were so perfect, as if they were made to kiss hers. She stood with her face only inches from his. Then she took him by the hand, and they headed back downstairs to the rest of the crew.

They spent a long night catching up on each other's lives. Sunny smiled, watching Jada and Born together again, laughing and talking. She thought about how her conversation with Jada had started, when she'd first gotten the flowers from Born. Jada had told Sunny that Born was the love of her life, and Sunny's reaction had been negative. She had wondered how Jada could feel love toward a man who had tossed her out on the street with no one to turn to. Sunny had seen the depths to which Jada had fallen, and she couldn't understand how Jada could come out of that situation feeling anything but anger toward Born. But as she sat and watched the two of them that night, laughing and smiling at each other, or catching each other's gaze as they talked, Sunny understood. Their love reminded her of the love she'd shared with Dorian. It was something unique, that she knew she would never have again with any other man. Sunny dated. She had several wealthy and successful suitors who would give her the world. But Sunny's world had been Dorian, and no one could bring him back. She didn't want to ever fall in love again. But she hoped, now watching Jada and Born together, that they would be able to salvage whatever was left of what they'd once had.

"So, Sunny, what are you doing these days?" Born asked. "I bet you got your hands full with Mercedes. All the little boys in school must be beating down your door."

"Mercedes goes to an all-girls prep school on the Upper East Side. Ain't no boys beating down shit." Sunny smiled. "Besides, I'm hoping she and Sheldon get married someday."

Jada laughed. "Wouldn't that be something?" she said. "Poor Sheldon. If Mercedes is anything like her high-maintenance mama, my baby's in trouble."

Everyone laughed, knowing that Sunny was the supreme diva. Sunny waved her hand at Jada, and then turned her attention to Born. "I'm modeling now. Nothing major, yet. A couple of runway shows here and there. Just some magazine ads, cosmetic ads, and shit like that. Baby Phat, Apple Bottoms, fashion layouts in *Essence* and *Vibe,* and all that. My friend Olivia has been hooking me up with some of her designer friends, and they seem to love my face." Sunny smiled, happy with her little claim to fame.

Jada smiled, too. "It's all that ass, not the face, that they love," she joked. Sunny stuck her middle finger up at her friend, and they all laughed.

"In the modeling world, I'm old," Sunny explained. "Most of the girls who get the big ad campaigns are in their teens and twenties. Either that, or they're household names who have paid their dues, and their faces are easily recognizable. I'm trying to change that. I'm thirty-six years old, and in my mind I'm still young. The fashion industry doesn't see it that way, though." Sunny shrugged. "Thankfully, I don't need the money. Every dime I make goes into a trust for Mercedes. When Dorian died, he left me all of what he had, and he damn sure had a lot! I don't have to work. I just want to."

Born nodded. "Well, it's good that you're doing what you always wanted to do. Dorian used to always tell me that you thought you were a supermodel."

Sunny laughed, remembering the days when she used to demonstrate her runway walk for Dorian, and he would tell her how sexy she was. She missed him so much, and she could tell by the look on Born's face that he missed his friend, too. "Dorian loved you, Born." Sunny's face and tone were sincere. "You were his favorite from the very beginning. Once he met you, it was like he found his protégé. Dorian used to always tell me that you were the one who would take over his empire. You were the one he knew would come out on top." Sunny smiled at Born.

He nodded. "Yeah. I thought it would be me and him on some Biggie and Puffy type shit for life. That was my man, you know?" Born's eyes got misty. "I just wish I could have stopped what happened. I feel like that shit is kinda my fault."

Sunny frowned and shook her head. "It wasn't your fault, Born. Nobody's to blame for that shit but Raquel. You didn't know that she was deranged. And none of us knew she had a gun. You tried. You shot the bitch in the leg! And for a sane person, that would have been enough to stop her. But Raquel was trying to kill me. Dorian saved my life. He saved Mercedes's life. And that's how he would have wanted it. I know it. Don't blame yourself." Sunny wiped one tear that drifted down her cheek. "He loved you, Born. He loved you a whole lot."

Born smiled at Sunny, and he felt better. At least she didn't blame him for Dorian's death. He hoped that someday he could stop blaming himself. Mercedes came in with Sheldon in tow, and Sunny explained to her daughter that Born had been a very good friend of her father's. Mercedes smiled big and hugged Born. "My daddy was a hero. He saved Mommy's life."

Born nodded. "Yup. I could tell you a whole bunch of stories about your father."

Mercedes's face lit up. "Really? Tell me!"

Born looked helplessly at Sunny, and she threw her hands in the air. "What, Mr. Big Mouth. You told her you got stories. Go on and tell her some stories!"

Mercedes tugged at Born's hand and pulled herself up onto his lap. "Tell me."

Born laughed at Mercedes's aggressive personality, and cleared his throat.

"Well, one time, me and your father were in Brooklyn . . ."

For the next hour or so, Born entertained Mercedes, and all the other folks present, with story after story about his adventures with Dorian. Mercedes was enthralled, and never took her eyes off of Born. Sunny, too, hung on Born's every word. Some of the stories were familiar to her. Dorian had told her some of them. But others, Sunny heard for the first time, and she smiled, reminiscing on her one true love.

The night wore on, and they all enjoyed the atmosphere. Everyone laughed and joked and talked until the wee hours of the morning. Sunny had everybody laughing. Mercedes fell asleep in Born's arms, and Sheldon fell asleep in Jada's. They carried the two of them to Sheldon's room, and laid them down. Jada tucked them in, and they went back to the living room, where everyone was beginning to grow sleepy.

By the time Born got ready to leave, at close to two o'clock in the morning, he and Jada had rekindled their friendship, and agreed to see each other again soon. She walked him to the door, and he stood there smiling down at her. "Thanks for inviting me over here," he said. "It was nice being back around you and Sunny again. Your son is so handsome, and Mercedes is beautiful." He reached over and touched Jada's cheek lightly, tracing his finger across the silky texture of her skin. "I'll see you again real soon."

Jada smiled, and relished the feeling of his hand against her face. "Okay."

Born turned and left, and Jada shut the door. She turned around to find Sunny standing behind her with a smile plastered on her face. "You got your second shot, girl," Sunny said. "Don't blow it."

Sunny turned and headed to the bathroom, leaving Jada standing alone—still feeling Born's strong hand caressing her cheek.

Epilogue
LOVERS AND FRIENDS

Things were never quite the same for any of them after that night. Born and Jada rediscovered the reasons they'd become such good friends in the first place. Though neither of them was in any rush to take things too far too soon, their chemistry was unchanged. Anisa hated that Born and Jada had made amends, and she was upset that he'd forgiven her. Anisa gave him hell whenever he brought Ethan around Jada and Sheldon. Born told her, truthfully, that he and Jada were just friends. He also made it clear to Anisa that he owed her no explanations about his private life. His relationship with Anisa had long been over. And deep in her heart she knew that he had never really been hers to begin with. Still, Anisa held on, hoping that he'd change his mind. But in truth, she knew that Jada had won Born's heart after all.

Sunny became reacquainted with Dorian's brothers as a result of Jada and Born becoming friends again. Up to that point, Sunny had always been cordial yet distant with the brothers, because she didn't like their inquiries about how much money Dorian had left behind. She wanted no discussion about Dorian's money. When they came to see Mercedes, Sunny always met them curbside, and dropped her daughter off with little conversation. But once Born started coming back around, that began to change.

Sunny was happy to hear that the uncles were busying themselves with D.J.'s success. Born had him poised to go platinum with his debut

CD, and Dorian's brothers were eager for a lifestyle of fame and fortune on a legitimate level. Born became the mediator between them, and he convinced Sunny that she could come back around their crew without worrying about people going after her money. She and Mercedes's uncles made amends, and Sunny was glad that their attention was diverted to what D.J. would inherit rather than what Mercedes would. Sunny and Jada found themselves attending barbecues, and reacquainting themselves with Dorian's brothers and their crew. These connections proved to be valuable when Sunny and Jada finished their novel, aptly titled *Truth Is Stranger Than Fiction*. They'd based it on their own trials and tribulations in the game, and it was as entertaining as it was fact-based.

In order to help them drum up support for the novel, Born helped them secure a meeting with Monarch Publishing. They aced it, signed a nice book deal for not one, but two novels, and drummed up so much of a buzz that the book was on back order before it was even released. This was due in large part to the spot Born booked for them on Mindy Milford's radio show.

Mindy, the scandal-obsessed radio personality, started the interview off nicely enough. She described the two women to her listening audience, pointing out that both of them were iced out in brilliant diamonds, and wearing designer duds. She told them both that they were very beautiful women, and Sunny and Jada smiled and thanked her. Then Mindy asked about the book, and what the story was about. Jada gave a brief synopsis, and the interview seemed to be going well. Mindy seemed to be behaving. But out of nowhere, she attacked. Mindy asked them both point-blank if they had ever dabbled in cocaine use.

Sunny had looked at Mindy like she'd lost her entire mind. But she recovered quickly. "Yes," Sunny had deadpanned. "I did. That's how I'm able to write about it so well. The character in the book—Charlene—she goes through a lot of things I went through, things that lots of young ladies are going through. That's why the story's called *Truth Is Stranger Than Fiction*."

Mindy cut Sunny off, and cut right to the chase. "But is it true that *before* you started dating award-nominated actors, you were once the wife of a major drug kingpin in Brooklyn?"

"What the fuck does that have to do with this book, Mindy?" The censors worked eagerly to bleep out the expletives in Sunny's tirade. "Why does that shit matter? Who cares about all that? The book is called—"

"*Truth Is Stranger Than Fiction,* that's the name of the book everyone," Mindy's voice boomed in the microphone. "I encourage everyone to go out and buy a copy, because it is beautifully written."

"Thank you," Sunny said, firmly.

"You're welcome. And I think it's so impressive, because the whole time you were living so fabulously you were getting high every day—"

"Mindy, why you trying to make me fight you in here today?" Sunny was pissed, and her voice conveyed that. "I didn't come in here to talk about my life. When I write that book about my life, you'll be the first to know."

"Well, I'll look forward to reading it. Because the things I've heard about you and your lifestyle back when you were getting high, *honeeeee!* That's something we all want to read about!" Mindy pressed a button, and sound effects filled the speakers. Fake applause filled the airwaves. "Is it true that you were pregnant with the football player Michael Warren's baby?"

"I'm not answering that," Sunny said. "Let's talk about the book, Mindy. The book!"

Mindy nodded. "Yes. The book is going to be a bestseller. The streets are already buzzing. But not nearly as much as they will be once you write that life story of yours. I'm sure you'll mention the fact that your child's father was murdered at your baby shower by his other baby's mother—"

"Bitch!" The next sound heard in the studio was the sound of microphones coming off, and the censors bleeping out the words Sunny was yelling. The phone lines lit up.

Mindy defended herself, insisting that as a public figure Sunny should be prepared to open her personal life up to scrutiny. Sunny gave her hell, and the censors worked hard to block out Sunny's curses. Still Mindy pressed on. "I'm giving you a forum to answer the rumors. The streets are talking."

Sunny stepped back to the mike once more, and said, "Well, the streets should shut the fuck up then. Read the book, and shut the fuck up."

Sunny stormed out and Jada shook her head. Jada leaned in close to the mike, and said, "*Truth Is Stranger Than Fiction*, in stores now. Find out what all the fuss is about."

And that's exactly what plenty of Mindy's listeners did. The segment got a big reaction from the syndicated listening audience, and it became the subject of plenty of the phone calls. It turned out to be great exposure, and the book was a national bestseller. Sunny and Jada were on their way, and they had Ava—their attorney—handling their business.

Meanwhile, Born was leading D.J. to the promised land, and for the most part all of their children were happy and healthy. For all of them, the whole situation was surreal. None of them had expected things to turn out as they had.

All of them now worked in an industry where the drug game was often glamorized and held up as a badge of honor. And they all knew the ugliest side of what that lifestyle entailed. Lucky for them, they had managed somehow to escape the game's clutches. But all of them still bore the scars of numerous battles. All of the good times had come on the heels of suffering. They had survived only because they'd learned the power of forgiveness. Their would-be fairy tale may not have ended happily ever after, but it came pretty damn close.

Jada had her life back, and she had Born's forgiveness—his friendship. They never shared anything more than an occasional kiss. And an awkward silence always followed that. Both of them were afraid. He was afraid of losing control, and she was afraid of letting him down. Jada was determined in her heart that she would never get high again. But she knew that Born wasn't so sure about that. He doubted her, and rightfully so. And Jada wasn't sure if she could ever find enough ways to convince him. Born had a wall around his heart, and she knew that she had helped lay every brick within it. So even though she loved him more than ever, she allowed things to move at his pace, and hoped that someday she could completely regain his trust. And his heart.

Their connection was still unmistakable. They laughed together often and called each other several times a week. Once in a while, they had dinner together, and whenever their eyes met across the table, it was like magic. It was like music. True friendship knows no bounds. And they were grateful that at least their friendship had survived all the pain caused by white rocks, glass pipes, and powdery white lines.

Qty	Selection	
____	**Criminal Minded** • Tracy Brown • 0-312-33646-2	$14.95
____	**Eve** • K'wan • 0-312-33310-2	$14.95
____	**Hood Rat** • K'wan • 0-312-36008-8	$14.95
____	**Hoodlum** • K'wan • 0-312-33308-0	$14.95
____	**Street Dreams** • K'wan • 0-312-33306-4	$14.95
____	**Lady's Night** • Mark Anthony • 0-312-34078-8	$14.95
____	**The Take Down** • Mark Anthony • 0-312-34079-6	$14.95
____	**The Bridge** • Solomon Jones • 0-312-30725-X	$13.95
____	**Ride or Die** • Solomon Jones • 0-312-33989-5	$13.95
____	**If I Ruled the World** • JOY • 0-312-32879-6	$13.95
____	**Nasty Girls** • Erick S. Gray • 0-312-34996-3	$14.95
____	**Extra Marital Affairs** • Relentless Aaron • 0-312-35935-7 . .	$14.95
____	**Inside the Crips** • Colton Simpson • 0-312-32930-X	$14.95
____	**The Black Door** • Velvet • 0-312-35825-3	$14.95

TOTAL AMOUNT $_____

POSTAGE & HANDLING $_____

(\$2.50 for the first unit, 50 cents for each additional)

APPLICABLE TAXES* $_____

TOTAL PAYABLE $_____

(CHECK OR MONEY ORDER ONLY—PLEASE DO
NOT SEND CASH OR CODs. PAYMENT IN U.S. FUNDS ONLY.)

TO ORDER:

Complete this form and
send it, along with a **check
or money order,** for the total
above, payable to V.H.P.S.

Mail to:

V.H.P.S.

Attn: Customer Service

P.O. Box 470

Gordonsville, Va 22942

Name:_____

Address:_____

City:_____ State:_____ Zip/Postal Code:_____

Account Number (if applicable):_____

Offer available in the fifty United States and the District of Columbia only. Please allow 4-6 weeks for delivery. All orders are subject to availability. This offer is subject to change without notice. Please call 1-888-330-8477 for further information.

*California, District of Columbia, Illinois, Indiana, Massachusetts, New Jersey, Nevada, New York, North Carolina, Tennessee, Texas, Virginia, Washington, and Wisconsin residents must add applicable sales tax.

🦅 **St. Martin's Griffin**

SECRETS EXPOSED, RIVALRY UNLEASHED, LOVE LOST AND FOUND...

"Brown keeps the drama flowing and the pages turning as the love triang[le] converges explosively in Atlanta."
—*PUBLISHERS WEEKLY*

THE RISE AND FALL OF TWO MEN OUT TO CONQUER THE WORLD, AND THE WOMEN WHO LOVED THEM TOO MUCH

"*Criminal Minded* is hands down, the best book I've read in a long time. Tracy Brown has created a masterpiece... a banging storyline."
—K'WAN, BESTSELLING AUTHOR OF *STREET DREAMS*

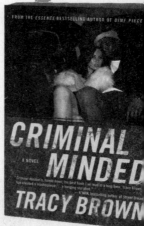